Ruth.

Enjoy.

P J Culd

Praise for *Praying Dove*

Phyllis Jo Arnold's *Praying Dove* artfully weaves together page-turning plot lines of love, sailing, mountain climbing, treasure hunting, and political intrigue to present an epic-like story of the Corn People's transition from a mythopoeic to a modern world.   Along the way, its impressionistic landscape blurs boundaries among things, nature, and people, sweeping one up into a world larger than the temporal self. It promises hope and brings light to a world grown dark beneath a black cloud of materialism. Arnold reminds us that stories can have magic and that, most importantly, their magic matters.

> Dr. David D. Joplin, *English Department, Monterey Peninsula College*

Praying Dove was a pleasure to read with every word so delicately chosen. The story is full of relatable characters and tangible emotions. The journey was awe-inspiring and Arnold's voice of gentle inner peace flows between each page.

> Neecy Twinem, *Award Winning Children's Book Author and Illustrator*

"a splendid, sprawling yarn at once ecologically sensitive and emotionally satisfying; a loving waltz to the voice of the earth"......

> D. Mason Weiner, M.D.

Bravo, Phyllis Jo Arnold! *Praying Dove* is one 'can't stop reading novel.' Your amazing control of the multiple storylines intrigues the reader as joy, love, fear and corruption are weaved skillfully into an adventurous and unpredictable plot. One twist after another unfolds into a finale of quiet satisfaction, leaving the reader filled with an unconditional appreciation of others. Well done.

> J. Logan Arnold, *bestselling author of The Salesman and the Farmer.*

PRAYING
DOVE

PRAYING DOVE

PHYLLIS JO ARNOLD

BRIO PRESS
12 South Sixth Street # 1250
Minneapolis, MN 55402

Distributed by Interface Media Patners

Manufactured in the United States of America

10 9 8 7 6 5 4 3 2 1

Book Artwork and Cover Design by Shelley Thornton

International Standard Book Number
ISBN 13: 978-0-9826687-5-7 (paper)
Library of Congress Control Number:2010935345

This book is dedicated to my best friend and loving husband, Pete Arnold. His never-ending encouragement and support have helped bring this book to fruition. Because of his passion for life, my world is filled with adventures that spark my imagination into words.

Characters and their Relations

King Eighteen Rabbit, *ruled the Xukpi People in Copan Central, twenty-seventh ruler before Roaring River*

Smoke Shell, *nephew of King Eighteen Rabbit, first king of the Corn People, married* Water Lily Jaguar
    Round Flower, *son*

Upturned Eyes, *Spiritual Leader under Smoke Shell*

Two Birds, *leader of the Corn People prior to Roaring River*

Roaring River, *born* Willow Leaf, *commonly called* Grandfather, *married* Horse Woman, *called* Running Filly
    Yellow Spotted Eagle, *daughter*
        Moon Jaguar, *daughter, married* Willy Stevens
            William Dancing Wolf, *son, called* Billy
            Falling Rock, *son, called* Rocky, *married* Red Feather
        Moon Shadow, *daughter,* married Fish Tail
            Praying Dove, *daughter, married*
            Andrew Thornton, *called* Drew
                Andrea Little Rabbit, *daughter, called* Andi
        Mat Head, *son, married* Singing Lavender Roller
        Jumping Toad, *grandson*

Winston Woodrow
    Abigail Woodrow, *daughter, married* Bartholomew Thornton
        Robbie Thornton, *son, married* Ruth Cunningham
        Andrew Thornton, *son, married* Praying Dove
            Andrea Little Rabbit, *daughter*
        Hope Thornton, *daughter, married* Logan McKnight

Matthew, *Kilimanjaro Guide*
Luke, *Matthew's brother*
Max and Tina Short, *rescued from the sea off sailing vessel Wind Got Us*
Teodor Lopez, *Honduras Governor*
Colonel Luis, *Lopez military head*
Tony Cirrus, *lumberjack*
President Jose Azcona Hoyo, *president of Honduras*

Copan Valley, Honduras

DURING A MOMENT OF REPRIEVE, MY MOTHER slowly opened her eyes. Like a ship breaking out of a thick, murky fog into crystal clear skies, her consciousness shifted from the intense ordeal that had been consuming her. For the first time in what seemed like hours, Moon Shadow became mindful of her actual surroundings instead of being entrenched in the unrelenting process her body was going through. She appreciated the cool cloth her sister dabbed across her forehead and the calming caress of her grandmother's touch, kneading the cramped muscles in her thighs.

Knowing the next contraction was imminent, she strove to release the tension in her body. Her gaze fell upon a lone dove perched on a low branch in the Spanish cedar tree she was leaning against. Moon Shadow was curious about the bird's behavior. She noticed its head was lowered in silence, not tucked beneath its wing in slumber. It appeared to be concentrating with focused stillness. Closing her eyes during the next all-consuming contraction, she saw the image of the dove etched in her mind. As her muscles cramped, a rush of blood reddened her face and my skull crowned; my mother knew I was to be called Praying Dove.

That particular night, the radiant full moon was haloed by an enormous green glow.

"It is an omen," rejoiced Horse Woman, my mother's grandmother. The omen told her that I was the chosen one to follow in the footsteps of our great leader, Roaring River, and become the next medicine woman and leader of the Corn People. As a tribe, we felt enmeshed with the powerful, life-sustaining corn spirit; hence our tribe was named after the large maize crops we grew and were dependent on for food.

In the pre-dawn hours, just after my birth, Horse Woman rushed from the women's hut to tell Grandfather, her husband, the news. Though his name was Roaring River, to most everyone in our tribe he was Grandfather. He was the cohesive foundation that gave support and strength to our people. He held us together through the second half of the twentieth century, while most other tribes had long ago disbanded. Horse Woman was excited to give her husband the message that I had been born under the powerful moon halo.

"It is not possible that a girl would be sent to carry on the traditions of the Corn People," he bemoaned. Turning his back to his wife, he tried to go back to sleep. He lay on the jaguar, deer, and raccoon fur pelts that padded the packed dirt floor of his one-room hut.

In Grandfather's home, shelves lined the four walls around him. They were stacked with old bottles and ceramic bowls in a collage of shapes and colors. Each held a particular part of a medicinal plant. Leaves, stems, flowers, and roots had been dried and stored in the containers for future use. Bunches of fresh plants were tied together and hung to dry from the ceiling, giving off a full array of both earthy and floral scents. Horse Woman snuggled in behind Grandfather and quickly fell asleep, but sleep evaded him.

Lying motionless, he tried to come up with an avenue to dissuade Horse Woman's belief in the portents of the haloed moon. Deep in concentration, he didn't move until after Horse Woman awoke and went to the women's hut to check on Moon Shadow. I lay suckling on my mother's breast as she rested.

In Horse Woman's absence, Grandfather knelt in the center of his room next to the small fire pit where he brewed healing teas and tinctures for our tribal members. He turned his gaze up toward heaven. His long, straight hair trailed back from his unusually high forehead down to his waist, like a shield of feathers on a gray gyrfalcon's back.

The morning sun blazed through a colorfully appliquéd curtain in the eastern window. The rays transformed into a thin, vibrant, multihued path dancing in the light breeze across the floor, over Grandfather, and up the far wall. A mockingbird, perched atop an elderberry bush outside the window, flaunted his versatility by singing a string of playful tunes. Grandfather didn't see or hear any of this. Nothing disturbed his focus. Even though his gaze was toward the ceiling, he didn't even see the palm fronds that formed the roof.

Looking for guidance about his new great granddaughter's destiny, he intently shook a gourd rattle in each hand. He asked his spirit ancestors to show him that he was correct in believing his successor would be a man, not a woman. As far as he knew, there had never been a female leading the Corn People, and he couldn't imagine it was time to change that lineage.

But instead of seeing confirmation of his belief, he saw me in an apparition as a young woman, skillfully performing healing techniques and spiritual teachings for our tribe. In that vision, he also saw something that took his breath away. He couldn't believe his eyes. A white man stood at my side, helping me with the daily organization of our people. Grandfather could not understand why this man would be with me. Because of this perturbing vision, he was determined to teach me to become a skilled healer and spiritual guide. He wanted to prove to our ancestors that I didn't need outside help.

Through my childhood, there were several meaningful turning points. One was the year I came of age and my moon cycles began. Once a month I stayed with the other women in the women's hut, the only round hut in our village. I found the time spent just with women to be soft and all-encompassing. The roundness of our energy enveloped us in a nest of refuge and bliss.

Sitting on the dirt floor, I sang with the others as I rhythmically wove palm fronds in and out on the mat I was making. Back and forth I rocked with the beat of the song and the movement of weaving. This repetitive motion took me deep into meditation and I become sensitive to my internal knowing.

In this deepened state, I asked God to show Himself to me. In my mind's eye, I saw Him as four weathered men with long hair. Ceramic beads and feathers hung from the ends of their braids. With their backs toward one another, and each facing a different direction, they sang forth the creation of pure raw energy. God's celestial voice came from everywhere and nowhere all at once, merging with the voices of my sisters. I knew the image of the men was just a visual expression for my benefit. God was not actually four men, but simply the source of energy from which all else is formed.

I opened my eyes. A smile spread across my face as I looked around the circle at my sisters. Our love filled the hut with an almost visual glow. Each month I found myself looking forward to the waning of the full moon and the time spent isolated with the other women of our tribe.

As the song we were singing ended, we all simultaneously giggled.

"Look at that mess," Moon Shadow said, laughing at the mat I had in front of me.

I looked down and laughed too. The weft fronds were loose and protruding way beyond the warp fronds. It seemed almost impossible for me to stay focused on what my hands were doing. Most of the weavings or xanabs, soft leather sandals, that I made were dismantled and reassembled by one of the more able women.

Yellow Spotted Eagle came to my rescue.

"No problem," she said, sitting down next to me. "Just pull it a little tighter."

Now, years later, that image of God comes back to me. Sometimes when I am busy trying too hard to help someone in need, I am reminded of the all-pervasive simplicity of God. Only then am I able to quickly let go of the complications that hold me from my pure, creative nature.

Some of my fondest memories of Grandfather were the nights we sat together on the hand-carved wood bench in front of his stick and mud hut. Those evenings, the night air smelled pungent—heavy with smoke from the communal cook fire in our village and with the intoxicating oil of the great eucalyptus tree growing behind his home. The eucalyptus leaves gave off their strong aroma particularly at dawn and dusk, filling the air with an exhilarating, spicy smell. Night after night, sitting on that bench, Grandfather conveyed stories to me, pointing out their importance for my future leadership. Many other nights, not a word was spoken, but the transference of knowledge still flowed to me from his powerful presence.

One night on the bench outside Grandfather's hut, I asked him again why he had been named Roaring River. I had questioned him before on this subject, and he had always said he would tell me another time, but he never seemed to get around to it. To me, his name didn't fit his calm, caring nature; he was always soft-spoken, nothing like the roar of a river.

"I'll tell you that story," he said after my prompting. That particular evening the obsidian sky hung low. Instead of growing animated like Grandfather usually did when telling a story, he became very still. Shadows danced from the firelight in bursts of orange and red across his deeply creviced brown skin, like the topography of a great canyon at sunset. To look at him, you would have thought he was older than the canyon itself. But his spirit had the light, airy innocence of a child's.

That night, in Grandfather's stillness, I feared he had suddenly died. With concern, I knelt down in front of him so I could look more closely at his face. To steady myself, I put a hand on his knee. My touch brought him back to the moment, and he slowly opened his eyes. He gazed directly into mine and smiled. With relief that he had not passed on, I smiled back.

"There is a great spirit," Grandfather said, as he lifted his head, "who will come for us." Returning to my seat next to him, I hoped he was beginning the story about the origin of his name. As I settled in to listen, I leaned over to pat the stray white dog that lay at my feet. Grandfather called this dog I had befriended my lost sister. Several years earlier, my mother gave birth to a beautiful daughter who never took a breath. Grandfather told me her spirit had returned to be with us in this handsome white dog.

To Grandfather, each animal had a particular personality and held its own type of magic. That night when he continued to speak, I realized he was presenting me with a different story altogether— "a lesson," he called the tales he told. I was not surprised that he wasn't telling me about the origin of his name, because he shared very little of his past personal life with me, but I was disappointed. During our evenings sitting together, he told me mostly about our ancestors and the chronicles of our beliefs. Occasionally he talked of the future, at which time he seemed to be far away, even though he was sitting right next to me.

Raising his gaze to the heavens, Grandfather said, "It is foreseen in the stars—a time when the Mother Earth splits in two." He appeared to be listening to something. I looked in the direction of his gaze, trying to perceive what he was focused on. A shooting star fell across the Great Bear constellation, momentarily leaving a line of light in its wake. I knew Grandfather was thinking this fleeting line, dividing the sky in two, was akin to how quickly the earth would be split. When things like this happened, I wondered if Grandfather had pulled the star through the sky to enhance the meaning of the story he was beginning to tell or if it was purely a coincidence.

"When some people step out of harmony with nature, their contrasting energies from those who still walk in tune, will split the world in two," Grandfather said. "The earth will no longer be able to withstand the pull between the human beings that live in harmony with our Mother and those that don't. The conflict is mounting and has almost reached an intolerable level. For the human beings living in accord, the time of separation from the others will be a joyous day. We will live in peace with Mother Earth once again. She will be happy and care for those who care for her. The others, on their own new world, will not be happy.

"They will not know that they are not happy, for they do not have an experience of true happiness," he continued.

"They will feel a sense of relief because there will no longer be a clash with those of us who move with singing hearts. During the split of the earth, a heavenly spirit will descend and guide us in our new world of peace. This spirit will be seen by all, spreading a blanket of joy across the face of our Mother." Pausing for a moment, Grandfather turned his gaze to look deep into my soul. Continuing he said, "This I tell you, my child, is not that many moons from now."

Feeling inadequate to be the one responsible as the story bearer for our tribe, I asked, "What if I forget these lessons you are telling me, Grandfather? What if I'm not able to lead our people the way you have?"

Taking my soft hand in his hard, weathered one, he warmly said, "The knowledge from these tales I tell you, and the knowledge your heart knows on its own, will always reside within you, my little darling. Only when it needs to be remembered will it travel up to your thoughts; then you will be able to speak the words that others need to hear. There is never a needed story that is lost or not remembered."

As Grandfather spoke, my mother and her sister came walking

arm-in-arm in our direction. A squirrel carrying a scrap of flat bread scampered across their path. Leaping on the trunk of a large Spanish cedar tree, he scurried up and spiraled around. In a slow stroll toward us, Moon Shadow and Moon Jaguar were engrossed in the present moment of the tranquil evening.

When Grandfather was finished speaking, he slowly put his hand-carved wood flute to his lips and skillfully played a slow, methodical tune. My mother loved to listen to the pining cry made by this wooden instrument. Grandfather's old, thickened fingers didn't look as if they would be able to tenderly caress the flute into song, but they gently stroked her wooden belly until her voice rang to the stars.

During those long, sultry evenings sitting on the bench outside his hut, Grandfather showed me the way of the awakened soul. I was taught to follow in his path, bringing messages from beyond this world into the present. Others in our tribe frequently joined us in the evenings, but it was known he was recalling these tales for my benefit. With his direction, I lived a life of meditative prayer, becoming the eyes and ears of knowing for our entire tribe. Over the years, Grandfather instructed me in how to sit in silence until my own mind released its continual, repetitive chatter and expanded into the All-Knowing.

When I was a young woman, Grandfather took me aside and told me about the day I was born and about the vision he saw of me leading our people. He said he was proud that I was the chosen one to carry on the traditions of the Corn People.

But after a moment of silence, a very confused look came across his face and he said, "In that very vision, there was another standing at your side." Grandfather knew that the future would be more complicated. After looking into my eyes with deep concern, he continued, "The apparition was of a white man." He described him as looking ghoulish and frail. Over the years Grandfather questioned this vision. Yet, every time, he was always given the same answer, "The white man would benefit from our tribe, and we would benefit from his joining us too."

"I am finally convinced you must find him," Grandfather said to me. "I've been told our tribe needs help from his family. Without them, there will be no tribe for future generations."

"Don't you think I am capable enough to lead our people?"

"Of course I do," he said tenderly. "But without his help, you will have no tribe to lead."

There had not been two people ruling the Corn People at one time since Smoke Shell was king. During the same time period, Upturned Eyes was the spiritual leader. This, Grandfather told me, was many, many moons ago—twenty-seven rulers before Grandfather, to be exact—and never had there been a leader who was not born of our tribe. By this time in my life, when Grandfather told me about his vision, he believed in my ability to see beyond this physical world. With his confidence in my gift to predict the future, he asked me to look forward for him.

I immediately saw the white man Grandfather was referring to. The man did not look well, yet I could feel his spirit and it sang a harmonious tune. I immediately knew the importance of finding this man, but I didn't know where to start looking. During the following decade, I thought frequently of the vision of the excessively thin, white man Grandfather called "The Bald Skeleton."

Since the time when I was young, not much has changed in the Copan Valley. The vegetation looks the same, our crops are in the same places, and our huts haven't been altered much. But we are exceedingly more aware of the rest of the world. Tourists frequently travel through the valley, leaving evidence of the developing world. We no longer wear only handmade clothing. Commercially made cloth had been introduced into our village several decades earlier. Each hut is also in possession of at least one plastic water bottle and various other items that indicate we are in the twenty-first century, rather than the tenth. But our way of life and community has not really altered much over the centuries.

And now, this exact spot on the bank of the Amarillo River, where I sit with my family, was Grandfather's favorite location to meditate. When he was alive, he would spend long, searing summer afternoons here. In this small clearing, tall, soft grass padded the earth. While sitting here, Grandfather would say he was listening to God speak through the river. When I sat here with him, he would instruct me to lie back on the shaded grass, be very still, and listen to the space around the voice of the river.

"In the silence around all else, God speaks," he would tell me, holding a finger up to his lips, motioning me to be quiet and listen instead of questioning him for an explanation.

These fond memories of my childhood were disrupted when a mail carrier entered the clearing where we were having a late afternoon picnic and handed me a letter.

After reading it, I took a deep relaxing breath. I lay back in the soft, tall grasses and looked up into the canopy of branches above me. Two beautiful blue and yellow macaws with long, trailing tail feathers flew from one tree to the next. Their brilliant colors were so precious to see in the monotony of green in the copious rainforest the Corn People call home. With the news in the letter, my mind drifted back to the particulars of my life three years ago, and I brought to my conscious awareness the details of those people who played the roles that were necessary for me to turn in the direction of "The Bald Skeleton." The month that I met him, my life as I knew it took an abrupt shift and changed forever.

While staring up into the canopy of branches above me, I slipped into a light trance-like state. From this state, I could see beyond my small consciousness, and I instantly tapped into Hope and Logan McKnight's lives, two intuitive conduits whose seemingly remote existence was paramount for the future of the Corn People.

From the communal bank of All-Knowing, this story unfolded before me...

The Crossing

A TOUGH LITTLE SAILBOAT PITCHED INTO A menacing storm off the east coast of Florida. Blustery winds tossed it from side to side and whistled a haunting trill through the shroud cables that held the mast upright. An intense burst of air grabbed the reefed mainsail and threatened to slap the boat down on her beam-end. Just before dusk, massive thunderheads, weighted down with moisture, approached from the north and threatened to release their volatile energy. Hope and Logan McKnight were on their way from Florida to Elbow Cay, in the northern part of the Bahamas, when this storm, which had not been in the forecast, grew with winds gusting up to forty-five knots.

Lightning lit the heavens as it shot from one black cloudbank to another. Deafening thunder immediately followed as Hope's shoulders and the hair on her arms rose. The ominous clouds ripped open and poured water down in sheets, drumming the coach roof of their small boat.

The McKnights had both come from nautical pasts and had many sailing hours on the water, but seldom had they been confronted with the weather shifting so quickly and with so little warning. While the Gulf Stream current swiftly plowed north, the wind tried to push the water south. With the convergence of wind and current, spume sprayed horizontally through the air.

Hope sat on the windward side of the cockpit with her feet firmly planted on the other side. Gripping the lifeline stanchion next to her for stability, she tried to duck in time, so as not to be drenched by the waves flying over the canvas dodger and into the cockpit. In the slight pause between two breakers, Hope glanced forward to the bow of the boat and noticed the cap on the chain hostel, a pipe that feeds the anchor chain down below deck, was off, simply hanging by its line. Every swell they took over the bow was now funneling water down the chain pipe opening, filling the chain locker. Water worked its way from the chain locker into the bilge, keeping the emergency bilge pump constantly running and overtaxed. Hope knew something had to be done to ease the load on the pump so it wouldn't burn out. She also knew she would have to be the one to take care of it, as Logan was steering the boat.

Focused on the state of the sea in front of him, Logan clenched his angular jaw in unison with the sharp movement of the helm. He fought to keep the boat in perfect alignment with each approaching comber to minimize the chances of being thrown over onto their side and to prevent burying the boat's bow into the next oncoming wall of water. Even still waves of water gushed over the boat as if it were an insignificant twig bobbing on the churning ocean's surface.

Hope screamed so Logan could hear her over the deafening roar of the waves, the wind, and the rain.

"The chain hostel cap has come off!"

But before she could finish her thought, another wave flew over the dodger and hit her in the face. Gasping, she abruptly stood up. Grasping the dodger's rim, she leaned out of the cockpit to spit the gagging saltwater from her mouth.

Logan strained on his toes to look over the coach roof at the chain hostel cap.

"I'll go forward!" she yelled, turning toward Logan and motioning toward the bow of the boat with her head.

"Wait!" Logan shouted. His heart sank. He wanted to protect Hope, but for now there was nothing he could do but watch his adored companion risk her life for their safety.

Taking a moment, he looked Hope squarely in her eyes and gave her a sad partial smile, as if to say, "I'm sorry." He knew it was urgent to cover the chain hostel, so he shouted after her, "Be careful, Hope! Make sure you're clipped in!"

Hope looked down, inspecting her lifejacket tether that was clipped to the jack line. The jack line spanned the entire length of the boat and allowed her to securely maneuver from one end to the other while tied to the deck. Confident the tether was secure, she looked out into the churning ocean to evaluate the swells. Hope tried to determine their pattern and whether or not they were coming in typical sets so she could choose the appropriate time to go forward. But it seemed as if they were only getting larger, and there was no rhythm to their configuration. Small, bumpy waves bounced toward the east while large, jagged, cresting breakers marched to the south. After dodging one unusually large wall of water that partially filled the cockpit, Hope took a deep breath and hoisted herself out of her comparatively secure position onto the deck. Inching her way forward, she scooted on her knees, clinging to the lifeline with her left hand and the grab rail on the side of the coach roof with her right.

With the crashing of each wave on the boat's deck, Hope lowered her head, closed her eyes, and repeated to herself, "Hold on, Hope. You can do it. Just a little bit further."

Each time a wave slammed into them, the boat quivered from the impact. The force of the wind flattened Hope's foul weather gear to her body. Unable to wipe the saltwater from her face, it burned her eyes and blurred her vision.

Wedging herself between the coach roof and the caprail, Hope reached her right arm around one of the stanchions. Bracing it in the crook of her elbow, she could use both hands to unclip her tether from the jack line. With trembling hands, she reached the tether around the outside of the stanchions and reclaimed it onto the jack line. All the while the waves and wind threatened to rip her from the small, floundering vessel and simply fling her into the churning water. With every inch she went forward, her chest constricted tighter and tighter with fear.

At the bow, Hope positioned herself in the middle of the vessel. She reached from one side to the other, holding onto the lifelines on either side. With her knees spread wide, she slowly let go with her right hand, intent on replacing the chain hostel cap, but the steep pitch of the boat stole her attention, and she grabbed for the lifeline again.

The water rose in front of her as the bow lifted at a terrifying angle up the face of a mammoth wave cresting toward the bow. Logan's pattern of steering was to keep the boat at a slight angle to the approaching wave so the boat wouldn't go straight up the face or dive straight down the back. Traversing the pinnacle, Logan angled down the backside just as an offbeat wave came from the starboard side of the vessel. The wave pushed the boat so hard he was unable to keep it from going directly down the back of the twenty-foot wall of water. The bow of the boat submerged with Hope hanging on.

Logan yanked the wheel as hard as he could and screamed with frustration, but there was nothing he could do. It didn't matter how hard he turned the steering wheel to starboard, the wave overpowered his attempt, and the boat turned port.

"No! Damn it! No!" Logan screamed, banging his hands on the cranked wheel.

For several seconds, Hope was completely submerged. The sailboat fought to the surface of the water as another smaller wave crested over the bow of the boat. This surge of water hit Hope on the back of the head with such force it slammed her face into the deck. She let out an uncontrollable shriek as she gulped for air. In the bucking chaos behind the roar of water and wind, Logan screamed to her.

"Hang on!"

The fear and deep concern in his voice were palpable.

Hope knew she had been hurt, but still first in her mind, she knew she had to replace the cap before returning to the safety of the cockpit. She clenched her teeth to fight back the rising terror in her throat. Persevering until accomplishing the task, she put the cap in place and then eased her way backwards along the coach roof. The further she scooted aft, the more her emotions overpowered her.

"Hope, I am so sorry. Are you okay?" Logan called.

Her tears bled into the rain and ocean spray. Her muscles shook from adrenaline pumping through her veins. Observing Hope's trembling body and seeing the blood drip down her chin, Logan assumed she was hurt much worse than she was.

"What can I do?" he shouted, unable to console her or even look at her for long because he had to stay intent on steering the boat.

Gritting her teeth, Hope took control of her fear-riddled mind. She knew it was imperative she keep her wits about her and be ready for any further emergencies. She wiped the tears from her eyes and took several deep breaths, calming her thoughts. She utilized the mental control she had developed from years of meditating. Hope quickly turned her focus to arriving in the Bahamas unscathed.

"I'll be fine," Hope called out to Logan. "What's my chin look like?"

Beneath her rain gear she was drenched to the bone and shivering. She wanted dry clothing. She wanted to look at her chin in the mirror because her blood, mixed with water, made it appear as if she was bleeding profusely. But she knew if she went below deck, she would probably get thrown around even more and it was below deck that she always got seasick in rough weather. Hope wedged herself in behind the corner of the dodger to get out of the wind. She dabbed at her chin with the cuff of her long-sleeve T-shirt.

"It looks like a scrape, so it's not a deep cut!" Logan shouted toward her. "Are you hurt anywhere else?" Logan felt awful. He felt it was his duty to protect Hope, and he had failed.

Hope shook her head to indicate no.

"I'm sorry. I tried," Logan said. He wanted to go to her, but he couldn't let go of the helm.

She knew he was doing the best he could, just as she was. They were both doing what needed to be done, and that was all either could ask for.

"I'll be okay," she said. "You did a great job recovering."

"No, babe, you are the one that did a great job!" Logan proclaimed. "I couldn't control the boat."

Hope held tight to the dodger frame and closed her eyes, willing her muscles to relax and her nerves to calm.

Earlier that week the McKnights had been excited and filled with anticipation as the compelling smell of salty sea air filled their desire to be free.

"Yes! We're on another adventure!" Logan shouted from where he stood bracing himself with the mast. "Rock 'n roll!" he shouted, raising a fist into the air.

From behind the wheel, Hope smiled and nodded her head in agreement.

"Rock 'n roll," she mimicked.

Secretly, Hope was dreaming of lazy days, reading novels, and snorkeling over pristine coral reefs, not an adventure-filled escapade into the unknown. She fantasized about island food, cold rum drinks, meeting other cruisers who were also pursuing a simplified life, and having time to allow her mind to amble. But most of all, Hope was looking forward to continuing her lifelong quest; she was excited to learn the spiritual beliefs of the indigenous people they would encounter on their travels. She was hoping to search out teachers who would help her find universal truths.

Even though the McKnights had tried not to, they had fallen into the life of hectic consumerism that the rich western world embraced. Feeling less than fulfilled from the acquisition of stuff, they decided to leave behind their chaotic lives of telephones, traffic and fast food. Now they were hoping to have a simplified life on their boat without being bombarded by advertisements encouraging avid consumerism.

The call of the sea pulled on Logan's heart. Longing for a life of extreme adventure drew him out into the world of water. In love with Mother Ocean, Logan did not feel complete without her. Even when he was in the mountains, far from the sea, he heard her seductive, watery voice and ached to be with her.

As a kid, Logan's parents had to drag him out of the water when it was time to go home after family excursions to the beach. Since he grew up just four miles from Pompano Beach in Florida, the lure of the sea made him figure out how to get to the ocean on his bicycle when he was merely ten. By the time he had his driver's license, it was impossible to keep him away from the water. When he was a teenager, Logan went surfing and free diving every minute he could. If a storm was blowing in and the waves were perfect for surfing, Logan would beg his mother to call the attendance office at his high school and make an excuse for his failure to show up to class.

"Mom, the wind's blowing out of the west today," he would beg. "The waves will be breaking in perfect curls. By this weekend, you know it will just be chop."

Logan pleaded with his mother while his surfing buddy stood at the back door waiting for Logan's thumbs-up to skip school. Knowing what an easy ride Logan's mother was, his buddy had already loaded their surfboards on top of his old red Rambler.

Because of surfing, Logan missed so many days during his junior year of high school that the school principal called the house one day to make sure Logan hadn't contracted a serious disease. The principal knew that Logan's extremely toned upper body, his dark tan, and his sun-bleached blond hair were not at all indicative of an ill person; but still, he had to call and ask. The basketball coach also knew Logan wasn't really sick all the days he missed basketball practice. He wished he could excuse Logan's absences so he could keep him on the team, but he couldn't break the rules for him. So, even though Logan was one of Pompano High's best basketball players, the coach cut him from the team. Logan barely noticed the loss. He was so consumed with surfing that school and basketball were just distractions.

Hope, on the other hand, longed for an easy, slow life. She wanted a life calm enough that she could hear her personal creative thoughts and enjoy the splendor of her individual mind. When left on her own, Hope was entertained by her own observations and insights. She called these moments of introspection when she allowed her thoughts to carry her away the "ultimate in home movies." Together Hope and Logan assumed that a cruiser's way of life was just their style, but obviously for different reasons.

The day they left Florida, the weather forecast sounded favorable for a two-day run to the Bahamas. The prediction for the next forty-eight hours was for a south-easterly wind to slowly clock around to the south and then to the southwest. This would gently push them through the Gulf Stream to the northern Bahamas. Before dawn they raised the sails on *Ladyhawke* and headed east. As the land behind them shrank from view, the sun rose in the sky, creating finger-like rays through the moist air.

Ladyhawke was happy when she was in the ocean. Her spirit seemed alive as she danced across the water.

"Doesn't it feel great to be going?" Logan shouted, emphasizing 'great.' He took a deep breath and filled his nose with the untamed smell of the sea.

"It makes me feel alive," Hope replied. They were both elated to be living the dream they had entertained since they met four years earlier.

By noon, just twenty-eight miles off the coast and not yet to the Gulf Stream, Logan noticed the predicted southerly breeze was quickly sweeping to the west. The wind had increased in force, blowing in gusts up to twenty-five knots and swiftly pushing them from behind. Lazy ocean swells lifted the stern of *Ladyhawke*, allowing her to surf down the face of each wave. The motion of the boat, in perfect tempo with the aquatic world and the airstreams, gave them the illusion of flying.

Down below deck Hope checked their position on the GPS. They were right on track, but she noticed the barometric pressure had significantly dropped from the morning's reading. Viewing the clear blue skies, Hope questioned if she had correctly written down the previous barometer reading.

"As long as this wind stays west," Logan said, sticking his head down the companionway, "we're okay, but if it starts blowing from the north, we're in for a rough ride once we hit the stream." Logan knew it was highly likely that the wind would continue to shift once it started its clocking maneuver. Hearing Logan's concern, Hope checked the barometer again. Sure enough, it was still dropping

Back in the cockpit, she also noticed the wind had shifted directions. It was coming from the northwest and continued increasing velocity. These quickly changing winds confused the ocean swells and created restless, jumping blocks the size of boxcars. Gone were the evenly distanced, predictable swells they had experienced earlier.

By late afternoon, Hope and Logan had entered the northward-bound Gulf Stream, an ocean river fifty miles-wide. Flowing at four knots, it was pulling warm equatorial water from the Caribbean up along the eastern seaboard all the way across the northern Atlantic to Europe. Hope knew she had to compensate for this current in her navigational figures. Otherwise, instead of making landfall in the Bahamas, *Ladyhawke* would sail north of the island chain unable, in the strong current, to make the necessary southing needed to get back to land. Hope made the calculations and entered the waypoint into the GPS.

"Try to stay on twenty degrees," Hope instructed.

"Will do, babe," Logan said, adjusting the sails to the new heading.

Ladyhawke was bucking dramatically, compared to earlier. "It's as I feared," Logan said. The northwest wind continued to clock;

now blowing straight into the northbound current. The sea state had deteriorated. "We'd best hunker down. Let's put in a reef. We'd better get ready for a long ride."

While Logan steered, Hope put two reefs in the mainsail and winched the headsail down to a little triangle not much larger than a bed sheet. Logan and Hope worked together, struggling to keep the boat on their rhumb line. Just when they thought they had the boat stable and the sails reefed small enough for a safe passage in extreme weather, Hope noticed the loose cap on the chain hostel.

Fighting the Gulf Stream and clawing into the wind for eight straight hours, Logan and Hope took turns hand steering, not trusting the autopilot to handle the erratic size and configuration of the waves.

In the wee hours of the morning, the wind clocked all the way around and lessened to about twenty knots, once again blowing out of the southeast. The McKnights were exhausted, crusted with saltwater and shaking from hunger. Relieved to have endured the storm and made it across the Gulf Stream, Logan attached the autopilot.

In the small confines of the galley, Hope put a kettle of water on the gimbaled propane stove, securing it with fiddles. While the water heated, she charted a new course corresponding to the new wind direction and sea state.

"Veer off seventeen degrees to the east," Hope called up to Logan as the ocean floor rose from over eight hundred fifty feet, the maximum depth their sounder would read, to twenty-eight feet. They had entered the Bahamian Banks, the shallow, submerged, carbonate platform that makes up most of the Bahamian Archipelago.

Logan adored Hope for her confident ability to handle every aspect of the boat. After adjusting the autopilot and the sails to coincide, Logan walked from stern to bow shining his flashlight on the rigging and lines to make sure nothing had chaffed or broken during the bucking ride they had just endured.

As their soup cooled, Hope slumped on the cockpit bench. A tear of exhaustion seeped from the corner of her eye as she snuggled into Logan's chest and he wrapped his arms around her.

"I'm just so thankful the boat is finally riding smoothly," Hope sighed with relief.

"We made it, honey," Logan said, pulling her closer to him. "I'm sorry it's been so hard."

"It is what it is," she said, finally able to relax in his embrace.

Ladyhawke settled into a rhythmic glide in the shallow water of the Abaco Sea that was protected by a string of islands over one hundred miles long. On the Bahamian Banks, in the transparent water, shoals and reefs came within a couple of feet of the water's surface, demanding that *Ladyhawke* stay on her rhumb line to assure she didn't hit bottom.

"Why don't you go down below and get some rest? I'll wake you in a couple of hours," Logan said, after they had eaten.

Without saying a word, she headed down the companionway stairs. Hope felt numb, without emotion. At the bottom of the steps she removed all of her foul weather gear and her drenched clothing, not wanting to take her wet things any further into the boat than necessary. By the time the weather had calmed enough that she could take her rain gear off, Hope's soggy clothes had warmed from her own body heat.

She washed the salt and sticky seawater off her skin in the galley sink. Crawling into the quarter berth behind the navigation desk that Logan and Hope had planned on using in shifts all night, she curled into a ball. At 3:30 a.m., the slow rocking of the boat and the rushing of water under the hull made a soothing lull that allowed Hope to quickly drift off to sleep.

Just before the sun popped above the horizon, Logan came down and gently nudged Hope awake.

"I can't keep my eyes open any longer," he said.

Hope pulled herself out of a dreamless sleep and reluctantly pried her body from its warm cocoon of bedding.

Logan took her place before the sheets had time to cool.

Dressing in dry clothes under her foul weather gear, Hope checked their position on the GPS.

"Sleep good," Hope said, kissing Logan on the forehead, before going up the companionway ladder.

Clipping her lifejacket tether to the jack line, Hope took a look around the boat to make sure all of the lines and sails were functioning properly. Scanning the horizon for lights or visible boats, she noticed, off in the distance, the lights of a ship on her portside. It appeared to be moving to the west, not on a collision course with *Ladyhawke*.

With a mug of coffee, she sat in the cockpit and watched the sun pop its head out of its watery covers and birth a new day.

Dawn was Hope's favorite time to be sailing. It reminded her of her childhood, sailing in the Chesapeake Bay with her father, Robbie Thornton. She sat with the tiller in her hands as her father untied the lines that held his small, classic, wooden day-sailer Mystic to the dock. They had sailed together so many times that they had worked in unison, without talking, to raise Mystic's small sails. Robbie's thin, tall, angular form almost looked like another mast standing on the deck. Even as a child, Hope had taken after her father's thin, lanky physique.

Together they watched the kaleidoscope of colors roll across the sky as the light from the budding sun bloomed above the horizon. She often wondered what he was thinking about back then, but she would never know. He had passed on a couple of years earlier.

Now the rising sun on the bow of *Ladyhawke* gave Hope the anticipation of a fresh start and the expectation of landfall before the sun set again. The wind continued to blow out of the southeast, but it also continued to diminish in speed. The anemometer read twelve knots. Still, they were traveling at about seven knots.

Bathed in the beauty of the sea and the radiant sky, Hope easily relinquished the terrifying episode of the day before. She reminded herself that most sailing was non-eventful, with gentle breezes, clear skies and manageable waves. Even so, she felt the scab covering the scrape on her chin, and her teeth automatically clenched remembering yesterday's bumpy ride. She forced her mind to shift to the beautiful rising sun instead of her recent fright. The fine string of clouds in the east glowed pink and lavender against the yellow and green bruised sky.

Hope was at peace in the rhythm of *Ladyhawke* as the boat charged forward. The GPS showed they were barely forty-seven miles from Green Turtle Cay, their first Bahamian landfall. Hope calculated they would be anchored in about seven hours if the conditions didn't shift again.

A few hours later Logan poked his head up the companionway and asked, "How's it going?"

"The wind has continued to lighten," Hope replied as she stood and gracefully stretched her long arms into the air, "but we're still on track. I've shaken all of the reefs out of the mainsail. We're still going about six knots."

"Let me make something to eat," Logan yawned. "Then you can take another nap. Would you like some oatmeal?"

"That'd be great," Hope sighed, trying to run her fingers through her stiff, salty hair and making a face of disgust as it stuck up unevenly.

The sun had warmed the chilly night air and Hope had already removed her warm clothing. Taking the opportunity to shower while Logan was busy in the galley, she removed the handheld shower wand from the port lazarette and adjusted the temperature. Slowly she lathered her body and rinsed away the remaining salt. Turning to pick up her towel from beneath the dodger, she realized Logan was watching her with a pleasant smile on his lips.

When Logan caught her eye, he gave her a big grin and said, "You are so beautiful, Hope." He loved to watch her move. Her short auburn hair playfully outlined her girlish face and sparkling eyes. Hope's charming grace sashayed when she moved, like a willow tree in a light breeze.

But the fact that he noticed her at all was a bit uncomfortable for Hope. She never liked to be the center of attention.

Logan couldn't resist. While the water for the oatmeal heated on the stove he stepped up into the cockpit and wrapped his arms around Hope's naked body. Logan held her tight.

"Mmm, you smell good," he said, kissed her on the neck and worked his way down to her small, firm left breast.

Hope kissed the top of his head and let out a sigh of desire.

Logan was thoroughly enjoying himself when the teapot began to whistle, pulling his attention back to the galley. They both giggled at the disruption.

"It can wait," Logan said, nuzzling his nose into her chest.

Hope giggled and gently pushed him away, saying, "Oatmeal?"

Logan hated the interruption, but he prepared the oatmeal and finished it off by adding a handful of dried fruit and walnuts to each bowl.

"I'll go take a nap," Hope stated, after eating. She went below, relaxed into the sea berth and quickly fell fast asleep.

Logan whistled to himself while he adjusted *Elmo* to coincide with the GPS rhumb line. *Elmo* was the name they had given the wind vane, a wind-operated steering device mounted on the stern of the boat. Streamlining the sails with the wind allowed them to pick up a quarter-knot of speed.

After reading the section of the Bahamas Cruising Guide that was related to Green Turtle Cay, Logan was confident of the best angle to enter the cut in the reef into the anchorage. The warm sun rose above his head in the cloudless sky and lingered at the apex. He was thrilled to see their plan had been achieved—to arrive at the bay when the sun was directly overhead.

"Hey, sleepyhead, time to get up. We're almost there," Logan said, poking his head down the companionway.

Hope rolled over at the sound of his voice and looked up toward the cockpit. The bright sun made her squint, like emerging from a movie theater in the middle of the day. Its intensity seemed out of place to her at first.

Taking the steering from *Elmo*, Logan turned the boat into the wind so Hope could lower the sails.

"I think the water looks deeper on the left side of the cut," Hope called from the bow. After successfully directing Logan through the opening and into the anchorage, they inched their way through the maze of shallow sand bars. With the sun at a ninety-degree angle to the clear water, it was easy to see where the coral and sand bars were.

"We can squeeze in over there," Hope said, pointing to a wide spot between two smaller boats. When they were in position, Hope lowered the anchor and chain-rode into the water. Logan put the boat in reverse and pulled back hard to ensure the anchor had set and dug deeply into the sandy ocean floor. Reaching down over the bow, Hope secured the nylon snubber to the anchor chain so there would be no annoying grinding noise in the cabin below.

Out of habit, they straightened *Ladyhawke* before going ashore. Dirty dishes were washed; bedding that was spread out in the salon was folded and put away; halyards and jib sheets were neatly coiled and hung; and *Ladyhawke* became a proper little sailing yacht.

Hope brought two glasses of tea up to the cockpit.

"We survived," Logan said with a chuckle, raising his glass to Hope.

"Thank God," Hope said, raising her glass in return. She couldn't believe she almost saw delight in Logan's expression as he remembered the severe weather they had sailed through. She shook her head, relieved to be safely anchored. Hope would be happy if she never had to sail in a storm again but Logan seemed to perversely enjoy the challenge.

They went to shore in their small inflatable dinghy. It was time to officially check into the Bahamas, since they were now a foreign-flagged vessel.

"Whoa!" Hope giggled and tried to walk a straight line as her sea legs wobbled.

Logan playfully shoved her and they both lost their balance. Every time they looked up, they felt like they were back on the boat. The sky swayed from side to side, and their stance automatically widened for stability.

Inside the immigration building, the air-conditioner strained to keep the air cool. A large, dark-skinned Bahamian woman stood behind the reception counter. Her straight tan skirt fell just below her knees and spread tightly across her full rear. Sewn to the sleeves of her tan blouse were several official-looking badges and pinned to her lapel were more official-looking symbols. A name-tag on her chest read "Lil." Her attire made her look authoritative, but her happy-go-lucky attitude made her seem like an old friend.

"Hey, how's it goin'?" she asked.

"We're tired, but we're here," Logan answered, handing her his documentation papers.

"You've arrived in paradise. Come join the party," Lil said, shaking her hips as if she was dancing. She quickly filled out their entrance papers.

"Now head on over to Isabel's and have yourselves an Island Splash," she said, recommending they start their stay with a specialty drink consisting of five different rums and a dash of fruit juice.

Hope and Logan were drained from the crossing so they made it an early evening and went back to *Ladyhawke*, vowing to try an Island Splash another day.

"You'd better enjoy this barbequed bird," Logan declared as he prepared chicken on the grill that hung off the stern rail of *Ladyhawke*, "because from now on, we are going to be eating from the sea." Presumably he was referring to all of the lobster and fish he planned on spearing.

At dusk they settled into the cockpit with a bottle of wine. Hope reclined into Logan's arms and engulfed his lips in a lingering kiss. From the cockpit, they watched the sun's rays filter down through a layer of mist in the air. The water beneath them leisurely rocked the boat from side to side. Through the hazy air, it was possible to look directly at the sun as it set. The sun seemed to move slowly toward the horizon, but once its lower edge touched the surface of the water, the fluorescent orange-red ball slipped quickly beneath the edge, vanishing until another dawn. In the afterglow of twilight, everything took on a magical aura, as if it were radiating its own light instead of reflecting the sun. Slowly, the almost-full moon rose above the horizon, and stars popped through the silky black sky. In the arms of her lover on this clear night, anchored off a small tropical island, Hope had arrived in her own dream.

Perfect Day in Paradise

"WHOO WHOOOO WHO WHO," AN EURASIAN collared dove's coo penetrated the aimless drift of Hope's awakening mind. For a moment she thought she was in her childhood home with a mourning dove calling for a mate in the oak tree outside her bedroom window. Then, smiling, she realized she was peacefully nestled with Logan in the forward berth of *Ladyhawke*, while her mind momentarily relived the first hair-raising exploit on their sought-after aquatic voyage. Water lapped at the boat's hull, and a pleasant breeze filtered in through the hatch above their heads. *Ladyhawke* sat anchored in the quiet waters of White Sound Bay, surrounded on three sides by Green Turtle Cay. Inch by inch the boat shifted to the side as the morning tides changed directions and the chain snubber groaned. Curled close to Logan's warm sleeping body, Hope drifted back to sleep.

The tender mating call came again, "Whoo whoooo who who." Once more, Hope was drawn out of her envelope of unconsciousness. The melodic cry beckoned her to get up and greet the new day. Gradually, she eased out of bed so as not to awaken Logan.

A lone, shirtless boy walked in the sand along the water's edge, flinging stones and broken shells into the water with a long crooked stick. The air hung heavy with moisture. *Ladyhawke*'s deck was slick with condensation. The sun's emergence above the horizon promised a beautiful, cloudless day in the crystal clear waters of the Bahamas.

On the varnished teak and holly sole in the galley, Hope stood below sea level. The port lights she looked out were barely four feet above the water's surface. The sounds of sloshing water reverberated through the walls of the cabin.

The simplicity of boat life fit well with Hope's personality. Everything she required for living life was contained within this small space. All the belongings she needed to be happy were within a few steps and an arm's reach. Even the man she loved was just a few feet away.

Hope brought a kettle of water to boil and poured it over coffee grounds in a French Press. When the brew was wafting a rich aroma through the cabin, she poured Logan a cup into his favorite mug that read, *You Mocha My Dreams Come True.* Then she poured herself a cup, adding several splashes of milk and a drizzle of honey.

"Are you really asleep or are you playing possum?" she teased, as she brought the steaming cups of coffee to the forward berth. "You're missing a beautiful day. Would you like coffee in bed or up in the cockpit?"

"Hmmm…" Logan groaned without opening his eyes. "Maybe the first cup in bed." He was always slow to start in the morning.

Hope set the hot cups of coffee on the richly varnished teak nightstand. She propped pillows behind Logan as he scooted sideways to lean against the ash panels of the ceiling that, on a sailboat, are the side walls.

Logan was no stranger to the boating world either. Because of his inability to focus on anything but the sea, his passion for free diving and sunken treasures turned into his career. *You Lose It, I'll Find It,* his underwater salvage company, contracted with international companies and the U.S. Government to retrieve all sorts of things from the bottom of oceans or lakes. His working vessel, *Maggie*, carried his one-man submarine and side-scanning sonar with monitoring screen.

To Logan, his job was pure bliss. When he was not employed to excavate something from the bottom of a body of water, he spent endless days scanning the ocean floor for sunken ships and the hope of ancient treasures. Logan enjoyed his job so much that weeks seemed like days when he was working with his submarine. Packing to move onto *Ladyhawke*, Logan couldn't bear to leave all of his treasure-hunting gear behind, so he grabbed his sonar equipment at the last minute and mounted the display screen in the cockpit.

"Let's go snorkeling!" Hope exclaimed excitedly before she slid her long legs into the high berth and sat beside Logan to drink her coffee. "You won't believe how beautiful it is outside."

Logan ran his fingers through his sun-streaked hair. He finally opened his eyes and with a glare, he grunted, "I just woke up."

"I know, but you should see it outside," she said emphatically, exuding enthusiasm while ignoring his scowl. Her playful, carefree attitude filled the cabin with youthful excitement. "You can't sleep your life away."

"The morning won't be gone in a half hour," he said as he took a long sip of coffee and sighed. "There's nothing like a good cup o' joe in bed. Except…"

He flirtatiously raised his eyebrows as he gently scratched himself beneath the sheets.

Hope giggled. "Oh my God, some things never change," she said rolling her eyes. "Don't you think it's really amazing we're finally living the dream? It seems like we've been planning this trip for a long time."

"Since we met," Logan said.

"And now we really have an entire year to play." Hope couldn't believe their good fortune. "The only thing on our calendar is meeting up with Billy and Rocky in Honduras at the end of March."

Hope and Logan had met William Dancing Wolf and Falling Rock in Mexico four years earlier on the same trip that they had first met each other. Since then, the four of them had met annually to vacation together.

"We're out here doing the dream," Logan finally grinned, drinking his coffee as his consolation to the alternative things he would rather be doing in bed.

"Spear fishing, spear fishing, spear fishing," Hope quietly chanted.

"Do you hear something?" she said louder, teasing him.

"No, what?" he came back, scowling at her with his eyes, but smiling with his lips. "I haven't had my second cup of coffee yet."

"Okay. Okay," she said as she crawled out of bed and walked the few steps to the galley for more coffee.

Logan genuinely smiled as he watched Hope from behind. He loved the way she pampered him and made him feel special. He also acknowledged the continual zest for life she exuded, always bringing excitement to their lives.

With two cups of coffee down, Logan leapt out of bed, ready

for a morning of spear fishing. Hope checked the tide table on the GPS to determine when there would be sufficient water in the shallow bay to leave without scraping *Ladyhawke*'s belly on the sand bars. It was already midway on a rising tide, perfect time to pull anchor and head to Elbow Cay where they had heard the diving was good. If they didn't leave the bay now, they would have to wait twelve hours until the tides were right again. They quickly pulled anchor and sailed out of the bay.

The sailing was crisp as they proficiently maneuvered between the small islands in the Abaco Sea. Two hours later they slipped into Elbow Cay Bay and anchored *Ladyhawke* beside the other boats in the anchorage. Eager to go spear fishing, Hope and Logan quickly got into *Sharpy*, their dinghy, and scouted around the northern tip of the island, looking for a dive-worthy reef.

The docile sea was smooth, allowing Hope to see deep into the translucent water, down to a wobbling collage of colors she knew from experience to be coral on the bottom of the ocean. Hope stopped the small boat just to the side of what appeared to be a perfect reef as Logan rolled off the side of *Sharpy* into the water. He took along his Hawaiian sling, a handheld slingshot apparatus with a five-foot spear.

Swimming with his mask, snorkel, and extremely long fins along the top of the water, he followed the jagged reef's edge looking for signs of edible fish or lobsters. Beneath him, large purple fans swayed in the slowly undulating water. Giant brown brain coral, with their maze of ridges, were tucked beneath the expansive fans. Lavender stone pipe sponge sprouted beside giant anemones ten inches wide. The anemone's pink and purple tentacles swayed with the movement of the water, waiting to paralyze and engulf sea creatures as large as a black, spiny sea urchin. Tiny transparent cleaning shrimp hid from predators in the anemone's tentacles and picked organic particles off its body. Secured to the coral rock, little bunches of Christmas tree worms bent in the current.

Logan was at home in the water. He easily submerged into this alien world and the rest of humanity drifted away from his mind. He was "on the hunt," as he called it, looking for fish for the grill. As he dove down to take a closer look at a particular fish, Hope visually followed his white T-shirt. It was the only color that didn't blend into the colorful aquatic world. Even so, she could barely distinguish him from the reef as he wove in and out of the coral heads thirty feet below.

Exploding out of the water, Logan breathlessly announced, "There's a triggerfish down there that's huge. I'll see if I can get it this time."

"Dinner's coming," Hope replied in a singsong tone. "Here fishy, fishy, fishy." Logan replaced the snorkel in his mouth, shook his head at her playful lyrics and headed down again.

Hope kept the dinghy above Logan. Twice he surfaced before he was able to position himself for a clean shot. He knew he would only have one chance to fire his Hawaiian sling, before the fish got spooked and swam away. So, on his third descent he quickly moved into position and let the spear fly. *Whap.* It was a perfect hit. The triggerfish struggled to swim, but it had no chance with a five-foot spear driven completely through its body. After filling his lungs once more, he kicked hard to get down to the struggling fish.

"Nice!" Hope shouted, when Logan surfaced with the large triggerfish impaled.

"Big one!" Logan shouted as he handed Hope the spear and she removed the fish from the shaft into the dinghy. She held it down on the bottom of the boat with her bare foot, careful not to get stuck by the rigid dorsal fin, as the fish fought to spin free. The unique dorsal fin of the triggerfish, if pulled forward, held stiff under any amount of pressure; but if pulled backwards, the fin released like the trigger of a gun.

Logan flipped into the dinghy close behind the speared fish—a precaution, just in case the smell of blood or the squeal of the injured fish had attracted the local reef sharks. Any sign of an injured fish meant an effortless meal for a shark and Logan definitely didn't want to be in between the shark and his next meal.

"Grilled triggerfish for dinner tonight," Hope said with glee. She could already imagine how the fish, brushed with lime juice and olive oil and seasoned with fresh dill, would taste.

"What a blast!" Logan cheered, taking Hope away from her fantasy. "I don't see any sharks, do you?" Even though he knew the smell of blood could attract a shark for quite some time, his enthusiasm took over. "Oh, what the heck. I'm going in."

"What if we go find another reef?" Hope asked. Not allowing Logan time to get back in the water, she pulled the ripcord and started the dinghy engine. "We aren't taking any chances."

"Okay," he acquiesced.

As they motored across the flat sea, Logan grinned.

"God, I love this!" he shouted, raising his hands in the air.

Logan turned to Hope and gave her a high-five.

Hope motored the dinghy past the bay and headed south. At the edge of another coral reef, she threw the small dinghy anchor and its rope-rode over into a patch of sand. Both Hope and Logan jumped into the water. Once in, Hope turned in a three-hundred-sixty-degree circle to get her bearings and scan for sharks. The coast looked clear. Now she was free to cautiously enjoy the beauty around her. Golden brown elkhorn coral intertwined their stiff jagged branches beneath a large school of blue striped and margate grunts. Their yellow and blue striping shifted in unison, resembling an intricately choreographed ballet. One lone, shy spiny puffer fish cautiously swam above the grunts.

The puffer nervously kept one eye on the human intruders. Hope enjoyed seeing spiny puffers inflate themselves, so she tormented the fish by repeatedly swimming too close for his comfort. Finally, the puffer sucked in a large amount of water, filling up like a balloon and sending his quills straight out at attention. His small fins quivered trying to swim away from Hope. When the fish disappeared from her view behind a large brain coral, Hope's attention turned to a hawksbill turtle a few yards away. The turtle time after time broke chunks of brain coral off the reef with its bird-like beak of a mouth. Directly below, she saw a trumpet fish hide its long, skinny body along the shaft of a purple stove pipe sponge. There it waited to ambush a small fish prey by sucking it into its mouth in one quick motion.

Upon closer observation, she spotted a prehistoric-looking, long snout sea horse also hiding in the sponge. Its outer, hard skeletal structure made it look like it was armored for battle. Using its dorsal fin to propel itself forward, it contented itself by consuming tiny brine shrimp whole. Next Hope was caught off guard by a long, silver, torpedo-shaped fish hovering twenty yards away. She instantly feared it was a shark, but with a scrutinizing look, she could tell it was a five-foot-long barracuda. Staring at Hope, it opened and closed its threatening mouth, displaying its sharp, menacing teeth. Hope knew the stories. Barracuda didn't attack people very often, but still the sinister fish gave her the creeps. She remained cautious.

Logan, on the other hand, ignored the colorful tropical fish and looked only for edible ones.

Submerged in this watery world of unusual shapes and colors, Logan and Hope were foreigners. They seemed to be trespassing in a universe where they weren't particularly welcome. But their fascination and total attention to the sea brought them back to it over and over again.

Hope Town, Elbow Cay, Bahamas

HOPE YAWNED AND RUBBED HER EYES. A SHIVER shot up her spine as she massaged her arms to ward off the chilly morning air. A mild cold front had blown in during the night and the cool breeze on her face was invigorating, like jumping into a mountain stream.

A thin layer of clouds striped the northern sky. From *Ladyhawke's* cockpit, Hope looked around at the other boats in the small bay and imagined the morning rituals of the people aboard. Being so closely moored to other boats was almost like living in an apartment complex. Hope could hear voices coming from her neighbors, but she wasn't quite close enough to understand what they were saying.

The delicious aroma of baking bread drifted across the bay from shore. Hope stuck her head down the companionway and looked into the forward berth to make sure Logan was still asleep before boarding *Sharpy*. She maneuvered through the crowded bay, taking the small skiff to the city dock. Skillfully cutting the engine, she allowed the boat to drift up to the dock. Before she could tie the painter to a cleat, a fellow boater reached down and took the line from her so she could easily crawl ashore as he held the dinghy tight to the dock.

"Thank you," Hope said, taking the painter from the stranger. Before securely attaching the line, she pushed the dinghy away from the dock so the boat's hypolon rubber material wouldn't rub on the barnacle-encrusted pilings.

"Which boat are you on?" the thin, weathered man asked. The boating world held a friendly crowd, always socializing and wanting to talk about life at sea.

"*Ladyhawke*," Hope responded, pointing in the direction from which she had come.

"Oh, she's a beautiful boat," he said with sincerity. "I noticed her coming into the bay yesterday. What kind is she?"

"A Fair Weather Mariner 39," Hope told him with an air of confidence.

From the quick shake of his head and his eyes darting upward as if trying to recall the make, Hope could tell he wasn't familiar with the boat.

"She was designed by Bob Perry," she offered, thinking the name might shed some light on *Ladyhawke*'s basic design. Most sailors recognized Bob Perry as an excellent naval architect. And it did seem to convey a particular knowledge. The man nodded affirmatively.

"A bunch of us boaters are having a little gathering tonight up by the Hope Town Lodge pool. Come and join us?"

"Sounds great. What time?" Hope asked as they both started walking down the dock toward shore.

"We usually get together around five," he responded.

"I'm sure we'll be there. My husband and I just got to the Bahamas a couple of days ago and we would like to meet other cruisers," Hope said as she turned to the left at the end of the dock and he turned to the right.

"My name is Jon," he said with a quick wave.

"I'm Hope. Thanks for the info."

"This is your town," he added, turning to make eye contact before walking south.

Jon's face was windswept and craggy but his eyes sparkled with joy. Hope watched his relaxed saunter as he strolled down the sidewalk following the coastline. She momentarily saddened with the thought of her father, knowing he would have enjoyed a cruiser's life.

Jon was right. She had the same name as the town. Hope was amazed at herself for not noticing the connection before.

Striding down Back Street, a narrow cobblestone lane, Hope followed her nose through the village. The slender walking street was lined with quaint, brightly-painted, clapboard houses and stores. Lush flower and vegetable gardens protruded through the picket fences framing their petite yards. The slow-paced, eighteenth-century fishing village, balanced upon the slender spine of the quarter-mile-wide island, was almost mystical in its old-world splendor and charm. The protrusion of the thin island above the water looked like the archeological excavation of a large prehistoric dinosaur's back, partially dug out of the earth.

Hope peered in the windows of the small gift stores and restaurants as she walked. She passed a very small fire station—so small that it looked like it displayed a miniature fire truck, not a true emergency vehicle. The fire truck had been ingeniously designed to fit down the narrow streets, originally built for pedestrians, and occasionally used by golf carts.

The smell of fresh bread was heady, and Hope's mouth was watering. She came to an abrupt stop when she spotted a man through the open door of a small room behind a grocery store. He was taking loaves of bread out of an oven. As Hope watched him, she tried to determine the likelihood of the bread being for sale.

Hope stepped up to the door of the bakery and innocently asked, "Is the bread ready? Is it for sale?"

The baker, who was also the owner of the grocery, slowly looked up from the pan of bread he held with oven mitts and gazed at her with expressionless eyes. He paused for a moment as if to determine whether she was worthy of his precious hand measured, mixed and kneaded bread.

Quietly, he said, "It just came out of the oven. It's too hot to bag."

Back at work, he turned each of the bread tins over to release the steaming loaves out onto a cooling rack.

Hope felt like she was interrupting him, but she wanted to know when it would be ready. Meekly she asked, "Should I come back in an hour?"

"It will be gone in an hour," he said without looking up.

Frustrated with the lack of information, Hope wasn't sure how she should proceed. Silently, she watched the baker. He had been known to completely ignore tourists and not sell his bread to them if he wasn't in the mood. Something about Hope must have struck a slight cord of appeal in him because when he was finished taking the loaves out of the pans, he turned toward her and said, "You can take one now if you don't put it in plastic."

"Oh, no," Hope said with excitement. "I don't need plastic."

With an oven mitt, he carried a loaf of bread through the back screen door of the grocery to the cash register and laid it on a stack of napkins. Hope followed his lead. The baker then walked back into his tiny bakery without saying another word.

The cashier was just as non-communicative. She looked up at

Hope and said, "That'll be three dollars." Hope paid for the bread and picked it up with several napkins so as not to burn her hands. She walked through a narrow pathway, exiting the front of the small grocery, avoiding the stacks of boxes of bottled water, soda and juice on the front porch. The exposed boxes were a sure sign of the lack of theft on the island.

Hope carried the loaf of bread in front of her chest, clutching it with both hands as though it were a giggling baby she was playing with. She sat down on the bench in front of Captain Pete's, a small diner where locals hang out. Laying the bread on the napkins in her lap, she ripped a chunk off and delighted her taste buds with a bite. It was amazing. The soft, warm bread was as good as it smelled. Its buttery crust melted in her mouth.

Hope sat on the bench for several moments watching the people go by as she ate the bread.

Before she knew it, she had eaten half of the loaf. By then, the bread was cool enough to wrap what was left in the napkins and place it in her knapsack.

From the galley, Hope could hear Logan moving around in the forward berth. She had returned to the boat.

"Cute little town," she said loudly as she put a teapot of water on to boil. "We've been invited to a boaters' get together tonight."

With the confusion of a groggy mind, Logan rubbed his head. "What are you talking about?" he asked.

"I took the dinghy to shore. Oh, and Logan, I found a bakery. You'll have to have some of this bread. Anyway, there was a guy on the dock that told me about the get-together."

Logan lowered himself out of the berth and walked into the salon in his boxers. "You've already been to shore?" he asked.

"Yeah. You were sleeping and I could smell the bread even out here. I wanted to see if I could find where the smell was coming from. And I did. Here, taste this," she said, removing the half eaten bread from the knapsack and handing it to Logan.

"But it's half gone," Logan said indignantly.

"Oh, no. I only ripped off a little chunk," Hope said pursing her lips and rolling her eyes, allowing Logan to know she was lying.

Squeezing into the galley with Hope, Logan removed a tub of butter from the refrigerator and a jar of honey from a cabinet. He slowly mixed a glob of the butter with some of the honey in a bowl while the water for their coffee heated. The bread was now the perfect temperature to slowly melt the butter in the honey mixture, allowing it to soak into the nooks and crannies. Logan also couldn't stop eating the bread; he ate the remaining half of the loaf before it completely cooled.

As soon as the morning air warmed, Hope and Logan loaded their diving gear into *Sharpy* and left the bay in search of another delicacy from the sea. Scooting around the rocky eastern shore, they found a series of coral reefs to explore. Hope threw the small anchor over the bow of *Sharpy* onto a narrow, sandy strip.

Logan kicked his flippers hard to get over to the edge of the reef in the swiftly moving tide. From the surface, he watched for any waving antennas or other lobster parts protruding from beneath the rocky shelves. The Caribbean spiny lobster was a curious crustacean. It frequently stuck its head out of its hiding hole to keep track of the creatures in its vicinity.

A queen conch slowly traversed the sand at the edge of the coral reef creating a path in the swaying sea grass. A small school of snapper got Logan's attention. He knew they would be good for dinner, but his mind was set on lobster. Hope noticed a beautiful queen angel and floated above it to watch its continual inquisitive maneuvers, poking at the coral with its hardened mouth for a bite of food.

After looking in every crack and under every shelf, Logan proceeded to the next coral formation ten to twenty yards to the south. He scrutinized the reef, looking for an elusive lobster. After an hour of swimming, diving and scanning the coral beds, Logan began to think he should have shot a couple of the snappers he had seen on the first reef that morning. He stuck his head out of the water and looked around to get his bearings when he noticed Hope quickly swimming in his direction. She looked up, got his attention and motioned to him to follow.

"I found a lobster!" she shouted and started swimming back in the direction from which she had come.

Logan loaded his spear into the sling as he kicked his long flippers. Hope led him back to the place where she had spotted the lobster in hiding. Sure enough, there was a pair of large, thick antennae sticking out from under a rock outcropping in the middle of a small reef. Logan tried to determine how he was going to get down into the small hole with his spear to snag the lobster. To get a closer look, Logan slowly lowered himself into the opening. He had to talk himself into going head first without knowing what was actually in there. It was probably the one and only thing that Logan was afraid of—being confined in a hole or cave and not knowing what he would encounter.

The opening in the reef was just barely large enough for him to get his chest and torso down low enough to get the spear in position. His excitement doubled when he saw the size of the lobster. It looked like a small dog up on its hind legs, protecting its hole. Up for a quick breath of air, Logan once again lowered himself into the hole, this time letting the spear fly. It was a perfect hit, but it must not have killed the lobster because the spear disappeared deep into the hole.

Logan had to surface again for a breath of air. Diving into the hole, he grabbed the end of the spear and pulled. He thought it would come right out with the impaled lobster, but the spear slipped through his grip and stayed where it was. Logan reached deep into the hole again. Grabbing the spear with both hands, he yanked. Still it didn't move. After another breath of air, he dove again, this time standing on the rocky edge of the hole. Straining to reach down to the spear, Logan yanked the shaft, pushing with his legs off the ledge. Still the spear didn't budge.

Logan swam back to the surface and paused for a moment catching his breath. With horror, he watched as the spear jerked from side to side and fell deeper into the hole. A good-sized grouper then swam out in front of Logan. Moments later, he cautiously lowered himself to the brim. Fearing what else he might encounter, he peered in from the edge to try to find where his spear had disappeared to, but it was nowhere to be seen.

"I've lost it," he said, when he came to the surface.

"What do you mean?" Hope asked, treading water just a few feet away.

"I don't see it," he said, sounding discouraged.

With another big breath of air in his lungs, he twisted from side to side, scanning the interior of the hole. He maneuvered himself to peer under every ledge he could find without sticking his head too far into the opening. But still he saw no lobster or spear.

Logan swam all the way around the small reef system. On one side there was a ledge about two feet above the sandy bottom. He cautiously dove down and looked under the rock outcropping. About ten feet in, he could see his spear lying on the sand, no lobster in sight. Above the spear, out of the shadows, came a large green moray eel. It slithered out of its hiding place, baring its razor-sharp teeth to him. He fought to back himself away from the approaching fish. He wouldn't take the chance of diving through the small opening and scraping his belly on the sand, while not knowing what else he might encounter besides the moray. Logan dove repeatedly, trying to figure out how he was going to get his spear back. Each time he peered beneath the rocky ledge, he looked into the mouth of the eel.

"Now what?" Logan asked. "How am I supposed to get my spear back with that eel lying on top of it?"

Hope laughed. It seemed so silly to her when she saw how afraid he was to go into small spaces when it seemed like nothing else scared him.

Logan dove into the water one more time and peered under the ledge at his spear lying in the sand.

"I would have to swim eight to ten feet under the coral before being able to grab the end," Logan said, shaking his head with a shiver of disgust. "Then I'd have to back my way out."

He could no longer see the slithering green eel. He knew it was in the coral, but he couldn't tell where. As much as he tried to talk himself into swimming beneath the rock outcropping, he couldn't do it. So he made a mental note of the reef's location in comparison to the land. He was determined to rig up a retrieval device so he could come back the following morning and reclaim his hunting tool.

Dejected, Logan and Hope drove the dinghy back to *Ladyhawke*.

That evening they took *Sharpy* to the Hope Town Lodge dock. Behind the petite lobby was a courtyard with a pool and outdoor bar situated at the pinnacle of the island. They felt like they were on top of the world, able to see in all directions. To the east they could see down to the pristine, white sand beach that followed along the edge of the deep blue Atlantic Ocean. To the west was the emerald green bay where all of the boats were moored.

The waiter served the patrons drinks while dancing to the music of Barefoot Man, a local musician who sang his own songs about island life. As Hope waited for beers, a song blared out of a boom box. The lyrics were explicitly about sexual bumping. The waiter completely stopped the efficient serving of drinks to throw his hands in the air and thrust his hips while biting his lower lip. The women in the crowd went wild and cheered him on.

For a fat boy, he has the moves, Hope thought and smiled to herself.

Hope noticed the man from the dinghy dock that morning. He was standing next to a beautiful, young woman that Hope assumed was his daughter. She was also very thin and small framed.

"Hope, this is my partner, Lynn," Jon said, grabbing the arm of the woman next to him.

The introduction momentarily confused her, because she assumed the woman had to be his daughter. Hope turned to Logan and took his hand while introducing him.

Before long, Logan was telling Jon about the lost spear and the disappearance of the lobster.

"Are you going diving tomorrow?" Jon questioned.

"Yeah, I have to get my spear."

"Do you mind if I tag along?" Jon smiled.

"I'd love the help," Logan replied. "Tonight I'll make something with my extendable boat hook that I can stick under the reef to retrieve the spear." Logan assumed that because of Jon's advanced age he was just going along for the ride, and he would enjoy snorkeling while Logan got his spear and went hunting.

From experience, Logan had learned to be tentative when talking to sailors about his previous experience on boats, even though he had sailed an extensive amount. Having gone from Maine to Bermuda, then on to the Virgin Islands, Logan felt he was an experienced sailor. From there he had continued down the Windward and Leeward Islands to Trinidad and Venezuela. Skirting the northern shore of South America, he visited the Aves and Los

Roques Islands before reaching Aruba and Bonaire. Only when prompted did he mention these achievements, because it seemed whenever he was asked, he got excited and went off on a tangent reliving his adventures.

Inevitably he would find out later that his meager experience was nothing compared to the vast accomplishments of those questioning him. Often the one asking Logan for his story had sailed around the world—maybe twice, or without an engine on a twenty-five-foot boat. Logan's extensive circumnavigation of the Caribbean on a forty-foot boat with a forty-four-horsepower diesel and another experienced sailor aboard paled in comparison.

When the crowd began to break up, Hope and Logan walked past the tall sea grass, down the steep embankment of sand to the almost black water of the Atlantic Ocean.

He grabbed Hope's hand as they walked along the shore.

"Do you remember when we met?" he asked.

"Of course! How could I forget our week in Puerto Aventuras?"

"I knew when I first saw you that you were the one," Logan said squeezing her hand.

"How did you know?" Hope asked.

"It was those perky little boobs," Logan said.

"Nice!" Hope exclaimed sarcastically and hit him with the sandals she was carrying.

Logan put his arm around her shoulder and pulled her close to him.

"I'm just kidding," he said. "I just knew. I had this strange feeling that you would have my kids. Before then, I never thought about having kids."

"Do you still think about it?"

"At times like this, I do," he said, stopping in the ankle deep water to give Hope a kiss. "I love you, Hopie. When we get home, I think we should try to have kids."

"Kids? How may do you want?"

"Oh, maybe a couple."

"I'd like that," she said, snuggling close to his chest.

The following morning, Logan picked up Jon for their excursion.

They maneuvered the dinghy back to the reef system where he and Hope had been the previous day. After hooking *Sharpy's* anchor in the soft sand beside the reef, Jon put his mask and snorkel on and lowered himself into the water. Logan collected his retrieval device and prepared himself for the dive.

By the time Logan got in, Jon was coming out from under the reef's edge with Logan's spear in hand. He had swum into the small crevice and grabbed the spear before reversing his way back out of the tight opening. Logan couldn't believe it. This wiry old man had more nerve and flexibility than he did. He now saw Jon in a different light.

"Thanks, man," Logan said. He began to wonder if Jon was one of those men with an extreme number of sailing adventures that he just wasn't talking about because he was too busy asking Logan about his.

"Let's find dinner," Jon said.

They each went their separate ways looking for edible fish. Within moments, Logan spotted a moderately large grouper and began to pursue it. He tried not to threaten the fish as he followed it from the surface of the water, watching it traverse through the spectacular topography of brain coral, elephant ears and elkhorn coral. Wanting the fish to stay calm so he could get into position for a clean shot, Logan kept his distance until he saw the perfect opportunity. Stretching the rubbers on his sling, he positioned himself directly above the unsuspecting grouper. Logan took a deep breath and submerged into the water. He was lucky and drove the spear through the fish with his first shot.

Swimming back to the dinghy with the grouper on his spear, Logan noticed Jon was also approaching the dinghy with his spear up and a beautiful triggerfish struggling on the end. Logan shook his head with amazement, once again having to shift in his mind what a seventy-five-year-old man was capable of. Logan pictured his father, who was just sixty-four. He couldn't imagine him having the stamina or ability to dive and hold his breath long enough to pierce a fish.

Logan reached the dinghy first and leaned over the edge with the spear ready to release the fish off the shaft to the bottom of the boat. When he looked down, he noticed there was already a large snapper lying on the dinghy floor. Jon had not only retrieved his spear from a tight place Logan wasn't willing to go, but he had also shot two fish in the time it took Logan to shoot one.

Relaxing into the bottom of the dinghy, they leaned against one of its blown up side tubs and propped their feet on the opposite one. Logan grabbed two bottles of water from his cooler and handed one to Jon.

When Logan went back into the water to pursue more fish, Jon stayed in the dinghy. Jon didn't feel the need to shoot more fish than he and Lynn would eat in the next couple of days. Relaxing in the warmth of the sun, Jon leaned back, closed his eyes and began to drift off.

For half an hour Logan swam close to the dinghy. At one point he found two very large lobsters in a small crevice about twenty-five feet down. They seemed to be wedged in so tight that he couldn't quite see how to pull them out once they were speared. He dove repeatedly trying to solve his predicament. While coming to the surface for a breath of air, he felt as though a mallet hit him from behind, knocking what little air he had left out of his lungs. Luckily he was close to the surface of the water, so he was able to make it to the top before he gasped for air. Spinning around, the dorsal fin of the culprit—a ten-foot-long reef shark, was an arm's length away. Logan swam as fast as he could in the opposite direction, back to the dinghy. Grabbing its side, he kicked hard, and in one swoop, he was up and over the side.

"What on earth?" Jon asked, laughing and shaking off the wave of water that Logan had brought into the boat with him. "What are you doing?"

"Sharks," Logan said out of breath.

"What?"

"Sharks. There was a shark down there trying to see if I was going to be his next meal," Logan said as he struggled to get his flippers and mask off.

"And what did he determine you were?"

"I don't know. I didn't stick around long enough to find out."

"I guess we should have moved to a new location. The sharks smell the blood from the fish we've speared," Jon said, with disbelief. In all his years of diving Jon had never been threatened by a shark.

Leaning forward, Logan tried to reach the middle of his back with his hands, but his well developed upper body muscles made it difficult for him to manipulate his arms to reach the tender spot.

"Jesus, that hurts," he grimaced.

Jon pulled him to the side. A large, dark red spot was forming on his rib cage. "Logan, what happened down there?" Jon asked.

"I was diving on a pair of lobsters," Logan said, still trying to reach the center of his back. "Yeah, man, you should have seen them. They were huge."

"I'm glad you weren't shark bait. Hope would have been pissed if I returned without you," Jon said chuckling, making light of the serious situation.

"We've got enough for today," he said leaning over the bow of the dinghy and hauling in the rope-rode and anchor.

The next three days in Hope Town passed like the first one. The sun shone intensely in the cloudless sky, and Hope and Logan swam for several hours. Each night they ate the catch of the day.

By the fifth day, the wind shifted to the north and cooled, and the sky filled with big billowing clouds. At two o'clock in the afternoon the clouds broke loose, and rain washed the dust and salt from *Ladyhawke*'s deck. With the shift of weather, the McKnights knew it would soon be time to pull anchor and move with the wind to their next playground. Sheets of rain danced across the water in the bay. Hope and Logan prepared the cabin of the boat for sailing. All of their belongings, such as books, silverware, dishes and laptop computer, were secured so they couldn't become dangerous projectiles when the seas got rough and the boat rolled wildly from one side to the other.

NOAA, the weather forecast on the VHF, predicted the rain would stop by the next morning, but the northern wind would continue for several days—perfect conditions to make the run to South Caicos, which was four hundred eighty-seven miles. Their sailing plan was to go due east for about thirty hours or around one hundred fifty miles, to make the needed easting. Then they would turn south toward the Turks and Caicos Islands.

The overcast sky hung low in the early morning mist when Hope went forward to the bow and proceeded to hand-over-hand haul in the chain and anchor. A whooshing sound, like the air in a tire being released, caught her attention. As she looked for its origin, she saw a dolphin off the starboard bow. It snapped shut its blowhole and rolled over to look up at her. Hope adored dolphins. Her heart instantly melted anytime she saw one. To her disbelief, the dolphin began to help her pull up the chain. He went to the sandy bottom and scooped it up with his dorsal fin, allowing Hope to pull it onto the deck effortlessly.

"Logan, look over the bow!" she yelled with enthusiasm as the dolphin dove again to the bottom and lifted up the following section of chain. Over and over, the dolphin dove and lifted until Hope had almost all of it on board with just the anchor stuck in the sand below. The dolphin then tried to lift the anchor with his fin, but couldn't. Next he dug his nose under the anchor claw and pried it up until he loosened it from the ocean floor. Then he was able to bring it to the surface for Hope while she, still effortlessly, hauled it aboard.

Laughing and cheering, Hope exclaimed, "Thanks, buddy!" The dolphin came to the surface of the water one more time and rolled to his side looking up at her. It was as if he smiled mischievously, waved good-bye with the shake of a flipper, and swam away.

"Logan, can you believe that?" she asked, pointing to where the dolphin had gone down in the water.

Logan smiled.

"Amazing," he said. "Simply amazing."

As the dolphin swam off, Hope stepped up onto the bow rail and steadied herself with the forward headstay. From there she was high enough off the water to see the shallow coral heads or brumbies (as the locals called them) and direct Logan safely out into the open waters. Logan pointed the bow of the boat into the wind, Hope winched up the mainsail and the sails filled. Then, they maneuvered through Man-O-War cut, a small opening in the reef that surrounds the Bahamian Banks, into the Atlantic Ocean. Logan adjusted the block on the traveler for an appropriate angle to the wind as he turned the boat east. Hope winched the headsail out, and *Ladyhawke* picked up speed. Logan was already smiling, feeling the pure bliss of the wind in his hair and the freedom of being out on the sea. *Ladyhawke* dipped her shoulder and plowed forward with the rolling waves, taking the two explorers on their next adventure.

With perfect sailing weather, there wasn't a lot to do after they trimmed the sails and set the wind vane to steer them to their charted waypoint. This was freedom in its classic sense—no phones, no cars, and no jobs to clock in at—just the two of them and the open sea.

Two days passed and they were now heading due south. Hope turned on the VHF for the daily weather check. It automatically tuned to Channel 16, the emergency channel, where there was silence, so Hope flipped through the others. She stopped on Channel 22, the all-purpose weather channel for the surrounding area. The weather forecast hadn't changed since the last time she listened. They could still expect northerly winds at eighteen to twenty-four knots and seas of three to five feet. She switched the radio back to Channel 16 and stood up from the nav-station with a stretch like a hound dog upon waking.

Trying to find something to do to pass the time, Hope picked up the book, *Life and Teaching of the Masters of the Far East,* and sat back down at the nav-station. She had just opened the book, hoping to be inspired, when suddenly she heard "Mayday! Mayday! Mayday!" coming from the VHF speakers.

Not believing her ears, she intently listened to see if it would come again. And it did. Another frantic "Mayday! Mayday! Mayday!" was barely audible over the radio static.

Heartbreak

MATTHEW WAITED AT THE CORNER BUS STOP. When the bus arrived, the Chagga tribe piled in, filling the seats and standing in the isle. Ashanti, Matthew's three-year-old granddaughter, sat on his lap as she danced her handmade cornhusk doll across his knee.

From the front of the bus, Zola began to sing, "Holy, holy, holy, Lord God Almighty! Early in the morning our song shall rise to thee."

"Holy, holy, holy, merciful and mighty! God in three Persons, blessed Trinity!" the rest of the group sang loudly in return. With the windows open, the bus rolled down the dirt streets on its way to the Lutheran church.

"Holy, holy, holy, Lord God Almighty! All thy works shall praise thy name in earth and sky and sea," Zola sang.

"Holy, holy, holy, merciful and mighty! God in three Persons, blessed Trinity," the others answered.

"Babu," Ashanti said, leaning into Matthew. "Mama sings like an angel."

"Like an angel in heaven," Matthew replied, cradling her cheek in his hand and pressing her head to his chest.

Sunday was Matthew's favorite day of the week. After church his family gathered for a big meal and relaxed under the large umbrella-shaped acacia tree behind his home. He felt comfort surrounded by them. From where he sat on a stump leaning against an old tree, he observed the preparations around him. His eighty-six-year-old mother sat on another stump and ground dried corn in a large wooden bowl—the same bowl he remembered her using when he was a child. His wife seared thin strips of goat meat on a small fire in their outdoor kitchen. His eldest daughter, Zola, shelled beans as Ashanti crawled on her back, wanting attention.

His teenaged twin daughters stood together looking in the same direction, and then, as if on cue, both turned to look the other way. It was as though they were mentally seeing and thinking in unison.

He knew his eldest son with his wife and their son, Samuel, would soon walk over from their neighboring house. Just moments earlier, he had watched his younger son enter their front door calling out to retrieve them.

From where he sat, Matthew could also see his brother and his family walking up the trail toward him carrying pots and bowls filled with food they were bringing to share. Luke, Matthew's brother, always seemed to have a barrel of banana beer for the occasion. To Matthew it was a perfect day.

The following morning Matthew was up early. He walked from his village to the entrance gate of Mount Kilimanjaro Park where he worked as a mountain guide. The park regulated all guides and porters as to how often they could climb the mountain and how much weight each was allowed to carry. This was Matthew's allotted week to work. It created an income for his family that he felt was needed.

After being assigned two American couples to guide up the mountain, he gathered the fourteen porters and the cook he had scheduled to assist him. The climb went smoothly. Everyone made it to the top with minimal complications. Five days later, on his way down the mountain, he was thankful for the beautiful weather they had and the thought of coming home to his family put a smile on his face.

But Matthew returned home that Saturday evening to devastating news. A great number of people in his village, including his mother, had come down with severe stomach flu. They had abdominal cramps and blazing headaches. It didn't appear that any of their traditional herbal medicines were helping.

Matthew sat on the floor next to his mother's cot. He felt helpless as he held her hand and looked into her yellowed eyes. Even before she had gotten sick, she was weak from her advanced age, but now she seemed barely able to lift her head for a drink of water.

"We've tried everything we can think of," Matthew's wife explained to him. "She's been sick for three days now."

He looked back toward his mother. She had closed her eyes.

"She doesn't seem to be in as much pain today," she continued.

"Yesterday she moaned all day about the hurting. It was awful to watch. We've tried everything, Matthew."

Matthew stood and put his arm around his wife's shoulder.

"It's just the flu. She will get better," he said with encouragement.

"I don't know, Matthew," she said. "This is different."

And she didn't get better. Six weeks later, she couldn't even swallow water. Weighing no more than sixty pounds, she died in her sleep. She wasn't the first to have died from the devastating flu. Already it had become an epidemic and a team of doctors came to see if they could help. They set up several large canvas tents in the soccer field, which became their makeshift emergency room. It seemed like overnight they had brought in a portable medical station with generators to create the electricity they needed and a large water purification station.

They quickly set up a portable lab, refrigerators, computers, cots and a 'round-the-clock staff of doctors and nurses. The Chagga people were grateful for their help, but still people were dying.

Every other week when Matthew left to climb the mountain, he feared for his friends and relatives, not knowing which ones would be sick when he returned. Three weeks after his mother had died, he returned home from work to find Ashanti cradled in her mother's arms with a wet cloth laid across her forehead.

Matthew fell to his knees to be with his daughter, whose face was twisted and distorted with grief. He placed his hand on his granddaughter's beautiful cheek. His heart sank. He shook his head with despair.

"Why?" Matthew muttered, not looking for an answer.

"Why?" he repeated, turning his eyes toward the ceiling.

The medical team tried several drugs on Ashanti. One seemed to take the symptoms of nausea and pain away, but she was so lethargic, she rarely moved from her mother's lap. Over the next several weeks her condition worsened. Her frail little body withered away.

"Sing for me, Babu," Ashanti said to Matthew as her dreary eyes closed. "Sing to me, like the angels in heaven."

Tears dripped from Matthew's eyes as he quietly sang, "Oh Lord, my God, I cry to Thee; in my distress Thou helpest me. My soul and body I command into Thy hands; Thine angel send to guide me home and cheer my heart when Thou dost call me to depart." The words softly slipped from his lips while he smoothed his dear granddaughter's thin hair away from her tiny forehead.

Ashanti died in Matthew's arms that night. Her little body was buried next to his mother's under the acacia tree.

Kilimanjaro

BEFORE GOING TO THE SIGN-IN HUT AT THE BASE of Mount Kilimanjaro, Matthew raised his gaze to the gray sky. The day seemed to reflect his mood. Drizzle seeped from the clouds and dripped down his cheeks, mixing his tears with heaven's, but his expressionless face concealed his pain.

"Good morning, sir," Matthew solemnly greeted Drew Thornton, the solo climber he was to guide up the mountain that week. "Are you ready for an adventure?" he added, wiping the moisture from his face with a hand towel.

"I'm looking forward to the challenge," Hope's brother answered, sincerely shaking Matthew's hand. Drew had come to Africa to observe the influence of global warming on Mount Kilimanjaro's icecap. Being a freelance journalist specializing in environmental issues, Drew frequently visited foreign countries to study the effects man had on the environment. At heart Drew was a naturalist, focused on living in harmony with the earth. He was a proponent of eliminating wasteful consumption and his motto was, "Less is more." He looked for ways to simplify his already simple life.

Through a break in the cloud cover, Matthew pointed to Kilimanjaro's visible peak.

"Yes, sir, we will be standing on top of her in just five days," he said, beginning to look forward to a week on his beloved mountain, not immersed in the continual dread he felt about the devastating plague taking its toll on his tribe.

Drew looked toward the mountain as his mind drifted to the pictures he had seen in an old National Geographic. The pictures had been taken on Peter MacQueen's failed attempt to climb to the top of Mount Kilimanjaro in 1908. In his mind he compared the 1908 pictures to the present view of the mountain and was alarmed at the distinct difference. The icecap had remarkably dwindled in size.

Drew was amazed at how far away the snow-covered peak looked. Even so, he was determined to climb the world's tallest stratovolcano at nineteen thousand three hundred thirty-one feet.

"This will be a great week," Drew added, excited to finally be on the mountain he had been studying from afar.

After handing over his gear to hired porters and keeping only a daypack to carry for himself, Drew followed Matthew's wiry body into the dense forest at the base of the mountain. As they wound through the trees, the aromatic forest smelled of damp wood. A multitude of small streams flowed down the meager crevasses in the densely-treed mountainside.

"My tribe, the Chagga people, used to believe the spirit of winter had captured this mountain and covered its head with a white blanket," Matthew shared with Drew as they walked. "They were hoping the blanket would stop the mountain from spewing flames and molten rock down upon the tropical foothills where we have lived for more than four hundred years." Coming from the Great Plains, the Chagga people had never seen snow. They couldn't imagine the white cap at the top of the mountain was frozen water. Just the few who were mountain guides had been high enough on the mountain to actually get into snow.

"Have you noticed a decline in the amount of snow over the years?" Drew asked, already in his journalistic mode.

"No, sir. I don't know if we get less snow, but the snowcap is definitely smaller. When I first became a guide," Matthew said, pausing to think back in time before continuing, "about twenty years ago, we always had snow at the summit camp. But now it is rare to have snow in camp. I bet this week we hike a mile beyond the camp before we get into snow."

From the trail, the sky was hidden from view by the dense canopy of huge camphor, agauria salicifolia, and macaranga kilimanjarica trees that lined the well-maintained path. Beautiful fern trees and large lobelia dominated the view at eye level. Matthew was beginning to relax on the mountain trail. He truly enjoyed sharing the adventure of ascending the mountain with foreigners. The drizzle had stopped seeping through the canopy and Matthew no longer needed it to conceal his tears. For the moment, his spirits seemed to have risen.

Matthew led Drew slowly up the mountain knowing it was best to go gradually, allowing their bodies to adjust with the change in altitude. "Polepole," Drew would hear Matthew say a multitude of times over the next week, which meant "slowly" in Swahili.

"It is the young inexperienced climbers who start off too fast, only to get altitude sickness and not make it to the top," Matthew explained. "Yes, sir, they think they are in great shape and invincible. They don't heed my warning to take it slowly. The slight incline at the bottom of the mountain is easy to run up. Without letting your body gradually change with the rising altitude, one is apt to encounter severe altitude sickness and have to descend before complications from the elevation become disastrous."

Drew knew Matthew was correct. He had read several accounts of people dying on the mountain from altitude sickness. He wasn't willing to take the chance so he slowly walked with Matthew, letting other climbers pass them on the trail.

"Why do you climb the mountain?" Drew asked.

After contemplating the question, Matthew answered, "Well, sir, I like to be a part of the fulfillment people experience when they accomplish the task."

"Are you afraid of the complications to your body?" Drew asked.

"Yes, sir, I know it has negative effects. But without this job, I wouldn't be employed. There aren't many jobs to be had. I am fortunate to have it. My brother, Luke, no longer can be a guide. He has been to the top over three hundred times. Now, his memory is not what it should be."

Matthew continued to slowly lead Drew along the path before asking, "What are you afraid of?" He knew his own true fear at the moment was of the plague, not this mountain.

Drew thought for quite some time before answering, "I'm afraid I'm not achieving what I came to earth to achieve."

"And what is that, sir?" Matthew asked, not knowing the concept that he had come to earth to accomplish anything. He was focused on the basics—making a living and providing for his family.

"I think I came to be an advocate for the earth," Drew said. "I have a gnawing inside that makes me feel like I am suppose to do something to help her. I feel that if I don't take care of the earth, I have failed. I feel I came to teach others what they can do to take care of our earth."

Stopping to eat a picnic lunch Matthew pointed out a beautiful flower at the edge of the trail. "This unusual variety, impatiens kilimanjari, is found only on this mountain," he explained, "nowhere else in the world. It has an extra point on the stamen compared to other impatiens." It was part of Matthew's job to know the flora and fauna of the mountain.

Drew was mesmerized by the tiny flower. For the moment his mind had slowed down enough for him to feel connected to nature. When Drew was away from the influence of man and enmeshed with nature, he felt content.

Several hours later they arrived at the first camp where Drew's porters had set up their tents. At the campsite, there were already several other groups of climbers stopping in the vicinity. Kilimanjaro Park mandated where the hikers were to camp each night so as to utilize the provided outhouses. Thus, the mountainside wouldn't become a waste site. Even though the first day's walk was long, it had not been difficult. Drew was exhausted from not sleeping much the previous two nights. Still, when he crawled into his sleeping bag, sleep eluded him. Drew's internal clock was attuned to the east coast of the United States, a nine-hour difference in time zones with Kilimanjaro. His body thought it was morning, not evening, and he should be getting up, not going to bed. Even though he was physically exhausted, his fully awake mind kept him from sleeping. He tried to get comfortable on the one-inch-thick camp mat, so he could at least rest.

"Good morning," the cook's assistant said, unzipping the flap to Drew's tent at dawn.

"Would you like coffee or tea?" he asked, placing a tray with the makings just inside Drew's tent.

"Good morning," Drew said, rolling onto his side and propping himself up on one elbow. "Black tea with a little milk, please." He drank his tea before getting out of his sleeping bag.

The morning was beautiful. The sky was clear and it was a moderate temperature. After a large breakfast, Matthew continued to lead Drew up the mountain while the porters stayed behind to pack and clean up the campsite. Over an hour later the scrawny porters, with all of the camping gear rolled into tarps and piled high on their heads, ran in ill-fitting shoes past Drew on the trail.

It was the porters' job to make it to the next campsite in time to set up tents and prepare the evening meal before the tourists arrived. Drew could tell when the porters were close by, not only from the loud, jovial singing and joke telling, but from the strong smell that accompanied them. He related the porters' body odor to the smell of wild horses. They had an overpowering animal tang mixed with a bitter human stench.

After lunch Drew and Matthew encountered a group of Italian men with their guide coming down the trail.

"Hey, how was the top?" Drew asked, wanting to know firsthand how the climb had been.

"Oh, not so good," one volunteered. They quickly admitted they hadn't made it all the way. "We've been sick." From the altitude they were nauseated and threw up because of intense pain in their heads. On their third day of hiking, they were so miserable that they all agreed it was best they turn around and head down.

As Drew continued up the trail, he turned to watch the four healthy-looking men descend.

"They look like they should have been able to make it," Drew said to Matthew with concern. Hearing about their failure made him a little uneasy.

"Yes, sir, you should be apprehensive," Matthew responded. "This mountain can be mean-spirited. But as guides, we are paid by the tourists, and we must do what they choose, even when we think it is dangerous. That is why several people die each year trying to make it to the top when they are not fit enough for the mission." Matthew shrugged it off. He had seen many people struggle to the top that should not have taken the risk.

"Before I was born," Matthew shared from his heart, "Lutheran missionaries came to our village and converted my parents to Christianity. My father told me about the missionaries when I was a child. He explained to me how they saved our souls and brought peace to the Chagga people. Before the missionaries came to Kilimanjaro, the different clans within the Chagga tribe fought with each other, burning down each other's stick and grass huts and stealing livestock from one another. But since the Lutheran missionaries converted most of the Chagga people to Christianity, we rarely fight."

Matthew was very proud to be a Lutheran; it made him feel superior to the other Tanzanians who hadn't been exposed to Christian beliefs. Because of the missionaries, several Chagga tribesmen had learned English and were educated in ways the other tribes in Tanzania were not. With this exposure to the English language, they became the chosen ones. They were able to become mountain guides for the American and European adventurers who wanted to take the challenge of climbing the elusive volcanic peak.

On those long days of walking at extreme altitudes, Drew was glad to become absorbed in the tales Matthew told. This external focus took his mind off his aching thighs and the blister forming on his left heel. Drew could feel the rich soul of the continent; he was feeling enmeshed with his surroundings. He was enthralled by the passion the Chagga people felt for the land and each other. Drew felt their deep dependency on one another. The Chagga people truly needed unity of the tribe to survive, and that created a cohesive community that Drew had never experienced in the United States.

"The missionaries brought Jesus to us," Matthew told Drew with conviction. "If they hadn't come, we would still be without faith or the ability to go to heaven." Matthew's belief seemed pure and simple to Drew. He didn't have complicated theological questions about the meaning of the Bible as some who delve into religion tend to have. It was as if Matthew had been given a child's Bible storybook to learn from instead of the complete one. Everything he knew about the scripture seemed to be in a simplified version. Drew figured it was because Christianity had only been his lineage for two generations. The teachings were untainted and straightforward to Matthew. "Love thy neighbor. Accept one another. Follow Jesus. He is the way and the light. Pray. Be good. Do no harm. Treat others the way you would like to be treated." Matthew shared his belief with anyone willing to listen. To him his religion had greatly influenced his life, and he wanted everyone to experience the immense good fortune he felt.

Drew had a hard time sifting through everything he had heard or read about Christianity to easily get down to the basics the way Matthew could. Drew viewed most of Christianity as a list of hypocritical, controlling rituals without much benefit. But when

Matthew put his belief so simply, Drew could honestly say he also believed and tried to live his life within the parameters Matthew was describing. And there on the mountain, Drew felt connected to God. When feeling this unity he had a deep appreciation and intuitive understanding of the environment. He knew every action in nature had an equal and opposite reaction. With his holistic view of the world, he believed the universe was the development of a collective intelligence.

After walking for several hours in silence Matthew stopped by a large boulder and sat down. "Yes, sir, I remember the day my parents came to me. I was making banana beer by the central water spring that runs through our village," he said. "My father said it was time for me to marry. They wanted to know my choice for a wife before they made their final choice for me. I was filled with joy the following day when they announced who they had chosen, because it was who I would have picked.

"According to tradition I went to my future wife's village and gave her a beautiful snail shell necklace with red and blue glass trading beads. Because of her delight with the necklace and our engagement, she played her part in the traditional tribal courtship by dancing naked all day with bells tied to her legs. Then for three months, I did not see my fiancée. Her parents kept her in the house so they could fatten her up before the wedding ceremony. The fatter they could get her, the wealthier her family would appear.

"During those three months, I finished the home I was building next to my father's—the house we still live in today."

"Do parents always pick spouses for their children?" Drew asked.

"Yes, of course. Most young people don't have the knowledge yet to make a decision they will have to live with for the remainder of their life."

"I wonder who my parents would have picked for me if we had that tradition in our family?" Drew wondered aloud.

"Are you married?" Matthew asked.

"No, I'm not," Drew answered.

Matthew and his wife were married in the Lutheran church with a Chagga medicine man presiding over the ceremony. Even though Matthew called himself a Christian, he and most of the Chagga people still pulled the threads of their ancient beliefs into the fabric of their lives, intertwining folktales of the Kilimanjaro mountain gods with their Christian beliefs.

As they climbed higher on the mountain, Matthew and Drew passed through the low-lying, dense rainforest. Smaller ericaceae and proteaceae shrubs took over the landscape, leaving behind the tall, powerful trees. The higher they hiked, the sparser vegetation became. Soon they were walking over crushed rock with only small lichens and tiny plants in the crevices.

During the day, clouds blew in from the north. "Oh great mvua mungu," Matthew prayed to the rain god at their evening meal. "Spare us while we walk upon the mountain slopes. Bring rain down in the valley where it is needed." Rain was vital for the growth and health of the crops that fed the people and produced valuable commodities to trade in the market. The prayer for rain had been at the center of their tribal beliefs for so long that it was one prayer Matthew hadn't let go of or replaced with a Christian one.

That night, like every night on the mountain, Drew lay in his tent mesmerized by the rolling, bubbling sounds of the porters' Swahili as they talked amongst each other. When their story telling momentarily stopped, the air burst into free, uncensored laughter. Drew couldn't understand what they were talking about, but their mirth was contagious. He found himself stifling his own giggles and feeling like he was eavesdropping. The porters told stories to each other well into the night. As the undulating words created a hypnotic state for Drew, he slipped halfway between sleep and consciousness.

During those long, lonely, sleepless nights, Drew realized how deficient he was of deep feelings. He was saddened by the awareness that he didn't have any friends to share the kind of closeness he saw the porters sharing. Though he was overloaded with acquaintances and business associates, he felt no one knew him deeply.

Camaraderie, passion to serve, simple happiness, and joy emanated from each and every one of the porters. Drew had never seen such purity of emotion and he felt he was missing out on the bonding they shared.

After four days of hiking, the elevation had risen from less than five thousand feet to over fourteen thousand feet. When Drew crawled into his sleeping bag at dusk, he tried to stay warm and ward off a high altitude headache that had persisted for the past twenty-four hours. He was completely exhausted from lack of sleep, and the continual days of hiking that never seemed to end.

Tonight he was to be awakened at midnight to make the last trek to the top of the mountain. The thought of only having a few hours to rest was more than he could bear. But, they needed to make it to the top of the mountain before the morning sun had time to thaw the ice covering the loose scree on the trail. Drew lay in his tent at dusk and closed his eyes. Once again, his sleep was fitful.

At midnight, the cook's assistant came to Drew's tent. In his singsong voice, he tenderly called out, "Oh Drew, it is time to get up," as he unzipped the tent flap and presented the tray of beverages. Exhausted, Drew rubbed the back of his neck while his tea steeped. Before he left his sleeping bag, he slowly drank the cup of tea, hoping to calm his throbbing head. The warm caffeinated liquid did seem to help.

Expecting it to be frigid at the top of the mountain, Drew put on every ounce of clothing he had brought. Emerging from his tent he was greeted by Matthew's cheerful smile.

"Power for up," he said, as he pointed to the heavy canvas dining tent that was covered with brightly colored fabric patches. Drew knew what that meant, because he had heard it every day he had been on the trail. When he wasn't hungry and would have preferred not eating, his guide and the cook encouraged him to fuel up with warm food. At such extreme altitudes he had lost his appetite, but the experienced climbers knew how important it was to continue eating if he was going to make it to the top.

The stars appeared to be close enough to grab. With the full moon directly overhead, Matthew led Drew up the final ascent of the mountain. The porter Drew had nicknamed Smiley also accompanied them. The happy man had a broad smile that appeared whenever Drew spoke to him, even though he couldn't understand much of what Drew was saying. The climb was steep, and the air was thin. Drew was glad he had worked out with a physical trainer for the past six months. He was in the best condition he had ever been in, yet his lungs still burned from the lack of oxygen, and his legs ached.

Feeling like he was in a trance, Drew put his feet in Matthew's tracks. Each step was barely a foot in length and abutted the one before it, as they inched their way upward. Though the climbing got tougher and the air continued to thin, Matthew and Smiley began to sing Lutheran hymns.

"A hymn of glory let us sing. New songs throughout the world shall ring." They did what they could to distract Drew and keep his thoughts off what he was doing.

"Alleluia! Alleluia! Christ, by a road before untrod, Ascendeth to the throne of God. Alleluia! Alleluia! Alleluia! Alleluia! Alleluia!

"To whom the angels, drawing nigh, why stand and gaze upon the sky? Alleluia! Alleluia!"

Other mountain guides also began to sing, making it sound like the mountain was returning their call and echoing the words back to them.

"I need to stop again," Drew said, gasping for air. He had begun counting their steps between each break, and they were down to only one hundred at a stretch.

Finally, they crested the peak. At that moment, the sun magnificently popped over the far eastern horizon, illuminating the top of the icecap. In the thin, crisp atmosphere, the sun appeared larger and brighter than normal. Drew looked out over the vast African plains surrounding the lone standing mountain. From that altitude he could see the curve of the earth on the horizon. He felt empowered, yet so small and insignificant at the same time.

Smiley cheered, giving Drew a hug. Drew momentarily felt as if he belonged. Tears of exhaustion, joy and awe-struck spirituality streamed down his cheeks.

"Sir, we must hurry," Matthew said, putting an arm around each of his companions in a group hug. "The sun is already beginning to melt the ice on the trail. Take what pictures you need and let's get going."

Drew wiped the tears from his cheeks as he tried to concentrate on what he had wanted to photograph. He tried to go through the list but his mind wasn't working very well. Of course, he had another hiker take a picture of him with Matthew and Smiley. Then he captured a magnificent photo of the sun sitting on the curve of the earth. All around him he took pictures of the snow, the few rocks that were sticking up above the icecap, and the worn trail they had just ascended.

Drew paused to take another look around in all directions when Matthew grabbed his arm, saying, "Quickly, sir, we must go down." From experience, Matthew knew how important it was to beat the morning thaw and any complications the hikers might get from the high altitude. From the oxygen deprivation, Drew's fingers and toes were tingling.

Drew took pictures from every angle and direction he could imagine. Then he carefully took the small thermos he had brought and filled it with snow, chunks of ice, and a few small rocks.

Moving slowly, because the throbbing in his head intensified with any quick or abrupt movements, Drew descended behind Matthew. Even though they placed each step they took very cautiously, they still slid. The loose gravel and sand created small landslides. Drew's legs felt like rubber; it took all his concentration to stop from sliding down the mountain.

Crumbling to a seated position as soon as he could see their camp, and feeling relieved he had made it, Drew put his head in his hands. He was so tired he wanted to cry, but tears didn't come.

"Come, sir," Matthew coaxed him into his tent. "Come lay down." With utter exhaustion, Drew collapsed onto his sleeping bag. Because of the high altitude and the pounding in his head, sleep still eluded him. He lay motionless with all of his clothes on, including his hiking boots, but only for the short time it took the porters to pack everything except Drew's tent and belongings.

"It is time we continue down the trail," Matthew said, ducking his head into Drew's tent.

Picking a steep trail that made it hard not to practically run, they descended below seven thousand feet before mid-afternoon. The porters had once again beat Drew and Matthew to camp. The cook was preparing the final trail dinner while Drew and Mathew had some cocoa.

"Tell me more about life here in Tanzania," Drew said, sitting next to Matthew outside the dining tent.

"Well, sir, we are going through a hard time right now," Matthew said, lowering his head.

For decades there had been little disease in the Chagga community. The Chagga tribesmen were hearty people and seemed to have natural immunities to many ailments. They felt fortunate AIDs had not infiltrated their community the way it had so much of Africa.

"Many people in our village have become seriously ill," Matthew said. "Before we knew it, several died. Immediately a team of doctors showed up. They have been administering drugs to try and find a cure."

"Is that typical for doctors to come to you instead of you going to a doctor's office?" Drew asked.

"No, sir, we don't use doctors very often. Our medicine man has always been consulted in the past," Matthew answered. After taking another sip of cocoa, he continued. "We've been told there is a bacterium in our drinking water. I can't imagine where it came from. Our water comes from an underground spring. It has always been clean water. It is why my ancestors settled here."

Drew could feel the sorrow Matthew was feeling, and he wanted to help him. He wondered why he had not heard of the grim plague before now. If it was big enough for a group of doctors to be assigned to the plague, why hadn't he read about it in the news? Drew was concerned for his friend.

When he crawled into his sleeping bag that night the rolling sounds of the porters' Swahili penetrated his dreams, and he finally slept soundly. Drew awoke the following morning relaxed and feeling like he had really accomplished something big. The final day of hiking was all downhill. The atmosphere was energized and talkative. The porters walked behind Matthew and Drew, not needing to hurry to set up another campsite. Once again in the lush rainforest, Drew felt a longing to know the deep, heartfelt union he had sensed between the porters and Matthew.

During one of their breaks Matthew motioned for Drew to be quiet. He was listening to a slight rustling in the canopy of branches above their heads. Moments later a colobus monkey appeared above them, obviously accustomed to being fed by the tourists. From the lowest branch above the trail, the monkey stretched his hand out toward them. Drew removed his daypack and rummaged through it to find the one protein bar he had left. He took the wrapper off the bar before handing it up to the monkey. The colobus then scurried into the thick branches of the tree and out of sight.

By the time they reached the exit gate to the park, Matthew sensed Drew's hesitation in parting so he invited him to be his guest in the Chagga village the following day.

Turn for a Rescue

HOPE HEARD THE MAYDAY RESPONSE LOUD AND clear. "This is the Bahamian Coast Guard responding to a Mayday on Channel 16. Please come back. Over." The methodical drone of the Coast Guard Officer's voice penetrated the air in *Ladyhawke*'s small cabin.

"Coast Guard, this is the sailing vessel *Wind Got Us*. Our boat is taking on water. We need help," a frantic man's voice returned.

"*Wind Got Us*, what is your location? Over."

"We are at 25°43"N, 75°18"5'W. We hit a cargo container that's sliced open the hull of our boat. Our bilge pump can't keep up!"

Hope could hear the terror in the man's voice and her eyes widened with concern.

"Logan, come down here!" she shouted, not wanting to leave the radio. "You've got to hear this."

"How many people are on the vessel? Over," the Coast Guard responded as Logan descended the companionway stairs and stood next to Hope.

"It's a Mayday," Hope said.

"Just my wife and me," the frenzied voice responded.

"Stay calm. Could you give me your names? Over."

"Max and Tina Short. We are from Annapolis, Maryland. We have been sailing in the Caribbean for two years, and we are on our way to the Bahamas." The words poured from his mouth as fast as he could say them. Even though his voice sounded frightened, he seemed fairly organized to Hope.

"Let me repeat your position, 25°43"N, 75°18"5'W. Is that correct? Over."

"Yes! Yes! That's it!"

"The closest boat we have in your vicinity is six hours away. What emergency equipment do you have on your boat? Over."

"We have a fully provisioned life raft, EPIRB, life vests, portable water maker . . . I don't know. We have all sorts of things."

"Very good. Stay calm. Be prepared to deploy your life raft if you can't keep the boat afloat. Do you have a portable VHF? Over," the Coast Guard asked.

"Yes! Of course!"

"Take it with you when you get into your life raft. How about a portable GPS? Over."

"Yes!" Max screamed.

"Take that with you, also. Make yourself an abandon ship bag now, with important papers, food, water, the VHF and the GPS. We are preparing a helicopter as we speak. Stay on this channel and we will be back in touch. I am going to announce your position to any other ships that might be in your area. Stay calm and be prepared to get into your life raft if necessary. Over."

"Water is everywhere! I knew this would happen!"

"Stay calm. I will get back to you as soon as I report your location. Over."

A moment later, the monotone voice of the Bahamian Coast Guard came over the VHF loud and clear, "There is the report of a sailing vessel taking on water at 25°43"N, 75°18"5'W needing emergency assistance. If there are any vessels in the vicinity that could help, please come back. Over."

"They must be within a few miles if we can hear them on the VHF," Logan said, already plotting *Wind Got Us'* location on his chart.

"Look, I think they're right here," he continued pointing to the chart on the navigation table. "I think they said 25°43"N but I'm not sure of the other coordinate. Call the Coast Guard and ask them to repeat it." But they didn't have to make the call because the announcement started to repeat itself.

"There is the report of a sailing vessel taking on water at 25°43"N, 75°18"5'W needing emergency assistance. If there is any vessel in the vicinity that could help, please come back. Over."

"I got it this time. Let's see. Yes, we are close. Wow, we are only six miles away. Hope, we should help," Logan said in a hurry as he reached for the VHF mic.

"We should," Hope said, just as eager to be of assistance. "I would want someone to help us."

"Bahamian Coast Guard, Bahamian Coast Guard, this is sailing vessel *Ladyhawke* responding to the ship in distress," Logan said loudly into the VHF mic.

"Bahamian Coast Guard responding to sailing vessel *Ladyhawke*. Over."

"We heard you announce the Mayday from *Wind Got Us*, and I think we are only six miles from their location."

"*Ladyhawke*, what is your location? Over."

"25°40"N, 75°15"7'W," Logan answered, reading the GPS.

"Yes, you are 5.87 miles from *Wind Got Us*. We would appreciate any assistance you could render. Over."

"We will turn and head their direction," Logan said.

"Please stay on Channel 16. Over."

"*Ladyhawke* standing by on Channel 16."

Hope charted a new rhumb line from their position to *Wind Got Us*' position.

"Sailing vessel *Wind Got Us*, sailing vessel *Wind Got Us*, this is the Bahamian Coast Guard. Over."

A few moments passed before Hope heard Max scream, out of breath, "This is *Wind Got Us*!"

"We have received a message from the sailing vessel *Ladyhawke*, which is within six miles of your position. They are willing to turn toward your coordinates. Over."

"Oh, thank you," Max said, his voice trembling. "The bilge is completely full. Water is beginning to come up above the floorboards. Our pumps can't keep up. We are going to lose her."

"Stay on Channel 16. That is how they will contact you. Did you hear their transmission a few minutes ago? Over."

"No."

"Your transmission is not as clear as theirs. I'm sure you will be able to communicate with them when they get closer to you. Until then I will relay for you. Over."

In the cockpit Logan took the steering back from the wind vane and hand steered. Hope pulled the headsail in and tightened the boom to the center line of the boat so Logan could make a sharp turn to the new heading a little north past due east. When they were on course toward *Wind Got Us*' location, Hope let the headsail back out and adjusted the mainsail to pull them as quickly as possible in the direction of the sinking vessel.

Ladyhawke reluctantly turned from the fresh breeze run, the smooth downwind glide she had experienced for the last two days. Tucking her shoulder and shifting her port beam to the north, she resisted the oncoming wind, as Hope and Logan demanded she bow toward it and barrel into the approaching waves. *Ladyhawke* tried to keep her power and speed intact, but to Hope's dismay, she began to look like a cormorant struggling to take flight. With the direction of the wind and the waves, they could only progress forward at about three and a half knots per hour. Hope was worried because they couldn't sail in the exact direction they needed to go. They would have to tack at least once and sail for two hours before reaching *Wind Got Us'* location.

"Let's try the engine," Logan said. Maybe it will give us enough power to go over the waves instead of slamming into each one."

Hope reached down and turned the start button. The engine roared to life.

But, try as they might, it didn't help. With engine power, they now hit every oncoming wave even harder, burying the bow deep into each approaching swell, drenching the decks of *Ladyhawke* all the way back to the cockpit. The boat came to an almost complete standstill with every impact.

With the engine back off, they trimmed the sails again, adjusting the lines by a fraction of an inch at a time. When they were convinced they were sailing as fast as they could, Hope went down below deck. Speaking into the VHF's mic she said, "Bahamian Coast Guard, Bahamian Coast Guard, this is sailing vessel *Ladyhawke*." She wedged herself into the nav-station seat and held on. The boat rocked from side to side and pitched forward and backward all at the same time, corkscrewing in the waves.

"*Ladyhawke*, this is the Bahamian Coast Guard. Over."

"We have turned our boat on the tightest course we can sail in the direction of *Wind Got Us*, but because of the wind direction we can only go about three and a half knots," Hope said as she looked over at the GPS and read the speed-over-ground indicator. "We will have to tack at least once before we reach *Wind Got Us'* location. I estimate it will take us about two hours."

With the hatches closed, the air in the cabin was stale and stifling. Hope could feel the dreaded sea queasiness swelling in her stomach. Her strength drained from her muscles with each twist the boat took. Hope tried to center her attention on the conversation, but her vision blurred, and her mouth filled with silky smooth saliva. Every tilt of the boat made her stomach contract, and the muscles in her body tightened with tentative anticipation. She tried to focus as a thin layer of perspiration broke out over her upper lip.

"What is your exact location? Over."

Again Hope turned to the GPS in the ceiling next to her. As the boat heaved, she tried to keep her eyes on the screen long enough to figure out what she needed to display their position. Confusion took over with her seasickness. Attempting not to think about her stomach and striving to put her attention on the situation at hand, she pushed the page key on the GPS until it displayed their current position.

"We're at 25°40"3'N, 75°15"9'W."

"Thank you for your help. I will relay your message to *Wind Got Us*. You are still the closest vessel to their location. Your assistance is appreciated. Over."

Hope cut the conversation short, saying, "We'll stay on Channel 16. Over." She dropped the mic on the navigation desk without replacing it in its holder and bolted for the cockpit as vomit rose in her throat. She just barely made it to the leeward lifeline and leaned over before she threw up.

"Oh God, I hate this," she mumbled to herself before she heaved again.

"That came up quickly," Logan said as he kept the boat as tight to the wind as she would sail.

Hope slumped on the cockpit bench and looked out at the horizon, trying to find something to focus on that wasn't moving.

"Ohhh," she moaned, wiping the sweat from her forehead. She was discouraged and felt like all of her energy instantly dissipated. She wanted to close her eyes, hoping the world would go away. She couldn't believe how swiftly an idyllic sail could deteriorate into a stressful, nauseating ride.

"Here, come steer the boat. That will make you feel better," Logan said as he stood to the side of the wheel.

She knew he was right, but the thought of having to move was not a pleasant one. She would rather have crawled into a hole. Now her head throbbed around her eyes and every movement of the boat bit into her soul. Her zest for sailing and life in general shifted from pleasant monotony to thoughts of wanting to magically levitate off the boat and get to shore, or better yet, find herself washed overboard so she could end it all. With thoughts like that in her head, she knew she needed to change the situation. After a few moments, she gathered her strength, pulled herself up and stood behind the helm.

Logan got her a ginger soda and wheat crackers along with a couple of pieces of candied ginger. She put her mind on steering the boat and on the soothing effect of the ginger.

Logan went to the navigation desk to look at the chart and determine where they should tack. Instead he stopped to listen as he heard Max scream over the VHF, "We can't stay on the boat. The water is filling the cabin."

"Move to the cockpit with your abandon-ship bag and prepare the life raft for launching. Hold out as long as you can. *Ladyhawke* is progressing in your direction. Over."

Rummaging through the miscellaneous electronics Hope had individually wrapped in plastic bags and placed in the navigation table, Logan found the portable VHF.

Ocean spray relentlessly doused the boat. Hope continued to steer so they wouldn't have to allow for the lag time the autopilot took to adjust the rudder

From behind *Ladyhawke*'s wheel, Hope could see the oncoming waves and predict their impact. With the ability to foresee the next movement, she could begin to shift with the boat and become one with its dance. By keeping her knees soft and flexible, she could move from side to side and up and down as the boat traveled beneath her. The continual motion that repeated itself brought to mind her grandfather's horse farm in upstate New York.

Balancing on the boat was very similar to riding Clancy. As a young girl, she fluidly moved with each of Clancy's muscular contractions, foreseeing his next step. Covering the rolling landscape, she and Clancy became one. Hope smiled, remembering the desire to compete with her brother when they mounted horses. For several moments after climbing into the saddles, the two riders walked side by side making small adjustments in their stirrups and settling into place. Then looking at each other from the corner of their eyes, the children lowered their heads for less wind resistance and swatted their horses into a full run, racing down the trail in front of them. Ducking beneath tree limbs, shifting up and down, anticipating the next deviation on the path—it was all like observing the patterns of the oncoming waves and moving in accordance with them.

Hope got lost in her mind. The motion of the water became Clancy's galloping stride. She pictured Drew upon Lightning, his gray Arabian that had turned pure white with age. As a child Drew had dreamed of being a jockey. He would pretend Hope was his competition and ride for all he was worth. But like the rest of his family, his size never allowed him the option of competing professionally on horseback. By the time Drew was fourteen years old, he was five feet ten inches tall. Before he was through growing, he had slightly surpassed his father at six feet four inches.

Gripping *Ladyhawke*'s reins, Hope could smell a fleeting whiff of acidic horse sweat drift over the waves of the seascape before her.

Wind Got Us **Down**

"ONLY TAKE WHAT IS NECESSARY FOR SURVIVAL. Forget the rest. *Ladyhawke* should be in your vicinity within the hour." Hope and Logan listened to the monotone voice of the Coast Guard Officer on the VHF.

"I can't get..." Max said before Tina screamed, and the sound of a large splash came to an abrupt stop as the VHF went silent.

Twenty stress-filled minutes passed while the Coast Guard tried to reach the Shorts with no success. Finally Max's voice came back across the VHF, "Coast Guard, Coast Guard, this is Max Short. We are in our life raft. *Wind Got Us* is barely floating."

"Can you give me your current location? Over," the Coast Guard Officer dryly responded.

"You'll have to wait a minute. I have to turn on the GPS." Moments later Max gave new coordinates for their location, which Logan plotted on their chart. Because of the wind and the roll of the waves, *Wind Got Us* had drifted a little to the south, which was good for Hope and Logan. Now they wouldn't have to chop into the waves as far north as they had anticipated.

Max's frantic voice was once again heard on the VHF speaker, "There it goes. The bow is lifting out of the water. The cockpit's filling. I just knew this would happen... The boat just went down."

The calm, steady voice of the Coast Guard returned, "Just stay calm. *Ladyhawke* will be there soon. We have your location and you are safely in your life raft. Over."

Logan took over the steering while Hope went forward to the bow. She scanned the water through binoculars, looking for the life raft.

"We should be right on track," Logan said after they tacked. "They have to come into view soon." Until then, Hope and Logan hadn't really tried to spot *Wind Got Us*. They had been too busy manning the boat.

During the frantic commotion of getting into their life raft, Max and Tina hadn't even noticed the approaching *Ladyhawke*.

When the opening to their floating tent turned directly toward *Ladyhawke*, they could plainly see the approaching sails.

"*Ladyhawke*, *Ladyhawke*, this is *Wind Got Us*, can you see us?" Tina asked with a nervous snicker into the portable VHF.

"*Wind Got Us*, this is *Ladyhawke*. We have to be close. We can't see you yet, but maybe you can see our sail?" Logan returned. He knew it would be easier for them to see the tall mast of *Ladyhawke* than it would for Hope to see their life raft bobbing between the waves.

"Yes, we can see you!" Tina screamed into the handheld. "If you continue on the same course you will pass to the north of us."

Logan called to Hope, "Do you see them yet?"

Hope shook her head.

"Hope is trying to find you with the binoculars. Hang on, we're coming," Logan said into the VHF.

"There they are!" Hope screamed. "There they are!" She pointed toward the bright orange life raft on top of a wave before it went down in a gully and disappeared. They were about a mile off the starboard side of *Ladyhawke*'s bow.

"*Wind Got Us*, we see you. We're coming."

"Oh, thank you. You really are going to reach us," Tina said with palpable relief in her voice.

"We're glad we were close enough to help," Logan said as he maneuvered *Ladyhawke* over the final leg of the rescue.

In only a few minutes, it was time for Logan and Hope to turn into the wind, drop their sails, and start the engine for better maneuverability. Logan trailed a long line into the water and instructed Max over the VHF to grab hold of the line as they circled them. Hope cut the engine and they coasted to a stop.

"Hold on! I'll winch you in!" Logan shouted, because the Shorts were now close enough to hear him without the electronics.

Logan wrapped the bitter end of the dragline around the primary winch. The waves and current were strong. Without the power of the winch, they never would have been able to pull the life raft up to the boat.

"Wow, we really found them," Hope said under her breath to Logan with a sense of surprise. "This seems so anticlimactic to such a serious situation. These folks just sank their boat. Imagine how we would feel if it had been *Ladyhawke*."

Logan shook his head in agreement, not wanting to expound on her comment now that Max and Tina were in hearing range.

Max handed their abandon ship bag and a large black garbage bag up to Logan and he then let Tina crawl up the ladder.

"I guess we just let the life raft go?" Max asked Logan.

"I guess," Logan said. "I don't know how we would take it with us now that it's inflated."

"Oh… Thanks, you guys," Tina said with a huge sigh of relief once she stepped into *Ladyhawke*'s cockpit. "How long would we be floating out there if it weren't for you?"

Hope reached over and gave her a big hug. Tears of relief rolled down Tina's cheeks and her middle-aged, athletic body began to tremble. Hope eased her into a seated position and sat next to her with an arm around her shoulder.

"You are safe now. Can I get you something?" Hope said, wanting to make them feel at ease.

Tina shook her head no, as she covered her tears with her hands.

Max stared at his life raft as he released its painter. At first, it trailed *Ladyhawke* as if she were still attached. But slowly the boat picked up speed and left the life raft behind. Max mumbled to himself, "There it all goes."

"Bahamian Coast Guard, Bahamian Coast Guard, this is *Ladyhawke*," Logan said into the VHF mic.

"*Ladyhawke*, this is the Bahamian Coast Guard. Over."

"We have successfully rescued Max and Tina from their life raft."

"Thank you for your assistance. We will call off all other rescue attempts. May I speak to Mr. Short? Over."

"Bahamian Coast Guard, this is Max Short."

"Mr. Short, we will record the last location of your boat. You must now file an official report to the Bahamian government within thirty days. Do you have a pen and paper? You will need the file number for your report. Over."

Hope motioned to Max that she had a pen and paper.

"Go ahead," Max said into the mic.

Max couldn't believe how matter of fact everyone was being.

Don't they get it, he thought. *I just sank my boat. Everything I own is on the bottom of the ocean.*

"Thanks," Max said shortly. He was beginning to get angry.

"Bahamian Coast Guard standing by on Channel 16. Over."

"*Ladyhawke* standing by on Channel 16. Over," Logan said into the mic.

Hope turned the boat south, once again moving with the wind and the waves in a rhythmic glide.

"When we got in the life raft, our boat went down so fast," Tina remembered, wiping the tears from her cheeks. "I couldn't believe it was happening. We've planned this life for years, and now *Wind Got Us* is gone. We don't even have any pictures."

"I did bring the laptop," Max said, shaking his head in disbelief. "If it didn't get wet, at least we have the pictures I've downloaded."

Tina numbly nodded her head in acknowledgment; Max sat down hard next to her.

"Our boat is gone. I knew something bad was going to happen before our trip was over. What did we expect?"

"Oh Max, you always think the worst," Tina said.

"All of our possessions are on the bottom of the ocean. How can it get much worse?" Max said. "It seems so ironic. I wrote my PhD thesis on 'Shipwrecks in the Caribbean' and now my boat's one of them. It's only fitting."

It was as if Logan woke up with that comment.

"We have the ability to go get things off your boat. I've got a submarine." Pausing for only a second and remembering where they were, he continued, "But as you know the water out here is over five thousand feet. I guess my sub won't go that deep."

Max looked at him with a puzzled expression. "You've got a submarine?" he asked.

"Yeah, I rescue sunken objects for a living. I own a search and rescue salvage company."

"I can't imagine anything on my boat that would be worth the time or money to get. Even if your sub could go that deep," Max said as he rubbed his forehead with his broad fleshy hand. "I would have thought the boat would go down in a storm if it was going to sink."

"It probably would cost more than it's worth to rescue your belongings, unless you have a few hundred gold bars stowed away," Logan admitted.

"I would have loaded them into the life raft if I did." A sarcastic smile slipped to Max's lips, imagining his life raft filled with gold.

"Believe me, Tina and I would be swimming along the side of the raft," he added, raising a dark, bushy eyebrow beneath his thick, black hair and looking over the stern rail at a small speck on the horizon—the last view he would have of his life raft.

Hope busied herself. She pulled out the settee and made a large, comfortable berth in the salon for the visitors. Max and Tina took showers and put on the dry clothing they had brought in the large garbage bag. Hope was thankful they were able to grab a few articles of clothing because hers and Logan's would not have fit them. Hope was much taller than Tina and Max was bigger around than Logan.

After a warm bowl of soup, all four settled into the cockpit with boat drinks made of island rum and fruit juice.

"The sun was just beginning to rise," Tina recalled. "And then that god awful sound of ripping fiberglass." She paused for a moment in disbelief.

Tina's voice cracked with emotion when she continued. "Max yelled at me, wanting to know what the noise was. I didn't know, but something told me it was very wrong."

"I jumped out of bed when I heard water running down the inside wall of the boat," Max said. Bile had risen in his throat as he tore the interior of the boat apart trying to get to its hull. As Max stood to demonstrate his ripping actions, it occurred to Logan that Max was made to be on a boat. His legs were short and stocky. His center of gravity was low, reminding Logan of a tree.

Max continued, "I found the gash. It was about three feet long on the portside of the boat just below water level. I ran to the head and grabbed all of the towels I could find and started stuffing them into the gash."

"I could just barely see it submerged beneath the water," Tina whispered. "A large cargo container. It looked like a railroad car, or something. How could we hit it at just the right angle to slice a hole in the side of our boat? How could we?" She leaned over and put her head on Max's chest as he wrapped his arm around her shoulder.

"The Coast Guard's records state," Logan said, "there are over seven thousand cargo containers lost annually. They float for months, until they finally fill with water and sink."

It was a sailor's nightmare come true. The four sat in silence as the stars ignited in layers upon the dimming sky. That night the wind and the sea quickly lay down, allowing the new passengers some much needed sleep. Max and Tina crawled into their berth. Logan and Hope took their usual night shifts. They observed the famous constellation of Orion appear above them and slowly slip over the western horizon, monitoring the passage of time.

With new batteries in her night vision headlamp, Hope read during most of her shifts. *Elmo* was doing a great job steering. Every few minutes, Hope would stand and scan the horizon for ship lights, but the few she saw never got very close to *Ladyhawke*. The night passed quietly.

At dawn Hope went to the galley to prepare a pot of coffee as the rest awoke to calm, crystal clear skies. The sea now barely moved as a congealed whole, and the wind puffed out of the northwest. They slowly sailed south through Caicos Passage.

"I can't imagine still floating out there in our life raft, if you hadn't come," Tina said to Hope as she stood in the galley. Once again, tears seeped out of her eyes.

"Oh Tina, you're safe now," Hope said, wishing there were something more she could do to make her feel better. "That's part of the law of the sea; we all help each other out here. I'm sure you would have helped us if we were in your shoes."

Tina nodded her head in agreement. Then abruptly Max screamed from the cockpit, "No!" The boat lurched to the right. Both Tina and Hope grabbed for the hand holds to steady themselves.

Logan and Max had simultaneously seen something large floating just to the port side of *Ladyhawke*. Logan grabbed the wheel and forced it hard to the right, over-powering the wind vane to avoid a collision.

Both Hope and Tina struggled up into the cockpit. As the sails flapped, the boom swung hard to the opposite side of the boat, making a loud bang when it reached the end of the mainsheet. Tina looked over the edge of the boat in the direction Max was pointing. A large eye appeared in the water.

"It's a whale, Max. Look, it's a whale!" Tina exclaimed with relief and a lighthearted chuckle. Like Hope, Tina was always delighted whenever she saw sea life.

Normally Tina didn't take much seriously. Almost everything she said was punctuated with a giggle or a snicker. With yesterday's incident past, slowly her happy nature returned.

The whale surfaced and exhaled through its blowhole, shooting a v-shaped spurt of water high into the air. Everyone squealed with glee until the shower fell back down and covered the boat with a rank, rotten, fishy smell. In unison everyone groaned, "Gross!" The whale took a dive, elevating its black triangular fluke high in the air. With a powerful flop, it disappeared below the surface.

"Oh my God! What a stink!" Hope cried as everyone tried to wipe whale snot off themselves onto something else. But everything was covered with the foul slime.

"Hope, come here and steer the boat away from the whale's last sighting," Logan said. Then he went to the back lazarette and retrieved a hose. Hauling it to the bow of the boat, he hooked it up to the raw water deck-wash spigot and started hosing the boat down.

"I can't believe how bad that smells," Tina said, laughing again. She leaned over and gave Max a playful slap on the back; in return he gave her a dirty look, trying to discourage her lightheartedness.

"Don't go down below before you wash off," Hope said. "We would never get the smell out of the boat."

Both Max and Tina went forward and allowed Logan to hose them off fully dressed.

"I don't think that helped at all," Tina said with a smile. "I still stink."

"I guess," Logan said, teasing her.

"Hey, you stink too," Tina said.

"It's just my manly smell," Logan said, sticking his nose in his armpit. With a mischievous smile, he covered half the hose end with his thumb and sprayed her even harder.

Screaming and laughing at the same time, she tried to grab the hose from Logan. But every time she got within reach he sprayed her in the face, which made her step back and laugh even louder.

Max came back to the cockpit and dumped a large amount of soap into a bucket. Returning to the bow, Logan filled the bucket with water. They all started scrubbing themselves with the soapy water.

"I'm sorry," Tina said, as she started taking her clothes off and putting them in the bucket. "I guess you have to lose all modesty when on a boat."

"I don't think we have much choice. That smell's going to gag us," Logan said as he took off his shirt.

"Hurry up!" Hope shouted. "It's got to be my turn. This stuff is starting to dry on me."

"Put *Elmo* on and come up here," Logan laughed. "Hey, get some shampoo and body soap. Bring some towels and washcloths, too."

When Hope emerged with the supplies, the three others were in their underwear, splashing soapy water at each other.

The whale snot had opened the door to laughter.

As the day wore on, the four of them continued to ease into a comfortable space with each other. Logan questioned Max about his knowledge of shipwrecks in the Turks and Caicos Islands, their next landfall.

"Well, I guess one of the more interesting stories I remember right off the top of my head is about two pirates from England back in the early 1700s who were women. You know who I'm talking about?" he asked Logan, but then answered himself. "Mary Read and Anne Bonny. The story is, they would act like damsels in distress to get the captain of the boat they were interested in to come help them. Read's crew was already waiting in the water, just out of sight, ready to board the un-captained boat and take the crew captive long enough to loot their goods. The biggest haul on record was when they captured the Spanish treasure ship *Gwen Emma*, captained by Enrique Maduro. There weren't many female sailors in the 1700s, let alone female captains, and especially not female pirates."

"You know, there are more than a thousand recorded shipwrecks in the Turks and Caicos Islands," Logan said, adding his brief knowledge of the area. "Most of the wrecks I've read about only had salt going out of the islands and provisions coming in for the slaves who were working the salt mines."

"Yap," Max said, nodding his head. "The treasures the women pirates took from the *Gwen Emma* were thought to have gone down with *Josephine*, Mary Read's boat, in the hurricane of 1743, considered the hurricane of the century.

"The hurricane wiped out all of the vegetation from South Caicos north to the Abaco Islands in the Bahamas. *Josephine* was never found or heard of after that hurricane.

"Lots of people have looked for *Josephine*, but nobody's found her."

"Let's go look," Logan said.

"If they couldn't find her, what makes you think we can?" Max asked.

Logan shrugged his shoulders, "You never know."

"There was a cave on Sand Cay that the English Captain Delaney found," Max continued. "It was filled with gems, gold and silver coins with an estimated worth of one hundred thirty thousand dollars back then. I think it was the women pirates' stash. Can you imagine what that would be worth today?" Max's excitement was surfacing. Logan had gotten him talking about his passion.

"Delaney was a member of Queen Victoria of England's Lordship and was said to be en route with his booty back to England in October that year, but he never made it. During that time period there was another hurricane that struck a week or so after Delaney left Sand Cay on *Elizabeth Anne*. I suspect he realized, with his falling barometer reading, that the storm was approaching, and he tried to make it back to Provo and the protection of Turtle Cove.

"Nobody ever heard from him again. He had to have gone down somewhere off the Grand Banks east of Grand Turks," Max said with confidence.

"Yes, but you know," Logan said, "I've read about Birch's Lookout where hundreds of boats have hit the banks and gone down. Even though it is a known reef, boats still hit it and disappear in its vicinity. But those wrecks have been raked over by treasure hunters for decades. If Delaney's boat had *Josephine*'s treasures, it had to have gone down someplace where people haven't looked."

"You may be right," Max agreed.

"We've got to be able to figure it out," Logan said. "We've got the technology."

"It's a long list of possibilities, Logan. Too many variables," Max said.

"But Max, what if we're lucky and we estimate a location where no one else has looked and we find it? What if it is outside of national water and the treasure is ours?"

"And what if Delaney's find was not *Josephine*'s loot?" Max speculated, getting wrapped up in Logan's infectious enthusiasm. "What if *Josephine* went down with everything she stole over the years? She's got to be out there somewhere, too."

Max mirrored Logan's excitement temporarily and then pushed the notion of truly finding a sunken treasure out of his imagination, not believing it feasible.

"That's a big ocean," Max said emphasizing "big" and looking out to sea. "And it was a long time ago. We'd never find them."

Max rarely allowed himself to dream outside the possibility of black and white logistics.

Logan agreed on the surface. But underneath he was a dreamer. *What if...* he thought. *Just, what if?*

The setting sun created a golden path on the surface of the water as *Ladyhawke* slipped into the southern bay of South Caicos. Max helped Logan clean the topside of the boat and they took showers in the cockpit as the women started dinner and took showers in the head. Spaghetti and meatballs was on the menu. When the men sat down at the table with Hope and Tina, they poured a round of wine and toasted new friends.

"*Wind Got Us* went down in history. Literally down. Forever to be recorded as a shipwreck herself," Max said, a little bit proud of that fact.

At dawn the next day, Logan was out of bed making coffee before Hope, something he rarely did. He hadn't been able to sleep much thinking about the possibility of finding one of the sunken boats they had talked about the day before. Locating his charts of the area and the tide and current tables, he set his single side-band radio up and attached it to his computer, logging onto the Internet. Logan checked the old boating records to determine the exact date of Delaney's departure from Sand Cay. He also found the estimated wind speed and position of the hurricane thought to have taken his boat. Logan was unwavering in his attempt to figure out where Delaney's boat might have gone down and maybe even Mary Read's.

When Max got up, Logan briefly pulled him back into his excitement. They scoured the charts trying to figure out the most likely outcome of the treasures on both boats.

"Oh, Logan, you're just dreaming. It's not worth your time or effort," Max said, not wanting to get his hopes up.

"But it's a dream worth pursuing. I've been lucky in the past," Logan said.

"You are one of the few," Max agreed.

After a late breakfast, Tina started pushing Max to gather his few belongings so they could go to shore.

"We need to figure out what's next. Besides, we're like whale snot," she chuckled. "I'm sure we're beginning to stink. We all need to check in and report our sunken boat."

It was midday when Logan ferried the Shorts to shore in *Sharpy*. The sun beat down with a vengeance onto *Ladyhawke's* deck and made walking without shoes a hot affair. Hope stayed on the boat to finish organizing and cleaning after the long sail from the Abaco. Occasionally, Hope caught a whiff of whale snot wafting through the air. After her upper lip curled from the putrid smell, she smiled with the memory of that day when the ice was broken, and it was evident the four of them would become friends.

When Logan returned to the boat, they embraced the afternoon, inhaled the warm Caribbean air, and relaxed in the cockpit. Sitting in the shade of the bimini, Hope read a novel and dozed. But Logan couldn't relax for long. He was fixated on finding Mary Read's or Delaney's boat. He worked on his charts drawing out potential routes Delaney could have taken. From his research of *Josephine*, he tried to predict where she must have gone down. His calculations appeared the same as all the others before him. He assumed she took her stolen treasures to the bottom of the ocean with her. But, there must be something I'm missing, he thought.

Bringing his charts up into the cockpit, he looked over at Hope and suggested, "What if we stay here a while and scan a few areas? Maybe we'll get lucky."

"Okay with me, but I thought you were on vacation," she replied.

"I am. This isn't work," he said, giddy with excitement. "This is fun."

"I'm game. What do you have?"

Logan quickly unrolled his charts and showed her several scenarios Delaney's fate could have followed, plus the one most predictable outcome for *Josephine*.

"Let's go find Max and Tina," Logan suggested after showing Hope the chart. "Max might have some suggestions I haven't thought about."

"I could use a trip to shore," Hope replied.

They asked about the Shorts at the only hotel on the island. Sure enough, they had checked in earlier, but they weren't in their room. The desk clerk suggested they look at the only pub on the island, Caicos Corner Bar and Barbeque.

He directed Hope and Logan down the street three blocks where they were to turn left into an alley behind the yellow, wood-framed house in bad need of a paint job. They found Max and Tina sitting in lounge chairs, drinking beer under a palm frond palapa in what appeared to be the back yard of someone's house. After sitting down next to them and ordering a round of beers, Logan once again unrolled his chart and showed it to Max and Tina.

"We have returned," he said with a playful smile, looking over at Max out of the corner of his eye.

Max intently studied the chart before saying, "You know they have a series of old charts in the Mariners Museum in Provo. I'd like to go look at them and check out the preferred routes that boats took back then. That way we could narrow down our options."

Logan was elated when Max showed renewed interest.

"I can get a puddle jumper from the small airstrip here on South Caicos to Provo. Planes leave every morning at nine." Tina had already called the airstrip, knowing they would first have to get to Provo before flying back to the States.

"So you're in?" Logan said barely able to contain his excitement.

Max looked at Tina for her approval.

"Why not?" she said. "It's not like we have a lot else going on."

Max agreed. "I could use a sunken treasure about now to go along with my sunken boat."

They all laughed at his comment.

Logan took a big swig of beer and turned to Hope.

"We're on an adventure, babe," he said, raising his eyebrows flirtatiously.

Hope gave Logan a big smile.

"I wonder if the museum would have charts of the hurricane's path, so we can put that into the equation," Hope mused.

"I'll check it out," Max said.

Back on *Ladyhawke*, Logan and Hope watched as the local fishermen returned from their day's outing. Each small skiff carried two men and their catch of the day as the sun approached the western horizon. One after another the boats went directly to the seafood processing plant at the dock.

Logan watched from the cockpit with curiosity as one fishing boat approached *Ladyhawke*. It was, by far, much fancier than the other fishermen's boats.

The fisherman shouted with a thick, island accent, "Hey, mon. Want to buy some lobsta or fish?"

"What do you have?" Logan asked, standing up to look over the lifelines into the fishing boat.

The fisherman leaned down, allowing his long bleach-blond dreadlocks to cover his face as he pulled a filthy towel back exposing a pile of lobster and red snapper in the bottom of his Boston Whaler.

"Where'd you get those lobsters?" Logan asked.

"Oh, 'bout five miles," he said, pointing out to sea by jetting his chin in the direction all the fishing boats had been coming from. "On the reef, mon."

"Can you show me where you got them?" Logan questioned, hoping he could find the best location for spear fishing so he could catch a few of his own.

The skipper took a quick look around at the other fishermen in the area and quietly said, "Ya, mon. I could take ya tomorrow. But, ya don't tell no one I be showin' ya. And it will cost ya." And then after a pause while he checked to see how close any of the other returning fishing boats were, he whispered, "Sixty dolla U.S." The wild-looking black man was acting as if he were doing something illegal, and he probably was.

Logan looked over at Hope and smiled. And then to the skipper, he said, "Okay. What time?"

"Oh, 'round nine. Not too early, not too late," he said in a sing-song voice as he stuck his fingers into his mounds of dreadlocks and scratched.

"It's a deal, mon," he continued and reached up to shake Logan's hand.

As he pushed off *Ladyhawke* he pointed to his bleached hair and said, "I'm Goldie Locks."

"Great, my name is Logan. I'll see you tomorrow, Goldie Locks."

After the deal was made and the skiff was headed to shore, Logan said to Hope, "If anyone around here knows any old pirate stories, I bet that fellow does. I'll get the scoop from him while he shows me where the lobsters hang out."

A Day with Goldie Locks

AS THE EARLY MORNING SUNRAYS SHONE IN THE hatch above the forward berth of *Ladyhawke*, Logan heard each fishing boat leave the dock and motor past. After rising, he prepared a dive bag for himself with his mask, snorkel and fins. He placed a jug of drinking water, sunscreen and his favorite towel in the bag. But at nine o'clock, Goldie Locks was nowhere to be seen.

Finally, almost an hour later, Logan spotted Goldie Locks and two young boys coming his direction in an old, derelict boat.

"Take a gander," Logan said to Hope under his breath. "What do you make of that?"

She looked up from the novel she was reading. "Oh, boy," she said with a lot of sarcasm in her voice. "What happened to the fancy boat he had yesterday?"

"I don't know," Logan said.

The small outboard engine on Goldie Locks' boat sputtered and missed as he approached *Ladyhawke*.

"Hey mon!" Goldie Locks loudly greeted Logan. "Ready?"

"Almost," Logan said as he ducked down below.

From the shade of the bimini, Hope watched as Logan reached into the navigation desk and grabbed the portable GPS, a chart, a hand-held VHF and a flashlight, putting them in the waterproof dive bag with his other gear. From the galley he collected another bottle of water and a couple of granola bars.

When he looked up the companionway at Hope, he said, "You never know."

Handing his now-heavy bag to one of the boys, Logan climbed over the lifelines, and lowered himself into the old rundown mo-torboat.

Logan gave Hope a look that said, *I can't believe I got myself into this one.*

Hope pressed her lips together to stifle a laugh. She was glad she hadn't agreed to go on the outing.

"These are my boys," Goldie Locks said, as Logan pushed off

from *Ladyhawke*. Goldie Locks gave the engine a little gas and the outboard died. Logan looked back at Hope and rolled his eyes.

"Keep the radio on Channel 16 so I can call," he said, not even masking the dubious tone in his voice.

She nodded her head in agreement.

Goldie Locks pulled the engine cover off and adjusted the choke. After several tries, he got the engine running roughly again.

The loud uncovered engine skipped and sputtered. Goldie Locks and his passengers rode without speaking. At an undefined location, the local skipper slowed the engine and came to a stop. Logan pulled his hand held GPS out of his bag and logged their position for later reference.

"I'll check it out," Goldie Locks said as he jumped into the water. He tied the end of the long painter line attached to the bow eyelet around his waist so he wouldn't drift too far away from the boat.

Logan took a mental note of the strong current direction. It was taking the boat away from South Caicos at a pretty fast clip. They were moving almost due south.

It seemed like ten minutes that Logan and the boys waited for Goldie Locks to surface. When he did come to the top of the water for a breath of air, he had a small sea turtle in his hands. He handed it up to his oldest boy.

"What are you going to do with that?" Logan asked him incredulously.

"Eat it, mon," Goldie Locks said, matter of fact.

"You had better not let Hope see it. She would be pissed," responded Logan, drawing the word "pissed" out as if it had three syllables. Hope was on the board of directors for the Sea Turtle Relief Program in the Florida Keys. She was passionately involved in preserving the endangered species.

"No, mon, we won't really eat it; we'll take it to the Turtle Conservatory. Research. Ya know?"

"Don't let Hope catch you." Logan said, knowing Goldie Locks was lying about the Conservatory.

"Is the water worth getting into?" he questioned.

"There's a few lobsta and groupa, mon. Would I be bringin' you here if there weren't?"

That was all Logan needed to know. He grabbed his snorkeling equipment and dove into the water. He was pleasantly surprised. In every crevice, there was at least one lobster. Most of them were shorts, too small to legally keep, but in plenty of supply. Logan swam around the sparse reef system that had been damaged from too much fishing. Finally, he found two larger lobsters.

Consumed in the pursuit of capturing the two lobsters, Logan didn't pay any attention to what Goldie Locks and his boys were doing. When he got back on the boat, he found twenty to thirty short lobsters on the bottom of the boat. Once again, Logan questioned him about the legality of his harvest, and once again, Goldie Locks lied about a make-believe conservatory on the island.

From there Goldie Locks drove them a quarter of a mile further south, stopped the engine and dove into the water. Logan was quick to follow. He found an eighteen-inch black grouper hiding in the shade of a dead coral outcropping. In the water, he became so consumed with his own hunt that he quickly forgot about the uncensored raping of the ocean that Goldie Locks and his sons seemed to have no guilt over.

Several hours later, Logan had saved five different coordinates on his GPS, and they headed back toward shore.

Slowly motoring across the flat seas, Logan quizzed Goldie Locks about any folktales he might know with reference to female pirates. And sure enough, he did have a tale.

"Everyone knows that when them female pirates came to town, they be loud and rude," Goldie Locks said, shaking his head like a wet dog. His naturally oily skin shed the saltwater and he was quickly dry. "Back then it was rare for a white lady to be in the islands, 'specially a pirate lady. But, in them days the island men put up with them bitches 'cause those chickie pirates spent money like it were water. I heard they were really someting to look at, too. My pappy say his great granddaddy knew they were wanted for piracy in Provo, but he and the others never turned them in 'cause they liked the money those rough girls spent on the island. I tink they had an agreement, my kin didn't turn 'em in to the Provo deputy as long as they spent money here and didn't steal from locals."

Logan couldn't tell how much of what Goldie Locks was telling him was truth or fiction.

"Most were afraid of them girls," he admitted. "If anyone pissed 'em off, the Captain was known to cut the balls right off a man as the other held 'im down with a knife to his troat." As he talked, Goldie Locks picked up the gas tank that was attached to the outboard engine and jiggled it for content. The engine sputtered and Goldie Locks grabbed an old tennis shoe that had been meandering across the bottom of the boat all day, floating in the couple of inches of water that sloshed back and forth. Sticking the shoe underneath the back corner of the gas tank, they continued for a short time until the engine gave its last sputter and died.

"Oh well," Goldie Locks said, knowing they had just run out of gas and not thinking it a big deal.

On *Ladyhawke*, Hope was just drifting off to sleep in the cockpit when she heard, "*Ladyhawke, Ladyhawke,* this is *Ladyhawke* Mobile. Over."

Down at the navigation station Hope spoke into the VHF mic.

"*Ladyhawke* Mobile, this is *Ladyhawke.* Go to Channel 68," she said, adhering to proper VHF protocol of not staying on Channel 16 unless it was an emergency.

After turning the VHF to Channel 68 she heard Logan say, "Take the binos and look off the portside of the boat in the direction we took off this morning and see if you can see us."

"Okay, let me go look," Hope responded. "I'll be right back."

Hope went up to the cockpit with the binoculars in hand and peered to the southeast.

"Yes, Logan, I see you," she said into the mic back at the navigation station.

"We ran out of gas. Can you put the spare gas can in the dinghy and bring it to us?"

"Sure," Hope said, stifling a giggle. "I'll be right out."

"Thanks, babe," he muttered with a snicker.

Hope wondered what Goldie Locks would have done if Logan hadn't been on the boat with him. How long would he have drifted out there with his two boys before someone noticed he hadn't returned home that night? She was always amazed at the islanders' lack of concern for dangerous situations, or maybe it was their lack of fear for death they displayed.

Hope lowered the tank of gas into the dinghy. So as not to get wet from the spray *Sharpy* made at full throttle, she stood up and steered the boat with the throttle extension in hand until she arrived at Goldie Locks' boat.

As the shadows elongated and the western sky turned red, Hope and Logan returned to the only bar in town, Caicos Corner. Right on schedule, a twin prop plane circled low above the island.

"That must be them," Logan said when he heard its engine.

It took Max and Tina no time at all to get a taxi ride to Caicos Corner just a couple of miles from the airport.

Before they even sat down, Max said in a low voice, "We might be on to something. Delaney probably went much further south than most people think. The hurricane he would have encountered was much larger than the majority of hurricanes. I doubt most treasure hunters would expect him to sail as far south as he probably did. I have a new prediction. I bet he went down south of all the Caicos Islands. I bet he made a mad run for it. The wind would have taken him west, and he would have been trying to go south to get out of the hurricane's way. I bet he was blown into the banks southwest of here."

"Do you really think so?" Logan said, unrolling his charts on the table. "That's sure different from the general consensus. If he did obtain damage in the shallow banks, the hurricane would have then pushed him further south and west. Somewhere in this area," Logan said, circling with his finger an area southwest of South Caicos.

"That's where I believe *Josephine* went down too," Max said.

"Let's go!" Logan shouted as he stood to leave.

"Shhh. Hold on. Hold on. Sit back down," Max said not wanting to alert the others at the bar, but he may have been too late.

Tina noticed a gnarly-looking man sitting at the table next to them. The man seemed almost motionless and too quiet for the typical beer-drinking patron. She thought she caught him glance in their direction out of the corner of his eye, trying to sneak a peek at their chart. She suspected he was listening to their conversation. And there was something about him that looked familiar—like she had seen him before on their travels. But that wasn't unusual. After cruising the Caribbean islands for the past two years, they frequently ran into the same people over and over again. It became common for them to recognize the other patrons in a restaurant.

Maybe, she thought, *he was one of the other passengers on the small plane we just got off.*

"We can't leave now," Hope said. "We need to figure out how far it is and how long it will take to get there. There is no need for us to get out there in the middle of the night and just slosh around until the sun comes up."

They all sat quietly while Hope figured the distance to their desired location. Tina kept an eye on the man sitting at the next table. After calculating the direction of the wind and the prevailing current, Hope estimated it would take them almost four hours to sail to the location they wanted to scan.

The Thrill of a Sunken Treasure

AT DAWN THE FOUR EXCITED TREASURE hunters were pulling up *Ladyhawke*'s anchor and heading to the coordinates they had circled on Logan's chart the night before. The early morning sun hid behind the bank of clouds on the eastern horizon.

"Over to the left!" Hope shouted.

Logan carefully maneuvered the boat by engine power over the shallow banks along South Caicos' southern shore, avoiding the coral heads that rose to within inches of the water's surface.

"Now to the right." Standing on the bow pulpit seat, Hope could see large starfish on the sandy bottom.

Once beyond the shallow banks, *Ladyhawke*'s sails were raised and her engine was turned off. In the moderate wind, the Genoa, the forward sail running from the bow to the top of the mast, filled with a loud snap and heeled the boat over on its portside. *Ladyhawke* slipped into a rhythmic glide.

Three hours later, Logan called to his crew to take the sails back down. With the engine just barely above idle, he turned his sonar equipment on and started slowly scanning the ocean floor for shapes that might possibly be sunken boat parts. The depth sounder registered between two hundred fifty and three hundred fifty feet. Logan knew it was too deep for traditional diving equipment, but not too deep for his submarine. At those depths, the sonar displayed a steady gray haze with no distinguishable shapes.

The ocean floor abruptly rose to just under a hundred feet and the familiar bumps of coral appeared on the monitor screen. Max squeezed in behind Logan, hoping for something that might be a shipwreck to appear on the screen.

Music blared from the cockpit speakers. Logan bellowed, along with Jimmy Buffett, "Yes, I am a pirate two hundred years too late. I'm an over-forty victim of fate. Arriving too late. Arriving too late... I made enough money to buy Miami, but I pissed it away so fast. Never meant to last. Never meant to last."

Max joined Logan and Jimmy on the next verse, "I go for younger women, lived with several a while."

Logan suddenly stopped singing. He froze in position, staring at the sonar monitor. Grabbing the throttle he brought the motor to neutral. Hope knew those signs and assumed Logan saw something he was interested in, so she also stopped mid-movement to wait for him to say something.

On the sonar screen Logan saw a shape that looked exactly like the bow of a boat. He put the boat in reverse to trace back over the area they had just passed. He logged their position with the GPS by pushing the MOB, man overboard button. Again he traversed the same area. While pointing at the screen, he loudly asked, "What's that? Huh? What's that?"

"It looks like a coral reef in the shape of a 'V'," Max said while Tina and Hope squeezed in behind the men to get a glimpse. They all shrieked with excitement, releasing the adrenaline that had been building since they left South Caicos that morning.

"It can't be. It's never that easy," Max said with his usual pessimism.

"My grandfather always said I was luckier than a two peckered billy-goat," Logan said, laughing. "But we really don't know if it is one of the boats we're looking for. Gramps also said 'Don't count your duckies before they quack.'" Logan's grandfather was a true central-Florida backwoodsman.

Now the treasure seekers had a decision to make, continue to look for other possibilities or head to Provo to pick up air tanks and return to this location. The likelihood of finding what they were looking for in the first hour of scanning wasn't very probable, according to Max, so they all agreed to continue traversing the mapped out area.

By mid-afternoon they came upon another visual that looked awfully promising. Since it was in two hundred thirty feet of water, it would take extreme diving gear or Logan's submarine to investigate; they were equipped with neither on *Ladyhawke*. By dusk, they had located three more areas that appeared to have ship part shapes. None were as dramatic as the first, but were still good possibilities.

As the evening sky turned a deep royal blue and the first planet appeared with a steady glow in the western sky, they hiked the sails and let *Ladyhawke* slip into a comfortable glide over the three-foot swells on the ocean's face.

The men trimmed the sails, trying to get the most performance out of each. Frustrated that they couldn't get the boat to move fast enough in the light winds to satisfy their mounting enthusiasm, they started the engine.

Under a carbon black sky dripping with layers of stars, they ate dinner in the cockpit. The Milky Way looked like a smear of glitter across a piece of ebony felt.

"We might be on to something," Logan said, coming up into the cockpit, while Max was on watch. He was too excited to sleep.

"That's why I agreed to go for tanks," Max said. Even he couldn't come up with a cynical statement.

While underway, they made a pact not to tell anyone else about their efforts. Together they had become secretive treasure hunters.

Mid-morning the following day, they docked *Ladyhawke* at Turtle Cove Marina in Provo. Once on shore, Hope and Logan went to the PADI dive shop and rented eight full air tanks. While in the dive shop they were very vague as to where they were going to use the tanks, not letting on about their search for shipwrecks.

"I know we all want to get going," Hope said, "but if we leave now, we will have to motor in circles until it's light tomorrow morning."

"What do you think?" Logan asked, as he put the tanks on *Ladyhawke*. "We should leave about two to get there at daybreak the next morning?"

"I think so," she answered.

They sailed with a reefed down mainsail and half rolled in headsail into a light chop and winds just off the nose of *Ladyhawke*. By nightfall the seas had picked up and the winds were shifting to the west. Logan spotted a bank of squall clouds moving their direction. At midnight they were in a rain-storm. The winds picked up to twenty-five knots. Being veteran sailors, it was amazing that not one of the four had remembered to check the weather forecast.

Hope turned the single sideband radio on and listened to the weather channel. Luckily, the storms were spotty and predicted to dissipate by morning. The rain continued, coming down at an angle drenching the cockpit and Logan on his watch. Down below deck the other three were trying to get some rest as the boat banged into the choppy swells. The noise in the cabin was unnerving and made it almost impossible to sleep.

By dawn, they each had a pile of drenched foul weather gear from their turn at watch. The wind and the rain finally stopped, leaving the boat rolling back and forth in the confused seas. The sails slapped without enough wind to keep them taut. After trying every angle and combination possible, Logan started the engine.

"I can't take it any more," Logan said. "Tina, can you steer while I take the sails down?"

"Let me help," Max offered.

By mid-morning the surface of the water was almost as smooth as glass. The cool night air had rapidly heated up, and the sun glared off the water. Now the only movement of air was from the boat advancing across the water with engine propulsion.

Finally, at 11:30 a.m. they reached the area of the primary wreck they wanted to dive. The four flipped for the first dive. Hope and Logan won. They organized their diving gear and put on their wet-suits while Tina maneuvered the boat into position over their initial sighting. Hope stepped off the boat, cool water seeping through her wetsuit. The sound of her regulator dispersing air to her mouthpiece was invigorating. Hope and Logan gave each other the diving okay symbol, placing the fingers of one hand on top of their head. Then they proceeded to deflate their BCDs, buoyancy compensator diving equipment, and descended into the water, releasing the pressure in their ears as they went.

The familiar view of coral and tropical fish appeared below them. Just a few feet from the bottom, Hope wove her way around large blooming elephant ears that fell deep into a great crevasse of coral and stone.

Tina eased the boat momentarily into gear and then out, before easing it into reverse, all the while keeping the "V" shape on the monitor screen.

Max checked the extra air tanks to make sure they were still se-curely tied to the stern rail. He coiled the headsail sheet and tucked the reef lines into the folded mainsail. Then there was nothing left to do, so Max and Tina sat perched in the cockpit like crows on a rooftop, waiting for something to happen.

A large shadow appeared on the reef below. Rolling over to look toward the surface of the water, Hope saw *Ladyhawke*'s hull and an elegant spotted eagle ray. The ray gracefully flapped its wing-like fins and smoothly soared through the water. Then, to her amazement, a school of a dozen rays materialized out of *Ladyhawke*'s shadow and swam above her like giant birds. She was fixated on their grace and slow, fluid motion. Tilting their eyes downward to observe Hope, the rays were as curious about her as she was about them.

Logan didn't even notice the large fish; he had gotten to the reef and was already taking pictures and examining his find. Hope swam in his direction as two eight-foot-long reef sharks appeared in the crevasse below her. She nervously watched the sharks swim out of the crevasse and circle back to take another look at Logan. She knew there wasn't much she could do if the sharks' intent was to eat him. She took some relief in the fact that reef sharks are very territorial and seeing two together meant it was not breeding season. That was the time in which they were more apt to attack.

Submerged in the silt on the bottom of the ocean was the front half of a boat. It was hard to tell if the boat had broken in half and the aft section was somewhere else, or if the whole back end was submerged in the sediment. The part of the boat they could see was completely covered with coral and barnacles. Logan removed the knife from the holster around his ankle and scraped a section of coral from the boat's hull. Immediately he was disappointed. He could tell the boat was fiberglass, a material that didn't exist in either the 1700s or 1800s. He pointed it out to Hope and they both lost all earlier enthusiasm.

"Here they come," Tina said, watching over the edge of the boat.

"Well?" Max said as soon as Logan took his mask off but was still treading water.

"It's fiberglass," he said in a very dejected tone.

"We have six more tanks. Let's go check out the other sights," Max suggested. He knew they could go down one hundred eighty feet without complications if they stopped at thirty feet on their way up to decompress a bit. At one hundred eighty feet they should be able to see enough of the wreck that's at two hundred thirty feet to make a good judgment as to whether it is worth further pursuit.

When they arrived at their second coordinate, they ate lunch so Logan could spend a bit more time on the surface before going down to one hundred eighty feet with Max. Tina and Hope kept the boat in position over the wreck, and the men descended with an extra regulator and a third tank of air. They had the spare tank of air tied to a thirty-foot line off the stern, with a heavy weight belt attached. From experience they knew they wouldn't have enough air in their primary tanks to stay at thirty feet long enough to get the nitrogen out of their bloodstream after such a deep dive.

Max and Logan got close enough to the wreck to determine that it wasn't what they were looking for. It was a sunken ship, but not an old one. They could tell the boat was made out of steel, not a material used on either Mary Read's or Delaney's boat. So up they went, slowly making their ways to the spare tank of air. They adjusted their BCDs to keep them buoyant at that depth while they passed the regulator of the spare tank back and forth, breathing the full tank's air capacity down to five hundred psi. Then they ascended to the surface of the water.

At the third wreck, which registered on the depth sounder at three hundred ten feet, they knew they wouldn't be able to see enough at their maximum dive depth of one hundred eighty feet to determine whether it was what they were looking for or not. Also, both Max and Logan had exceeded their allotted dive time for that day. They weren't willing to run the risk of getting the bends from nitrogen poisoning and having to be flown to a decompression tank. So while at the site, all they could do was look at the suspicious shape on the sonar screen as they traversed over it several more times.

Logan was in his element; he could stay and look for shipwrecks indefinitely. But he knew that without his submarine it would be impossible to excavate a treasure if one were found. And the sub was the only way to check the deeper possibilities. Logan was excited and disappointed at the same time. He was an impatient man, easily frustrated when he wasn't immediately able to do what he wanted.

Logan vowed to himself and the Shorts that it would be his next project when he returned to work after his year-long sailing sabbatical with Hope. He would bring his submarine to the Turks and Caicos Islands and search for the two sunken ships. As Logan made this promise, he visualized himself bringing *Josephine*'s treasures up from the bottom of the ocean.

Conspiracy in Africa

DREW EMERGED FROM HIS HOTEL ROOM IN Arusha to putrid air. It was thick with smoke from burning garbage in the multitude of small cook fires behind each makeshift shack that tightly packed the outskirts of town.

"How are you?" the cab driver asked, practicing his limited English on Drew.

"I am fine. Thank you."

"It is a, a, um, a beautiful day. Correct?"

"Yes, it is a beautiful day," Drew smiled as he answered the driver.

Then after several moments of silence, the driver asked, "Are you on safari?"

Not knowing that the word safari meant vacation to most Tanzanians instead of a wild animal hunt, Drew replied, "No, I came to climb Kilimanjaro."

"Yes, yes," the driver said, enthusiastically pointing in the direction of the mountain.

Leaving the city they drove out into the countryside down dusty dirt roads before coming to the entrance of the Chagga village. Matthew was waiting for Drew's arrival with several of the village children. They were eager for the American's visit. Matthew shook Drew's hand in greeting and the children tentatively gathered around him.

The large camera case that hung from Drew's shoulder became a big curiosity to the children. Swarming around him as he opened it, they fell over each other to peer within. Drew removed the camera and turned it from side to side for the children to examine. Samuel, Matthew's grandson, held his hands out. Drew gently placed it in his hands, but didn't let go of the delicate instrument.

"For me?" Samuel asked.

"For the moment," Drew answered, smiling at his innocence.

On the surface, the lush valley appeared to be an affluent African village. The children had clothing on and some even wore shoes.

"Good morning, sir," Matthew said. "We are so glad to have you visit."

"Thank you for inviting me," Drew answered.

They passed by the village school, which was a neat row of three one-room, cinderblock buildings with nicely crafted paintings on the exterior walls. One of the paintings was of a very detailed African map; another had an anatomical human in several stages of dissection. The third building was covered with geometrical shapes and algebraic equations. The cafeteria was a separate cinderblock building with a dirt floor and a fire pit in the center.

"Only if someone has a good harvest do the children have lunch at school," Matthew explained. It all depended on donations.

They walked down a dirt trail between gray cinderblock houses with corrugated metal roofs. Some of the houses were finished with hand-made stucco covering the cinderblocks. Several actually had electricity running to them from the central electrical line. Spring water also ran in an open trough through the center of the village. A few villagers had diverted water with piping to their own homes so they had a gravity-fed spigot.

Loose hens and roosters pecked at minute seeds and insects. An occasional grazing goat or cow was staked in a grassy patch. The wealthiest Chaggans owned pigs. Between the homes were gardens planted in layers. Beneath the banana trees grew yams and tomatoes. Among the corn stalks, beans and beets flourished. At first glance everything looked normal, until Drew noticed the rows of new graves and the number of people lying in the shade of the large acacia trees. When Drew walked by the lounging Chaggans with Matthew, they all looked up but they didn't have the strength to get up or engage in conversation.

"When our tribe settled here," Matthew explained, "each man took a plot of land to call his own. On the land he built a house and raised crops and livestock to feed his family. As his children grew, he divided his land amongst his sons so they would have land for their families. Because of this continual division of land we no longer have enough property to support our families. We have to seek employment outside of the village to earn money to supplement our crops."

"But you said employment is scarce," Drew said.

"Yes, sir. It is. Very few have a regular job."

Matthew was a proud, ambitious man. He, his wife, and their children had been hard workers who, as he put it, had become entrepreneurs. He owned the only liquor store in the village. Matthew took Drew to a cinderblock building about eight feet square where he stored cases of beer. Matthew's bar was a picnic table in front of the beer shed where villagers came to drink the room temperature brew and gossip. Matthew's family also owned the only beauty salon in town, where his oldest daughter cut hair. It was an even smaller cinderblock building with one window. Inside, an old wood chair sat in the center of the room. On a small table sat a large toothed comb and a set of electric clippers that were powered with an extension cord draped through the window. Everyone in the Chagga tribe had the same haircut; men, women and children all had a close buzz. Their kinky black hair barely colored their scalp right after a cut.

Matthew had done well for his family. But, even he was feeling the pain of loss. With his mother and granddaughter already taken by the plague, he was now in fear for his children. The Chagga village was not jovial the way the porters had seemed on the mountain trail. There was a stillness that blanketed the valley. Hopelessness had come over the people like a black looming cloud. Even with the arrival of the doctors, hope had not been restored. The shots and medication the medical team was administering didn't appear to make a difference. People were still getting sick at an alarming rate. Only a very few seemed to miraculously spring back to health and recover. When someone appeared to have a positive reaction to a medication, the medical staff just took more notes.

Drew sat down at the picnic table outside Matthew's beer

shed while the proprietor brought him a warm Tanzabeer. From where he sat, Drew could see the line of graves spread across the hillside like wildebeests during a spring migration, one behind the next. Within moments Matthew's brother, Luke, joined them and began asking Drew for his suggestions on what they could do about the plague. Drew was a journalist, not a doctor. He couldn't supply them with an answer, but he was overwhelmed with sympathy. He took on the project of helping them find an answer like he would take on a research story he was writing, analyzing it from every direction.

"Tell me what you know about the illness," Drew prodded.

"I'm told it begins with an intense headache," Luke said. "Nausea then follows for days, and then the headache and nausea seem to subside, but the sick never return to health. We've been told that there is a bacterium in our water."

"They quickly lose the ability to swallow food," Matthew added. "Their throats constrict somehow. Eventually they can't even swallow their own saliva."

As their bodies dried out in the African heat, crusted mucus filled their mouths and stiffened their tongues. Slipping into comas, their partially opened eyes glazed over. Both brothers had watched the energy drain from the flesh of their loved ones like the recession of flood waters after a monsoon, leaving their skin cracked and grayed.

The draining of life's vital force took its course from beginning to end in a brief period. The epidemic had wiped out over a fifth of the Chagga people in just four short months. At first it was only the elderly and infants that were dying, but now the healthy, strong, working age villagers were getting sick and beginning to pass on as well.

Drew took a deep breath and let it out with a sigh, wishing he knew what to do. Slowly he shook his head from side to side having a hard time believing what he was hearing. At one end of the soccer field, Drew could see the large medical tents that Matthew had described.

The more Matthew and Luke explained their dilemma, the more Drew began to feel uneasy. There was something about their story that didn't seem to add up. Where did this bacterium come from? Why hadn't it been diagnosed and named? Why was it only inflicting their tribe? Why did some get better, but most did not? And why did the doctors come immediately to try and remedy the problem? Drew wasn't buying it. Something felt wrong to him. He knew there was a story here that hadn't been told; yet he believed Matthew and Luke. He believed they hadn't figured it out themselves.

After exhausting all the information that the brothers had, Drew went to the main medical tent. He was immediately greeted by Dr. Ghazi Hakem, who appeared to be in charge. Ghazi seemed friendly enough and was quick to answer Drew's questions with short, vague answers. Drew left the tent feeling like he didn't know anything more about the plague than what Matthew and Luke had already shared with him.

Upon leaving for the city, Drew promised Matthew he would stay in Tanzania for a few days and try to help figure out what could be done to fight the plague.

At his hotel room, Drew searched the Internet, but couldn't find anything about the plague or the mysterious bacterium. It appeared the plague hadn't even made the news in Tanzania. He then emailed his mother in Panama where she was a nurse in the Peace Corps. He described in detail what he was seeing in the Chagga village and asked if she had ever seen anything like it in her travels as a nurse in third-world countries.

Her response alarmed him.

Drew,

Don't ask too many questions. It is not for you to research. Please drop it and go home. You may be stepping beyond your bounds...

This response was not what he expected. *Why wasn't she more concerned about the Chagga people?* he wondered. It wasn't like her to turn and walk away from people in need.

The following morning, Drew returned to the Chagga village and went straight to the medical tent hoping to get a clear picture as to what the doctors planned on doing. Across the room Drew could see Dr. Hakem sitting at his computer. At the top, in bold letters, was CDR Pharmaceutical. As soon as Dr. Hakem noticed Drew was standing behind him, he turned his computer screen off.

"We are busy," Dr. Hakem said in his thick Middle Eastern accent as he ushered Drew out of the tent. "Yes, yes, come back later."

Drew knew something was going on that shouldn't be. He began to question everyone who would talk. It seemed there had been a small group of men hiking the hills above the Chagga village just a few weeks before people began to get sick. Many of the Chagga people didn't trust outsiders and always blamed tourists for any problems, so they were instantly to blame. But what could the Chagga people do even if the tourists were the culprits? The Chagga tribe was dying off, and it took most of the energy of the healthy people to care for the sick.

The more information Drew gathered and the more questions he asked, the more nervous the doctors became. Then, out of the blue, Dr. Hakem surprised Drew with an invitation to join him for dinner in Arusha. Drew hoped that at dinner, he would open up and shed some light on the disease.

When he arrived at the appointed restaurant, the hostess ushered him into a private sitting room where Dr. Hakem and a lady were quietly talking.

"Yes, yes, come join us. It is nice to have you," Hakem said, now seeming to welcome Drew's presence. "Have a seat, yes? Please meet Dr. Lucrecia Lu. She has just arrived."

"It is nice to meet you. You can call me Lucy," she said, extending her hand toward Drew.

"Likewise," Drew said, shocked at her English because she spoke without a foreign accent, even though her name and appearance made Drew think she was from China.

"I hear you climbed Kilimanjaro," Lucy interjected as Drew sat in the chair across from her. Hakem lifted an open bottle from the center of the table and poured a glass of wine for Drew, raised his glass to his guest, and tipped his head in a silent cheer.

"Thank you," Drew said, raising his glass and taking a sip. "Yes, I did manage to make it to the top of Kilimanjaro, but the last leg of the ascent was grueling. If it weren't for my guide and my porter, I never would have made it."

"Someday, I would like to climb Kilimanjaro," Lucy said.

"Is this your first time to Tanzania?" Drew asked her, wanting to shift the conversation away from himself.

"Yes, it is," she responded.

Wow, Drew thought. *I really need to eat something. This wine is going to my head unusually fast.* He rubbed his forehead and the back of his neck as he broke out in a clammy sweat. Trying to focus his eyes, the room began to spin, and he felt himself tumbling. Hakem rose to his feet to help Drew as he fell out of his chair.

The next morning Drew awoke with the intense African sun shining on his face through the small window of a hotel room in downtown Arusha. He immediately closed his eyes again. An image of Lucy sitting in a chair next to him pierced his mind. The throbbing in his head was intense enough to make him want to vomit. For a moment, he thought he was hallucinating, and then he heard her voice.

"Drew, are you okay?" Lucy asked when she realized he was conscious.

Gritting his teeth, not wanting to scream from the wretched pain, he tried to hold onto consciousness and not slip away; the searing pain took him again and he was unresponsive.

The intense sun now blazed straight overhead as the temperature rose. Drew awoke drenched in his own sweat, which had soaked the bed sheets and halfway through the mattress. He felt as if he had an internal sun baking him from the inside out.

Again, he heard Lucy as he tried to focus in the direction of her voice. "Drew, I'm over here. How are you? What is happening?"

Drew's tongue was swollen and his jaw felt paralyzed, making it impossible for him to speak. He closed his eyes and drifted back into unconsciousness.

Hours later, he again awoke. He was aware of someone speaking to Lucy. It was Dr. Hakem. Without opening his eyes, he tried to stay conscious and focus on their conversation.

Hakem was talking. "Yes, the bacterium is having a most intense effect on him."

Who? Drew wondered, *who was reacting intensely?* He did not realize they were talking about him.

Drew felt his eyelids being lifted and a bright light being shone into his eyes, but he couldn't blink or move.

"Yes, it is yellowish," Ghazi said, looking at the whites of his eyes. "Increase his IV. Without Latrixal, he won't survive. Yes, we must get him back to the States before he dies."

"How much Latrixal should I administer?" Lucy asked.

"Start with only two units. Yes, yes, that should get him up."

Drew drifted off again. It was two days later when he finally awoke. He could now clearly focus on the ceiling above him. It was dark outside, but he could see in the room because there was a small lamp in the corner that was lit. He looked toward the lamp and saw Lucy asleep in a recliner, with her reading glasses still on and an open book in her lap. The searing pain in his head had been replaced with a dull ache behind each eye. The sheet he was lying on was still soaked, but he was no longer sweating. His eyes were tired and burned. But his mind felt remarkably clear.

His memory was vague and not complete. He no longer trusted Hakem or Lucy and he feared for his life if he stayed in their company. Slowly he removed the IV from the back of his left hand and silently slid out of bed. He found the clothes he had been wearing the night he fell to the floor in the restaurant; they were draped across the back of a folding chair by the hall door. He slipped into his boxers, noticing they were loose around the waist. He thought he must have lost several pounds from dehydration. He quickly picked up the rest of his clothes and tiptoed out the door into the hallway.

In the hall he quickly finished dressing. The smells of urine and burning hashish accosted his nose and instantly brought his headache and nausea on again. In the center of the hall, the carpet was worn down to the wood underlayment. The walls were filthy and smeared with what looked like blood.

In the lobby he slipped past the front desk attendant, who was also asleep behind the counter. When he entered the street, he wasn't sure where he was. He walked from one street lamp to the next, avoiding the shadows of the night, until he came to a busy street. Even in the middle of the night, several people still milled around. He found an old taxi parked at the curb with someone asleep behind the wheel. Drew knocked on the hood, startling the sleeping man. The driver agreed to take Drew to the hotel where he had left his belongings the evening he met Hakem and Lucy for dinner. In his hotel room, he quickly took a shower and gathered up his things. Just before dawn he had another cab driver retrieve Matthew from the Chagga village. He didn't feel safe enough to go to the village himself.

The sun was just beginning to give light above the horizon when Matthew entered the small open-air restaurant at the hotel where Drew was waiting.

"My friend, how are you feeling?" Matthew asked with deep concern, genuinely happy to see Drew. "Dr. Hakem said you had become ill."

Drew quickly looked around to make sure there was no one else in earshot before saying, "I think I was drugged, Matthew."

"No, sir. How would that happen?"

"Not only drugged, but infected with the same bacterium that has been plaguing your tribe. I don't trust Dr. Hakem."

"Oh, sir, but we must. Who else do we have?"

"Something is going on here that doesn't seem right. I think they are trying to dissuade me from prying. I just spent four days in a drug-induced haze. I can barely remember time passing. I was shocked to look at my watch and realize four days had passed since I met Hakem and Lucy for dinner."

"No, sir," Matthew said shaking his head, not wanting to believe what he had just heard. "Dr. Hakem is trying everything he can to help." But even as Matthew was saying this, he remembered the day he overheard Hakem and one of his colleagues talking about the effect of different drugs on the infected. At the time Matthew shrugged it off, not wanting to believe his own suspicions.

"I know Hakem has a cure for the plague. I just can't remember what it is called."

As the two talked at a back table in the restaurant, Drew began to sweat again. Sweat was seeping from every pore in his body.

Noticing it, Matthew said, "Drew you must come back to the village with me. Maybe Dr. Hakem can help you."

"No, Matthew, I must go home. The cab driver should be waiting outside for us. He will take you back to your village and me to the airport." Drew was hoping to make it home while he still could.

That morning when Matthew walked into the medical tent, he could hear Dr. Hakem before he could see him. He was very angry. He was shouting at Lucy.

"You are kidding me. How could you sleep? How could you? You, go find him."

Matthew ducked out of the tent. He now knew Drew was right. But what was he to do?

The Dominican Republic

AFTER A QUIET, UNEVENTFUL CROSSING TO Grand Turks, they anchored *Ladyhawke* on the southwest shore in Hamilton Bay. Now the McKnights were poised for a direct sail to the Dominican Republic, their next destination.

"Please keep in touch," Hope said to Tina at the dock.

"Maybe we can meet down island," Tina said, as she hugged Hope good-bye. "We'll miss you guys."

"It's amazing how a disastrous situation has brought us together," Hope said. "I feel like I have known you for a long time."

"It's not good-bye," Logan said. "It's hello to new friends."

"Safe travels, Two Peckered Billy-Goat," Max said to Logan with a grin.

A good weather window for sailing to the Dominican Republic came quickly. The following afternoon Hope and Logan pulled anchor and set sail into a moderate chop and a brisk wind. Hope quickly made up a sea berth for them behind the nav-station and prepared a pot of pasta for dinner. Logan charted a rhumb line to follow and hooked *Elmo* up to steer them south. At dusk the western sky turned a radiant pink and orange while a small bank of clouds in the east turned lavender. *Ladyhawke* slid into a rhythmic glide over the evenly spaced, four-foot waves.

During Logan's midnight to three a.m. shift the winds began to pick up. Tethered to the jack line, he went to the mast and lowered the mainsail to the first cringle and hooked it to the ram's horn. Putting a reef in the sail, he cinched the lines tight. He proceeded back toward the cockpit when an off-beat wave abruptly lifted the boat as his foot hooked into a loose line. Logan fell hard, smacking his mouth on the handrail. In the salon, Hope was awakened by the loud noise.

"Logan, what happened?" Hope asked when she saw blood dripping through his fingers.

"I fell," his voice was muffled through his hand as he sat down in the cockpit.

"Let me see," she said. "Oh, Logan, you split your lip open. Let me get some ice."

"I broke a tooth, too."

"Bad?" Hope asked.

Logan opened his mouth and Hope grimaced at all the blood and the view of only half of Logan's left front tooth.

"Let's get the bleeding stopped first," she said. "I don't know what to do about the broken tooth."

With a wet washcloth she tried to clean the blood from Logan's face, hands, and arms. She then wrapped an ice cube in a clean cloth and handed it to him. He touched it to his lip and then quickly jerked it away. The electric shock from putting ice next to his chipped tooth weakened his muscles to the core.

"Can you put it on your lip without touching it to your tooth? We've got to get the bleeding stopped."

Logan tried to put the ice to his lip, but again he jerked it away.

"Come lie down," Hope soothed.

She helped him get comfortable, lying with his head elevated.

"Maybe this is cool enough to help stop the bleeding," Hope said, as she handed him a wet washcloth without ice.

Hope didn't want to leave Logan's side, but she knew she was now in charge of the boat. Up on deck she scanned the horizon for lights. All was clear. Then stepping back into the cabin to the nav-station she charted their position. They were still on course.

Making sure the bleeding had slowed, she went back into the cockpit, clipped her tether to a pad-eye, and started her watch a little earlier than planned.

Several times through the wee hours she went below to check on Logan. It took a while, but the bleeding eventually stopped and he fell asleep. Hope let him sleep the rest of the night and into the morning.

Just outside of Luperon Bay, Hope woke Logan.

"How are you feeling?"

"Mmmm," Logan groaned without opening his mouth.

"Can you get up and steer while I take the sails down?" she asked.

From the mild exertion of moving, Logan's lip began to bleed again, and he had to hold a rag to his mouth as he steered.

Luperon Bay was disappointing. The water was muddy and

thick with sediment. Boats were tightly anchored next to each other, and Hope felt overwhelmed with the congestion of humanity and the oppressive heat.

The day was gray, and rain drizzled through the hot, muggy air as Hope made it to shore in their dinghy. She hurried down the dock, on a mission to quickly clear Customs and Immigration, and more importantly—find the name of the best dentist in town.

Heavy vegetation hung low along the road, looking dismal in the overcast sky and droopy from the weight of moisture. Trash lined the road and the smell of rotting plants clung in the air. The area was poor and disheveled.

Dirty, wet children aimlessly walked along the road, looking blankly at Hope as she passed. Their eyes were slightly yellowed from dehydration and parasites. Even in her non-pretentious attire she looked entirely too clean and was obviously a foreigner. The children looked at her as an outsider, but they expected outsiders. Luperon was a common place for ocean-crossing sailboats to make shore for provisions. Many boaters ended up staying for long periods of time because of its inexpensive supplies and lack of regulations on the length one could stay. Hope didn't see the appeal. For her, the filthy water and pollution outweighed the inexpensive lifestyle.

Having quickly checked in with Customs and Immigration, Hope walked along the main street. It was lined with stores catering to life on a boat—fruit and vegetable stands, rigging supplies, canvas repair, cushions, electronics, refrigeration repairs, and sail makers.

Choosing to enter the canvas repair store, Hope was glad to see an American-looking woman at a sewing machine. When questioned about a local dentist, the woman had an answer for her immediately.

"His name is Klaus Von Ark, a German dentist who moved here several years ago when he fell in love with a local woman," she informed Hope in a simple American accent. The seamstress took a break from her duties, found the dentist's address and phone number in the local phone book, and wrote it on the back of a shop card.

"You're welcome to use our phone to call him, if you like," the seamstress offered. Hope accepted.

Dr. Von Ark wanted to see Logan immediately. Hope thanked the seamstress and quickly headed back to *Ladyhawke*. Within moments, she had Logan in the dinghy and took him to shore, where they caught a taxi to the dentist's office.

Dr. Von Ark greeted his new patient with a warm, relaxed smile. He looked very tan in his hiking shorts, worn polo shirt, and Teva sandals. He questioned Hope as to how the accident had happened before he had Logan try to open his mouth. Because of the swelling and split in his lip, Logan was only able to open his mouth a crack for Dr. Von Ark to look inside.

"You sure did break it off. Where did you guys come from?" he said, looking up at Hope for an answer, not wanting Logan to talk.

"We just sailed in from the Grand Turks," she informed him.

"Well, I'm afraid the work I need to do is going to require Logan to open his mouth wider than he can right now," he said to Hope.

Looking over at Logan, he continued, "Your lip is going to have to heal a little so I can get my tools in your mouth. We don't want your lip to keep splitting open. Let's give it a few days to knit. It will look better and heal with less scarring if we don't have to put stitches in. I suggest you go back to your boat and rest. I'll make an appointment for you to come back in a week. We'll see how you're doing then."

Hope's spirits fell as she realized they were going to have to stay in Luperon for awhile.

"In the meantime, you're going to have to be on a liquid diet," Dr. Von Ark continued. "Make smoothies or put soup in a blender. Make sure everything you drink is body temperature. Any fluctuation of hot or cold will make your tooth feel like it is on fire. I'll give you a prescription for the pain; you might need it to sleep. How is the pain now?"

Logan separated his lips a tiny crack and slowly slurred, "If I don't move or talk or open my mouth, it's tolerable." But since he had just opened his mouth to speak, air hit his tooth and pain shot a visible jolt through his body. Dr. Von Ark shook his head, understanding his predicament while filling out a prescription for a pain medicine.

A week of lying around *Ladyhawke* seemed like three when it was finally time for Logan to return to Dr. Von Ark's office. Most of the swelling had gone down; his lip seemed to have healed to the point that he could open his mouth enough for the tools that were needed to make an impression of his teeth.

"I have a Nor'sea 27," Klaus said, referring to the small sailboat he owned. He was trying to distract Logan from the pain. Logan had his mouth wide open and could only acknowledge by a slight nod of his head.

"I keep it in Samana Bay, located on the southeast side of the island," he continued. "It is beautiful there. The water is clear. It is nothing like Luperon."

Klaus talked about his Dominican wife and her family. Knowing Logan couldn't respond to what he was saying, he talked as if he were alone. He told Logan how corrupt the Dominican Republic's government was and how one's status in the country was determined by whom one knew.

"Life for the average person, without a lot of money or connections with people in power, is very difficult. The government could easily make or destroy a person's life."

Logan's tooth was beautifully repaired. With each visit they learned more about the Samana anchorage. It didn't take Hope and Logan long to decide they wanted to move their boat to Samana Bay. When they finally got a weather window to make the one-hundred-fifty-mile sail around the northeastern tip of the Dominican Republic, they were pleased by the isolation and the beautiful, dense, tropical vegetation along the shoreline. In the bay, the water was a clear, royal blue. It was just as the doctor described.

Their hopes were high that at this new anchorage they could settle into a peaceful life for a few days. But for some reason, it still didn't feel right. Both Logan and Hope couldn't just relax and enjoy their surroundings.

Hope kept saying, "Something's wrong. I just don't know what."

As they prepared grouper filets on the grill the first evening in Samana, they kept looking into the darkness, feeling as if someone was watching them.

Fighting for His Life

DREW SLEPT THE ENTIRE EIGHT HOURS IT TOOK to fly from Kilimanjaro to Amsterdam. His dreams were centered on the primal pounding of a ritual drum. The beating was the throbbing inside his head. Once again, he was profusely sweating.

The flight attendant had to awaken Drew when it was time to get off the plane.

"Pardon me, are you okay?" she asked as she shook his shoulder. But it became obvious he wasn't well when she felt his wet clothing and looked into his extremely bloodshot eyes. "Would you like me to get a wheelchair for you?"

Drew nodded his head in agreement. After everyone else had exited the plane, he stood up and was helped off. But he left the outline of his body in the chair. He had sweat all the way through his clothes and into the fabric of the coach seat.

Before boarding his final flight to Baltimore Washington International in Maryland, he managed, with a lot of effort, to change into dry clothes in the men's restroom. In the handicapped toilet stall, he had to sit down in his wheelchair several times, closing his eyes, becoming motionless, and waiting for the agonizing pain in his head to calm down to a manageable ache. If he moved too much, his head felt as if it would explode, and he feared he was on the verge of passing out.

Leaning back in his chair on his connecting flight, he immediately fell asleep, even before the plane took off. At BWI, another wheelchair attendant helped him retrieve his luggage and get into a taxi that took him directly to the Johns Hopkins Hospital. It was known as one of the best hospitals in the nation—the same hospital where Drew's mother had worked as a surgical nurse when he was a child.

In the emergency room, the attending nurse knew Drew's mother and immediately admitted him into a room. He was thankful he didn't have to wait in the excruciatingly long line of patients with colds and skinned knees. Without delay, they began running tests to determine what was needed to make him better. Within an hour Dr. Tom Mercer, a work associate and friend of Drew's mother, was in his hospital room taking over his care. Drew asked Tom to call the emergency number he had for his mother in Panama.

"I have it in my backpack somewhere," he said.

"I know how to reach her," Dr. Mercer replied.

"I've been poisoned," Drew tried to explain for what seemed like the one-hundredth time.

"With what?" questioned Dr. Mercer.

"I think it is a bacterium."

"Who poisoned you?" Dr. Mercer asked.

"I don't know who they really are," Drew said, closing his eyes. "They told the Chagga people they were doctors." Drew took a deep breath, trying to muster the energy to continue talking. "They were evasive when I asked them directly what company they worked for. I saw an email Dr. Hakem was reading one day. He closed the screen immediately when he noticed I was standing behind him. The only words that stood out on the page were 'CDR Pharmaceutical'. I know Dr. Hakem has the antidote for whatever they poisoned me with, but I can't remember what it is called. I've tried and tried. My mind is not as clear as it should be."

"I've never heard of CDR Pharmaceutical. Let me do some research," Tom responded as he quickly walked toward the door. "Continue running the tests analyzing his blood." He directed his request to the nurse on duty as he exited the room.

Drew had already been hooked up to an IV that pumped fluids into his body to try and replace the liquids he had lost. The nurse also injected intravenous medicine into his IV for pain, obviously to just mask the symptoms, not to do anything to cure his ailment.

His blood test did detect anaerobic bacteria that infiltrated his blood, but it was not a known bacterium to the lab technician.

They immediately rushed him over to radiology and performed a CT-scan to determine if there was an abscess anywhere in his body that could be the source of the infection. To their surprise, there were many abscesses in his digestive tract and internal organs. The bacteria were causing tissue destruction, quickly replacing the healthy tissues with masses of hard capsulated abscesses filled with infected pus. It was not the typical Bacteroides Fragilis, Peptostreptococcus, or Clostridium bacterium. But it was definitely a bacteria—a large cell formation without a nucleus.

In the O.R. Drew went under emergency surgery. Dr. Mercer inserted a microscopic camera into his abdomen, followed by a large syringe to drain pus from the abscesses. After they drained most of the larger ones, they used ultrasound to break up the abscess casing. But as fast as they could drain and break up the bundles of abscessed bacteria, new ones appeared in their place—only larger, with a thicker encasement.

The team of doctors now working on Drew's case realized they weren't improving his situation, but instead potentially worsening it. They tried a new avenue, administering a large dose of antibiotic into his IV, thus hoping to control the spread of the bacteria. This may have been helpful, because when Drew awoke in the recovery room, he appeared to be more stable. It seemed that, for the moment, the antibiotic was working.

They put Drew in the ICU and secluded him in an isolation room, fearing the spread of this unknown bacteria to the rest of the hospital.

Dr. Mercer entered Drew's room and uncharacteristically locked the door behind him.

"Drew, I've talked to your mother," he said. "She is flying home on the next flight out of Colon. She will be here tomorrow evening." Drew said nothing. He was remembering the email he received from his mother while in Tanzania. She was right. He stuck his nose where it shouldn't have been.

"How are you feeling?" the doctor asked, taking his stethoscope from around his neck in preparation to listen to Drew's heart.

"I'm exhausted," Drew said, barely able to open his eyes. "I still feel drugged from surgery." He continued to lie motionless on the bed. "If I don't move, my head doesn't hurt… it just feels full."

"That will pass. I'm hoping the medicine will control and eradicate the infection," Dr. Mercer said as he leaned over and listened to Drew's racing heart. It was beating twice as fast as normal.

"Drew, I've been on the Internet looking for CDR Pharmaceutical. It doesn't exist. When I Google CDR, Chemical Defense

Research Department shows up. Another site led me to CBR, Chemical Bioterrorism Response. All sites that had any mention of CDR were high security and they wouldn't let me in without clearance. Are you sure CDR Pharmaceutical is what you saw on the screen?"

Drew knew in his heart the infection and the appearance of the supposed doctors were suspicious. He knew he had been deliberately infected with the bacteria by Hakem and Lucy. Drew didn't want to think of them as Dr. Hakem and Dr. Lu anymore, because they didn't deserve the titles, and those probably weren't their real names anyway. His heart sank, knowing the prognosis for the Chagga tribe. He knew he had to do something to help them, but with the sedative still in his blood, he couldn't think clearly.

"I've got to get back over there and warn Matthew. They don't deserve to be guinea pigs for the research of some corrupt organization." As Drew said this, he tried to pull himself into a seated position but couldn't muster the energy.

"This is not your battle, Drew. I would just drop it and focus on getting yourself well," Dr. Mercer said. "I'm not sure if what you are saying is true or not. I can't imagine a corruption so deep they would experiment on a tribe. What I do know is you are very sick and you cannot do anything for the Chagga people if you die."

"I have to do something," Drew said as he closed his eyes in thought. He knew there was something he could do, but he just couldn't concentrate long enough to come up with what it was before the drugs took him back to sleep.

Dr. Mercer left Drew's room truly concerned for his life. The information Dr. Mercer pulled up on the Internet was enough to make him not want to get involved. He only wanted to focus on finding a cure for Drew. He intended to let it lie.

Drew awoke in the middle of the night, shivering and soaked in his own perspiration again. Every sheet and blanket on the bed was saturated with fluids that oozed out of his skin as fast as fluid could be pumped into his veins through the IV.

Drew was dreaming about the heart of Africa. He began to wonder if all of Africa had been a dream. There were parts of Africa he wished were a dream because they had become a nightmare as he struggled for his life; yet there were other aspects of the place he loved—the deep connection the Chagga tribe felt for each other, the primitive, uncivilized countryside, and the tribal cultures that spanned centuries. Drew wondered, *How could one place have such extreme good and bad?*

In Drew's dream, he was a withered old man climbing Kilimanjaro with Matthew's grandson. He was walking up the trail very slowly, because slow was as fast as he could walk. Drew led Samuel up the mountain like Matthew had led Drew. On the mountain, Samuel listened while Drew reminisced about his long and meaningful life. Drew told him that he had learned to stop doing life long enough to enjoy being alive. Drew listened to himself tell this to Samuel and knew it was true. Now in the hospital bed, Drew hoped he would live long enough to be able to tell others about how meaningful his life had been.

Lying in the hospital bed, he could feel the deep-rooted heart that pulsed through the soil in Africa. He truly felt like he had left a part of himself there. He could feel the rudimentary beat of life itself emanating from the continent. The ancient land felt deeply precious. With sadness, he hoped it wasn't just a dream. He hoped the small tribe of Chagga people really did have a fundamental unit, a caring family that extended back in history for many generations.

In the middle of the night, Drew felt the loneliness that dominated the United States. Suffering from the anaerobic infection and feeling physically depleted, he felt desperately alone. Here in his home country, he couldn't find the feeling of "United" like the name might suggest. The only pulse Drew felt was the rhythmical pulse of the relentless heart monitor. Despair and hopelessness radiated from every cell in his body. He could feel his vital life force slipping into nothingness. Drew was scared.

Perhaps it was the anesthesia wearing off, but his mind was becoming lucid. Drew realized he needed to contact the journalistic community and let them know what was going on in Tanzania. Someone had to get to the bottom of the deception that could potentially wipe out an entire village, a village that had survived for generations and a tribe that was much older than the United States itself. Drew couldn't wait until morning. He didn't care what time it was, he got on the phone and called his friend Steve Jennings, a news anchorman. He woke Steve out of a sound sleep and told him what had happened in Africa.

Before he hung up, Steve was committed to gathering a crew of journalists and cameramen to head out to Tanzania. Drew wished he could accompany them on the mission, but he knew he didn't have the strength.

Later that morning Dr. Mercer made his rounds and checked in with Drew. His temperature had broken and his heart had slowed to a tolerable rate; but still, it was not as slow as Dr. Mercer had wished. He ordered more blood tests to monitor the severity of the infection and another CT-scan to observe the abscesses.

The results from the lab were favorable. There appeared to be fewer bacteria in his blood and his white blood count was reduced, indicating the infection was under control. But when the X-ray technician looked at the CT-scan, he was shocked. The abscesses had enlarged and increased in number. It appeared the antibiotic had helped to control the bacteria in Drew's blood, but not the growing number of cysts that were beginning to hamper the function of his organs.

The concerned doctor continued to research on the Internet, hoping to find information relating to an unusual abscess-producing bacteria and what might be done to eradicate it from Drew's body. With frustration, that evening he returned to Drew's room with no new information.

As soon as Ruth arrived at BWI, she took a taxi to Johns Hopkins Hospital. She had talked to both Drew and Tom Mercer several times throughout the day during her flight layovers. Drew was awake when she entered his room, but he was exhausted beyond words. He barely had the strength to lift his own arms to hug his mother when she leaned over to embrace him. Ruth was the ideal specimen of a woman in her seventies. She was strong, lean, and flexible. Her eyes sparkled from her nicely tanned face. Anyone could tell by looking at her that she was a very healthy and happy woman.

Drew melted in his mother's arms. He could feel it again; the bond of love he had felt in Africa. Tears seeped from the corners of his eyes and ran to his ears. Leaning back from Drew, Ruth grabbed both of his hands in hers.

Shaking them, she said, "We will get through this together. You have the best staff of doctors in the world on your side. We will discover the cure for you." Ruth was a strong woman, but even she was fighting to control tears as she looked down on her diminished son.

Drew nodded his head in agreement. His mother brought hope to his world. Her positive nature changed the energy in the room. His fears lessened.

Wedding Day

WHEN WILLY STEVENS FIRST CAME TO THE COPAN Valley, he thought he had died and gone to heaven. There were more plant varieties in one square mile of Honduran jungle than in the entire state of Indiana, where he was a botanist.

One day, when Willy was intently gathering plant specimens, he heard Moon Jaguar, my mother's elder sister, singing in the distance. He stopped to listen to the melodic sounds drifting his way through the thick, sultry air. Typically Willy was too absorbed in plant life to even notice a chattering troop of spider monkeys in the trees overhead, let alone a voice singing off in the distance. But Moon Jaguar's voice seemed to be calling to him.

His curiosity took over. He stopped picking plants and gradually started walking down the path in the direction of her voice. As it grew louder, it seemed to fill the forest with its richness. Willy stopped when he saw a young woman kneeling by a stream, intent on doing her laundry. Moon Jaguar slowly swayed back and forth as she pushed and kneaded the clothing on a flat rock. Her plump body moved fluidly—free and unencumbered from stress or tension. He couldn't pull his eyes away from her long, loose hair that swayed from side to side on her beautiful mola blouse.

The mola was an intricately appliquéd picture of a jaguar lying under two coconut palms with a very large full moon rising in the background. Willy was taken aback by how completely at home she was in her surroundings. The heartfelt longing in her voice vibrated through Willy and touched his soul. Now standing just a few feet behind her, Willy was mesmerized. Moon Jaguar abruptly stopped singing and looked up from her laundry. She froze. Only her eyes moved while scanning the landscape in front of her, looking for the intruder that she could feel. She listened intently to the noises around her as she slowly turned around.

When her soft black eyes met Willy's, they locked. For a second she didn't move, not knowing if she should trust the stranger, but curiosity about his green eyes abolished any concern she was feeling.

At first she didn't register that Willy was white—only that he was not from her tribe. She continued to stare for several seconds until finally she burst into laughter.

Surprised by her response, Willy's trance was broken. He had not thought about how silly he must look. His arms were full of plants. Flowers hung out of his backpack. He was chewing on a long sprig of grass, and there was a large red hibiscus flower stuck in the brim of his hat. Willy's strawberry blond hair and pale skin were not conducive to the heat or sun in Honduras. His face was covered with freckles and red splotches. His skin was pulled tight over his wiry muscled body. The definition in his arm and leg muscles was exposed. All in all, he looked like a scarecrow, with plants spilling from him in every direction.

Moon Jaguar's laughter made Willy chuckle. "Hola," he said, assuming she spoke Spanish.

"Hola" was one of the few Spanish words she knew. Of course she spoke Chol in her tribe. She stopped laughing long enough to send a greeting in return, "Hola."

A slow smile spread across Willy's face as she burst into laughter again. It must have been contagious because Willy started chuckling; that made her laugh even harder at the breathy, braying sound he made when he laughed. On and on they laughed until she finally walked over to Willy, reached up, and pulled a bright green tree frog off the top of his hat.

"Wow," he said with surprise, not knowing the frog had been hitching a ride. And then both Moon Jaguar and Willy burst into laughter again.

"My name is Willy," he finally said in Spanish.

She shook her head. "No, Willy," she corrected. "Hijo de Flores" which meant "Son of Flowers."

As her laughter wound down, she said in Spanish, "My name is Moon Jaguar," then continued in Chol. "I am the granddaughter of Roaring River, chief and medicine man of the Corn People."

And with that, she took his hand and started leading him down the path along the edge of the stream. She seemed completely focused as she left her laundry behind and led Willy away. Though surprised with her actions, he was curious and showed little resistance as he followed her. As of yet, his travels in the Copan Valley had not taken him down this particular trailhead.

Moon Jaguar walked swiftly with determination. Almost a quarter of a mile down the path, the jungle opened up into a lush valley. Directly in front of them were towering rows of maize. Here Moon Jaguar and Willy skirted along the edge of the grain field.

The rows of maize abruptly stopped and flourishing rows of beans took over. Interspersed in the beans were squash plants and banana palms. Beyond the beans Willy could see a small village of approximately twenty-five mud and stick huts. Back then, the village seemed to be much more primitive than Copan Ruinas, where Willy had been staying just a few miles to the south.

Moon Jaguar and Willy walked down the center of the village. Between the small huts were beautiful gardens hanging heavy with fruit. Dirt walkways connected one hut to the next. Mother hens, with their small chicks, pecked the ground for insects and worms. Powerful roosters strutted, showing off their dazzling combs and defending their territories.

In the center of the village was a large communal area with a fire pit for cooking. Surrounding the pit were large palm frond palapas. There the village inhabitants gathered to make tools, weave cloth, prepare food and hold social events or spiritual rituals.

Two younger girls came running toward them, and Willy began to get a little uncomfortable. For the first time, he questioned what he was doing—allowing himself to be led into this strange village. But his fascination outweighed his concern for danger.

The girls talked to Moon Jaguar. Hearing their conversation, he immediately realized they weren't speaking Spanish. The only words that he could understand were "Hijo de Flores." When Moon Jaguar said his new name, the other girls giggled. Willy was spellbound by the girls' beautiful clear brown skin. They joyfully skipped in circles around him. One of the young girls grabbed the strap on Willy's backpack and swung it back and forth. They seemed to have no fear of him, only playful curiosity. It reminded him of the children in Copan Ruinas who ran to his side every afternoon when he returned from the jungle to see what he had gathered.

The people in Copan Ruinas, however, spoke Spanish and had

quite a few more modern conveniences. Their homes were rough stucco with handmade tile roofs; several had electricity and crude forms of running water. There were even a couple of phones in the village. Most of the houses in Copan Ruinas had their own fagon, which was a type of wood-burning stove for cooking. In contrast, the Copan Valley had no electricity or running water, and the Corn People cooked communally on a large fire in the center of town.

Moon Jaguar continued to lead Willy to the far side of the common center. Stopping at a hut that was slightly larger than the others, Moon Jaguar stood just a few feet from its door, facing it, with Willy's hand still in hers. She glanced over at Willy and smiled with an air of confidence. Within a few moments, the heavy, woven flap of wool that covered the entrance to the hut opened, and a beautiful older woman stepped out.

She was gorgeously adorned with colorful feathers and beads sewn to her appliquéd blouse and skirt. Her hair was braided and piled high on her head. Large wooden combs bejeweled with emeralds in the shape of falcons held her hair in place. She looked regal, both in her dress and her stature. She greeted Moon Jaguar by rubbing cheeks with her, and then exchanged a few words before stepping back inside.

"My grandmother, Horse Woman," Moon Jaguar said as she looked up at Willy and smiled.

"She is beautiful," Willy replied. He was taken aback by how healthy and strong everyone in the tribe appeared.

A few moments later the flap opened again and Horse Woman summoned the two to enter. Then she stepped out and left them. Inside the hut the dirt floor was covered with soft fur pelts. Sitting near the far wall was an elderly man. He had distinguished gray braids hanging on either side of his head. His face was deeply creased from age, but surprisingly, his eyes were still extremely alert and inquisitive, his body still agile and limber.

A large, intricately beaded chest piece draped from his neck and a simple loincloth hung around his waist. Loose skin swung freely from his upper arms. Tied around his head was a dyed leather headband painted with a picture of a river and the surrounding jungle. A thin strand of leather with polished rocks dangled down his back. Lying on the fur next to him was a carved wooden rod about fourteen inches long, made into a rattle with small beads strung along one side. A very thin jade rock lying next to it was used to play the beaded rattle.

Willy looked around at the shelves that lined the walls. Every imaginable type of leaf, flower and root had been dried and stored upon the shelves. Hanging from the roof were more bundles of plants tied together with leather straps. It took a few seconds for Willy's eyes to get accustomed to the dim light within the hut, but as they did he focused on the old man sitting in front of him who was joyfully talking to his granddaughter.

"Welcome," Roaring River said in Chol. "Come, sit down." He motioned to Willy as he pointed to another fur on the floor.

Moon Jaguar led Willy to the fur. As she sat down she pulled him to a seated position next to her. Willy laid the bundle of plants he had been carrying on the ground.

"Who is this you have brought to me?"

"This is Willy," Moon Jaguar said. And then with a giggle she corrected herself, "Son of Flowers."

Grandfather smiled, "Yes, Son of Flowers it is."

"He came to me by the stream while I was washing the clothes. He has come to be with us. I am certain of that."

"How do you know this? Has he told you so?"

"No, but I cannot let him leave."

"What do you mean?"

"He is the one I have been waiting for. You have said it is time for me to marry, but I have not wanted to until this very moment. I have always been so happy by myself, but now I am happier."

"Does he also want to marry you?"

"I am sure. I can tell by the way he looks at me."

Willy was enthralled. He had no idea what they were talking about. But he knew from the way they were looking at him that he was the subject of their discussion.

"He doesn't understand us," Grandfather said half as a question and half as a statement.

"He speaks Spanish, not Chol. As you know, I have learned to speak a little Spanish," Moon Jaguar said, proud of herself.

Grandfather closed his eyes and hummed a rhythmical chant for a few moments. When he opened his eyes he said, "Yes, he is the one. It is good he is interested in plants. Tell him of your plans to marry and the ceremonies will begin on the next full moon." It was only ten days away.

Moon Jaguar turned to Willy and said in Spanish, "Grandfather has approved of you and we shall start our marriage vows with the rising of the full moon."

Willy scooted back to the edge of his fur pad. Marriage? He couldn't believe his ears. He wondered if he was translating the Spanish correctly. He shook his head and said, "Married? I don't understand."

"Did you not come here to marry me?" she asked.

Willy thought for a moment. Why had he allowed her to lead him into the village? What was he doing here? Was there some connection? Was there some force guiding him? What was the magnetism he felt when he first saw her? Why had he allowed himself to drop his defenses, and why was he even thinking about this possibility? Marriage?

"I'm not sure," Willy said. He was confused. Ever since he heard Moon Jaguar sing in the jungle, he felt as if he had entered a dream, as if the drama was unfolding for him without his conscious participation. "I didn't purposely come here to get married. But…" His voice faded away.

"What is he saying?" Grandfather asked.

Sadly, with her eyes turned down, Moon Jaguar said, "He is not sure if he wants to marry."

"Then he must go to the men's hut and wait there for the answer to come."

Scooting back next to Willy, Moon Jaguar told him what Grandfather said. Standing, she gently pulled him to his feet and led him to the men's hut. As if in a daze, Willy went along.

Willy was bewildered by the situation, not panicked or threatened. He wasn't fearful or scared. It was almost like he was searching for a reason why he shouldn't marry Moon Jaguar. The presumption of marriage seemed so obvious to her. He was instantly drawn to her, but in his culture that only meant it was likely that they would start dating. Here it was obviously different.

Moon Jaguar nodded toward Grandfather as she and Willy left his home and walked to a long, thatched-roof hut at the far west end of the village. Willy could hear yearning flute music coming from within. Moon Jaguar brought him to a standstill in front of its door. Again she stood looking at the woven cloth that covered the entrance. Within moments, a very fit looking tribe member, in his early manhood, drew aside the entrance cloth to the men's hut. Moon Jaguar immediately told him why she was bringing Willy to the hut.

"Son of Flowers, this is my brother, Mat Head," she said. "He will take you into the men's hut so you may become one with your path."

Willy stood there silently, still allowing curiosity to be his leader.

Mat Head asked Willy to enter. Inside the hut, he motioned for Willy to sit on a woven reed mat, one of many mats forming an oblong circle on the packed dirt floor. There were already several other men sitting in the circle. The evocative flute music continued.

The other men appeared to be in a deep meditative state. Mat Head sat down and immediately closed his eyes like the others.

Willy had studied the history of many Honduran tribes. He was captivated by everything he had read, but the drama that was unfolding in front of him was certainly more than he had dreamed. Without even asking, he was being allowed to experience the intimate interactions of the Corn People. Willy was curious about Moon Jaguar's clarity when it came to wanting to marry him. He wanted to know how she knew he was the one she was to spend her life with. He didn't feel like he was being pressured to marry her; he felt he was being given the opportunity to find out whether or not marrying Moon Jaguar was the path he saw for himself.

Though hot and humid in the hut, Willy shivered as he closed his eyes. He felt slightly intoxicated by the incense smoke that filled the room. The music seemed to expand in his head, taking him outside of himself into a sort of communal awareness with those around him. A strong sense of directed simplicity overpowered him as one of the men in the hut began to beat rhythmically on a large, leather-skin drum.

In his relaxed mind Willy saw himself as a large tropical flower, open and exuding beauty and joy to all he came in contact with. He saw Moon Jaguar also as a flower next to him, and they were in a field of many beautiful flowers. The flowers danced in the breeze. He realized his marriage and his years of studying plants and ancient cultures were not the most paramount aspects of his life. He saw that the most important thing he could do was to spread joy across the planet. And it didn't matter what he did to spread that elation as long as joy was what he contributed to the world.

After an indeterminate length of time, the musician lowered the flute to his lap and began singing a hypnotic chant while the drumming continued. Slowly several of the other men also began to chant, while others picked up dried gourd instruments and played them like rattles. On and on the heartfelt music continued throughout the afternoon.

At dusk, the music ceased. When Willy opened his eyes, the hut was full of men, sitting in the circle. Willy had not been aware of them entering the hut nor the passing of several hours.

Mat Head turned to Willy and spoke to him in Spanish, "Now we shall eat."

As Willy heard this he realized he was very hungry. He had not eaten all day. So, he willingly stood, stretched and followed Mat Head out of the hut into the center of the village where the women and children had already gathered. As he approached, Moon Jaguar spotted him and stepped to his side.

"After I eat, I must go back to my room in Copan Ruinas," he said to Moon Jaguar.

"You cannot enter the jungle alone at night," she told him, her voice carrying a note of concern. "You would not be safe. I want you to stay here tonight."

As he peered out into the darkness of the surrounding jungle, Willy knew she was right. He wasn't even sure if he could find his way back to Copan Ruinas even if he wanted to risk encountering a lurking puma or other wild jungle creature.

"Where will I stay?" he asked.

"Mat Head will let you stay with his family," she offered.

Willy knew he didn't have much choice. He looked into her eyes and saw straight into her tender heart of kindness. Her innocence was so pure; she didn't have complicated layers to decipher to get to know who she was. Her emotions and spirit were completely exposed to his view. Slowly he nodded his head in agreement. He felt safe here in this village; he felt secure and content with this woman. *Strange,* Willy thought.

Giddy with pleasure, Moon Jaguar grabbed his hand and took him toward the fire pit to where the tribe was gathering. A large pot of richly-aromatic spiced beans sat next to another large pot of creamy maize and mutton stew. Tropical bass impaled on wooden skewers sizzled and hissed above the glowing embers of the fire.

Moon Jaguar ladled a hefty spoonful of each dish into a shallow bowl and topped it with a perfectly grilled chunk of fish. She then took a small stack of flat cornbread and once again led Willy away from the crowd of people, this time to a small bench several yards upwind from the fire. Moon Jaguar motioned for Willy to sit next to her and share her bowl of food. She took a piece of bread, dipped it into the stew, and held it up for Willy to take a bite.

The rich flavor was the best he could ever remember tasting. It made him smile. *Marriage,* he thought again, still trying to be rational.

Moon Jaguar's sister, Moon Shadow, and her husband, Fish Tail, sat down next to them with their food.

"Moon Shadow is swollen with rising spirit," Fish Tail proudly said to Willy, referring to his pregnant wife.

The rest of the tribe slowly ate and talked with each other as the fire embers burned down. Not understanding Chol, Willy listened to the texture of their language. It reminded him of a bubbling brook, flowing and rolling and splashing with bouncing, joyful fluctuations. Eating seemed secondary to the continual conversation. Willy marveled at how life's twists had brought him to this village. *Marriage,* he thought again, shaking his head and chuckling to himself. *Now that's not what I was expecting to find in this jungle.*

Throughout the meal, Moon Jaguar tried to keep Willy informed of what those around them were saying. Several of the men were reenacting the day's fishing experience. And as usual, there was a humorous story involved that gave everyone a good laugh. No one was in any hurry for the meal to be over. Not a single one of them had an appointment to rush to. All of their friends and family were already gathered around. No one had bills to pay or chores to do. There were no televisions beckoning them into isolation. They were completely content exactly where they were.

As it got late, the tribe started to disperse to their individual family huts. Moon Jaguar asked Mat Head if Willy could stay with him for the night. And of course, as she knew would be the case, he was welcomed.

As Singing Lavender Roller, Mat Head's wife, prepared a bed for Willy, Mat Head explained, "If one chose to marry a member of our tribe, it was expected for the groom to kidnap his bride and take her to live with him. This would show his desire to marry her. The Corn People would mourn her disappearance; but while she was gone we would prepare for her wedding, praying she would be safe and return in time for the ceremony. And, of course, the groom would bring her back the night before the full moon so she could spend the entire twenty-four hours before the wedding in the ceremonial hut with the other women. During the bride's kidnapping, it was customary for the groom to live with her as a husband lives with his wife."

Willy realized Mat Head was speaking as though Moon Jaguar and he were getting married. He wondered how this could be such a simple decision for them. It seemed so monumental in his world. *Maybe it should be a simple decision, a simple commitment,* Willy pondered.

The next morning Moon Jaguar walked with Willy back to the rock where her laundry still laid. With an uncomfortable good-bye, he promised to return before the week was up. Moon Jaguar watched as he walked backwards out of sight. Their eyes were locked until the path turned and they no longer could see one another.

In his rented room, Willy preserved and classified the plants he had picked the day before. He was distracted as he worked. He couldn't stop thinking about Moon Jaguar and the Corn People. He finally lay down on his bed and closed his eyes trying to deliberate the meaning of their chance meeting in the jungle. His heart ached. He knew something special had happened to him; yet he was confused. He longed to have a simple life like the Corn People, but he was also driven to study and become the botany professor he always dreamed of being.

He questioned if he could be happy staying there and marrying Moon Jaguar. He was amazed that he was even allowing himself to consider the possibility. He had never met a woman who moved him so much, and within such a short period of time. He realized he had felt more satisfaction and serenity in the past twenty-four hours than he ever had before.

Willy dozed off, and his conscious mind melted into a dream. He found his awareness was present in an old cabin. He was watching as Moon Jaguar and a man were having a heated conversation. In the dream, Willy wasn't in physical form, yet he was in the room, just observing. Moon Jaguar and the man weren't aware of his being there. Willy instantly assumed the man to be the one Moon Jaguar would marry if Willy chose not to marry her.

A loud clap of thunder got their attention and everyone turned suddenly toward the raging storm outside. The three quickly moved to the front porch to watch the rain beating down the grass in front of the cabin and forming a new river flowing to the Rio Amarillo. The wind was intense. Branches were breaking off the trees and flying through the air at immense speeds. A large gust of wind grabbed Moon Jaguar and threw her from the porch; the wind and the water pushed her toward the river. At the embankment she grabbed hold of a young willow shoot and clung to it for safety.

The river had turned into a deadly torrent. There was no escaping its power. Holding tight to the willow shoot Moon Jaguar struggled to keep on shore. Two huge arms formed out of the river embankment and grabbed her, throwing her forcefully into the raging waves. She was quickly pulled into the tumbling foam and disappeared beneath the water.

Willy knew Moon Jaguar was being swept down the river to her death. She was struggling to the surface for a breath of air when two more arms came out of the water, grabbed her and pulled her head under again. In the dream, Moon Jaguar's husband stood on the porch and watched as she was drawn away.

Willy realized she was going to drown. Now he felt panic. He would rather face his own death than to let her die. In the dream he had a choice to save Moon Jaguar's life. He quickly entered her body so she would not have to die. In Moon Jaguar's body, Willy relaxed and let the water arms pull him under the surface. He leaned back and inhaled a big breath of water. But instead of dying, Willy awoke with a start, gasping for air. He sat up quickly. His eyes sprang open.

For a second he thought he saw Grandfather, just hovering over his bed. But the image faded and he was left with the feeling of being alone in his room.

In a daze, Willy rose and walked out into the cobblestone street. It was dawn. He had slept all afternoon and through the night. Before he knew it, his legs were taking him down the path toward the Corn People's village some five or six miles away. He ran faster and faster until he was sprinting. He moved with agility through the jungle like a cat on a mission. He continued to run until Moon Jaguar's village was in view.

With deep, quick breaths, he swiftly walked to the center of the village where several women were gathered. Though in the cool of the morning, perspiration dripped from his body and soaked the T-shirt he wore. Frantically he turned in circles looking for Moon Jaguar, but he did not see her. He didn't know what he was going to say when he did, but he couldn't stay away. The dream seemed so real to him. He had to know she was safe.

One of the younger girls he had seen the day before pointed over Willy's shoulder. He turned in the direction she was pointing. About two hundred yards down a dirt path were two women walking together. Willy immediately recognized Moon Jaguar and Moon Shadow. He stood still and watched them for a few moments. He was relieved to know Moon Jaguar was safe.

He marveled over her simple, relaxed nature. He questioned himself. What had come over him? Why was he reacting this way? Was this love? One thing he knew: his thinking was not sane or based on reason.

Moon Shadow noticed Willy standing by the fire pit. She guided Moon Jaguar's gaze toward him. When Moon Jaguar saw him, she stopped walking and a smile spread across her face. For several moments neither she nor Willy moved.

Willy took the first step and started walking toward Moon Jaguar. Moon Shadow nudged her sister into motion and Moon Jaguar started walking toward Willy. Moon Shadow stood where she was and rubbed her swollen belly knowingly. The closer Willy and Moon Jaguar got, the quicker they walked. They were practically running when they reached each other. Willy reached out and took each of Moon Jaguar's hands in his.

"I have come to your village to marry you," he said, surprising even himself when the words left his lips.

What did I say? he thought to himself. *Could it be true?* Yet even as he was questioning it, the words felt so true he could not change them. And before he knew it, he confirmed in his own mind they would marry.

Moon Jaguar leaned her head back with her face aglow in the early morning sun. Willy thought she was the most beautiful woman he had ever seen. Looking into his eyes she said, "I am pleased. I am pleased. I am pleased."

He knew he was also pleased. Willy would be the first white person to marry into the Corn People's tribe.

Throughout the day Moon Jaguar and Willy casually walked through the valley and told each other stories of themselves. They walked past the pen where the tribe's livestock lived when they weren't out grazing with the herdsman. The pasture was surrounded by wooden posts that were stuck in the ground every three feet. In the fertile soil and hot humid air, the posts had sprouted and were in the process of becoming trees. Lots of heavy barbed wire was used between the posts to confine the sheep and burros.

Every afternoon that week, Willy broke away from his work and walked to the Corn People's village to spend more and more time with Moon Jaguar. The more Willy learned about Moon Jaguar and her relatives, the more he wanted to know. She was so warmhearted and kind. She was funny and playful. She was loving and affectionate. Willy was truly falling in love.

Three days before the full moon, Willy came, as usual, to spend the afternoon with Moon Jaguar. They walked back to the stream where they first met. Moon Jaguar leaned over the edge of the water scooping up a handful of water and playfully splashed it on Willy. It was cool and refreshing in the muggy hot air.

Willy slipped his shoes off and stepped into the stream, leaned over, and dipped both hands full of water. "Two can play this game," he said as he threw a large splash in her direction.

Without hesitation she stepped into a shallow pool along the stream's edge and started frantically throwing water on him. Moon Jaguar was laughing so hard that all it took was a slight nudge by

Willy and she sat down in the water. Quickly she grabbed his leg and pulled him down beside her. Pausing for a moment, their eyes locked. Willy leaned over and kissed Moon Jaguar on the lips. She grabbed him around the neck and kissed him in return. They rolled along the water's edge embraced in a passionate hug. Slowly they removed each other's drenched clothes and threw them to shore. Willy sat staring at her large breasts that looked like melons hanging from a vine suspended around her neck. He relished the feel of her soft, round body beneath his hands.

The jungle around them was brimming with wild calls. Locusts purred in a group as a whole, pulsating from one tree to another. The stream bubbled and babbled as it took on the shape of every rock it rolled over. Off in the distance, howler monkeys yelled to one another with their deep, resonating voices. Hummingbirds whirred from one flower to the next. Golden turkeys strutted and gobbled along the far shore. The music of the jungle softened and slowed.

Willy and Moon Jaguar sighed and cooed with the universal language of love, tenderly discovering each other's body. Spontaneous moans rolled from their lips and harmonized with the frogs as their bodies slid together. With a deep inhalation, the jungle's music quickened and grew. It then expanded and intensified, building and growing until the entire jungle was filled with an enormous excitement.

Willy did not walk Moon Jaguar back to her village that afternoon. He kidnapped her. He took her to his rented room in Copan Ruinas. They made love until the sun was high in the sky the next day.

The evening before the full moon, Willy and Moon Jaguar walked back to the Corn People's village. The elder women of the tribe quickly swept Moon Jaguar up and ushered her off to the women's hut.

Mat Head took Willy to his hut for the night. In the morning, he and several of the other young hunters took Willy out on a traditional wedding hunt. He was to show his skills at providing for his soon-to-be wife and, hopefully, new family. Willy and the other men tracked a small herd of deer to the embankment along the Copan River where the animals came to drink every morning. Mat Head pointed to the largest deer, the one he thought Willy should shoot. Willy slowly removed an arrow from the quiver on his shoulder and strung the arrow onto the bow. Aiming, he let the arrow fly. From lack of hunting experience, he completely missed the deer. Instead, the arrow struck a tree just a few feet from the spot where the deer were drinking. It was enough to scare them into flight, and they scattered in the thick brush.

By early afternoon, Mat Head had spotted two more deer lying beneath a small thicket of willows. Silently he pointed them out to Willy. Willy tried to remember the basic archery skills he had learned in high school as he reached for another arrow. Aiming just behind the largest deer's shoulder, he let the arrow fly. He missed again; the arrow hit the deer in the nose. Both deer rose up and started running away. The injured deer's face bled profusely, which luckily made it easy to track. But she wasn't mortally wounded, so she traveled at great speed.

The men tracked the injured deer all afternoon. An hour before dusk, they realized they were back at the Copan River where they had started that morning. Willy spotted his deer with the arrow still in her nose. She was trying to take a drink. Once again, Willy notched an arrow, drew his bow, and let the arrow fly. This time, he shot the wounded deer right behind her left shoulder, and she fell where she stood.

The full moon was about to rise. Willy stepped into the river and quickly took a bath so he wouldn't miss the beginning of his own wedding. The others cleaned the deer and started hauling it back to the village.

A ceremonial fire had been prepared in the town's center. The women were brightly dressed in their finest clothes as they finished the last of the feast preparations. From the south, Willy and the other hunters walked into the village, carrying his offering of deer meat. Grandfather came from the north to the ceremonial center of the village, flanked by all the elders both alive and dead. Blindfolded, Moon Jaguar walked with her mother, Yellow Spotted Eagle, from the west. And from the east the full moon rose over the fertile valley.

Willy couldn't believe how beautiful Moon Jaguar looked. She wore a white free-flowing dress embroidered with white threads. Her hair was braided and wrapped in spirals atop her head intertwined with flowers. The rest of the tribe gathered in silence. Grandfather, Yellow

Spotted Eagle, Moon Jaguar, Mat Head and Willy all converged at the same time in the ceremonial circle. Grandfather shook his rattle. One of the elder men lightly beat on a large kettledrum.

After bowing his head in silence for several minutes, Grandfather looked at Willy and said. "It is a wonderful day to be wed. The ancestors agree with your union." As he said this in Chol, Mat Head quietly translated for Willy into Spanish.

With the acceptance of the ancestors, Yellow Spotted Eagle removed the blindfold from Moon Jaguar's eyes. She looked to her right where Willy stood next to her. Tears of happiness rolled down her cheeks. Willy tenderly held her hand, his heart racing with excitement. Grandfather proceeded to expound on love and how a good marriage would bloom when the two united were allowed to fall in love over and over again— always with the same person.

In a haze of drumming and chanting, Mat Head translated Grandfather's Chol.

"Do you, Willy, take Moon Jaguar to be your wife?"

"I do," he said, surprised that Grandfather was now using a familiar form of church wedding vows. Catholic missionaries had come to the Copan Valley several generations before and had left their mark on the Corn People.

"Do you, Moon Jaguar, take Willy to be your husband?"

"I do," she said.

"And so it is," Grandfather said and started shaking his rattle again. The tribe cheered and Willy grabbed his wife and kissed her again and again.

The feast started immediately with an elaborate array of dishes. Willy took Moon Jaguar in his arms, dancing in a circle to the energized flute and drum music.

Deception

TEODOR LOPEZ WAS GOVERNOR OF HONDURAS during the time that Drew was climbing Kilimanjaro. From Teodor's third floor office, he looked out on the shabby sandstone judicial building on the opposite side of 10th Street in downtown San Pedro. Sitting in front of his dilapidated oak desk, he leaned back against it and pulled his feet off the floor, balancing precariously on the back two legs of the chair.

Even though his eyes stared out the window, he saw only the images in his own mind. Lopez pictured himself living a continual vacation in Rio de Janeiro once his illicit deal was completed and the bribe money he was to obtain was safely transferred into his offshore bank account. He had always schemed for the day he would take his wife and two daughters to a better life. Over the years he had created many elaborate plots to hit the jackpot financially. None had materialized. But now his hopes were rekindled.

A month ago, Tony Cirrus, a lumber magnate, had proposed a deal that made the governor sweat with anticipation. Waiting for Tony to come and finalize their agreement, Lopez fidgeted with a glass paperweight encapsulating a silver bullet. He rolled it down his large, round stomach that covered most of his lap.

Over the past decade, Cirrus had moved his lumber operations from one Central American country to the next, always one step ahead of the law. He unscrupulously secured land dealings with corrupt government officials, harvested the lumber off the land and shipped it back to the United States. When the land was no longer of any use to him and devoid of most timber, he would sell it back to the government at a discounted price. With no trees for support, the topsoil sloughed off, filling the rivers with silt.

Tony had previously searched out the property he wanted to purchase in Honduras. Looking for large, old, exotic wood, he chose the Copan Valley as his next target. More research determined that Governor Lopez was a morally weak man who might accept his deal. A little over a month earlier, Tony had met the governor at a dinner banquet. After a few drinks, Tony took him aside and told him about the need to find land for his next lumber project.

He told Governor Lopez that he was willing to purchase the land in the Copan Valley for ten million dollars, knowing it was worth twice that much. Tony guaranteed the corrupt governor five million dollars under the table to push the deal through before anyone noticed and tried to stop the transaction. Instantly Governor Lopez was interested. He felt it was his opportunity to become rich. He calculated how to sell the land and skip the country before being caught. As Tony talked, he downed the glass of scotch he held in his hand and began to perspire from the excitement of making a deal.

There came a knock on Governor Lopez's office door. The dream of Rio de Janeiro was abruptly interrupted and his secretary stuck her head inside the office saying, "Gobernador, Señor Cirrus está aquí."

Being jerked out of his daydream, Lopez responded, "Please invite him in." Briefly standing to shake Tony's hand, he continued, "Tony it is so good to see you. Please have a seat." Lopez quickly sat again behind his desk not wanting to feel like a dwarf in comparison with Tony's height.

"Likewise, Teodor," Tony replied shaking the governor's hand with his big, burly grip.

After the door to his office had been securely closed, the governor said in a hushed voice, "The papers have all been prepared for your purchase." Opening a manila folder on his desk, he continued. "All you need to do is sign here. Colonel Luis has assured me everything is ready for you to start cutting Monday."

"Wonderful. My machinery will be moving in this weekend," Tony replied.

"As promised, we have a helicopter waiting to take us to view the perimeters of your property," Lopez continued. The governor had agreed to a quick closing on the land so Tony could begin harvesting the rainforest before nature activists or the rest of the Honduran government knew what was happening.

Governor Lopez and Colonel Luis sat behind the pilot and Tony Cirrus as the helicopter swept along the border of the chosen land.

"Fly over there," Tony demanded, spotting smoke rising from

the center of the Corn People's small village. As the helicopter got closer, he could see the village was still inhabited.

"I thought we had an agreement. All of the people were to be moved off the land by the time we signed the contract today. With them still there, the deal is off. There will be no extra money for speedy delivery. Take me back," he said in a huff, trying to manipulate the governor.

The overweight politician's round, fleshy face lit up like a red tomato as he turned to Colonel Luis. Trying not to shout, he clenched his teeth and spoke in Spanish with raging fire in his voice.

"You said you had removed them. You told me you had transferred them to San Fanaro. Do you make me out as a fool? They must be removed. I will personally check at dawn. Do whatever you need to do to get rid of them." This aggravation taxed the governor's already short breath and he began to wheeze. Perspiration ran down the side of his face. He reached for his collar and ran an index finger along the inside, trying to stretch the material away from his throat.

"I'm sorry. I have ordered them to leave," the Colonel said, nervously ringing his thin hands. "I thought they understood. I'm not sure why they are still here. I will take care of it as soon as we land."

"Remove them personally or I'll have your job," he scowled. Turning to Tony, he tried to calm his voice. Mopping his brow with a handkerchief he continued, "Consider it done. They will be gone by morning."

"And if they are not, there is no bonus," Tony said with aloof confidence. Continuing his bluff, he lifted his thin, pointed nose in the air and turned to look out the glass door beside him.

I can still vividly remember that day when the helicopter flew over the lush mountains here in the Copan Valley. For me, the day started when Grandfather pulled me aside and said, "Praying Dove, we will need tamamuri today. Can you bring some to my hut?"

Earlier that morning, two of the tribe's adolescent boys had carried Swinging Squirrel Monkey into the village. The three were supposed to be weeding the southern maize field. But instead, they were playing around, running through the tall rows of corn and hiding from each other. While playing, Swinging Squirrel

Monkey stumbled, fell into a shallow pit, and badly sprained his ankle. Grandfather needed bark from the tamamuri tree to make a poultice to reduce the swelling and pain in Swinging Squirrel Monkey's ankle.

"Of course I can," I told Grandfather. I knew of a few towering tamamuri trees down by the stream. Slowly, I walked down the narrow path that leads along the Copan ridge. Towering chico zapote, ceiba, mahogany, and Spanish cedar trees lined either side. A thick canopy of branches blocked most of the sun's rays from filtering down to the ground. The sound of locusts filled the air with a concentrated buzz. Yellow-headed parrots called to one another as they flew through the branches overhead. The scorched air was thick with humidity. I walked along a trail between volcanic cliffs and sedimentary hills in the canyon north of Rio Amarillo.

My sleek black hair was pulled into a single braid that trailed down the middle of my back past my waist. A solitary strip of leather adorned with several brightly painted clay beads was tied to the end. Back then, I had a girlish figure that made me appear younger than my thirty-four years. My features were delicate, my skin was the color of warm cocoa and my eyes were black and penetrating like those of a hawk. That day, I remember wearing a beautiful lavender and teal hand-dyed sarong tied around my waist. A loose fitting, hand-woven blouse the color of the sky freely hung on my shoulders. Slung across my back was a woven reed bag. Always looking for usable plants, I kept my eyes intent on the flora carpeting the forest's floor.

As I walked down the path on my way to the tamamuri trees, I came to an abrupt stop when I heard two men speaking English. It sounded like they were just a few feet in front of me, around a bend on the trail. At the same time, I heard the helicopter approaching; because of the dense vegetation, I couldn't see it in flight.

Even though my native language is Chol, I could understand what the American lumbermen were saying. Willy Stevens taught me English as a child. He married my mother's sister, Moon Jaguar, the same year I was born.

The sound of foreign voices made my flesh crawl as I flashed back to the government officials with machine guns who had entered our village ten days prior. They brought a message stating that the Corn People, our entire tribe, would have to move, and they gave no explanation.

"The lumber from this forest will make us rich!" I heard one foreigner say, as he walked through the jungle surveying the land they were preparing to harvest.

"How could it not?" the second man replied. "Look at all this teak and mahogany."

Startled by a broadwing hawk that screeched and flew from its nest in a large cedar tree next to me, I stumbled, falling into the nearby brush.

"Did you hear that?" one of the men said to the other.

"Hear what? The locusts just stopped whirring."

"Not that."

"Oh, you mean the bird making that ruckus overhead?"

"No, I mean the sound in the bushes."

"Oh, I'm sure that it's just a squirrel or something."

"That was too much of a commotion for a squirrel to make," the first man responded as he started walking down the path in my direction.

The helicopter flew overhead and I slipped silently into the dense jungle growth. Without a sound, I turned to face the path and peeked around the edge of a large mahogany tree. Hidden in the dense foliage, I saw the two men I had heard moments earlier.

Over the last twenty years the Honduran government had sold most of the land around our settlement to the archaeologists and historians that came to study the primitive ruins. The amount of land our tribe was allowed to farm and hunt kept getting smaller and smaller and each year it became more and more difficult for us to feed ourselves. Ever since Copan Central was excavated in the mid 1800s, explorers from all over the world had been walking through the countryside by our village. The two men on the trail were now walking slowly down the path, paying close attention to the sounds in the brush.

I stood motionless until I was sure they were gone. Back on the path I proceeded another hundred yards or so and then walked off the path down to the edge of the stream. I found the tamamuri trees I knew to be there. Looking to the heavens I asked God to enrich the plants with healing powers and thanked Him for providing daily for our needs. I tenderly chipped several chunks of bark off the trunk and placed them in my reed satchel. When I had gathered all I needed, I took the time to scan the rest of the small valley. I spotted a clump of wild yams, and before returning home, I dug up the sweet tubers to share with the others.

"Thank you, Praying Dove," Grandfather said, acknowledging me as I entered his hut.

In the midday heat I began to pound the tamamuri bark into a paste. As we worked, I told Grandfather about the two men I had encountered. The old man only grunted in response, continuing his work with the herbs.

When the paste was prepared to Grandfather's liking, he carried it over to Swinging Squirrel Monkey who was lying upon a fur on the other side of the hut.

Grandfather meticulously applied the paste to his injured leg. While administering herbs to tribesmen, Grandfather frequently took the opportunity to express his beliefs or tell myths passed on to him from his predecessor.

"The people in our tribe are the only descendants who have survived from the great disaster that killed most of the inhabitants of Copan Central over a thousand years ago," Grandfather began. "At the time, King Eighteen Rabbit ruled over the Xukpi People in Copan Central. King Eighteen Rabbit was a powerful man.

"On an unusually hot August day, Smoke Shell, King Eighteen Rabbit's nephew, solemnly walked down the banks of the once raging Copan River. The river had been the life source for his people. But now the riverbed was almost completely dry. Small pools of muddy, thick water were dispersed in the bottom of the riverbed. Only small trickles made it down the stream from its source. Leaves on the once-lush trees along the bank were drooping and turning brown. On a mammoth rock overlooking what was once a large pool of water, Smoke Shell sat down and sadly stared at the cracking dirt in the pool-bed.

"'What has happened to the waters of the sky?' he said as he looked to the heavens. It had not rained for an entire season. The prior year had been just the opposite. Torrential floods filled the Copan Valley and spoiled the tribe's reserve of food."

Grandfather saw Swinging Squirrel Monkey grimace with pain. He stopped the story long enough to shake a gourd rattle and cry out in chant. When Swinging Squirrel Monkey's expression relaxed, Grandfather continued with his tale.

"Smoke Shell saw a horned owl flying overhead. Horned owls were known to be the messengers from the underworld. The owl tipped a wing to Smoke Shell and summoned him to follow. The messenger led Smoke Shell to the entrance of a cave where Xibalba, the underworld, began. A few steps into the mouth of the cave, Smoke Shell slogged through a shallow pool of mucky silt. It was dark inside the cave and smelled of decay. Before Smoke Shell could step back out into the light he was jumped from behind by Hun-Came and Vucub-Came, the gods of death. They held him down so tightly he couldn't move or speak.

"In their death grip, Smoke Shell could barely breathe. There was putrid water all around him and death loomed everywhere. The gods of the underworld tried to tempt him to willingly stay in the underworld. They told him the river of life that ran along the edge of Copan's town center was soon to be filled with death. The Xukpi people would die from the water that once gave them life. Smoke Shell was told the sun god, the moon god, and all of heaven would no longer be nourished by the people of his tribe, which is what his people were born to do. The lack of being nourished would disappoint the gods; in return, the gods would no longer give the Xukpi people what they needed to exist.

"'If you stay with us, we will make you a god, as we are,' Hun-Came said. 'You might as well stay and rule the underworld instead of suffering the inescapable human death and becoming one of the masses in the afterlife. This summer, all of your tribe will die from the decay in the shallow waters.'

"Smoke Shell knew he was being shown the end of his tribe. He knew that it was inevitable and that he must free himself so he could warn their leader. He summoned every ounce of energy he could find, trying to liberate himself from the grip of Hun-Came and Vucub-Came. The more he tried to break away, the more trapped he felt, until he finally remembered to ask God for help. With His help, Smoke Shell had enough strength to break loose from the grip of Hun-Came and Vucub-Came.

"Smoke Shell ran out of the entrance to the underworld, up the drying streambed, and straight back to Copan Central. Immediately, he went looking for King Eighteen Rabbit. When he found him, he warned him of the forthcoming dangers.

"'We must prepare to leave our homes. It is time to relocate our village,' Smoke Shell cautioned. 'We have not been good stewards of our land. We have destroyed the balance of give and take between humans and gods. We have angered the gods and, in return, they have depleted our river of life. The small trickle of water that remains in the riverbed is putrid.' Then he tried to explain his experience in the underworld to the old king, but the king was leery of Smoke Shell's story.

"Over the years, King Eighteen Rabbit had put aside his belief and praise of God. He had forgotten he and his tribe would always be taken care of if he acknowledged God and followed the path he had been sent to earth to follow. King Eighteen Rabbit had decided to make decisions for himself and for the rest of the tribe that would increase his power and wealth, not create harmony and balance as a whole. He chose to rape the earth of its vital energy and enslave others to work for him.

"'You are not King. You will not decide when the tribe leaves its home,' King Eighteen Rabbit spoke with anger.

"Smoke Shell was shocked at the king's reaction because it was clear to him what they needed to do to survive. Smoke Shell instantly knew he must take his small family away from the valley and the control of King Eighteen Rabbit so they would have a chance to live. Smoke Shell gathered up his few possessions: an obsidian machete knife that his mother, the king's sister, had given him; a water gourd; a little bag of stone tools he used to make other tools; his hunting spears and snares; his small bag of fire tools; and two hand-woven blankets given to him on his wedding day.

"Early the next morning he led his wife, Water Lily Jaguar, and his infant son, Round Flower, in the direction of the rising sun.

Their journey was long, and for several weeks Smoke Shell struggled to keep his family safe. Mid-afternoon on the twenty-fourth day of travel, Water Lily Jaguar spotted a boy wandering down a path. The boy was very thin. He was gathering small sticks. Smoke Shell called to the young boy, but instead of answering his call, the boy ran into the forest. Smoke Shell and Water Lily Jaguar assumed he was not alone, so they followed in the direction he went. The further they walked, the less dense the jungle became, until finally it opened into a fertile valley filled with lush maize, beans, and chili plants. At the far edge of the crops was a small settlement with several thatch-covered huts.

"Smoke Shell and his family stood in the brush and watched the actions of the inhabitants. Theirs was a simple life. Bare-chested women ground maize and prepared food; naked children either helped or played stick games. There were only a couple of elderly men present. They were sitting together, making stone tools. Water Lily Jaguar thought they had left Copan Central with few belongings or adornments, but compared to this small settlement, they were lavishly dressed with their beaded cloaks and dyed sarongs.

"Through the middle of the crops, Smoke Shell could see fresh water gushing down a deep riverbed. The underground spring surfaced, becoming the Rio Amarillo. Moving cautiously, they left the protection of the brush and entered the small village. Thankfully the inhabitants didn't see them as a threat. They welcomed the newcomers, offering food and shelter.

"The village was just far enough away from the Copan River so as not to be dependent on its waters. In time, Smoke Shell's knowledge offered him great advancement in the small tribe. Being the nephew of King Eighteen Rabbit, he had been taught privileged information. He knew how to use the two-hundred-sixty-day ritual calendar that kept the gods on their side; the solar calendar of three hundred sixty-five days that helped them plant their crops; a lunar series that recorded the lunar month; and a Venus calendar that predicted the appearance and disappearance of the morning and evening star.

"Soon Smoke Shell was made king of the small village. As king, he insisted they never make pyramids or lavish structures like Copan Central. He was convinced it was the grand structures of the center that led the gods to destroy his people for trying to become gods themselves. He was the one to begin calling our tribe the Corn People. These are your ancestors," Grandfather said as he finished wrapping Swinging Squirrel Monkey's leg.

"You must always respect and take care of the earth," I said to Swinging Squirrel Monkey. "She will take care of you."

He nodded in agreement.

"I'm sorry I was playing when I should have been weeding," Swinging Squirrel Monkey said with regret.

As I handed Swinging Squirrel Monkey a cup of tea and gestured for him to drink, Grandfather started chanting. Accompanying himself, he again picked up a rattle and began shaking it over Swinging Squirrel Monkey's leg. I sat down in the far corner and tapped rhythmically on the skin of a water drum to create the vibration of healing.

In a sudden flare of commotion, Yellow Spotted Eagle burst through the door of Grandfather's hut.

"The soldiers have come back," she said frantically, her face showing she was close to panic. "They say we must leave. What does this mean?"

Grandfather and I knew exactly what it meant.

Moped Ride to Remember

THE OBSCURING DARKNESS OF NIGHT TURNED into day as Hope awoke. She twisted her head to the side and opened her eyes in the forward berth of *Ladyhawke*. The encapsulating womb that once had been her solace of protection and peace now felt disruptive and foreign. The boat no longer gave her a sense of happiness, and she felt only anguish when she thought of another day aboard. Everything about the Dominican Republic had been unsettling since the day they arrived, and now the mere idea of boat life seemed annoying. She felt distracted and her intuition told her something was wrong. She still caught herself frequently looking over her shoulder as if she was being watched by invisible eyes lurking in the shadows.

Hope's usual playful light-heartedness was subdued as she and Logan drank their morning coffee in the cockpit.

"Logan, I'm ready to leave," she said, looking up from her cup. "I don't feel comfortable here. This energy is starting to pull me down."

"I agree," Logan said with resignation, feeling beaten and irritable after a restless night.

It was Saturday, and they weren't sure the Immigration Office would be open to check them out of the country before reentering international waters.

Locking the dinghy with a secure wire cable to a cleat on the dock, Logan and Hope climbed the steep embankment to a muddy road that led into town. They walked in the heavy, humid air. Trash filled the shallow ditches along the road. The smell of rotting garbage accosted their senses. They trudged the mile and a half into town, passing several small shacks barely tucked into the thick brush along the way. Ahead of them on the road, chickens and roosters strutted and scratched at the dirt. As Hope and Logan approached, the chickens ducked deep into the undergrowth.

The McKnights heard a voice from behind them, and they both turned toward it with a start. Just like the chickens, they were uneasy in the exceedingly still surroundings, overreacting to even the smallest noise. The voice was only a mother calling to her children from the doorway of a small, disheveled shack that sat only a few yards off the road. The woman stood framed by the doorjambs with her hands on her narrow hips. Her penetrating black eyes calmly looked at the Americans as she once again yelled out for her children. Logan and Hope turned back in the direction they were walking, unable to figure out why they felt so uneasy.

Unfortunately, once they arrived at the Immigration Office, it was closed. A man at the small communications office next door witnessed their dispirited reaction as they tried to open the locked office door.

"Would you like me to call Martinez?" he asked, leaning out a large, open window. "Frequently he will come open the office on the weekend for an extra fee." His thin, bony arm looked scrawny in the baggy, short sleeved shirt he wore.

Hope and Logan exchanged glances.

"That would be great," they said in unison. They didn't want to stay in the Dominican Republic a minute longer than necessary. Leaning back inside the window, the helpful man picked up the phone receiver on his desk.

Hope swatted at the fleas and mosquitoes that swarmed her legs. She had gotten no less than a hundred bug bites, between mosquitoes and sand fleas, in just the few days they had been in the Dominican. The poison from their bites made her skin crawl. That, in itself, soured Hope on the country and made it hard for her to relax and enjoy her surroundings.

"He will come soon," the shopkeeper said to Logan when he hung up the phone.

"Thank you," Logan replied, sitting next to Hope on a dilapidated wood bench in front of the office.

Leaning her head back on the small wood building behind them, Hope let out a deep growl from between her teeth. Closing her eyes, she tried to imagine better times, hoping to ignore the insects gnawing at her flesh.

An hour later, an overfed man approached the communications building.

"Hey, Marcus," he said lackadaisically. When the thin man leaned out, the two looked like the ends of a spectrum—one short and round, the other tall and skinny.

"How's it going?" Marcus asked.

"Louie played good in the game today. Made it 'cross home base twice. Won, twelve to three."

"Great. How are Juana and the kids?"

"Fine, fine. Thanks. Where's Rosa?"

"She's doing chores at home."

Martinez stood outside the communication office, casually talking to Marcus as if he had nothing else in the world to do.

When he finally turned to the Immigration office and unlocked the door, Hope and Logan finally realized that he was their man. Looking at each other, their eyes bulged with disbelief at how Martinez seemed to be in no hurry whatsoever. Even though Martinez didn't acknowledge Hope and Logan, they followed him inside the building.

From behind the counter, Martinez slowly fumbled through the departure paperwork at a pace that made a snail look fast. Then he charged them an extra hundred dollars for his inconvenience—a hundred dollars they were glad to pay, if it meant they could leave the country and get back to the tranquility of the sea.

In town, Hope and Logan went to the fresh produce stand and picked through the already scavenged, old, bruised fruits and vegetables. They only bought the bare essentials and agreed that for a few days they could eat the canned and dried goods they already had on the boat.

The day became blistering under the intense midday sun. When they made it back to the dock with their groceries, they found two young Dominican boys in their dinghy rocking it back and forth, filling it with water. The boys spotted Logan and Hope at the same time that they were spied by the couple. Logan put his food bag down in the middle of the road and started running.

"What the hell are you doing?" he screamed. The boys jumped off the back of the half-submerged dinghy and swam to shore. Bailing water from the boat, Logan muttered, "Let's get outta here!"

Hope and Logan prepared *Ladyhawke* for an ocean crossing,

pulled anchor, and slowly sailed down the western shore of Bahia de Samana toward the open ocean. A narrow beach lined the edge of the fluorescent water. A pair of royal terns skimmed the water's face a few yards offshore, searching for minnows to abate their hunger. *Ladyhawke* slowly tacked back and forth at forty-five-degree angles, making slow progress toward the mouth of the bay, but utilizing the light breeze that seemed to persistently come straight out of the direction they wanted to go.

Knowing that as soon as they could turn west they would have a favorable beam wind in which to sail, Hope and Logan were now in no hurry. It felt good to be on their way with plans of sailing toward the sunset and another country. Seagulls flew overhead, calling to the sailors in anticipation of a snack the McKnights didn't have to give. Two bottlenose dolphins rolled and jumped in *Ladyhawke*'s wake, escorting the boat as it finally cleared the coral reef on either side of the bay's entrance. Once again they progressed into the Caribbean Sea. The warm wind, now on their beam, filled their sails and the boat heeled over into a comfortable glide. *Ladyhawke* seemed to like it. She tucked her shoulder and accelerated to eight knots. Small rolls of water gently lapped at her port hull, creating a lulling motion that beckoned the entire ocean into slumber.

As the last rays from the sun filtered over the horizon, Hope put fresh batteries in her night vision head lamp and snuggled into a beanbag. Safe behind the canvas dodger, she was ready to enjoy a good novel during her first three-hour watch. Logan crawled into the sea berth for a nap, and trusty *Elmo* steered them toward Roatan, an island off the east coast of mainland Honduras. On through the night they sailed at a moderate clip, Logan and Hope trading shifts on and off watch.

Early the next morning Hope went down below deck for a cup of coffee, connected the single sideband radio to her laptop and signed on to download her emails. As always, Hope was excited to hear news from home and from friends they had met while sailing. When she opened a note from her mother, Hope couldn't believe what she was reading. She almost collapsed with the devastating news about what was happening with Drew.

When Dr. Mercer came to Drew's hospital room again with no

new suggestions for a cure, Drew told his mother, "I want you to see if Hope can contact Billy."

Hope had told Drew stories about Billy's great-grandfather, Roaring River, and his uncanny ability to heal people. Drew wanted to know if Roaring River would have a cure for him.

When Hope had finished reading the email, she called to Logan who was beginning to stir in his berth.

"Drew is sick," she said. "They think he has been exposed to a deadly bacterium." And then Hope gave Logan a brief synopsis of the email she had just read.

"We have to do something," she said in desperation. Logan looked grim.

Hope quickly sent a note to her mother in return.

Mom,
I am so, so sorry. I will do anything I can to help.

As she typed, tears rolled down her cheeks, and Logan took command of the boat.

Logan and I were planning to meet Rocky and Billy in Honduras in about six weeks. We are slowly sailing that direction. Maybe we can speed things up. We intended to spend a month in the "Bay Islands" off the coast of Honduras. Then we planned to sail to San Pedro, secure the boat there, and take a bus inland to meet them where they grew up in the Copan Valley. I can talk to Roaring River to find out what he would recommend, but it seems our current schedule will take too long.

We are sailing along the northern shores of the Dominican Republic as I write to you. Let me know what you want me to do.
Love, Hope

Ruth must have been using the Internet on her laptop in Drew's hospital room, because Hope got a return message before she signed off. It read:

Hope,
If nothing changes, Drew will be dead in the six weeks it takes you

to get to Honduras. I hate to be so blunt, but we need to act quickly. I'm sorry but he can't wait. Dr. Mercer's team of researchers has been running tests around the clock and experimenting with drugs on the bacterium with no luck.

Roaring River is our last option for a cure. According to Dr. Mercer's team of interns, it doesn't look good. I hear them talk amongst each other. They think Drew has no chance unless we stumble onto something accidentally. They haven't been able to classify the bacterium that is infecting Drew. I can't believe this is happening. If there is a bacterium in this world, there should also be a cure. I believe the rainforest has more natural cures and medicinal plants than anywhere else in the world. I'm hoping Roaring River just might know something the Western medical world doesn't know. Drew thinks he was deliberately poisoned, but that is a whole other story I won't get into now. I've seen a lot of backwoods medicine work in Panama.

I'm afraid! Dr. Mercer and his staff only give Drew a couple of weeks to a month at best. We must find the cure ourselves.

Hope fired back a reply.

I will email Billy and see what we can do. Last I heard from him, he was in Indiana with his father, Willy.

Hang on. I will get back to you as soon as I hear from him. I'm sure he will help and meet me sooner.

Early that same afternoon, Hope got a return email from Billy.

Hope,

I am very sorry to hear about your brother. I would love to help you, if I can. I'm sure Grandfather would be more than happy to share the herbal recipes and the healing techniques he has used in the past. As I told you before, he has cured many in our tribe. You must come to Guatemala immediately if you want to meet up with Grandfather.

Our tribe has been ordered to move from the sacred ritual lands where we have lived for as long as any of our ancestors can remember—really, as far back as our tribal history goes. The Honduran government wants us to relocate to an unfertile piece of land that won't grow enough food to feed our people. The heart of the tribe aches. The elders are especially distraught. Grandfather is so saddened. Why can't they leave us alone?

We know the answer really; it's always about money. The amount of money our land is selling for will fatten many government officials' pockets. The conflict has started. I hear it was an ugly fight between a few young men in our tribe and the officials who were sent to escort us off our land. They threatened to kill or imprison everyone who did not leave.

That was two and a half weeks ago. I've been in the States with my father; I only know what Rocky told me in an email right after they left the valley. He simply said to meet him in Antigua at the Casa De Los Cantaros. That is where I am now. He said there was trouble, but I don't know to what extent.

He also said Grandfather had a vision. In the vision, it was clear to him that it was time for the tribe to leave Honduras and come to Guatemala. When they get settled in a secret cave Grandfather knows of, Rocky will come to get me, and I can join them. I guess from what I can piece together, the cave is about five miles from where I am in Antigua.

Grandfather has seen what he is calling 'the Shifting of the Wind.' He says it takes place in Antigua and he knows he must be here for it. I've asked around the village and no one else seems to know anything about 'the Shifting of the Wind.' Grandfather says this shift was foreseen in the heavens since before he was born. He is saying it is best to not fight for our land just now.

When they reach the cave, they will wait there until Grandfather knows the time is right, and then they will come to the city. But you know, Hope, I am surprised that Rocky hasn't come to get me yet. I really expected him days ago. I don't know where you are, but if you can get here before he does, you can go to the cave with us. You could ask Grandfather yourself how he might help Drew. But to do that, you must come immediately. I do not know where the cave is or if I will be able to be in touch with you after I leave Antigua. Come quickly if you can. I am staying at Casa De Los Cantaros in Antigua. If I have to leave before you arrive, I will leave a message for you at the front desk. Let me know of your plans.

I hope to see you soon. Be strong, Hope.
Billy

Hope stuck her head into the cockpit where Logan was fussing with *Elmo*. She told him of the importance of moving as quickly as they could.

Then, in typical Logan style, he replied, "Bring the charts out. We'll figure out exactly where our first port of entry is so you can fly out as soon as possible. I can bring the boat behind you to Guatemala."

After reviewing the charts, they determined the next port of entry was a full day and a half sail from where they were. There had to be another way. With close examination of the charts, they could see an island about ten miles south of their current position. Even though they had been sailing all night, they had paralleled the northern shore of the Dominican Republic and weren't far from land. They could still see the tropical mountains on the mainland. It looked as though there was a small area just behind the island where they could anchor the boat. The chart also indicated that there was a small village on the mainland opposite the island. With careful entry they just might be able to make it through the cut and tuck into the protected water behind the island.

Hope was thinking ahead. She wondered if their new dentist friend, Klaus, would be able to use his connections to get her signed back into the country and transported to the airport in Puerto Plata. Even though she dreaded having to go back to the Dominican, it seemed the quickest solution.

Hope emailed both her mother and Billy, telling them of their plans. With the sails lowered, Logan carefully maneuvered the boat between reefs and shallow shoals to a small bay. Anchored securely behind the small island, Hope slipped below deck to pack for her trip.

While Logan untied the dinghy on the forward deck, the roar of an engine made him jump. Quickly turning in the direction of the noise, he grabbed onto the stanchion amidships to balance himself. He couldn't believe his eyes. A small dented metal skiff with a plump middle-aged man and his scrawny-kid sidekick were approaching *Ladyhawke*, both in uniform, complete with twenty-year-old military rifles.

Logan stuck his head down the forward hatch where Hope stood packing a small backpack.

"Not our lucky day, babe. Federales are coming with guns. Best act sick. I'll tell them it's a medical emergency and see what happens."

Please, she thought to herself. *Not now. Don't let us get in trouble.* Hope now knew why she had been feeling so anxious in the Dominican Republic. It didn't have anything to do with the country; it was all about Drew. Hope's heart felt heavy. She knew she could help Drew if she could just get to Roaring River. Life was calling her to rise to the next step. Never had she felt that her actions were as important as she did at this moment. Hope felt that she was finally walking through the portal into the life she was born to live. Her smooth sail down life's emotional river had quickly jibed, and the turn was rough and jolting. But every rapid she sailed over now had meaning and importance.

Hope crawled into the front V-berth, gripped her stomach, slowly rocked from side to side and quietly moaned, pretending to be sick.

"Despacho, despacho," the heavy set Dominican officer said, as his derelict skiff bumped into *Ladyhawke*. Standing, he picked up the semiautomatic rifle that lay next to him. The young man who was driving the boat also stood and held onto the caprail of *Ladyhawke* to stabilize their small boat from the wake they had just made.

From the salon, Logan retrieved the prior clearance papers and brought them on deck. The official took them and read.

"What are you doing, stopping here? You have checked out of the country," he said in Spanish as his face flushed with anger.

Again Logan was glad he spoke some Spanish. He could understand what the federal was asking, but he took a moment to respond. He was trying to figure out the most logical way to gain entry back into the Dominican Republic, even though this small village was not a port of entry. He knew the laws were to protect the country and control the masses, but this was different. Hope and Logan were not criminals; they were just trying to get Hope to Guatemala as quickly as possible.

"I am sorry. My wife has a medical emergency. I need to get her to a doctor as fast as I can," Logan tried to tell them in his best "Logan Spanish" while he walked down the side of the boat toward the cockpit. The officer's sidekick pulled their skiff along *Ladyhawke* to follow him. Logan knew that if necessary, money always seemed to talk in third-world countries.

"No. You are not supposed to be in this country. You have already cleared Immigration. There are no doctors here, not even any roads to a hospital. You must leave," the officer demanded, glancing back at his sidekick who was nodding his head in support.

"There must be an exception for emergencies. Can we just come ashore to use the phone?" Logan pleaded.

"There are no phones here. The nearest phone is on the other side of that mountain," the officer said as he pointed to a steep hill covered with a banana plantation. The hill seemed to rise up forever. From where Logan stood it looked like one solid mass of banana fronds.

"Please let us come ashore so we can get my wife to Puerto Plata. There has to be some way," Logan pleaded.

The officer peered at Logan and motioned to his assistant to tie their painter to a cleat on *Ladyhawke*'s stern.

"We're coming aboard," he said.

Logan also went to the stern of the boat and eased the swim ladder down. He knew he should be as congenial as possible to the two men with guns. They seemed angry and agitated.

From the cockpit the older man descended the companionway into the salon as the younger man perched himself on the stainless steel stern rail. He sat holding his rifle ready.

Logan followed the round one down the companionway into the salon.

"I'm sorry but I don't feel like we have any other choice," Logan said.

The federal said nothing. He slowly scanned the salon without touching anything.

"Logan?" Hope weakly called out in her pretend sick voice from the forward cabin.

"Hope, I'm here," he said. "We've got company. I'm trying to get permission to bring you ashore."

The officer took a few steps toward her voice and stuck his head into the V-berth. Hope was ready with a grimace on her face and she rocked herself back and forth in the fetal position.

Turning around, the officer stepped into the head and gave it the once-over, before again turning back to Logan.

"Get in our boat. I'll take you to shore," was all he said before ascending the companionway ladder.

"Hope, can you get up? He'll take us to shore," Logan translated with tentative excitement.

"I'll try," she said weakly, moving slowly and acting very feeble. When the officer was back in the cockpit, she quickly finished packing.

Logan hurried around, closing the hatches and port lights. Behind Hope, he locked the companionway door and climbed down into the metal skiff, and the federales took them to shore.

The overgrown jungle fed into the sea on either side of the small beach. An old, weathered picnic table, a lean-to covering a wood fire pit, and a makeshift outdoor kitchen took up the entire clearing. Two distinct trails led into the brush from the picnic table. A little way down the trail to the right were several small huts, and the trail to the left led up the mountain into the banana plantation.

The round officer asked Hope and Logan to wait at the table while his assistant went down the trail to the huts. They sat and Hope stayed bent over, acting sick. A few minutes later, he returned with Lupe, an emaciated, dirty teenage boy, and his moped.

"Lupe's moped is the only way to the resort on the other side of the mountain," the officer explained. Hope and Logan agreed to let Lupe drive them, though they were unsure how the moped would carry all three.

When the senior officer saw how willing Hope was to get on the moped he questioned Logan about just how sick she really was. With some smooth negotiation and the slipping of a twenty-dollar bill to the federal, Hope and Logan were finally allowed to get on their way.

Then another twenty-dollar bill, this time to Lupe, would get them to the resort. Thank goodness Lupe was a frail teenager who probably only weighed one hundred pounds soaking wet, because he sat on the gas tank of the moped with Hope squished in behind him. As she sat down, her nostrils were assaulted by the raw, bitter stench of unwashed human, and she tried to breathe through her mouth. Logan perched behind Hope on the moped fender and put his feet on the back pegs. Hope's long, lanky legs wound over Logan's shorter ones. Squeezed together like teenagers in love, the three precariously took off through the jungle.

With every bump they hit, Hope was pressed even harder into Lupe's back, as Logan's weight pressed into hers. Back on the beach, the large officer finally cracked a smile and shook his head in disbelief as he watched the moped bounce through the low-hung branches up the tropical mountain trail. And if it weren't for the situation Logan and Hope were in, it would have been hilarious to them as well. Their legs flew off the pegs in all directions at every bump as they parted the branches.

At full throttle, the little bike squealed "ping, ping, ping, ping" up the narrow trail. Bouncing over roots and falling into water-filled trenches created mud sprays and all three were sprinkled with brown splotches. Almost coming to a standstill with each trench they hit, Lupe pushed on, determined to earn the crisp bill he had in his pocket.

Hope screeched as banana fronds slapped her in the face. And then she let out a full-hearted scream when a six-inch-long, yellow banana spider zoomed straight for her face.

"Gross!" she yelped, trying to wipe away a thick glob of spider web strong enough to catch small birds.

After a simultaneous, blood-curdling shriek that quickly faded into nervous laughter, all three ducked to avoid a huge black snake hanging from a branch in the middle of the trail. The bike wobbled from Lupe's distraction and almost fell over as his passengers shifted weight from side to side.

Twenty minutes later, with great relief, they popped out of the dense banana plantation onto the edge of a spectacular coral beach adjacent to a quaint, rustic resort. Several tourists sat in lounge chairs along the shore. Logan and Hope guessed they were European, because the women were topless. Lupe paid no attention, as if it were commonplace.

"You can get a phone inside," he said to Logan.

Peeling themselves off the moped, Hope and Logan unwound

their limbs from each other and walked around a small, oval pool. Soothing music played softly through the poolside speakers. An overgrown cobblestone path led to the small lobby.

Standing behind an old wooden counter was a thin half-black, Dominican man. Antiquated bookkeeping devices and hand-written registry papers were being used to keep track of the guests. Behind the clerk, a pegboard hung heavy with old-world skeleton keys for the rooms.

There was only one phone in the lobby for public use and it didn't even have a dial pad. The hotel clerk dialed the operator using a phone at his desk. Once connected, the call was transferred to the phone in the lobby. The McKnights had the operator place a phone call to Klaus' home, knowing it was Sunday and assuming he wouldn't be at work.

Hope and Logan sat in rugged bamboo chairs with dingy, faded cushions that smelled of mildew. Bamboo beams held up the large, palm-leaf ceiling that spanned the polished stone floor. The atmosphere was quiet and relaxed; life was slow there, as if they had slipped back in time. Hope had difficulty believing they were still in the same country as the one they had been in for the past two weeks. It was entirely different at this wealthy tourist destination, compared to the poor cruisers' bay of Luperon.

When the call connected, the hotel clerk motioned for Logan to pick up the phone in the lobby. They knew they had no right to ask, but they were certainly hoping Klaus' Dominican wife might have some strings she could pull to help get Hope back into the country at this non-designated entry.

"That's the way things work in this country," they remembered Klaus saying. "It's all about who you know and how much money you have."

"I've never heard of the resort or the village," Klaus said, after he took their call. "Let me get my map out. You know, Logan, it is illegal for you to be on land. The federales could seize your boat, and there would be nothing you could do about it. This is the Dominican Republic. You must be careful."

Klaus checked his map for a few moments before coming back to the phone.

"I see where you are on the map. It looks like there're no roads to the hotel," Klaus said.

"The desk clerk says all supplies and people come by boat," Logan confirmed. "He says there is a small path from the highway around the other side of the hill to the beach where *Ladyhawke* is anchored."

"Like I told you before, my wife does have connections. I will ask Martinez if he will come with me. He is an immigration officer and a friend of my wife's father."

"I think I know Martinez," Logan told him. "I think he's the same man we bribed yesterday to clear us out of the country in the first place."

"I think he's a little shady," Klaus said, "discreetly of course. He's the man we want on our side. If I could bring him to you, we could offer him a little cash to consider signing your papers to let Hope back into the country. But I'm not sure how I will get to you, short of that pathway the hotel clerk spoke of. Let me make a few phone calls and I will call you back."

For twenty minutes Logan and Hope anxiously sat in the hotel lobby until the clerk behind the desk motioned to them to pick up the phone again.

"Okay, here's the plan," Klaus began, as Logan and Hope put their heads together and both listened to the earpiece. "Martinez is willing to come with me, but it will cost you two hundred dollars. It's the best I could do. If you need some cash, I can help you out. I'll bring my four-wheel-drive truck. Martinez confirmed the whereabouts of a passable trail into the little village where you are anchored. It would be better to meet there, rather than a public area like the hotel. But don't go back to your boat yet. It will take me at least two to three hours to get there. When we arrive, I will send for you. The federales would just hassle you if you went back now. So for now, hide. You are extremely illegal in this country. Anything could happen and the government wouldn't care. You are the one breaking the law. Is the moped driver still waiting for you?"

"Yes," Logan replied.

"Good," Klaus continued. "Offer him a small cash bribe to return for you when I arrive. Tell him where you will be, out of view, mind you. Send him back to the small village. Good luck."

"Thank you, Klaus. You could be saving someone's life. We'll tell you the whole story later."

Lupe showed Hope and Logan a secluded part of the beach where they could wait alone. Logan asked him to go back to his village and wait for Klaus. He then told Lupe that when he safely returned them to the village he would give him another twenty dollars. Lupe agreed quickly. He excitedly took on the mission. In an instant, he and his moped disappeared into the jungle.

Time crawled as Hope and Logan sat anxiously waiting on the beach. The afternoon sand fleas viciously attacked Hope's bare legs. She tried to sit and swat at them, but they drove her crazy. She paced up and down the beach tracing a twenty-yard circle, making sure she didn't go down far enough for the other tourists to see her. About three hours and, quite literally over two hundred bites later, Lupe came running down the beach.

"Your friend has arrived. Your friend has arrived," he repeated.

That was the news they wanted. The three quickly headed toward the jungle where Lupe had left his moped. Back up and over the mountain they rode, now dodging the same banana palms in reverse. They were pros now, balancing on the bike. Somehow it seemed easier returning to the small village.

They were filthy by the time they got to where Klaus and Martinez were waiting. Exhausted from the tension and covered with insect bites, Hope looked a sight. Klaus stood next to Martinez, who was sitting at the picnic table and drinking a quart-size Presidente beer from the bottle.

As Logan slipped a twenty into Lupe's hand, Klaus approached and whispered to Logan and Hope, "Be patient, my friends, and let me do the talking."

And of course they did. Klaus led them over, close to where Martinez was seated and casually sat down across from him. Klaus idly chatted with Martinez, while Logan and Hope stood a few feet away.

Halfway through Martinez' second quart-size beer, he looked over at the two sailors and said, "Nice to see you again. Where is your exit visa?"

"I've got it right here," Logan replied, pulling it out of his shirt pocket. He also pulled two hundred dollars out and handed it all to Martinez. Logan had previously put the money with the exit visa when Klaus told him the price of this favor. Martinez looked at it, pocketed the money like it was the normal procedure, took a pencil out of his pocket, drew a line through the number two under how many people were on the sailing vessel *Ladyhawke* and wrote above it the number one. Then he handed it back to Logan and proceeded to drink the rest of his beer.

That was all. Scratch through the number two with a pencil. No initials or anything. Logan couldn't believe it, but he didn't argue. He quickly took the visa back when it was offered to him.

"You are illegal," Martinez said to Logan and made sure the large officer with the machine gun heard him. "You must leave immediately. Now!"

"Thank you, sir. I will," Logan said and returned the visa to his pocket.

Logan turned to Hope. "I will sail through the night," he said. "I should be able to get to Puerto Plata by afternoon tomorrow. I can clear Immigration there. I'm sure if I email Max and Tina, they would be more than willing to meet me in Puerto Plata and help me sail to Guatemala. When I'm in Puerto Plata I will email you and let you know the plan."

Martinez stood and Klaus came over to Hope and Logan and said, "It's time to go."

Hope kissed Logan good-bye and the federales ushered him back to their small skiff. Logan waved in the dimming afternoon light as Klaus, Martinez and Hope got into Klaus' truck.

Once all were seated in the front-seat bench, Klaus slowly drove down the one lane pathway. Pigs and chickens got up from their evening resting place and reluctantly moved out of their way.

Things seemed to be working, Logan thought, as he approached *Ladyhawke* in the federales' skiff, but then a wave of fear shot up his spine as he realized Hope was leaving with her fanny pack around her waist. The fanny pack carried both of their passports and all their credit cards.

When the magnitude of not having any identification hit him, he started yelling at the federales, "We have to go back. We have to go back."

The plump officer simply looked at him, pointed to his watch and said, "No." Logan tried to explain to him, but still the officer said, "No."

So Logan did what he had to do. He jumped out of the small boat and started swimming toward shore. Now the federales started screaming at Logan as they turned the skiff around. They followed along as Logan swam. He figured if the men were going to shoot, they already would have.

Once ashore, Logan ran to Lupe, who was sitting on the picnic table with his feet up on the bench and waving his money for all his friends to see. Logan was thankful he still had a bit of cash in his pocket. He flashed the boy another twenty-dollar bill. That was all it took, and after a quick explanation the two of them were speeding down the dirt trail where the pigs had just settled themselves again. The federales stood in shock watching Logan. They had failed.

After what seemed like forever, Logan and Lupe popped out of the jungle into a clearing, just in time to see Klaus' truck turn onto the paved highway. Lupe shrugged his shoulders. Knowing it was not very likely they would catch up with the truck now, he slowed the moped to a crawl.

Logan bellowed, "You must try, you must try!" as he flashed another twenty-dollar bill in front of Lupe's eyes. The moped seemed to sprout a new gear, one he hadn't used before. The small engine whined and screamed, trying to catch up with the truck. Progress was slow but they seemed to be gaining. Logan and Lupe eventually caught the truck and pulled up beside it in the oncoming lane. The driver and both passengers looked over. Total shock was evident on their faces.

Klaus quickly pulled over and Logan explained that Hope had his passport, money and all of their credit cards in her fanny pack.

"I could never check into another country," he exclaimed.

That was all it took. Hope, filled with the stress of the day, burst into tears. She handed Logan's passport and credit cards to him. Martinez gave them both dirty looks, but said nothing. He had his bribe money. What were a few more minutes?

Klaus said, "I'm glad you caught us. Be safe, Logan."

Logan turned and got back on Lupe's moped and waved good-bye again.

"He'll be fine," Klaus said trying to comfort Hope. "He knows what he's doing and he's resourceful."

She nodded her head in agreement as she wiped the tears away. Looking back over her shoulder she watched Logan disappear into the distance on the back of Lupe's moped. She knew he would be fine. It was just the last straw in a very tiring and stressful day.

Focused on the Past to Keep from Embellishing the Present

HOPE CLOSED HER EYES AND LEANED BACK IN the seat between Klaus and Martinez. She was exhausted. Her kidneys were working overtime to filter out all the adrenalin pumping through her veins.

"Are you all right?" Klaus quietly asked.

"Yes," she said, opening her eyes and giving him a sad smile. "I'm just trying to calm down a bit. It's been an intense day."

Klaus nodded silently.

While they were driving, Martinez filled out the necessary paperwork for Hope and stamped her passport admitting her back into the Dominican Republic. He got out of the truck in front of the Immigration Office and shook Hope's hand saying, "I hope your stomach, or whatever, feels better real soon. Good-day." Glancing at Klaus, he said, "Give my best to Margarita."

"I will. Thank you," Klaus said.

Pulling away from the curb, Klaus looked at Hope. "What's he talking about? Your stomach?" he asked.

Hope had forgotten all about her fake sick act for the federales. Of course they would have told Martinez. It was the first humor she felt all day. Hope told him the story of her supposed sickness and the real reason for her reentry as they drove to the airport in Puerto Plata.

"I think there is a red-eye flight that leaves for Guatemala City around 10:30," Klaus said. "If we hurry, we can probably catch it."

Hope wished she had been able to clean up a little before going to the airport, but she was willing to forsake clean clothes if it meant making the last flight of the day. After buying her ticket and saying good-bye to Klaus, she washed her face and arms in the restroom sink.

At a payphone, Hope made an international call to the bed and breakfast in Antigua and told them she was on her way. She was relieved to hear that Billy hadn't left for the cave yet. She then called her mother.

"Drew's body can't fight this much longer," Ruth whispered from Drew's bedside, not wanting to awaken him.

"What does his doctor say?" Hope asked.

"They are systematically looking for a cure."

Hope turned toward the wall, hiding her tears.

The plane to Guatemala taxied down the runway. Hope sat in coach next to the window. With every thought of Drew, her body tensed. Upon takeoff, a quick flurry of turbulence shook the plane, and several passengers let out startled screams or audible gasps as a swift wave of fear shot through the cabin.

Hope's mind temporarily transitioned from Drew to another nerve-wracking flight she had been on four years earlier—the one she had taken to Cancun on the day she met Logan. The trapped, stale air in that plane's cabin was also filled with tension, making the flight attendants move too quickly and the passengers feel anxious. Hope made herself focus her thoughts on the week she spent in Puerto Aventuras, a small resort town south of Cancun, Mexico. She thought if she distracted herself with pleasant memories, she would stop worrying about Drew.

Hope's travel agent in Colorado had told her someone would meet her at the airport with a van and take her to Puerto Aventuras. After asking several taxi drivers if they were going to Puerto Aventuras Inn and getting negative responses, she was informed by another tourist that she had to obtain a pass from the travel guides, inside the airport, in order to ride one of the unmarked hotel vans. The first guide she approached wanted to sell her a ticket for a ride to her hotel, but she knew it was part of her travel package. The second one pretended he couldn't understand her broken Spanish well enough to point her in the right direction. Finally, the third travel guide took her to a desk in the far corner of a long filthy corridor. She approached the desk withered and frustrated.

"Miss Thornton, I've been waiting for you," the travel guide said, knowing she was the last person on his list to be transported to Puerto Aventuras. Hope was startled because he knew her name. She glanced down at his name tag, which read 'William.'

Studying his face, Hope thought there was something peculiar about him. He looked Indian in lots of ways. He had beautiful, clear, brown skin and high cheekbones, but very penetrating green eyes. He was tall for a Mexican and his features were more delicate than most. What really surprised her was that he spoke American English without an accent.

In the Cancun airport, William had picked up Hope's luggage and led her back to the first van she had approached out by the curb. In Spanish, without an English accent, William told the van driver that Hope was to be taken to the Puerto Aventuras Inn. He then loaded Hope's bags into the van while a fast stream of words flowed from his mouth. Hope's two years of high school Spanish hadn't left her with enough skill to understand much when the language was spoken quickly.

"Have a nice stay. I will see you in a week," William said to Hope as he walked back toward the airport terminal. Hope's eyes followed his movement, questioning in her mind why he acted as if he knew her.

Hope was the last tourist to get into Julio's van to Puerto Aventuras Inn. She sat in the front seat to the right of the driver. They left the noisy confusion of the airport and headed out into menacing traffic down Cancun's narrow streets. Horns blaring and tires squealing made Hope feel for her seat belt to make sure it was secure.

Julio maneuvered the van through town to a very dilapidated highway with no shoulder. In some places, the ground was a good foot below the edge of the cement road. Hope had to divert her attention from the image in her mind of the van breaking an axle as it strayed just a few inches over the concrete's edge.

An hour later, the van turned off the main road in Puerto Aventuras onto a narrow, cobblestone drive lined with coconut palms and flowering oleanders. At the end of the cul-de-sac, the van stopped to drop the passengers in front of a beautiful marble staircase that led into the open-air lobby.

Once inside, the ceiling towered above Hope's head, and the same marble on the stairs continued on the floor of the lobby. It was hard to tell exactly where the transition from being outside to being inside took place. In the lobby, huge potted palm trees and tropical flowers enhanced the feeling of being outdoors. Wild parrots and barn swallows flew through as if they couldn't tell where the distinguishing line was either.

Though her energy was depleted from traveling, she quickly registered into the luxurious hotel. After going to her room, she slipped into her bathing suit. On her way to the beach, she walked past a round bar at the back of the lobby. The hotel pool was situated between the bar and the beach. It sprawled and twisted with playful curves around palm trees and under walking bridges. At one end of the pool was another bar where guests could sit on stools either in or out of the water while listening to the mariachi band that played just inside the alfresco lobby.

With renewed energy, Hope walked through the crowd of people around the pool. On the beach, she found an empty lounge chair and sat down. She took a few deep breaths to relax before coating her skin with sunscreen. Leaning back in the chair, she closed her eyes with a smile of contentment. Even though the intense heat from the sun almost burned the inside of her nostrils, she took another deep inhalation; it felt good compared to the frigid wind back in Colorado.

Hope joyfully anticipated spending a week alone contemplating her future. As she tried to quiet her mind, she became intensely aware of a buzzing sensation in her body. It seemed she continually reflected back into the past or projected forward into the future with worry, guilt, anticipation or desire. Rarely was she simply living in the present.

Within minutes she began to sweat profusely. Fortunately there was a vague, cooling breeze that allowed life to exist in such extreme heat without completely burning up or melting. Yet, something inside of her did begin to melt. Her mind started to slow. She felt the tension in her cells slip out with the sweat.

Hope began to review her life, which was her intention for this trip. She wanted to decide what direction she would take next. Her life was going well; she was very content living in the Rocky Mountains. She enjoyed riding her bike, running and hiking through the foothills and the Garden of the Gods right from her back door. With a degree in art history, it was natural for her to be the owner of a successful art gallery.

Slowly Hope opened her eyes and looked around with a soft gaze, taking in her surroundings without judgments. Little stilt sandpipers did their quick, scurrying dance in the wet sand along the ocean's edge, rhythmically moving with the water while it ebbed and flowed. Hope was hypnotized watching the oscillation of the water. Slowly her view went further and further out to sea until her vision stopped on two sailboats with spectacular, multi-colored spinnaker sails.

In the light breeze, the vessels leisurely moved toward the horizon. Drawn into the lull of the ocean's lazy motion, Hope drifted off into a dream of sailing. Because of her childhood exposure to boats, it was easy for her to imagine herself living a cruiser's life aboard a sailboat.

"Have you ever been out to sea?" Hope was startled out of her dream by the voice of a man who had sat down on the lounge chair next to her.

"Sort of," Hope said, surprised at his frankness. Slowly she began, not sure why she was sharing this with a total stranger. "I grew up in Annapolis and sailing was one of the ways I spent time with my father." Looking toward the sailboats again she added, "Have you?"

"Have I what?"

"Ever been out to sea?"

"Oh, yes," the extremely tanned man said. "I grew up in Florida. And now I spend most of my time on a boat searching for sunken treasures."

"Searching for sunken treasures?" Hope questioned with a slight chuckle, not quite believing him. She waited for an explanation.

"I own a salvage company," he said. "We retrieve stuff off the bottom of the ocean. I spend so much time in the water that I actually feel a little peculiar on shore."

Watching the sailboats, Hope could feel herself being drawn into the memories of sailing the Chesapeake Bay. She felt connected to her father on the water as she never had on land. She could almost hear her father calmly say, "Ready to come about? Come about," which meant to tack the boat from one course to another.

Slowly, Hope turned her gaze to the man sitting next to her and she realized he was off in his own dream, staring out to sea too. While she watched him watching the boats, she felt a growing curiosity about him. She was drawn to his clear skin; his bronzed, hairless body; his strong, well-developed limbs; the way his hair curled and fell on his forehead; the smallness of his waist; and the broadness of his shoulders. She was instantly taken by his calmness and his total absorption in the sea.

Sunken treasures, she thought, shaking her head.

He glanced over at her and caught her staring at him. She let out a nervous giggle. He smiled and said, "Hi, my name's Logan, Logan McKnight."

"Hi, I'm Hope Thornton," she replied as her face flushed, which it rarely did. Feeling embarrassed, she quickly turned her gaze back to the sailboats. With the rhythmic sound of the ocean taking her away, she pushed herself to resume her fantasy of worlds between the waves, even though she really wanted to stare at the extremely handsome stranger sitting next to her. A quiet week alone, she reminded herself. That is why she had come to Mexico.

Logan continued to watch Hope. She glanced over at his leg, not wanting to make eye contact and saw a quick sweeping wave of goose bumps cover it as he quivered. Finding his shiver abnormal in the intense heat, she quickly looked back out to sea, feeling as if she had just witnessed something she shouldn't have.

After a few minutes of fidgeting and uncomfortable silence, Logan and Hope allowed themselves to question each other and quickly determined they were both on vacation alone.

Hope learned that Logan was an entrepreneur who had just fallen into business, truly by mistake. He wasn't organized or analytical enough to make it in the business world, but he had a dream of recovering shipwrecks and a personality that could sell snow to an Eskimo. With that combination, his business flourished.

Throughout the afternoon Logan and Hope continued to probe into each other's lives with interest. Tension and laughter built between them and then was slightly released by a quick nudge or an occasional touch on the other's arm.

The afternoon quickly faded and slid into evening. They were enjoying each other's company so much they decided to meet for dinner.

After a quick shower, Hope slipped into shorts and a T-shirt and met Logan in the lobby of their hotel.

By the time they sat down in the taxi for a ride to Aventuras' large marina lined with restaurants and shops, their clothes were damp with perspiration and the humid air. The tranquil bubble they had developed on the beach was popped by the noise of racing cars, trucks, and buses that had long ago lost their mufflers and shocks. Honking horns and revving motors from cars jockeying for position at each traffic light quickened their hearts and made them extremely aware of the rat race of humanity.

Exhaust from unfiltered engines saturated the air. It was impossible not to breathe in the sickening pollutants. On their left, garbage lined the roadway: plastic bags, tin cans, old tires, broken glass, dirty disposable diapers, a broken-down recliner, a tennis shoe, an old cloth, a dead dog half eaten by turkey vultures, yellowed newspaper, and a kitchen table with two legs missing and a hole in the top. The garbage went on and on.

The wind had ripped the water-deprived palm trees to shreds. There was rubble from buildings that had been started, but never completed and fence posts with no fences. Amongst the garbage were palm leaf huts with several Mexicans sitting in the shade. Filthy children played in the parched dirt. Women cooked tortillas on open fires—small fires, so as not to heat the air any more than absolutely necessary.

And to their right, Hope and Logan glimpsed the ocean lapping at the shore between the large fancy hotels. These hotels had beautifully manicured lawns filled with sufficiently watered palm trees, hibiscus bushes, oleanders, geraniums, chinaberries, blue bonnets, and buttercups—all in bloom. Tourists on the ocean side of the street were mostly Caucasians dressed in designer clothing. The distinct contrast was disturbing.

The cab driver raced through the crowded streets to town, arriving at a restaurant. The waiters were happy to see more tourists. It was as if they saw them as walking pocketbooks, not fellow people. After the host sat them at a table overlooking very expensive fishing boats, their waiter proceeded to efficiently serve them a delicious dinner of spicy snapper with black beans and rice.

The evening was filled with a string of flirtatious gestures and remarks that bounced back and forth between the couple like an evenly matched tennis game.

Locking eyes with Logan, Hope smiled. He thought her smile

was charming. He was having a hard time taking his eyes off of her. She seemed unaware of her own beauty. She didn't wear a speck of makeup, no fancy clothes. And she didn't flaunt her body— the body of a tall, athletic, sensual women. Logan found it all curiously attractive.

Hope didn't emphasize her looks because she didn't like the attention she got from being attractive. She enjoyed the simple, athletic look, not the provocative, sexy image so many women wanted to portray. Hope could feel herself blushing again.

From their table, Hope and Logan watched the fishing boats return with the day's catch. Stiffened black fin tuna and dorado lined the dock waiting to be cleaned. Each boat displayed their fish on deck to make sure they had outdone the neighboring boats. The captains mingled on the shore with the paying clients hoping to book a trip for the following day.

Later that evening Logan and Hope slowly walked down the beach by their hotel. She knew it didn't make sense that she was as comfortable or as quickly drawn to Logan as she was, but she was.

At one point Logan stopped walking and tenderly took Hope's hand in his. He turned her so they were both looking out to sea. Once again, the peace and tranquility was compelling. For a long moment they stood in silence and watched the lazy waves lap at the beach. From where they stood, all the way to the horizon, the moon laid a path of sparkling glitter upon the blackened sea.

Later that night outside the door to Hope's hotel room, she leaned back and propped one foot up against the stucco wall behind her. Logan said "Good-night," and leaned toward her slowly to test her receptivity to a kiss. When he was within a few inches, he looked into her eyes and saw no resistance.

New Love

STILL WITH HER EYES CLOSED AND THE LOUD hum of the jet engines in her ears, Hope relived her first kiss with Logan. She had let out a sigh of desire with that first kiss. The rest of the world dissolved. She felt a quiver stirring in her heart. Her knees weakened and her eyes fluttered open as Logan slowly stepped back from her and sauntered down the open-air hallway. Hope watched from where she stood, leaning against the wall, wanting more. With a wave over his shoulder, Logan said, "I'll wake you in the morning." Hope stood for a moment outside her hotel room and watched Logan until he turned down the stairwell and out of sight.

When she awoke the next morning in Puerto Aventuras, even before she opened her eyes, Hope felt anxiety swell in her body. She felt the urge to sneak out of bed and leave the hotel. She thought about telling Logan, when he called, that it had all been a mistake and she really had come to Mexico to spend some time alone. But instead, there was a knock on her door. She opened it a crack and saw Logan holding a tray with a pot of coffee, a basket of rolls and a bouquet of flowers.

"I was dreaming of you," he said, raising his eyebrows suggestively.

Hope couldn't help but smile. She wondered if he had rehearsed that line.

"Good morning, Hope," Logan said as she opened the door wide enough for him to enter. As he walked past her, he gave her a gentle kiss on the cheek. Hope felt a spark of excitement in her stomach. His tenderness made the tension in her shoulders give away. She wanted to grab him and hold on, but she resisted, because part of her wanted to shut the door in his face and run from the intensity she felt in his presence. It was as if he were a fantasy come true and she didn't know if she should trust her feelings.

Hope and Logan sat on her veranda overlooking the hotel pool with the churning ocean beyond. Beautiful Spanish guitar music drifted up to them from the poolside bar.

"I remember lying in bed," Hope told him as she leaned her head back on the patio lounger. "My mother used to sing to me when I couldn't sleep. Her voice was so soft, barely audible over the tenderly plucked strings on her guitar. Playing was one of my mother's secret loves. While in Panama with the Peace Corps, she learned to play classical Spanish guitar."

She giggled to herself, remembering she was still in her pajamas and she hadn't washed her face or combed her hair, but neither of them paid any attention.

Logan also told Hope stories of his childhood. He told her that he and his mother lived with his grandmother during his senior year of high school when his parents temporarily separated.

"One afternoon Grandma had bridge club at her house," Logan said. "She played bridge on a regular basis with the same women she played with in college."

He closed his eyes, for just a moment, remembering the details. Laughing, he continued, "One afternoon they were in rare form. It was Hazel's birthday and Ann brought a bottle of champagne to celebrate. When I came home from school, I could hear them giggling out on the screened-in back porch where the card table was set up. The champagne bottle was empty in the kitchen, and I saw two more corks from wine bottles lying on the counter. It sounded like they were having a great time. I could tell the bridge game was beginning to fall apart when they accused Marty of cheating. She vehemently denied it and then they all laughed. In a moment of silence, one of them let out a huge fart. They burst into laughter so loud I literally jumped in the kitchen. They roared until Ann started protesting, 'Stop, stop, I'm going to pee my pants.'

"And of course she did. Which made the others laugh so hard that Hazel joined her and also wet her pants."

Still laughing, Logan said, "It was always a riot at Grandma's house. We had so much fun… I really miss her…"

Hope couldn't imagine her stuffy grandparents letting go and enjoying themselves the way Logan's grandmother and her girl-friends did. She wondered what it must have been like to grow up with a silly grandmother. Hope had always wished her grandparents weren't so serious.

Looking at his watch, Logan proclaimed, "It's noon. I'm starving. Let's go get lunch." The morning had vanished and Hope was amazed at how comfortable and natural it was to spend so much time with him.

Hope dressed in the bathroom before she and Logan jumped into a cab out in front of the hotel and accepted the driver's recommendation of the restaurant Del Sol, in Playa del Carmen, as a good lunch destination. From the hotel they drove north along the old scenic coastal highway. The view of the jagged shore was a dynamic cliff down to the crashing surf, reminding Hope of northern California where she frequently attended meditation retreats.

The restaurant was built on the point of a rock jetty. Surrounded on three sides by water, it precariously adhered to the stones beneath. Over the half-wall next to their table, they could look straight down fifty feet onto a small, secluded beach that was adjoined to the Hotel Del Sol by a steep zigzagging staircase.

A mild breeze blew in from the sea; the day was slightly cooler than the day before. In the peaceful, relaxed atmosphere their conversation paused as they both turned to gaze at the subdued colors of nature. The green-gray ocean lapped at the brown-gray sand beneath the blue-gray sky—all were dotted with specks of white to lift the gray gloom. The sky had its small, puffy clouds; the sea had the froth on the breaking waves; and the sand was lined with seagulls that hurried along the water's edge calling to each other like laughing school children.

In the midst of this grayness, Mexicans had become exceptionally colorful people. The walls in the restaurant were painted a brilliant blue. The trim that encircled the large, open-air views was painted a rich orange and the doors were tinted vibrant lavender. Each wood chair was high-lighted with intense colors of the rainbow, as were the tables. The wait staff was also brightly adorned with intricately embroidered blouses.

After lunch Logan and Hope returned to their hotel. Sitting under a palm frond umbrella, they passed the afternoon on the beach reading novels together.

Day turned to night. Logan and Hope went out for dinner again. Hope thought she should feel strange spending so much time with a man she barely knew, but in some odd way, it seemed like he was the reason she had come to Mexico.

After dinner, Logan put his arm around Hope's shoulder and they strolled along the shore. They watched the lights on the passing ships slowly move across the horizon. The smell of the ocean filled their nostrils with a rich and untamed perfume.

Seated in the 747, Hope got goose bumps remembering how much she craved Logan's touch that night four years ago. Yet at the same time, she had feared the vulnerability of being physically intimate with him.

Fateful Meeting

JOEL PLANTED HIS SHORT, STOCKY LEGS ON the dock with a wide stance. His broad, fleshy feet were calloused and hardened from years of going barefoot. Slightly wavy hair the color of rich, fertile, Nebraska soil curled at the nape of his neck. From the dock, Joel repeatedly threw a small circular net into the water; then, hand over hand he pulled it back out with baitfish in tow.

The sun was just beginning to cast long, wispy shadows in the emerging dawn when Hope and Logan met Joel and Jorge at the fishing docks. They had hired the fishing guides to take them on an excursion. The moist air brimmed with the calls of the awakening birdlife. From the last remaining dimness of night, pelicans and seagulls stretched before taking to the air.

They headed out of the bay on an older, center console, fishing boat. A VHF radio was the only electronic instrument onboard. There were no safety precautions taken: no life jackets, no life raft, no single sideband radio, no GPS and no fear. Jorge and Joel had taken this boat out thousands of times before; it was as habitual for them to go fishing as it was for a pelican to dive into the sea.

For two hours they motored away from land into nothing but blue. Jorge took the position of captain. He appeared to be older than Joel; his frame was smaller and less supple. His skin was loose. His eyes were foggy with cataracts from the years of exposure to the sun. Without a word, they both simultaneously knew they had arrived at their favorite fishing location. Jorge stopped the engine. Joel stood in the back of the boat, pitching handfuls of live bait into the water. Joel trailed baited fishing lines behind the boat as Jorge put the boat in gear. It was a rare and appreciated day. The water was like glass and there wasn't a speck of wind to disturb the air. The sun lazily pulled itself up into the sky through the early morning haze. Not a word was spoken. They trolled for an hour and a half without even a nibble. Devoid of words, Jorge looked at Joel who reeled in the lines. They raced off to a new location and twenty minutes later, they were trolling again.

In the stillness, the water oscillated just slightly as a whole. Joel threw in a baited hook, and it appeared to penetrate something much thicker than water. The ever-present quiet was eerie. Two more hours passed without even the slightest bite. The sun was now directly overhead and glaring off the water's surface. To ward off the intense sun, Hope slipped into a cotton gauze shirt and pants. From beneath her straw-hat, she looked out to where the deep blue sea met the royal blue sky. The heat made her feel woozy.

Sitting on the bow pulpit, Hope faced out into the water. She dangled a leg off either side of the boat and absorbed the pervasive calm into her soul. Very quietly she started singing her meditation mantra in a rhythmical song. Over and over Hope sang the Sanskrit words. "Om TaraNamah. Om TaraNamah."

Logan sat in the back of the boat waiting for a bite, practicing his Spanish on Joel, who patiently corrected Logan's grammar and pronunciation. Off in the distance Jorge spotted a large congregation of birds circling and diving into the ocean. He pointed it out to Joel who began reeling in the lines again. Birds meant fish, so off they went. As the bow of the boat lifted with the increased speed, a small wake rolled beneath Hope's dangling feet. In the roar of the engines, Hope sang her mantra louder and louder.

Hope giggled when she notice porpoises just below the surface of the water beneath her feet.

At full speed the boat approached the diving pelicans, laughing gulls, black-headed gulls, common terns and blue footed boobies. The birds' plunging and splashing made the placid surface of the water seem to boil. Jorge stopped the boat just outside the ring of diving birds.

"Hope, look!" Logan shouted, pointing to the starboard as a porpoise leapt out of the water.

And then, all four turned to see what had made the sound of a large splash in front of the bow.

"Look!" Hope shouted as more porpoises flew from the sea.

The boat was surrounded in every direction. Small harbor porpoises and larger bottlenose dolphins leapt from the water as far as the eye could see. No one moved to throw baited lines out. No one thought of anything other than what was happening in front of them at that very moment.

Once again, Hope giggled with merriment.

The once-still, docile water appeared to be giving birth to each porpoise as it emerged from its watery shell. It was as if the water itself were being transformed into life. In all the years of running fishing boats, even Jorge and Joel had never seen anything like this magnificent display of aquatic life. They all watched in amazement for twenty minutes, agog over the spectacular show. Slowly the gigantic congregation of porpoises began to disperse.

Back on the dock that afternoon, Joel cleaned the two dorado they caught trolling on their way back to shore.

"Gracias, Joel," Logan sincerely said, shaking his hand when Joel handed the cleaned and nicely packaged dorado fillets to him. Turning to shake hands with Jorge and give him a tip to share with Joel, Logan offered, "Would the two of you like to join us for dinner?"

The fishermen readily accepted; and the four walked up the dusty dirt road to Tequilas, a small, lime green building. Inside, the room was loud with conversation and music. Jorge and Joel knew almost everyone in the restaurant.

As they waited for their fish to be prepared, women swarmed around Joel, wanting his attention, which he gladly gave.

Tequilas prepared a spectacular feast for the fishermen. Half the fish was grilled with garlic and the other half was sautéed Vera Cruz style.

The old speakers in the corners of the dining room blared Spanish dance music. Frequently, couples rose from their seats and did a sexy salsa swing as the rest of the crowd cheered and clapped. The single women in the restaurant took turns dancing with Joel. He had mastered sensual moves that captured the young girls' hearts.

With a beer in hand, Jorge and Joel mingled with the diners and told everyone about the dolphin show they witnessed.

Logan held Hope in his arms while they slowly danced. It was hard for him to let her go between songs. The more he was around her, the more he adored her.

"Let's go cool off," Logan suggested. On the patio, he held Hope from behind. He inhaled her scent, pressing his lips to the back of her neck. Hope turned toward Logan and found his lips with hers.

Being out in the sun all day was beginning to catch up with both Logan and Hope. With full stomachs and their share of beer, they excused themselves to catch a cab back to their hotel.

Exhausted, Hope and Logan stumbled up to their rooms and said goodnight to each other in the hallway. As soon as Hope's head hit the pillow, she was asleep.

The sky was a brilliant blue the following day as Logan, with Hope at his side, drove down the coast on the way to Tulum Ruins. When they arrived at the ancient remains situated on a small plateau overlooking the turquoise water of the Caribbean Sea, the magnificent structures took them back in time. Hope and Logan walked in silence over the ground hardened from years of baking sun and voracious winds. They envisioned children running between the buildings and playing stick games where ritual sacrificial ceremonies took place.

Hope's mind quieted to an almost spiritual void as she took in her surroundings.

"Wow," she whispered in awe. "It's overwhelming."

Logan grabbed her hand and squeezed.

After slowly touring the grounds, they sat for a while on the rock wall to the east of the Temple of the Descending God.

Beneath the scorching sun, Hope couldn't picture people actually living at the site. It seemed overly exposed to the harsh elements.

"Where did the Mayans go for protection?" Hope asked.

"I don't know. We are out here in the open. That's for sure."

"The ground looks like what I imagine dinosaur skin to have looked like. It's all scaly and cracked."

Logan nodded his head in agreement.

"I'm thirsty. Can we go back to that little town we passed through?" Hope asked.

"Of course, let's go."

On a narrow side street just a block from Main Street, Logan parked the Jeep in Tulum Pueblo. They hiked up a steep incline to the center of town. Tiny storefronts lined the street for two blocks. Behind Mixik, a quaint little store, they found a small cafe. Walking through a beaded curtain, they entered a room with only four very simple tables with chairs crowded around them. At one end of the room stood a hand-painted bar with a dozen or so bottles of tequila and rum stored behind on a single shelf.

As Hope looked around the room, her eyes stopped and locked with those of a man. He sat quietly watching her from one of the tables. Hope gently tugged on Logan's sleeve.

"I know that man," she said under her breath, while continuing to look at him sitting across the room.

Logan followed her gaze and asked, "Who is he?"

"I'm trying to remem..." she whispered. She thought hard.

"Oh, I know who he is!" she said louder now, remembering. "He's the travel guide from the airport in Cancun."

As she recalled who William was, he raised his hand and motioned for them to come and sit down at his table.

Feeling a little awkward, Hope and Logan slowly walked to his table. They didn't have much choice; all of the other tables and seats were taken.

"Miss Thornton, how are you? I would like you to meet my brother, Rocky," William said, gesturing to the man sitting next to him.

"You can call me Hope," she said, shaking his outstretched hand. "And this is Logan."

"You can call me Billy," William said.

"Nice to meet you," Logan responded.

"Please have a seat," Billy offered, pulling a chair out for Hope.

"Thank you," she said shyly.

"Would you like something to drink or eat?" he asked as he motioned to a young girl behind the bar. "I would recommend the chicken tostadas."

The café had hand-plastered walls that looked as if they had been painted with tempera paint from grade school art class. It was thick and powdery like the color would run off if it ever got wet. Under foot, the dirt floors had been swept and walked on for so many years they almost seemed polished.

When the young waitress approached, Billy asked, "What would you like?" directing his question toward Hope and Logan.

"I would like tostadas and a beer, please," Hope said to the young girl, hoping she spoke English.

Billy translated into Spanish, because she didn't.

"Yeah, I'd like a beer," Logan said. "But let me try something else to eat. A little variety. Surprise me."

So Billy ordered pineapple tamales for Logan.

"Do they serve guacamole?" Hope asked.

Billy asked the waitress.

"Sí, sí, es el mejor en el pueblo," she said, smiling at Hope.

As the waitress left to get beers for all, Billy turned to her.

"How are you enjoying your vacation so far?"

She laughed, looked over at Logan and said, "It hasn't been anything like I had expected."

"And why is that?" he questioned.

"I imagined spending all of my time alone on the beach relaxing and reading novels, but instead, I met Logan. And honestly, we have been on the go nonstop," she told him.

"But has it been fun?" he questioned further.

She paused a moment before she answered, "It's been an unexpected gift."

"There seems to be adventure here in Mexico that there isn't in the United States. There is an element of mystery and wonder that just persists in the air," Billy said.

Hope's eyes lingered on Logan's before acknowledging Billy's comment. "I agree. Where are you from? You look Mexican-Indian, but your eyes look Irish," she said. "You speak perfect American English and perfect Spanish. I'm just curious where home is."

Billy said, "We are from Honduras. Our mother, Moon Jaguar, is of the ancient Xukpi tribe that inhabited Copan Central hundreds of years ago. We live along the Amarillo River in the Copan Valley. But our father is mostly Irish. He is a professor at the University of Indiana."

"What are you doing here in Mexico?" Logan asked.

"As Hope knows, I work at the airport in Cancun," Billy answered.

"I'm just visiting Billy," Rocky said. Billy nodded.

"What's your story?" Rocky asked, sounding very American and looking at Logan.

"Well, I'm also here on vacation," Logan began. "I live in Marathon, Florida. I own a marine salvage company. We salvage ship wreckage and sunken artifacts. We just finished recovering all we could find of the Rudolph Groing shipwreck in the Dry Tortugas. It took me years to find the shipwreck, let alone bring it up. Just as we were finishing categorizing everything, the U.S. government came in. They declared the shipwreck was in their waters and they expected a cut of the salvaged metals and the little gold that was found. Years of work and expense on my time and my nickel, and they want a cut." Logan was disgusted.

"I can relate. Our tribe is being unfairly hassled by the government, too," Rocky said. "Our ancestors have been living in the same river valley for as long as our family tree goes back. We can trace it at least thirty-seven generations. But the government has decided that our mountain range is the site of an important archeological find. They have been excavating around us for years now, shrinking our farming and grazing fields. It's only a matter of time before they will want to excavate the entire valley."

"They don't have the right to do that, do they?" Logan asked in an irritated tone, a little too loudly. Logan was transferring his frustration and anger he had about his own situation. "How have our governments gotten so out of control? They think they have the right to manipulate us by instilling fear in our everyday lives."

"A couple of years ago, our government did a study on our tribe because they heard we had members who were over a hundred years old," Billy joined in with antipathy. "They wanted to see if they could figure out why we were as healthy as we were. But, when we wouldn't allow them to observe our spiritual rituals, they started mandating laws to try and take control of us. They thought they could do this by making certain sacred herbs illegal to collect or have in our possession.

"They seem to think the way of life we have been living for as long as anyone can remember is detrimental to the environment and to the welfare of our children. They say the consumption of these secret herbs and the healing rituals we have performed for centuries are dangerous and possibly destroying the ecosystem."

"Can you believe it?" Hope asked, bewildered.

"No, I can't," Billy said.

"Do you know why your tribe lives to be so old?" Hope asked.

"I'm sure it's our entire lifestyle," Rocky answered. "It's how we think, what we eat, what we believe. It's who we are as people. Our great-grandfather is the Medicine Man and chief of the Corn People. He lives in a different dimension than most people. Even we don't understand all the things he does for the well-being of our tribe."

"Why doesn't he teach you what he does?" Hope asked.

"Because most of us are not at a level of understanding that would allow his teaching to mean anything." Billy said. "Praying Dove, our cousin, will carry on the ancient healing rituals. Grandfather has been teaching Praying Dove his techniques since she was a small child. She has done miraculous things since she was quite young."

"Is the chief of your tribe your grandfather or your great-grand-father?" Logan asked.

"He is actually our great-grandfather, but everyone in the tribe calls him Grandfather."

Hope was mesmerized. What a story, she thought. She wanted to know more. She wanted to take her knowledge of spirituality to the next step with a spiritual leader like the one Billy and Rocky described. She wanted to meet someone so special that most people couldn't understand what he knew.

"Have you ever seen his methods of healing work?" Hope asked.

"Of course, over and over. I've even seen people come from outside our tribe to ask him for help," Billy said.

"What exactly is it that he does?" Hope inquired.

"Well it's different for different people," Billy said. "In Western culture, you might diagnose several people with a particular heart disease, but Grandfather would see them as individuals and treat each one differently, even though they appear to have the same illness.

"Sometimes he has the person drink herbal teas; sometimes they are instructed to chant and do repetitive physical movements. Sometimes they are instructed to interact in a specific way with their relatives. Sometimes they are sent to a specific place just to wait for a message on their own. Over the years, Grandfather has instructed me to do lots of unusual things. I have gotten results every time, even though they are not always the results I thought I was asking for. Wouldn't you say the same, Rocky?"

"Most definitely," he responded. "Once, our mother told me to go talk to Grandfather about One Legged Bear, a boy who wouldn't stop kicking me. My mother always told me to ignore him and feel sorry for him because One Legged Bear had a hard life. He was born with only one good leg and just a nub for the other. It made him angry at the world. He had a small set of crutches his Uncle carved for him and he learned to run like the wind with those crutches.

"For no reason, he would run up to me, swing on his crutches with his good leg raised and plow it into me. Year after year, he kicked me every time he saw me. I finally went to Grandfather and asked him what I should do. He told me I should kick him back. He said I should kick him as hard as I could to pay him back for all the years of kicking me. So I did. The next time I saw him, I kicked him before he could kick me, but his crutch was in the way and my foot struck the hard wood. I kicked so hard that I broke my foot and couldn't walk for almost a month.

"One Legged Bear thought that was so funny he started to laugh. It was the very first time anyone heard him laugh! I think he laughed every time he saw me that entire month I couldn't walk. He no longer seemed angry. He now sees the humor in life in spite of his issues. He has become so lighthearted that Grandfather now sends people to him when they are depressed so he can lift their hearts. Since then, we have become best friends."

"What a wonderful story," Hope said.

"Oh, but it is not a story, it is the way of life," Rocky corrected.

"Have you ever seen extremely sick people be cured?" Even back then Hope was curious about what Grandfather could actually do.

"Of course," Billy said. "One summer our father returned to our tribe with his mother, who had a very advanced case of breast cancer. It had advanced to the point that her right breast was about three times as large as the left one and her right arm was beginning to turn black. The skin on her upper arm was starting to split. She was afraid of doctors and had refused any medical treatment back in the States.

"When Grandfather saw her, he immediately stood facing her and placed his hands on her shoulders. With his eyes turned to the heavens, he started screaming a chant while begging and crying to God for his help. He went on and on until Rose, our father's mother—she never wanted us to call her Grandma—started screaming and shaking herself. She crumpled to the ground where she stood.

Grandfather stumbled backwards away from her. He also collapsed and began coughing up black liquid. Rose sobbed uncontrollably. Horse Woman then took Rose into the women's hut where she nursed her with Grandfather's herbal tinctures and compresses. Grandfather retreated into his own hut to rest.

"Three days later when Rose came out of the women's hut, she was cured. The tumor in her breast had completely vanished and her arm wasn't swollen or black anymore. Her face looked more open and alive than I ever remembered it being."

And then Rocky turned toward Billy and said, "Don't you remember? We knew it was her, but she looked entirely different." Billy nodded his head in agreement.

"On the third day Grandfather also came out of his hut," Rocky continued. "He sat in the sun all afternoon. He looked exhausted. We weren't allowed to talk to him. But by the evening meal, he was back to normal and interacting with the rest of us."

"Then, for the first time, Rose wanted us to call her Grandma," Billy said, pointing back and forth between himself and Rocky. "That was hard for me to make the switch after so many years of calling her Rose."

"Oh, and remember the time Praying Dove laid her hands on Lazy Eye's stillborn child and filled the baby with the breath of life?" Rocky blurted out.

"She was always doing amazing things when we were children," Billy agreed.

Hope was beyond curious now; she wanted to know what Grandfather and Praying Dove knew, but she didn't even know the first step in getting there.

"Logan, it's been great," Billy said, shaking Logan's hand. "I knew when I saw Hope in the airport that she was someone I would enjoy being friends with, and you're an extra bonus."

"We've seemed to whittle the afternoon away," Logan said. "It's been real."

"Thanks, Billy," Hope said, giving him a hug. "I would love to meet your grandfather sometime."

"I have a feeling you will," Rocky said, wrapping his arms around Hope's shoulders.

Before Hope and Logan left for Puerto Aventuras they exchanged email addresses with William Dancing Wolf and Falling Rock.

Hope and Logan slowly walked hand in hand along the shore behind Puerto Aventuras Inn while the hot, oppressive air slightly cooled. The light of the moon reflected off the ocean. Hope could not look at Logan without wanting to kiss him. She knew the following morning she would be getting back on a jet and zooming off to Colorado, yet she felt a piece of her would be staying in Mexico with Logan.

They walked to a secluded cove at the end of the beach. Logan laid down the Indian blanket he had bought from a vendor in Tulum Pueblo and pulled Hope close to him. Hope adored the sweet musky aroma of his skin. Without words, they communicated. She sighed slightly with every exhalation. Logan stroked her hair and pulled her closer and closer. Their lips met with a kiss—a kiss of such heat and tenderness that Hope knew nothing outside of his lips against hers, his teeth grazing her bottom lip, the feel of her tongue teasing his, her breasts against his chest and the heat of desire rising in his loins against her belly.

Hope sensed his most secret desire and toyed with him. She teased him until he practically begged for release, and then after granting his unspoken dream, she whispered, "You taste of the ocean, salty and wild."

They lay on the blanket in each other's arms, and quietly shared their appreciation for the beauty the earth gave them and the warmth and tenderness they gave each other. Logan's arms were powerful, his voice was like black velvet, and his face was shaved so close he could glide his chin on Hope's neck for hours and it would feel like a silk scarf blowing in the warm night breeze, ruffling across her skin. Yet she knew none of these were the reasons she was drawn to him. She was drawn to his spirit that ignited a spark of fulfillment with hers.

In Hope's hotel room, moonlight streamed through the sliding glass doors, creating unusual patterns across their bodies as they lay on her bed.

"Won't you please stay at least a few days longer?" Logan begged.

With his head resting on her breast, he looked up at the delicate skin of her neck. From her neck he ran his finger down her sternum as far as Hope's blouse would allow and then he unbuttoned the top two buttons so he could slide his hand beneath the fabric. Tenderly he cupped her left breast in his hand.

Overcome with desire, Hope's back slightly arched.

"I have to go back to work," she reasoned.

Exposing her breast Logan nuzzled her nipple, encircling it with his tongue. Hope moaned a deep, guttural sound. Logan slowly moved down her body, unbuttoning the rest of her blouse to expose her stomach. He caressed and kissed the point where her ribs met, and he licked his way down her belly. Hope arched her back even more, giving herself to him. Allowing herself to be vulnerable, she ran her fingers through his hair. Logan unbuttoned her pants and nuzzled his nose into her mound of curly hair, taking in her aroma and feeling her wetness.

On every inhalation Hope felt rippling goose bumps coming from her core, exploding out her fingertips and toes. Every exhalation felt like warm water was running through her veins and out her mouth, materializing as a rolling moan. Each inhalation and exhalation increased in intensity. They became dizzy in their own opium-like fog.

Engulfed in the rhythm of their oneness, Hope lost herself in a scream of delight and melted into convulsions as the early morning sun's rays drifted through her room.

Antigua, Beautiful Antigua

GUATEMALA CITY TWINKLED LIKE CHRISTMAS lights nestled in the lush rainforest. As the airplane approached the runway, Hope saw the city as a living geometric pattern, glowing brighter and brighter the closer they got. In the terminal the passionate Spanish culture was apparent. Hope quickly relaxed into the casual atmosphere.

In front of the airport she found a cab driver willing to take her to Casa De Los Cantaros. They drove down an ill-kept, winding, mountain road with the windows open to prevent them from being poisoned by the exhaust escaping the large hole in the car's muffler.

Hope sat in the front seat next to the driver and periodically stuck her head out the window in search of fresh air. The bench seat was pulled as far forward as the car would allow for the driver's short legs. Hope's long legs pressed firmly against the glove compartment. From the radio speakers, Spanish love songs blared at full volume, which was necessary to be audible over the loud, un-muffled engine.

Consumed in his own world, the driver bellowed out baritone harmonies to each song. When they arrived at the bed and breakfast, Hope was relieved to still be conscious and grateful that she had not succumbed to the exhaust.

The taxi stopped in front of the renovated Colonial plantation. A narrow rock path lined with hand-made bricks meandered from the street to the front porch through a beautifully manicured flower garden. Hope carried her backpack and briefcase up the small wood stairs of the covered veranda. Before she reached the front door, Billy stepped out. He wrapped his arms around her. "It's so good to see you," he said.

"It's good to see you, too," she replied, relaxing into his embrace. "What a gorgeous place. How did you know this was here?"

"My father used to bring my mother, Rocky and me here for Christmas when I was a kid. It's a special place," he answered.

"I feel almost like I'm in a dream or a movie or something that is taking place in colonial days. The fragrance in the air even smells old," she said, pulling herself from his hold to look again at all the flowers lit by lanterns along the pathway. Hope stood watching the multitude of night moths drawn to the lights and the small bats darting through the air that were attracted to the moths. Katydids chirped in waves from one tree to the next with an intense, almost constant, drone.

At such a late hour, Hope was surprised to see the entire bed and breakfast staff standing just inside the door waiting to greet her. In the entryway, rough plank wood floors were covered with hand-woven rugs. Authentic colonial antiques, brought from the United States over a century ago, were used as everyday furniture.

There were only three guest rooms in the Inn, each with its own private bath. Billy already occupied one, Hope was to stay in another, and the third was not taken; they had the place to themselves.

On the canopy bed in her room, Hope ran her hand over the elaborate wedding ring pattern of the quilt. She admired the hand-made lace trim on the sheets and pillowcases. An exquisite, stained glass lampshade adorned the table lamp next to the bed. Tiers of lace covered the windows and obscured the view on the other side into shadows of light and dark.

Hope took a quick shower to wash the day's adventure from her skin before meeting Billy down the hall in the library for a nightcap. He was seated in the far corner in a high-backed leather chair. The walls of the library were lined with heavy oak shelves. The room smelled like old books, a combination of paper, ink and mildew.

"Would you like a glass?" Billy asked, pointing to a bottle of port. Two small, crystal stemmed glasses sat on the end table next to him.

"Sure," she said, as he filled them.

"Tell me about Drew," Billy probed.

"I'm worried," Hope said. "They've exhausted Western medicine and we're depending on Roaring River to come up with a cure."

"How did he get sick?" Billy asked.

"Well, he thinks he was poisoned somehow. I don't know the details."

"Why would someone poison him?" Billy couldn't imagine someone doing that on purpose. "That's like murder."

"I know," Hope said, as her stomach tensed with fear. "If Roaring River can't help, I'm afraid we don't know where else to turn."

"I expect he has an answer for you," Billy said.

"So tell me, exactly what is happening to your tribe?" Hope questioned. She wanted to direct the conversation away from Drew, because she knew if she talked about him much longer, she would cry. "I guess I don't really understand how they can tell you to leave your home."

"Well, from what I've been able to piece together, the government has sold the land that we live on. A while back, a colonel from the army came to our village and ordered us to leave. He said the Governor was giving us a small piece of land on the southeast shore of Honduras. It is mostly sand dunes. Not much will grow there. It would be impossible for us to feed ourselves. The tribe obviously didn't go. And I guess the Colonel came back and again ordered everyone to leave."

"That doesn't seem fair," Hope said.

"No, it doesn't. And in the middle of all this, Grandfather has seen a vision—a vision he has been calling 'the Shifting of the Wind.' He says this shift, whatever it is, takes place here in Antigua. That is why he is coming here. So, of course, most of the tribe is coming with him."

"That's loyalty."

"Two weeks ago, the tribe left the Copan Valley. It will be complicated for our tribe to travel. Very few of the tribespeople have passports. They have never needed them. The Honduran government acknowledges they are from Honduras, although they don't have any legal papers. The Guatemalan government will also be able to tell they are from Honduras and will certainly require passports to enter Guatemala. Rocky said the majority of the tribe planned to sneak across the border at night. Of course, the few who do have passports can enter the country legally.

"Grandfather is headed to a large cave just a few miles from here where they can stay until it is time to come to Antigua. When they are settled in the cave, Rocky will come and meet us here. I hope they are okay. I really expected Rocky to be here by now."

"It's amazing how devoted your tribe's members are to each other and to Grandfather. In the U.S., it is hard to keep a single family together, let alone an entire tribe. We all want to be our own leader, and we find it difficult to give someone else the authority your tribe gives to Grandfather. It's all about the almighty 'I' in the U.S.," Hope said, yawning.

"We have had to stick together to survive. As individuals, we never would have made it in the jungle," Billy commented from his knowledge of having lived in both countries at different times in his life. "It is different in the States."

"Which way of living do you think is the best?" Hope questioned.

"Well, I feel more love and the sense of belonging when I am with the tribe," Billy answered. "But I feel freer and more expansive when I am in the U.S. I also feel like I have more options and choices in the States. It's more complex there, but the complexity allows for opportunities. I seem to be processing information the entire time I'm in the States, whereas when I'm in the jungle, I'm very much in the moment. I feel more relaxed, and my mind is quieter when I'm at home, that is, in Honduras. I guess I still call Honduras home."

"It's funny, Americans take classes to learn how to be in the moment," Hope said. "But down here, it is almost as if inner peace and tranquility are emanating from the land."

"I know what you mean," Billy agreed, refilling Hope's glass. "Father and I have talked about how different we are in each country. I enjoy both states of being, as does Father. Mother, on the other hand, seems to want to stay in her tribal ways when she is in the States and doesn't seem to be able to switch into the quick-paced American way. It is hard for her when she comes to visit in Indiana."

"I like the tempo down here," Hope yawned behind her hand. "Oh, gosh, I'm getting tired. You know, when I go back to the States, I have severe culture shock. So much of what I see is sterile and pointless. The culture bombards the psyche with 'more is better'. I have always been drawn to a slower mode than most Americans. I have spent a large part of my life looking for the simplicity in an un-simple culture. It might not be there."

"Maybe it's because I have gone back and forth between both cultures for my entire life that it is easy for me to switch from one to the other."

Here the conversation paused. They both simultaneously took a deep breath and exhaled with a sigh as they settled deeper into their chairs.

"Hope, tell me about the boat," he said. "Do you like living aboard?"

After thinking for a moment, she said, "Well, it is a life of extremes. I'm either having the most spectacular journey with serene, idyllic conditions or the most terrifying, uncomfortable ride, fighting the power of nature. It never seems to be anything in between."

"Is Logan safe sailing the boat by himself?" Billy asked.

"I expect so. He certainly is capable, and the weather is supposed to be very calm for the next couple of days. But weather predictions are not always accurate," she said, remembering their Gulf Stream passing. "He should get to Puerto Plata sometime tomorrow evening, and then, hopefully, he will be able to get a friend to help him sail the boat here to Guatemala."

Having noticed her tan and apparent fitness, he gestured, "You look wonderful. It certainly appears life on a boat suits you."

"I enjoy it. It's good for Logan and me to spend so much time together. When in Florida, Logan is gone, sometimes for a month or more at a time. He's one of the lucky few who actually love what they do for a living."

Hope and Billy talked on until the hazy hues of dawn began to appear in the east.

Once in bed, Hope tossed and turned. She wasn't used to a large, soft, motionless bed. She had quickly become accustomed to the constant rhythm of the small, hard berth on *Ladyhawke*.

After just a few hours of sleep, Hope awoke. Before she opened her eyes, she heard voices in the garden outside her bedroom window. The loud buzzing of the katydids from the previous night had stopped. There was an almost sweet smell coming in the open window. It reminded her of honeysuckle, but was just a reminder; it was a sweeter and fuller bodied aroma than the honeysuckle back home. She allowed herself to leisurely get out of bed and indulge in the luxury of taking a bath in the large, claw-foot tub that sat in the middle of the bathroom adjoining her bedroom. She hadn't had a real bath since she left the United States two months prior.

Steam rose as she filled the tub with hot water. Hope stuck her face in the steam and inhaled deeply. After easing herself into the tub, she scrubbed her body until it was pink. Her cheeks glowed from the warmth.

From the lobby of the bed and breakfast, Hope used the payphone and called her mother to check on Drew. She was sad to hear that his condition had worsened, and they still hadn't a clue as to how to eradicate the infection. She felt uneasy putting so much of her faith in Roaring River being able to help Drew, but she didn't know where else to turn.

In the small, screened-in dining porch on the back of the Inn, Hope met Billy for a late breakfast. Bright yellow banana twits fluttered from one oleander or bougainvillea bush to the next. The tropical garden behind the bed and breakfast was as magnificent and meticulously manicured as the front. Beyond the flowering lilac bushes that bordered the garden, the pointed volcanic peak of Mount Agua pierced the hazy mid-morning sky.

After breakfast, Hope and Billy walked down the cobblestone streets in Antigua which had been made consistently smooth from years of cars and people traveling over them. Billy led her past several streets where local artists were creating elaborate mosaics of colored sawdust and flower petals that covered the entire expanse of the streets. Hope was fascinated by the focus and intricate detail the artists were putting into these striking creations, even though they would soon be driven over and scattered in the wind. Billy explained that this form of art represented the impermanence of individual lives on earth.

Each year the artists devoted the entire week before Easter to beautifying the city. Today was Good Friday, and the town square was already filled with people. They had come to see the magnificent, eight-hour parade honoring Jesus' life.

Plaza Mayor was filled with vendors selling their goods. In the open-air market, they displayed knit hats, hand-carved flutes, jade jewelry, wooden sculptures, weavings, hand-woven blankets, traditional Antiguan toys and countless piles of beautiful molas.

Hope and Billy stood on the worn stone staircase leading up to the city hall building. From where they stood, they had a good view of the intricately carved stone Catedral Metropolitana. The church was a fascinating combination of Catholicism and primitive ritual worship. From the open doors Hope heard the slow, rolling, monotone voice of an Indian priest chanting prayers in an ancient dialect. She was mesmerized by the sound. Copal incense puffed in waves through the open doors. A slow-moving line of people funneled in the front doors. The women were dressed in brightly colored, hand-appliquéd blouses and hand-woven, wrap-around skirts. The men were slightly less festive in dress. Most wore khaki pants with embroidered shirts.

The Honduran people were much shorter than Hope, so she looked over their heads and viewed them as a whole. The sea of black hair oscillated in a rhythmical dance, moving toward the beckoning prayers and dizzying incense.

Immediately after Mass, the band started signaling the beginning of the renowned Good Friday Procession. The earth began to quiver at the same time, almost as if it had been planned. The ground shook, and Hope watched the hard-packed earth roll as a shockwave passed through. The crowd and the band momentarily hushed. The tremor subsided as quickly as it came. Behind the cathedral, a large cloud of smoke rose above Fuego, one of the many volcanic mountains adjoining the highland valley. Bit by bit the music and conversations resumed, as if the small earthquake had never happened.

The procession continued with Roman centurions and cavalry, self-flagellating penitents, statues of saints on floats, high Catholic officials, brass bands playing dismal funereal marches and a large statue of the Virgin Mary. For the first hour, Hope and Billy watched the parade pass before them. Before it was over they began to wander through the Plaza. Late in the afternoon the parade concluded with a mammoth float of a black Christ carrying a cross. It swayed from side to side as over eighty bearers shifted back and forth to create the illusion of Jesus walking.

That night Hope was disappointed when there was no email from Logan. She assumed he should be arriving in Puerto Plata momentarily. She knew he probably wouldn't be able to send an email late in the day since she took their laptop and he would have to find an Internet café. But still, she was disappointed.

Can't Drop a Sunken Treasure

LOGAN PERCHED ON THE MOPED FENDER behind Lupe. Slowly they proceeded down the trail toward the beach. Lupe swerved back and forth, dodging the pigs that had once more resumed their cool places in the mud puddles.

The federales once again escorted Logan to his boat, asserting their meager but potentially dangerous authority.

Quickly Logan pulled anchor and started sailing toward Puerto Plata. He put the wind vane to work steering the boat, so he could put a reef in the mainsail. With the boat comfortably sailing toward his next waypoint, Logan went below deck, put on dry clothing and prepared dinner for himself. He checked the charts, logged his position on a paper chart and drew a rhumb line to follow.

The ride through the night was rough and wet. Logan busied himself reading the cruising guide for Puerto Plata and the entrance to Bay Side Marina. By three a.m. Logan had difficulty staying awake, so he brought an egg timer out into the cockpit. Snuggling into the beanbag wedged in under the dodger on the leeward side of the boat, he allowed himself to close his eyes. He knew the timer would awaken him every ten minutes, so he could scan the horizon for ships as *Elmo* guided *Ladyhawke* along the northern coast of the Dominican Republic.

At dawn he was glad to see the sun; in the light, it was easier for him to stay awake. From lack of sleep Logan knew he was not as coordinated as usual, so he very carefully maneuvered himself around the heaving vessel. He worked his way to the bow, making sure all the lines were organized and in place as he went. At the bow he retied the anchor on its roller and tightened the lines that held the dinghy to its chocks. Logan played with the angle of the headsail to pick up as much speed as possible. He was hoping to be in Puerto Plata before dark, and to do that he had to squeeze every quarter knot he could out of the wind.

With the sails down, he carefully maneuvered *Ladyhawke*

under engine power through the large cargo freighters in the big commercial port. He docked at the transient pier with his yellow quarantine flag flying, since the Immigration and Customs Offices had already closed for the day. Logan could see the sun quickly approach the horizon. Glistening orange and pink clouds scattered the sky. The vaguely undulating, inky bay reflected colors back, in circles of turquoise and lavender. The lazy water danced and swayed to the orchestrated closing of the day. Logan crawled down below and into the v-berth, where he immediately fell into a deep sleep.

The following morning, he went straight to the Immigration Office. He was never questioned when he presented the official with his Exit Visa—the one with the scratched-out number two and penciled-in number one. From there, he proceeded to the Customs Office and then on to an Internet café. He emailed Hope to let her know he had arrived. He then emailed Max and Tina Short, asking them if they were interested in sailing *Ladyhawke* with him to Guatemala.

Back on the boat Logan hosed the salt water off the deck and straightened the cabin below. That afternoon he returned to the Internet café and found a reply from the Shorts.

Logan,

It is so good to hear from you. We are still in Provo. You won't believe what we've been doing. We've become obsessed with finding either Josephine *or* Elizabeth Anne. *All we've done since you left is do research on the Internet and in the local historical museums. At the Mariner's Museum, we found the glitch in our estimation as to where* Elizabeth Anne *went down. After compiling all the information we have gathered, we now have two new locations where each of the boats might be. We can't be wrong this time.* Josephine *probably went down due north of where we were looking, maybe twenty miles or so. Delaney's boat probably went down west of South Caicos, not southeast. All of our new information is pointing in the same direction. We really think these calculations warrant a look.*

We would love to sail with you to Guatemala. What if you pick us up in Hamilton Bay and we spend one day scoping the new coordinates with your sonar and then we'll take off for Guatemala?

Logan, it would only take you an overnight to get here. We know we're on to something.

–M&T

Logan didn't even have to think about it. He shot an email back.

I'm on my way. All I need to do is fill my water tanks. I should be there by noon tomorrow. Bring air tanks if you can.

Logan couldn't resist. He would rather be looking for things on the bottom of the ocean than doing almost anything else. He knew Hope would understand; besides he was sure he could still make it to Guatemala before Hope was ready to leave for the United States. He quickly sent her an email telling her of his new plans. He told her if she needed to leave for Baltimore before he got to Guatemala, he would soon follow.

Barely able to contain his excitement, Logan ran from the Internet café to the dock and ripped the water hose out of the lazerette to fill his tanks. Then he remembered he had to check out of the country. He grabbed his boat papers and passport and ran back to the Immigration Office, knowing it was about to close for the day. When he got to the office, there were two people in line in front of him. From excitement, he pranced in place, not able to stand still.

Once the paperwork was complete, he went back to *Ladyhawke* and finished filling the water tanks. With his chores done, he immediately untied from the dock and was gone. Again Logan sailed through the night and into the following day, arriving at Hamilton Bay mid-afternoon. Max and Tina were waiting at the dock when he sailed into the bay. They anxiously waved to him before he even anchored. After Logan secured the hook, he stood on the bow of the boat as Max and Tina called to him with excitement. They impatiently watched Logan's time-consuming process of taking the dinghy off the bow of the boat and bringing it back to the stern where he lowered the outboard engine onto *Sharpy*'s transom.

When Logan finally made it to the dock, Max immediately

handed him their newly bought luggage and six rented air tanks. Once again, it was too late in the day to take off for Max's new charted locations. If they did, they would arrive around midnight and have to motor in circles until it was light enough to use the sonar.

Before dawn the following morning, the three set out for the newly circled area on the chart where Max presumed *Josephine* had gone down. The seas were barely rippling, reflecting a mirage of colors from the kaleidoscope of fragmented blues, yellows, pinks and lavenders in the early morning sky. By noon they lowered the sails so Logan could maneuver back and forth over the designated area using *Ladyhawke*'s small auxiliary engine to turn in tight circles meticulously covering the area of anticipation.

Logan intently watched the sonar monitor for suspicious-looking shapes. By mid-afternoon, they had found a prospective formation in the midst of coral at about eighty feet. Logan traversed over it several times while Tina looked over his shoulder at the screen. Coming to a complete stop, Logan said, "Well, we've got the gear."

While Tina kept the boat positioned on top of the formation, Logan and Max put on dive gear and got in the water. In the water they could hear the approaching engine of a motorboat, so they quickly dove down out of the way of the prop. What would a boat be doing out here? Logan wondered as he descended.

From behind the wheel, Tina watched the small dive boat come toward *Ladyhawke*. The driver was behind the center console, obscured from her view, but when the boat got within shouting distance Tina screamed, "I have divers in the water! Please stay back!" and as she said this, a man came up from below deck and briefly looked in her direction before he ducked down below again. Tina got a quick glimpse of his completely shaved head with a large tattoo on the crown.

Within the split second he was in view, she knew he was the mysterious man she had seen at the bar in South Caicos two weeks earlier—the man who appeared to be listening to their conversation about shipwrecks. Now she thought she could also place him as the same man she remembered seeing in the Mariners Museum last week. Always, in the past, he wore a baseball cap covering the tattoo. The man steering the boat also seemed to be trying to stay out of her view, so she couldn't get a good look at him. Instead of turning to leave the area, which would have been the most logical thing to do, the driver put the boat in reverse and backed away from *Ladyhawke*. That made it impossible for Tina to get a good look at the driver or the boat's name on the transom. But, as Tina watched them back away, a small wave tilted the powerboat to the side. Tina could just barely see the boat driver. He was a black man who appeared to have a large streak of blond in his dreadlocks.

Now Tina's skin crawled; a wave of uneasiness washed over her. "Come on you guys don't stay down too long," she said in a hushed voice to herself, wishing Logan and Max would hurry. Her apprehension was growing.

Finally when the men surfaced and boarded *Ladyhawke*, Tina immediately told them about the boat and the weird way they backed away to keep her from seeing the transom.

"Who are you talking about?" Logan asked when she told him about the strange man who kept reappearing.

"Well, I keep seeing the same guy," Tina answered. "I saw him when we were in the Mariners Museum in Provo day before yesterday. I assumed he was just another tourist who looked familiar. That's when I remembered seeing him at the table next to us at Caicos Corner the first day we were all there talking about searching for the wreck. Remember we had the charts laid out on the table? He was sitting at the table next to us by himself. I caught him looking our way several times. That day I thought he looked like someone trying not to look interested in what we were saying. But you know, I just bet he was."

"Why didn't you mention him earlier?" Logan asked.

"I guess I was hoping I was wrong and just being paranoid," she replied.

"If we can lose him now we're fine because the boat on the bottom is not what we're looking for," Logan responded as he looked with his binoculars through the clear Eisenglass windshield on the dodger. He was trying to hide himself behind the canvas, so the men on the powerboat couldn't see him looking their direction with binoculars. By now they had already retreated about a quarter mile to the north. Through the binoculars, Logan could tell both men were sitting in the back of the boat looking away from *Ladyhawke*. Logan could see the black man's hair clearly now.

With wide eyes he quickly lowered the binoculars and turned to Max and Tina with a jerk.

"The black man is Goldie Locks," Logan quietly said.

"Who's Goldie Locks?" Max questioned, confused.

"He's the guy who took me lobstering the first day you and Tina went to Provo. He knew I was looking for shipwrecks because I asked him about female pirates. It all fits. Was it after Hope and I left for the Dominican that you saw the other guy at the museum?" Logan asked, turning to Tina.

"Yes," she said as she placed the events on a timeline in her mind.

"Let's go to the other circled area to get away from them and hope they don't follow us," Max suggested.

Logan agreed, so they raised the sails to make it look like they were finished scanning with the sonar and sailed southwest with the wind, trying to lead the others diagonally away. Logan intentionally sailed *Ladyhawke* off course until he couldn't see the powerboat any longer and then turned north. An hour and a half later they were scanning with the sonar again right on top of Max's hopeful waypoint. Luck was with them, and by early evening they had spotted one more particularly well-defined shape on the monitor. They flipped for the dive, and Logan and Tina won. Max had to stay on board and man the boat.

Once in the water, Logan quickly determined the configured shapes that had been displayed in the sonar monitor were broken parts of a boat. It was often difficult to make out the ship's sections when searching for wooden shipwrecks. The wooden hull and deck would have long since disintegrated and rotted away, leaving only coral in the shape of the hull along with its metal fittings. From closer observation it became obvious to Logan this was a wooden shipwreck, the material of either *Josephine* or *Elizabeth Anne*.

At the forward end of what appeared to be the bow section, Logan noticed a five- or six-foot long accumulation of coral. It was shaped similar to that of a canon. As he got closer, his inspection revealed a very distinct shape. He could make out the features of a face. Logan carefully scraped away the hardened sand that covered the lower part of the face and neck section and revealed the outlines of two large breasts. Right between the breasts was another face. The large figurehead forged out of metal, had fallen off the bow of the boat and lay half buried in coral and sand. Logan took dozens of pictures with his underwater camera.

When Tina saw what Logan was taking pictures of, she almost choked trying to tell him that it was exactly the same image as the drawings at the Mariners Museum of *Josephine*'s figurehead. She quickly pulled out her underwater slate from a pocket in her BCD and wrote, "THAT BELONGS TO *JOSEPHINE*."

Logan looked at her in bewilderment, not knowing for sure how she knew. She pointed toward the surface. He agreed, and they rose. The second they surfaced Tina spit out her regulator and quickly told him about the drawings she and Max had seen in the Mariners Museum in Provo.

Back on the boat all three could barely contain themselves. Max couldn't believe what he was hearing. As Logan detailed the second face carved into the chest of the first, Max's eyes just about bugged out of his head.

"Logan, you are describing the picture we found in an old recreated log of *Josephine*'s. The two female faces were of Mary Read and Anne Bonny."

Max, who kept his cool, quiet demeanor at all times, couldn't believe himself; he had never been this excited. "I've seen drawings of what you're describing! I know it's them. I have to go down," Max said.

Using his binoculars, Logan scanned the horizon for boats. When he was sure there weren't any within view, he buddied with Max while Tina kept the boat above the wreck. At the base of the wreck, Max and Logan poked through the silt trying to come up with any other evidence of a treasure, hull identification, or something they could take to the surface. Most of the boat was either buried or missing. The ocean currents moved things around constantly.

After prodding around for as long as their air would allow, Max and Logan surfaced and crawled back onto *Ladyhawke*.

"Now what?" Logan asked with a mischievous smile. "Should we head over to your other coordinates and see if we can find *Elizabeth Anne*, or should we stick to one find at a time and try to figure out how to get my submarine out here?"

"I have no doubt that we have found *Josephine*," Max said emphatically.

"It's got to be," Tina agreed.

"So, I think we should get the submarine," Max continued.

While deep in thought, Logan's eyes stared out to sea. He nodded his head in agreement while thinking of the logistics of meeting up with Hope and Billy in Guatemala and getting his sub to South Caicos from the Florida Keys.

"Okay. This is what I think we should do. First we sail *Ladyhawke* back to Provo where I can leave her in a secure marina. I'll fly to Guatemala to meet up with Hope. Maybe she has found the cure for Drew. I have to go with her to Baltimore for a few days." Max nodded along.

"I will then meet you in Florida to get the sub." Logan's power-boat *Maggie* was equipped to transport the submarine. She could carry enough fuel to go from Marathon to Nassau. From Nassau, they planned to bump down the Bahamian chain of islands, filling the fuel tanks in Rum Cay before traveling on to Provo.

"There can't really be a valuable treasure down there," Max said, throwing his hands in the air, letting his pessimism return. "That's a lot of work."

"Sure there can," both Logan and Tina chimed together.

"Max, just the figurehead from *Josephine* is worth the effort," Logan laughed at Max's lack of ability to see the value of what they had found. Tina nodded.

"Maybe you should just forget about it," Logan continued. "I'll go get the sub by myself and see what's down there."

"I'll come," Tina volunteered.

That's all it took. Max admitted it was worth the search. He was in.

Turning *Ladyhawke* into the wind, they once again raised

the sails and headed for Provo to return the rented air tanks and securely dock *Ladyhawke* at the marina. As they were sailing, they spotted the dive boat that approached them during their dive. It was now anchored over the exact place the fiberglass wreck was located. Through the binoculars, the boat appeared to be without passengers. That night in Provo, they docked *Ladyhawke* at Turtle Cove Marina.

The following morning, they returned the empty air tanks to the PADI dive shop. While Tina was at the bakery buying a loaf of bread, she again saw the same man she'd seen at the bar in South Caicos, at the Mariners Museum a few days ago, and on the motorboat yesterday. He was standing on the corner across the street from the bakery when Tina emerged. Turning from her he quickly started walking down the street. At first, Tina was going to ignore him. But she couldn't make herself. She ran down the street toward him shouting, "Hey you, we keep running into each other."

He began to walk faster, while saying, "No. No, you must be mistaken. I've never met you before."

This only made Tina more certain it was the same man. There was something very creepy about the way he showed up all the time. He felt sinister.

Tina rushed back to *Ladyhawke*. Logan was packing for his trip to Guatemala when Tina arrived. She told him at once about the man on the street corner.

"Where's Max?" Logan asked. He hurried into the cockpit, hoping to see Max in the immediate vicinity. "We have to go get something off of *Josephine*," he whispered to Tina. "We need to claim the wreck and register it as a legal find before someone else does." He knew it was possible that creepy man had all of their coordinates. Not seeing Max, Logan turned to Tina and continued, "I'll go rent some more tanks. You go find Max. Meet me back here as soon as you find him."

"I think he's at the museum." Tina stated over her shoulder as she fled down the dock.

Logan and the Shorts once again headed out to sea, zigzagging in the opposite direction from *Josephine*'s coordinates to confuse anyone who might be following them. It took the rest of the day and most of the night to get back to the site.

Once in the water at daybreak, Max helped Logan poke around in the sand and silt along the base of the wreck. They were trying to come up with something—anything—that would officially declare their find. Nothing appeared. Almost an hour passed. Just before their air tanks were to run out, they surfaced and discussed trying to possibly raise the figurehead. But Logan didn't have the tools or the ability to preserve it once it was out of the water and no longer under pressure.

"It would be a shame to bring it to the surface and allow it to decompose just because we didn't preserve it properly," Logan told the Shorts. "I wonder if pictures of the figurehead would be enough."

"At the moment, that is all we have," Max replied.

"I wish I could talk to a friend of mine in Miami who works at the National Mariners Research Department. He would know what we need to claim this wreck," Logan said.

"Well, let's call him," Max said descending into the salon. With a big smile he unzipped his travel bag. Wiggling his eyebrows, he continued. "I knew there was a reason I bought this satellite phone in Provo last week."

"A satellite phone? Where'd you get that?" Logan asked as Max brought it up into the cockpit and turned it on.

"Oh, our daughter begged us to get one when she heard we lost our boat. So, I bought it at the cell phone store. Watch. It works great." They both watched the screen on the phone as it picked up enough satellites to make a call. When it was connected, Max handed it to Logan who dialed Miami.

"Randy Hilbens," a strong, confident voice answered into the phone receiver.

"Dolf, is that you? It's me, Logan."

"Logan the Great. Well, I'll be damned. Where are you?"

"I'm in Provo."

"How's the life of a bum?" Dolf asked jokingly.

Logan ignored the tease. "I've got a serious question."

Lowering his voice, Dolf whispered, "What happened, Logan? Are you okay?"

"Yeah, yeah. I'm great. What do I need to claim a wreck in the Turks and Caicos Islands? Do I have to bring an artifact to the surface like we do in U.S. waters or can I claim it with pictures of a distinguishing piece of the boat like in the Bahamas?"

"Photos will do in most of the Caribbean islands. Give me a moment while I look up the Turks and Caicos Islands specifically. The photo has to be dated and you have to be in the picture with the artifact. It might even help if you take your submersible GPS in with you and get a picture of the location of the object. Here it is. Yeah, a photo will do. What did you find?" he asked eagerly.

"Well, I can't tell you over the phone. I really need to keep this hushed. Don't let on to anyone I might have found something. We think we are being followed. I'll bring you up to date as soon as I can. I've got to go. Thanks."

"Only Logan the Great can go on vacation and find a valuable shipwreck. Be careful, buddy. Call me when you can."

"Rock n roll!"

"Say hi to my favorite princess."

"Hope's in Guatemala. But that's a whole other story." And he hung up.

"Okay, a picture will do," Logan said, handing the phone back to Max. "What a great buy."

This time Logan and Tina descended with full air tanks. Logan took meticulous pictures depicting the boat remnants and figure-head in every combination he could imagine. Then they surfaced to *Ladyhawke* with what they hoped was enough evidence to establish their rights to the wreck. Just in case, Logan decided to hold onto the pictures of the GPS headings until the last. Maybe the other photographs would be sufficient.

Refuge in Guatemala

SATURDAY MORNING HOPE WAS GLAD TO SLEEP late again. She met Billy at the bed and breakfast lobby and they leisurely drank coffee on the front porch. Small birds and bees flew around the flowering shrubs just beyond the veranda railing.

After touring a couple of old buildings in town, Billy and Hope walked to the Plaza and found a quaint open-air café to have lunch.

Just as they were finishing their meal, Billy looked down the street. "Finally," he said. "Look who's coming,"

Hope turned and looked in the direction Billy was pointing.

"Hey, he made it," she said, standing to get Rocky's attention. "Rocky," she called, waving.

He smiled with relief when he saw her.

"I was worried," Billy said, giving Rocky a firm hug.

"I know. It has taken longer than expected," Rocky replied. "What are you doing here, girl?" He gave Hope a hug.

"I need Grandfather's help. My brother's really sick."

"Grandfather is really acting weird," Rocky said, expressing his concerns. "He's been talking to the spirits a lot more than usual. He seems extremely distracted. I think something is up but I'm not sure what. We need to get back as soon as possible."

"Oh, it's great to see you," Billy said.

"I was surprised to hear you were in town," he continued, as he hugged Hope again. "They told me at the inn."

"I'm hoping Grandfather can help," she said.

"I'm hoping he can talk with humans when we get back to the cave. He's been off in a different world," Rocky said.

Before leaving for the cave, Hope checked her email one more time. She was relieved to read the message from Logan; he had safely made it to Puerto Plata. She still didn't know that he had sailed back to Hamilton Bay. She emailed him, letting him know she was off to the cave and, hopefully, to find a cure for Drew. She called Drew's hospital room and talked to her mother, briefly letting her know her tentative schedule.

Billy and Hope followed Rocky through the dense jungle as the sun's light transitioned to the west and diminished. The sounds around them shifted from day creatures to the nocturnal ones. The last mile they walked, Billy and Hope tried to stay close behind Rocky so they could see the trail in the illumination from the flashlight he carried. Hope was glad she packed lightly. She had left her laptop at the bed and breakfast to lighten her load even more. Everything she took fit neatly in her small backpack.

As they walked, Rocky tried to fill them in on the last day the Corn People spent in the Copan Valley.

It seems like life had shifted into an almost dream-state ever since Yellow Spotted Eagle came into Grandfather's hut the afternoon he was tending Swinging Squirrel Monkey's ankle. She told him the colonel had entered our village and wanted to speak to him. Grandfather stood and turned toward me.

"It is time, Praying Dove," he said, looking deep into my eyes, eyes he had come to rely on for wisdom. Sadness filled Grandfather's soul and radiated from every cell in his body. He knew something awful was about to happen. He turned toward the entrance of his hut knowing he couldn't put off the inevitable. He ducked his head and stepped high to exit through the small raised doorway.

I looked over at Yellow Spotted Eagle's face, pale from fear. Without words I took her hand in mine and followed Grandfather. By the fire pit in the village center the colonel was waiting for Grandfather. Mat Head also waited; he had been summoned to translate the colonel's Spanish into Chol for Grandfather. Colonel Luis and his assistant had arrived on ATVs. Their thin, well-toned bodies were clad in military uniforms, and a large machine gun was strapped across each of their chests.

"What do they want?" Grandfather asked Mat Head as we all watched in anticipation.

"I'm not sure. They were waiting for you," he said to Grandfather in Chol.

"We told you to leave. This land is no longer yours," Colonel Luis said.

Mat Head translated for Grandfather.

"This is our home. This is the land we have chosen and the gods have agreed by granting us the ability to provide enough food for our people to live," Grandfather told Colonel Luis. "This is where we have lived for more generations than anyone can remember."

News of the colonel's arrival had spread throughout our village and as Grandfather spoke, the men of the tribe were gathering behind the nearby huts, each armed with a bow and arrows.

Colonel Luis puffed his chest out, raised his voice and said in an unsympathetic and demanding tone, "This land has never been yours. It belongs to the State. Governor Lopez has now sold it. You must leave before dawn tomorrow. You have no choice. If you are still here in the morning, we will arrest you for trespassing. You will all be thrown in prison."

As Mat Head translated, the warriors of the tribe stepped out from behind the surrounding huts and gathered behind Grandfather as his support. Feeling threatened, both Colonel Luis and his assistant raised their guns. In one clean swipe of his hand, Grandfather knocked the colonel's gun to the ground, which prompted the colonel's assistant to start panic firing into the crowd. Of course our warriors fired back immediately, killing the assistant with their arrows. In the mayhem the colonel disappeared running into the jungle. Beneath the dust of the commotion lay the dead body of Colonel Luis's assistant, two machine guns and our tribe's member, Deer Eyes. No one moved. We were in shock. We could not remember the last time there had been violent human bloodshed in our village. We were lucky Deer Eyes' blood was the only blood from our tribe to seep into the dirt that day.

With dread in our hearts we knew we must leave our home. Without speaking, Grandfather went directly to his hut. Throughout the village we could all hear him scream. Raising his hands to the heavens, he vigorously shook his rattles. For twenty minutes he roared in his singsong voice before his arms fell to his sides and he was silent. Tears rolled down his cheeks and he bowed his head to the floor, touching his hands and his lips to the fur covering the dirt beneath him. In complete silence the rest of the tribesmen ran from one hut to the next, gathering up all the necessities and precious possessions they could carry. I could feel the tension of fear in the air. Panic raced through our village as we frantically readied to flee.

Grandfather emerged from his hut and announced it was time to leave our beloved homeland that had protected us for so many seasons. He told us the ancestors had shown him the path we must take. It would take us up and over the mountains into Guatemala. He said it was time for 'the Shifting of the Wind' to take place. The shift would take place in Antigua. He had to go there. He had no choice. He personally had to be in Antigua for the shift. This was his path, and those who felt it was their path also were welcome to come with him. He knew not everyone in our tribe would follow him to Guatemala. Some would stay behind. The Corn People would split for the first time in hundreds of years.

A few had already begun to disperse in their own direction as Grandfather spoke to those remaining.

That night the waning moon rose, golden and great on the horizon. Darkness pulled the animals of the night from their slumber. And the Corn People scattered in silence into the jungle, dragging branches behind us to scratch the dirt and erase the tracks of our soft leather xanabs.

When the moon was high in the sky, we gathered on the hill across the river, beyond the sacred burial grounds. We were careful to stay beneath the jungle foliage and out of sight. Grandfather knelt and prayed in silence for several minutes as the remaining tribal members made it through the jungle. We laid Deer Eyes high on an altar built out of branches that we gathered along the way.

I could already see a change in the devotion of the tribe. Its cohesiveness had begun to diminish. We were heading into an uncertain future, creating great anxiety and uneasiness in all the tribe's people. As Grandfather beckoned our ancestors to care for Deer Eyes' soul, I could hear the eerie scream of a jaguar far off in the distance. The jaguar seemed to have meaning for our departure; he was voicing the pain we were all feeling, but couldn't release for fear of being heard.

In a low-hanging branch, an owl quietly hooted, signaling us to move on, to move away from Deer Eyes so the owl could guide his spirit to the afterworld. We continued on our new journey in faith, following Grandfather's guidance. We crept through the dense, dark undergrowth beneath the canopy of branches that sheltered our path. We stayed in the shadows, dodging the moonbeams where they filtered through the canopy. I followed closely behind Grandfather. I could feel sparks of energy fly from the tips of his long gray hair as the night breeze blew it back toward me. In the miniscule tracks left by his adeptly prancing feet, he left a trail of himself behind in the valley where he was born. All night we walked in an attempt to distance ourselves from the colonel and his men, who were sure to come looking for us.

It was a relief to see daybreak the following morning and to know we made it through the night. The quiet of dawn was pierced by the incessant chirping of orioles as they foraged for seeds. Mockingbirds jumped from limb to limb above our heads, welcoming the new day with playful tunes. We drank the morning dew from the crooks and hollows of the trees.

By the time the first hues of dawn penetrated the forest, we had traveled a great distance from our village and were now in an unfamiliar land. Even still, we were constantly watching over our shoulders, fearing the threat of Colonel Luis. Grandfather quickly progressed, never seeming to falter or question the direction he was leading. By midday the forest was once again silent, and the intense heat of the day drained the energy from our flesh and dominated its power over us, making me momentarily question our survival.

We ate berries and seeds along the way, unable to stop and cook the maize we had brought or the rabbits we could shoot as we went. We chewed on the new shoots of the cedar trees and sucked the nutrients from the dried venison and rabbit we brought from home.

My legs began to ache, but I knew it would be pointless to complain because everyone's legs must also be aching. When I removed my xanabs to soak my feet in a stream during our mid-afternoon break, I noticed deep blisters on my heels. I was so tired, I felt like my mind had stopped thinking. I only occasionally thought about keeping my feet moving forward, following in the swift and skillful footsteps of Grandfather. He never seemed to tire; he was so consumed in his conversations with our spirit ancestors that he barely noticed the continual motion with which his body moved. The young children in the tribe needed assistance. Most adults struggled to carry a child along with their meager belongings. Very little was said to one another; we just continued to move forward.

As the colors began to mute in the waning evening sunlight, the intense whirr of locusts and katydids filled my mind, and I no longer missed listening to my own words bounce around in my thoughts. My stomach growled. It was time for our evening meal, but Grandfather did not hesitate in his progression forward.

In the shadows of night, the outline of another owl appeared above me in a Spanish cedar tree. As I passed beneath, it let out in a haunting cry. I feared its message would carry me to the underworld and the passing of life, so I looked away and ignored its call. Off in the distance I heard the cracking of dried leaves. For quite some time, the noise seemed to parallel the animal trail we were now following.

Another cry of a jaguar stopped me in my tracks. For a few moments no one moved. Even our breathing quieted. The animal's cry reminded us to be quieter. Slowly we continued. Occasionally I saw glowing red dots in the brush when moonbeams filtered through the canopy and lit upon an animal's eyes.

We traveled continuously, hiding deep in the jungle undergrowth to take short naps only during the day. On the third day of walking, we stopped when the sun was high above our heads. The creatures of the forest were all resting in the intense afternoon heat. From a small, clear stream running down the steep crevasse in the hillside, we replenished our water gourds and cooled our aching feet.

At the moment, we were not feeling the immediate threat of being followed. So, we gathered wood and built a small fire, cooking flat bread and maize stew with fresh rabbit that the men had snared in the woods. After eating, we napped for several hours before Grandfather instructed us to resume moving. I lined my xanabs with soft moss and lemon grass to cool the heat in the oozing blisters on my feet. I began to hear the women in our tribe engage in conversation as they walked. Several of the children began to carry their own weight and walk on their own. Grandfather started to pray and chant aloud instead of walking on in silence. We were now focused on where we were going, no longer fearing what might be tracking us.

I could feel unshed tears putting pressure on the back of my eyes. There was heaviness in my heart and hollowness in my soul that I couldn't discard. Grandfather was so absorbed in his own thoughts and his own process that I didn't talk much with him.

The motion of the forest around us was unnerving again as darkness fell. The smells of wild animals at night kept us gathered together for protection. We passed through an area where the urine of a male jaguar hung heavy in the damp night air. Feeling our way through the thick underbrush, scraping our legs on the branches and thorns, we heard Grandfather speak loudly to the spirit world. It seemed they were asking him to do something he didn't want to do. Most of the time he went along with their desires, but now he stopped walking, stamped his feet and shouted, "No, I am not ready. I will not do what you are asking." After Grandfather listened to the spirits' voices for a moment, voices I was not privy to, he began walking again and talking quietly as if resigning to a task he knew he must do.

Finally we neared the border of Guatemala. Grandfather gathered us together, instructing those of us who had passports to walk to the nearest border patrol and cross into the country legally. Grandfather would lead the rest into the jungle where they would sneak across the border. I headed for the border patrol station with Falling Rock, his wife, their daughter and Moon Shadow. Mat Head, his family and Moon Jaguar went as a group to the border patrol separate from us. We didn't want to pass across the border as a large group and draw attention. We each carried our small bundles, with the only possessions we now had. I was overly alert to my surroundings, feeling cautious and exceedingly protective of those I was traveling with. I began to feel responsible for the well-being of the members in our tribe, and without Grandfather's immediate guidance, I took on the role of leadership.

"Follow me," I said, trying to lead with confidence.

At the border there was a long line of cars being searched. When we approached, it appeared they were looking for something or someone in particular. We did not know who or what. We were praying it wasn't us. The small buildings at the border were rundown and dirty. Nothing grew in the hard-packed dirt or the cement that covered the ground. All vegetation had been completely trampled away long ago. Arrows pointed the way to a building where declaration papers needed to be filled out and presented along with our passports. When we entered the declaration building there was a large poster on the wall asking for the whereabouts of Roaring River, who was wanted for the murder of Private Manuel Chavez, officer in the Honduran military.

"Murder!" we gasped, and then averted our eyes to the floor trying not to attract attention.

When we caught up with Grandfather and the rest of the tribe, I told them that he was being blamed for Manuel Chavez's death. Grandfather shrugged it off. On he pressed toward the cave. He was driven to keep moving like I had never seen before. He had a strength that seemed to come from beyond him. Frequently he spoke out loud. He looked straight ahead, never questioning the direction he was going.

At noon on the seventeenth day of walking, Grandfather led us directly to the entrance of a large cave hidden behind thick brush. Until Grandfather ducked behind the thicket and disappeared into the cave, I couldn't see the entrance. Just inside we lit torches. We found one large room with several smaller coves, like fingers on a palm. It was an old cavern that had been carved out of the ground by an underground waterway that still ran along one wall. In the center of the main cavern we lit a small fire in a used pit. Smoke was released through the small opening in the ceiling. For the first time since leaving the Copan Valley, we began to relax.

In the center of the cavern, Grandfather stood and turned his face to the ceiling. As we all watched, he was illuminated by the sunlight coming in the hole above the fire. A single beam lit Grandfather like a spotlight on stage. Lowering his gaze to take in the tribe members who gathered around him, he held his arms out gesturing an all encompassing embrace.

"I come before you with a message from beyond. The time is upon us to observe the world anew, my sons and daughters, children of the Corn People. I stand before you with a heavy heart, knowing there is no return for me. The path has brought us to the flowing river of life we must journey down. The beginning has come to an end.

You, as a tribe, must start anew and wander the earth looking for your place upon it. I have seen the seeds sprout, the plants grow tall, the kernels fill, and now new seeds need to be planted before they are scattered by the wind in every direction the gods have created.

"Walk gently, my children. The shadows protect the vulnerable ones until they are strong and can create shadows themselves. I shall always be looking over you. Go in peace. Mix with the other seeds of the world. We will all be together soon."

Behind Grandfather, Yellow Spotted Eagle and Jaguar Lily stood clutching each other's hands while silent tears rolled down their cheeks. I looked to the eyes of those around me and felt, for the first time, that I was alone—alone in the midst of my family. No one would return my gaze. I saw distance from each and every one's soul. I felt for the most part we had already separated. My heart ached for Grandfather, knowing that he knew, better than the rest of us, what the outcome would be for our tribe.

In my sorrow I heard Grandfather speak again, as if he were answering my fears.

"Do not feel isolated and alone in this time of need. It is important that you unite and stay as a strong whole. The leadership that awaits you is powerful. Do not question their knowledge. 'The Bald Skeleton' is your friend. Look for him where you least expect."

As Grandfather said this last statement, people started mumbling to each other about a bald skeleton, wondering to whom he was referring. Memories flooded my mind, as I remembered all the conversations Grandfather and I had over the years about "The Bald Skeleton."

Becoming One with the Corn People

HOPE COULDN'T IMAGINE ASKING ROARING
River for his attention when the Corn People needed everything
he had to give. When she had left *Ladyhawke* just days earlier it
seemed like she was embarking on the greatest quest in the world.
She was off to find the cure for Drew; instead, she found herself
hiding out in a secluded cave in a third-world country, with illegal
aliens whose chief was wanted for murdering a military officer in
another country. She could barely believe her predicament. Yet, she
knew she needed to be with the tribe during their struggle. She also
knew she needed their help.

Billy and Hope followed close behind Rocky. They traversed
back and forth across the face of the steep hill. They approached
a large thicket of cat claw bushes on the side of the mountain.
Rocky pulled the brush away from the rock face. Behind the brush
they each squeezed into a narrow crack in the earth. The flashlight
illuminated a small passageway. Their shadows seemed grotesque
and misshapen, reflected on the rocks. Hunched over, they walked
down a short tunnel. Around a sharp corner they popped out into
a large cave. In silence, the Corn People were preparing sleeping
pallets and a small dinner. One by one, they recognized Billy and
came to his side for a hug.

When Moon Jaguar saw her son, she hurried to him, giving him
a warm, fleshy embrace. She closed her eyes and sighed, rocking
him back and forth. She was content and filled with relief that her
first-born son was safe and with her again.

"Where's Father?" she asked, speaking her native tongue.

"He couldn't come with me. He will be in Antigua next week,"
Billy replied in Chol. "Dad has contacted his friend, the Senator of
Indiana. He is hoping to pull some strings with the U.S. Embassy
in Honduras and find out why our land was taken from us and what
we can do to get it back."

"My heart sings. I am so glad you are here," Moon Jaguar said.

"I am glad, too," he replied as he took her in his arms again.

Turning her gaze toward Hope, she asked, "Is this the woman I have been waiting to meet?"

"No, Mom. This isn't Brenda." Switching to English he said, "But I would like you to meet Hope McKnight. You remember Falling Rock and me talking about Hope and her husband, Logan?"

Moon Jaguar nodded her head.

"She has come a very long way to get healing advice from Grandfather," Billy continued. "Her brother is very sick."

Moon Jaguar opened her arms to Hope and said in Chol, "She has a peaceful soul. She also has the gift of seeing. But she does not know how to use it." Hope leaned in and wrapped her arms around Moon Jaguar's shoulders as Moon Jaguar wrapped hers around Hope's waist and rested her cheek to her chest.

Billly smiled. The two were exact opposites to look at. Hope had a light complexion with blue eyes; she was tall, thin, toned and angular, whereas Moon Jaguar was short and round. She was the soft image of the universal mother with dark skin and coal black hair. Her eyes were so black it was impossible to tell where the pupils stopped and the iris began.

I watched the excitement around the newcomers from a distance. While in the arms of Moon Jaguar, Hope's eyes met mine. I could hear her soul purring a warm, opulent cry. Instantly I knew she was the sister I had always longed for. I walked to where they stood and Billy engulfed me in his arms. The sides of our cheeks met with such tenderness I heard myself sigh as I melted in his embrace. Being an only child, I was raised with Billy and Rocky as if they had been my siblings instead of my cousins. Loosening his grip on me and leaning back, he introduced me to Hope.

Hope's eyes did not leave mine even when Billy led her to Grandfather. She also felt our connection.

Looking up at Dancing Wolf, Grandfather whispered, "Drink this." In the middle of the cave Grandfather sat on a fur pallet next to the small fire. His presence seemed much larger than his physical size. In his right hand he held a dried gourd vessel.

"What is it?" Billy asked.

"The brew to make us invisible. Preparation for 'the Shifting of the Wind,'" Grandfather answered.

Without questioning Grandfather further, Billy drank a sip. He then started to hand the gourd to Hope, but Grandfather shook his head no and held his hands out to receive the gourd back.

"Hope's on our side," Billy said.

"I sense that, but she must first drink the cactus root nectar so she can become one with us. In the morning before we leave the cave, she can drink the brew to become invisible for the Shift and also travel in safety."

"Grandfather, Hope's brother is very sick and she wants to know if there is anything you can tell her that might help," Billy explained.

"This I know," he said, closing his eyes and reaching out with his spirit to find Hope's brother. "Your young friend will receive from our tribe what is necessary for her brother to continue on his chosen path. It is not to worry." Grandfather removed a small glass vial from a satchel lying on the ground by his sleeping fur pallet and handed it to Dancing Wolf. "Ask her if she is willing to become one with our tribe."

Billy translated Grandfather's Chol into English for Hope.

Hope was trying to absorb what Grandfather said about Drew. She looked confused as if questioning what Drew's chosen path was. Hope turned to Billy, who was now holding Grandfather's glass vial.

"I guess so," she said, answering Grandfather's question. "I don't really know what becoming one with the tribe is." But Hope trusted Billy.

As Billy led Hope to another fur pallet on the other side of the small fire, Grandfather motioned for me to follow him and guide Hope through the initiation ceremony.

After Hope became comfortable in her surroundings, I instructed her on how to drink the fermented cactus juice. "Face north," I said, pointing to the side wall of the cave. "Take a large mouthful of juice. Swish it around until the bitterness goes away and then swallow."

Hope turned to face away from the fire in the direction I pointed as Billy handed her the glass vial.

Hope took the lid off and smelled the fermented liquid. She looked from my eyes to Billy's before taking a mouth full. She seemed to be following blind faith at this point.

With the first mouthful, the pungent, sour liquid almost gagged her. The scowl on her forehead let me know she wanted to spit it out. I knew the bitterness would slowly subside and she would be able to swallow the juice. I then pointed for Hope to face east. As she turned to the entrance of the cave, I instructed her to take another mouthful. I had her repeat this procedure two more times facing south and then west. Each time she swallowed the juice quicker.

"Now take the vial and sprinkle a few drops in a circle around your feet, moving clockwise. This will assure our ancestors will enlighten you with the proper message tonight."

This act took Hope several moments to complete. It was as if she was moving in slow motion. I then had her lie down on the pallet of furs we had laid on the floor of the cave. Billy sat next to Hope's right shoulder and assured her he would stay with her all night. I sat to her left. Hope had no idea what to expect.

Hope closed her eyes for only a moment before she opened them and looked from me to Billy. She opened and closed them again several times before settling in and keeping them shut.

An hour later, Grandfather sat down next to Dancing Wolf and gently put his hand on Hope's shoulder. She gasped with a startle, being brought back to her awareness of the cave.

"I'm sorry to awaken you, Little Bird. I know it's the middle of your journey, but I felt there was something that needed to shift." Even though Grandfather said this in Chol, Hope could understand him as if he was speaking English.

She struggled to make meaning out of her experience. Words were hard for her to form.

"What are you dreaming?" Grandfather asked.

"Hmm," Hope thought. "At first I felt like I was falling backwards deep into the furs and the ceiling of the cave felt like it was moving further and further away." It was hard for Hope to speak. At times she wasn't even sure if the words were audible, but she knew her message was being conveyed to the three of us. She rolled onto her side and leaned on her elbow so she wouldn't drift back into the other world.

"When I opened my eyes, the tumbling sensation would stop. Well, only at first. Eventually it didn't matter if my eyes were open or not, I kept falling. I felt sick to my stomach.

"The definitions between things became soft," she continued, trying to remember the order of her experience. "There no longer were any sharp edges on anything. I felt myself melting into everything around me. I was no longer a separate entity. I no longer had control of my body. It no longer was mine." She ran her hands across the fur she was lying on, as if the action somehow grounded her.

"The furs on the floor seemed to move; they appeared to be breathing. Then the walls began to move making the room seem like it was shrinking and then expanding, as if the room itself was breathing. The walls..." she said, remembering how real it seemed. As she closed her eyes once more, she again had the sensation of tumbling backwards.

Forcing herself to open them, she tried to pick up where she had left off. "The walls. They seemed to take on a life of their own." Pausing for a few more seconds, Hope tried to remember what happened next.

"Oh, and then those eyes. Those eyes... Some place there was a pair of eyes that at first seemed like they were on your face," she said pointing at Billy. "Then the face got hairy and it seemed like they were the eyes of an animal. I think it was you.

"My sickness faded. The feeling of melting into everything became overwhelming. I started to move and watch myself move without knowing I was making myself move. Oh, it was weird." Hope swallowed several times, trying to clear some of the mucus from her throat.

"Then cold seemed to creep into me, but not through the air. The cold was an entity all its own. It was warm in the cave. My pee wanted out... Yes, I did have the sensation of having to pee, but my pee took on an entity of its own and it wanted out.

"My nose was cold, as if I were an animal. My nose began to run. I remember feeling nervous and jittery. My body began to shake. My skin became cool and when I thought it would be nice to have a blanket, I felt my skin grow a covering like down and feathers. Then wing feathers covered my arms. And I no longer was cold or sinking." Hope swallowed hard, trying to clear more of the mucus from her mouth, and immediately Billy handed her a bottle of water, as if he knew her every need. She drank deeply, feeling the water spreading through her body as it went down her throat and entered each of her cells.

"I was floating at the roof of the cave," she continued. "The wings on my arms lifted me with no effort on my part. I could feel myself gliding or soaring like a bird in a thermal.

"I looked down at you sitting next to my body and your eyes were definitely the eyes of an animal," Hope said directly to Billy. "Fur came out of the sides of your face and down your shoulders. I felt like I was losing any grasp on what I always thought was real, at least what I had been programmed to believe was real."

Grandfather leaned in close to Dancing Wolf and whispered, "She doesn't know you were born to the Wolf Moon?" Again Hope understood Grandfather as if he was speaking English.

They turned their attention back to Hope, as she continued. "Then I was back down here on this fur, and my nose was stuffed up," she said, with a sniff in through her nose so we could hear the congestion in her sinuses. "It was difficult to inhale. There were geometric patterns everywhere. The cave seemed to split into two separate rooms. I sat in one room and viewed the other as if it were a TV.

"My ears filled up with mucus, my nose was plugged; it became harder and harder to breathe. Each breath I took was an effort. I tried to speak, but words would not have been able to explain what was happening. I lay in the dark, on the floor, and beings began to show themselves to me." Hope got excited and sat up to explain the thrill of being surrounded by our ancestors.

"There were hundreds of these beings. They had all left their physical bodies. They were friendly. They tempted me to leave my body and join them. They told me how wonderful it was not to be confined to a body. They had the ability to be here with me, to be in the Florida sun, and to be on the moon. They had the ability to be everywhere at once, to be everywhere at any time, or to be everywhere all the time. All the time or any time is the same thing. It's all now.

"If I stopped thinking about each breath, I actually stopped breathing. I didn't want to die; I was afraid to die. I was afraid that if I left my body and joined the spirits, my physical body would die, and I would never be able to be Hope in this body again. But I was tempted. I continued to concentrate on my breathing. I made myself breathe.

"I was not ready to die yet. They told me death was just leaving physical form as we think we know it. There isn't really a death. The words 'life' and 'death' are words we use to describe change from one reality into the next. To them, the two words were interchangeable. Nothing dies; it just moves to another dimension.

"The spirits then asked me to make a choice—to live or die. So, telepathically I told them, 'I don't want to die.' Immediately my breathing started to come easier. My nose ran, my eyes ran and my ears crackled from the fluid that was building up in them. I felt as if death were not as close.

"The beings realized I was not ready to die and they slowly disappeared. Physical life became more appealing to me.

"And then I heard you calling me off in the distance. I was up above you watching you tap me on the shoulder," Hope said looking at Grandfather as she lay down again. "And then I opened my eyes and you were talking to me.

"I feel . . . I feel more alive. Life seems to have taken on a different meaning or dimension. I'm finally convinced that when I die, it will only be my physical body. 'I' will never die," she said as she rubbed her chest tenderly over her sternum. "The beings told me I saw them as a multitude of beings because my mind could not comprehend one being as massive or as powerful or as All-Knowing. In physical form we just have the illusion we are separate. We are all, always part of the same whole. Always. It's an illusion of being separate. Do you think that is true?" she asked, not really looking for an answer. We did not say anything.

"God, it was strange," she continued.

"The cactus root does not lie," Billy said.

Grandfather stood and said to Dancing Wolf, "There is more," as he walked around the small fire to his fur pallet and sat down.

"Just relax and close your eyes," I said to Hope.

Hope was glad to. I looked into Hope's mind and I could tell she would rather not stay focused enough to communicate in earthly ways. Immediately after closing her eyes, she could hear rain pelting the rock in rhythmic tones by the entrance of the cave. She drifted off as the pitter-patter turned into women singing, and then the rain started to pound with wild stallions galloping. The stallions' nostrils flared scarlet with bursts of steam swirling in the cool predawn air. Then their stomping became the raging surf that drew closer and louder with every beat.

It was a familiar beach, one she had walked down almost every day as a child. She knew each of its crannies and rhythms of change through the seasons. She was aware of each new intruder as it washed ashore. The appearance of the beach was even predictable the morning after a storm. Hope knew the beach as if it were inside her—as if the storms were her emotions churning the sand, preparing for the new arrival of ocean treasures that were the sparks of new ideas.

She heard a rumbling behind her. As she turned to look, seven stallions came running down the beach toward her. They were trampling the ground at the water's edge, kicking and splashing wet sand into the air. As they ran past her, a gust of warm, moist air blew in from the sea. Two hundred yards in front of her, the stallions disappeared around a bend; they vanished as fast as they had come.

In their wake, Hope noticed a small woman sitting on a blanket at the water's edge. Hope wondered how she had not been trampled in the stallions' path. The woman did not even seem to be aware that the stallions had nearly killed her.

Facing out to sea, the woman sat with her legs folded. The wind blew intensely, streaming her long gray hair away from her face. The voracious wind pulled sparks of electricity from her, lighting up the beach grass on the sand dunes behind her.

Hope stopped in her tracks and looked back to the entrance to the cave, but it was gone. She realized there had been music playing, which had quit as the wind stopped blowing. The music had been a perfectly orchestrated prelude that roared in with the wind, the stallions, and the crashing of the sea, and then concluded as they all dissipated. The older woman sat motionless and her hair now barely moved in the light sea breeze. Her eyes were just slightly open and her gaze was unfixed.

The woman appeared to be very old in some respects, but vital and timeless in others. She appeared poised. Hope was mesmerized by her presence.

The sea now calmly lapped at the shore. The tide was coming in slowly, inch-by-inch, as if it were testing the sand for friendliness. The atmosphere had completely shifted from just a moment earlier. There were no stallions, no wind, and no crashing waves.

She was drawn to the seated woman as a magnet is drawn to the North Pole. There was only one direction to go, one choice to be made and that was toward this intriguing person. Hope quietly sat down next to her and looked out into the ocean as her mind melted away. Just as Hope turned to look at the other woman, she turned to look at Hope.

"It is another glorious morning to be," the old woman intoned. Her hushed voice filled the air with resonating warmth as if her words were the heat in the air.

All Hope could do was smile. With delight, she knew she had just met someone very special. The woman telepathically conveyed to Hope that she called herself Running Filly, and she was brought into Hope's awareness to spark Hope's internal knowing.

Without saying a word, Running Filly conveyed, "The waters have risen and changed the way we have known the earth. Where there was once land, there is now water. Where there was once peace, there is now turmoil. Where there was once a system for living with nature, there is now destruction. There are many directions and choices to be made. The ways of the elders no longer flow with the river of life. The young know how to live in this world; with it, their spirits have shifted. They are able to change faster than the wind can swap directions. We must all give in to the rising of a new world. Like the tide, the waters have already risen and made a new shoreline."

After a timeless period of sitting on the blanket next to Running Filly, Hope was filled with knowledge, as if she had been reading an ancient scroll. When the words stopped flooding her mind, the space around her became quiet, and time seemed to stand still once again.

Hope turned her gaze toward Running Filly and became aware that she was observing without judgments. Instead of seeing through defined beliefs, she saw magnificent beauty everywhere she looked. Hope was observing the world, without the preconceived notion of what is. She was fully aware in the present.

"Now is not a reflection of yesterday; it is a new awakening every moment in space." Running Filly's words tumbled into Hope's mind. Hope could see how anything and everything was possible. "A universe with no limits is where we live."

Blinking only once, she fully awoke back in the cave. Grandfather was again sitting next to Dancing Wolf, peacefully communing with him, when he noticed Hope was watching them.

"She has brought us a message, Dancing Wolf," Grandfather said. And then turning to Hope he continued. "Please tell us what you've seen."

And so she did. "Before I opened my eyes back here in this cave, I heard Running Filly say, 'What we don't know about life is just beginning to reveal itself to us. Life is what we make it. It is our projection and our perception. Life is truly what we decide it will be. The spirits only go with you if you walk your path. Choose to awaken in the world instead of sleeping through life.'"

When Hope finished relating her experience, Grandfather stood and bowed to her. He then walked over to his pallet in the center of the cave and sat down. Closing his eyes halfway to see into both worlds, spirit and physical, he quietly spoke to those without form.

"He is pleased with your insight," Billy said.

Hope looked from Billy to me, our eyes locked in a tender embrace. I could feel her looking deep into my soul, as I was hers. Our connection bloomed into something larger than the two of us knew separately.

Slowly she turned her gaze back to Billy. "I have a headache," she noticed.

"Drink the brew to become invisible and your headache will go away," he said, handing her the gourd Grandfather had left for her.

As Hope drank the brew, Billy continued, "Grandfather was married to Horse Woman, who called herself Running Filly. She was a powerful foreseer for the tribe until her death. No one has seen her in a vision since. Many moons ago, she was seen calmly walking to the Grand Falls Cliff and stepping off. Her body was never found. Grandfather knows you were meant to be here with us. You have brought us a message, a message we have long awaited. He has also told me that we must go to Drew as soon as possible. Grandfather will not be going with us. He has asked Praying Dove to accompany you and me to Drew's side. She has agreed." As Billy said this, both he and Hope looked my direction and smiled.

The Unthinkable

GRANDFATHER SAT WITH HIS EYES CLOSED ON a fur pelt next to the small fire. He appeared restless in the dim light. The sounds of him chanting filled the cave with a rich, deep reverberation. Occasionally he accompanied himself with a rattle or drum he chose from the instruments that lay in a semicircle in front of him. Intermittently he stopped chanting and jolted his eyes open into a wide stare, as if startled.

Following the abrupt shift in his behavior, he would raise rattles, and vigorously shake them in the direction that he stared. His intensity captured the attention of all in the cave. And then, just as suddenly, he would close his eyes again and continue the resonating vocals, which echoed off the rock walls and answered his cries. His one-man orchestra was similar to the yipping of a single coyote sounding like an excited pack.

Throughout the day, the Corn People picked up on Grandfather's uneasiness and fidgeted in their own restlessness as they patched xanabs, brewed herbs, and washed clothing. The familiar, sweet smell of flatbread cooking on the fire was altered by the bitter stench of anxiety.

There were many unasked questions as to why Grandfather had brought us to Guatemala. Everyone wanted to know the importance of Antigua, but no one was willing to disrupt Grandfather's process to ask him. Only Jumping Toad, Mat Head's youngest grandson, had the courage to sit down beside Grandfather and wait until he slipped from his trance-like state before asking him, "Why, Grandfather? Why did you bring us to Guatemala?"

Roaring River turned toward Jumping Toad and tenderly replied, "It is my path, Jumping Toad. I did not have a choice. It is what is. I must do my part in 'the Shifting of the Wind.' The Shift will take place in Antigua." Then Grandfather darted his gaze from Jumping Toad toward the ceiling of the cave as he continued, "I have seen the rising of a new star."

Before Jumping Toad could question him more about the Shift,

Grandfather closed his eyes and quietly began to chant again. With this answer, there were only more questions.

A number of the men left the cave mid-morning to go hunting. Out in the open air, they were able to relax without the communal anxiety of the others. Several hours later, they returned with enough rabbit and fowl for a feast. The last of the maize we had brought from Honduras was prepared alongside the game. Everyone somberly ate in silence—everyone except Grandfather. He only stopped chanting long enough to talk out loud to the spirit world, saying things that didn't seem to have any relevance to our current situation.

The passing of the day was registered by the single sunbeam that entered through a small hole in the ceiling of the cave and traversed the floor as the sun journeyed across the sky.

Slowly everyone gathered, sitting in a circle. They felt sure Grandfather would soon speak, and they all wanted their questions answered. I sat next to Hope on the opposite side of the fire from Grandfather. She looked tired. I tenderly held her hand as we exchanged smiles. Nearly an hour passed and Grandfather was still heavy in a trance.

From the other side of Hope, Billy whispered to her, but just loud enough for me to hear. "Praying Dove is willing to help you find the cure for Drew; she knows the way of the healing heart."

Hope looked to me with inquisitive eyes.

"Tell me about Drew," I prompted in a hushed voice.

"He is my brother. He has been infected by an unusual form of bacteria that has caused his body to grow abscesses. His doctor predicts he has less than three weeks to live unless they can find a cure." Hope looked from me to where Grandfather sat rhythmically rocking himself back and forth, tenaciously drumming and chanting.

Hope described him as she last saw him, which was on a rafting trip they had taken together. At the time he appeared strong and tan. From the image she conveyed, I got a very vivid picture of Drew. When I tapped into his spirit, I saw a large lump of darkness, dark as a moonless night, buried deep in his chest. I could see the capsulated cysts pulling energy from his vital organs. I opened my eyes and looked into Hope's. I could tell she also felt Drew's pain and sadness.

"Why is he so troubled?" I asked her.

She shook her head, expressing her lack of knowing.

I knew all he needed was to release the resistance he had in his body. He must allow the life force to circulate with the communal energy of the universe so the heavenly light could speak through him in the manner he was born to express. In the past, the steps of healing were shown to me one at a time as I assisted the one needing my help. At the moment, I could only see how to begin Drew's process of healing, not the whole procedure. His response to the initial flow of energy would determine the next step in his healing, and that I could not foresee. I could feel the invasion of the bacteria that also needed to be stopped, but I knew that would be easy with the fruit of the great camu camu tree.

"It is time for us to move." Grandfather's voice abruptly changed from chanting to addressing the tribe. As he spoke, I squeezed Hope's hand, letting her know we would continue our conversation about Drew another time.

Lowering his eyelids halfway, allowing him to see into both the physical and non-physical dimensions, Grandfather continued, "Today is the day to release our brothers and sisters who have gone before us in spirit. Be free. No longer do as they did; choose a new path. Unlock your heart and follow the light that shines within you. Live as one with Mother Earth. Walk in peace, my children.

"We must leave the protection of the earth's arms and venture out to a new camp," Grandfather said, as he stood and motioned for the rest of us to gather our belongings and follow him. It didn't take long to bundle our few possessions.

At the entrance to the cave, Hope paused. Before ducking through the small entryway, she leaned against the rock wall and cleared her head of all that had happened in the last twenty-four hours.

"The spirits only go with you if you walk your path," she repeated to herself, still not sure what Running Filly meant.

She halfway expected to see the ocean raging at the entrance to the cave, as it had been in her vision-induced state. But outside the ground was solid and the sky was clear, with millions of piercing stars overhead. In the darkness, it was difficult to see more than the vague shapes that made up the landscape.

Quickly Hope turned her head from side to side as she alone heard the voice of Running Filly.

"I want you to live from the spirit, enjoy the physical, learn from your emotions, and know your soul's source," she cooed, as a gust of wind hit Hope in the face and the sound of prancing hooves played in the breeze.

Following Grandfather, we walked into the night. He prayed out loud for guidance, for peace of mind, and for his willingness to take the next step he knew he must take. When we arrived at the back of a box canyon, we broke for camp. Feeling vulnerable out in the open, we divided ourselves into groups and slept in shifts for a couple of hours at a time. This schedule reminded Hope of sailing through the night on *Ladyhawke*, and she sent a quick blessing to Logan for a safe journey to Guatemala. She still didn't know he had returned to the Turks and Caicos Islands and was planning to fly to Guatemala from Provo.

We camped in the canyon for two days, until Grandfather said it was time to continue on into Antigua.

Grandfather took ash from the fire pit and covered most of his face with the white powder. He asked me to braid his hair entwined with ceremonial beads and feathers, which I did. He wore his warrior's vest that hung heavy with protective artifacts and bundles of herbs. His soft xanabs were soundless along the animal trail that wound into town.

Remembering the night she had taken the fermented cactus juice, Hope asked Billy, "Why did Grandfather call me Little Bird?"

"When he first saw you, he said you flew in with a message. He knew before you ever drank the fermented cactus root that you didn't just come to him for answers, but you came to bring us wisdom."

"How did he know I was going to see Horse Woman?"

"I don't know exactly what he knew. I don't know whether or not he knew the message was going to be from Horse Woman."

Shrugging her shoulders, Hope said, "I'm not exactly 'little.'"

Both Billy and I smiled. She was right. She was a full head taller than the tallest one in our tribe.

"I think 'little' was a sentiment of endearment or reference to your young nature," Billy chuckled, "not your size."

Single file behind Grandfather, our tribe entered Antigua. We walked along the edge of the highway lined with stone buildings. My eyes feasted on the colorful clothing adorning the beautiful Antiguan people. But they did not return my look. It was as if they didn't notice our presence. I was captured by the electrifying field of energy encompassing Grandfather. I could hear a crackling noise as if sparks were flying within the bubble that surrounded him.

And then right before my eyes, the unimaginable happened. Grandfather extended his hands out in front of himself and tenderly said, "Slowly, dear, no more running. I am a tired old man." It appeared he then intentionally stepped out into the street in front of a truck barreling down the steep highway. His movement into the street appeared to me in slow motion. I could hear my own voice releasing a long, drawn out wail for him to stop as the truck struck, lifting him off the ground.

My broad experience of life narrowed to this one point, and I could see how we were all in this together, all interacting as a whole for the communal experience of now. Five, ten, twenty, thirty feet in the air, his body was tossed. His physical form seemed weightless, as if he were flying, but not for long. With the shattering of glass and the screeching of brakes, time resumed its natural pace. The truck driver quickly jerked his head from side to side, looking wide-eyed at the Corn People. He appeared to be startled by our presence, as if he hadn't seen us before this very moment. All spells were broken, including the spell of the invisible brew we had drunk earlier—the brew that Grandfather had told us would accompany 'the Shifting of the Wind.'

And with the breaking of the spell, Grandfather fell hard on the pavement like a tossed rag doll. Lying motionless, one of Grandfather's legs bent backward in an unnatural position. Thankfully, his arms created a cradle behind his head for a softer landing. As I rushed to his side, I felt a gust of wind behind me and with it the sound of prancing hooves. I veered to the side, expecting to be trampled by horses, but none were there.

As fast as the accident happened, the young warriors in our tribe ran to Grandfather and lifted his unconscious body upon their shoulders and trotted back in the direction we had come. The truck driver and the few locals who had seen the accident looked confused. I turned and ran behind the warriors who carried Grandfather down the trail, and all the way back into the cave. The rest of the Corn People dispersed and scattered into the crowd and the dense brush along the road.

In the cave, Grandfather lay upon a bed of furs. A small fire was built to take the damp chill from the air. In Grandfather's herb satchel I found the leather pouch of dried devil's tobacco, and began sprinkling it around his body in a clockwise circle, drawing in the vibration of healing. Kneeling next to his head I looked into Grandfather's peaceful face. He appeared to be sleeping, but I could feel his soul detaching from his physical form.

Raising my face upward with my eyes closed, I spoke out loud, "Help me, oh Great Spirit, Father of us all, to release my restrictions of unclear vision so I may allow the healing vibration of your pure nature to work through me and heal Grandfather's form."

I performed one of the ceremonies Grandfather had taught me, asking my guides to show me what was needed to help Grandfather. But for the first time, I had doubts about my abilities. Nothing I did felt right. I felt disjointed. I didn't feel like I was able to draw in the help I needed for Grandfather's healing. I felt alone, even though I could look with my physical eyes and see those who supported and loved me sitting around me in a circle. I felt powerless. Over and over I repeated the ritual Grandfather had taught me, but it seemed so trite.

That night, the last of our tribal members who had followed Grandfather to Guatemala returned to the cave. Everyone was quiet and somber. I could feel the fear and uncertainty that everyone was feeling.

For the first time in my life, I felt hopeless. It was such an empty and lonely emotion. I began to wonder if it was Grandfather's connection to the spirit world I was able to access in the past and that, without him, I was unable to read the messages brought from those that had passed before me.

Billy, Rocky, and Hope sat behind me holding hands, supporting my endeavors, but it wasn't enough. In front of me, Yellow Spotted Eagle, Moon Jaguar, Jaguar Lily, Mat Head, Singing Lavender Roller, and Moon Shadow huddled, swaying in unison, quietly muffling sobs. I couldn't stay focused. My energy was draining away from me, instead of filling me as it had in the past when I called upon the divine to lead me.

I prayed to the One God Grandfather had shown me. I chanted the healing words that had previously restored the sick to health. I washed his body with a healing herbal tea. I asked for guidance from our ancestors. And I prayed and I prayed and I prayed, until I had nothing left to give.

In my exhaustion I lay down and curled at the back of Grandfather as he lay in the fetal position. His body trembled. Only when I lay close behind him and held him tightly, with full body contact, did his trembling stop. I could hear Yellow Spotted Eagle praying out loud. She begged for Grandfather's life to continue and for him to resume consciousness.

A couple of hours later, I awoke from disturbing dreams of crushing boulders falling upon me and burying me alive. A deadening quiet had come over the cave. The stillness of night had penetrated every crack in the rocks. I could hear the heavy breathing of the slumbering earth. Even Roaring River's children had drifted off to sleep lying in a circle around his body.

In the dark quiet bowels of the earth, I once again slipped into a restless sleep filled with visions. I saw Grandfather's body effortlessly floating on his back in a sea of red. Without resistance, he moved with the blood current. I could tell he was listening to voices off in the distance. Beautiful music swung in and out of my audible perception. Grandfather was hot, and his own heat enveloped his body in a cocoon of warmth. My physical body pulled away from his intensity, but only a few inches, because he had intertwined his fingers into mine, gripping tightly to the hand I had around him.

I heard a pop that came from Grandfather's head, and the red sea ran from around him and off into a raging river; with it, the heat dissipated from his body. In my sleep, I instinctively pulled him closer to me as he quivered again with a chill.

The voices Grandfather was listening to got louder and he began to understand a few words that were being spoken. They began to become clear to me as well.

His attention was drawn to one voice in particular. Horse Woman was talking to another about Grandfather, not to him. They were discussing a path he should be shown. Horse Woman turned her awareness to Roaring River and said, "Hello, I'm here," when she noticed his attention was on her.

Grandfather looked toward the river of red that was getting further and further away. His spirit sat up and looked at me cradled around his body. He could see and feel my loving touch at the same time. His heart ached, knowing it was time for this chapter of his life to be over.

Horse Woman's voice beckoned his soul to a standing position. "I've been waiting for you. It's time we return," she said, holding a hand out to him.

I stirred in my sleep and Grandfather pulled my hand closer to his heart and whispered, "Thank you." Turning toward Horse Woman's voice, he rose above the fur pallet we lay upon. With a hand outstretched he slowly ascended toward the light in Horse Woman's voice. Fluidly he was guided like a river to the sea.

"It's been my privilege," I said instinctively in my sleep.

The sound of my voice drew Grandfather's attention back to his crumpled, worn out body in my arms. The sight of his body encircled by his children, grandchildren, great-grandchildren, and even great-great-grandchildren saddened him. He tried to let us know he was going to be fine, but his ascent continued to take him away. The Shift he spoke of had begun.

My eyes popped open with a start. I was instantly fully awake. I held my breath and did not move a muscle, listening for the familiar, tender voice that had told me, 'Thank you.' Grandfather's body made a rattling noise as his muscles tensed; he gasped for his last breath of air and then went limp. I pressed my forehead to his back and whispered, "No."

I continued to hold him in my arms as I cried for my loss. I wept silently until I no longer could breathe through my nose. I untwined my fingers from Roaring River's, our beloved tribal chief, leader of the Corn People, my maternal great-grandfather, and dearly adored teacher. Gently I rolled him onto his back. After gazing into his face for several moments, wanting so badly to perceive any sign of life but viewing none, I turned my eyes toward heaven hoping to find some sort of guidance from our non-physical counterparts.

I was relieved when I saw three large angels hovering close to the cave's ceiling. I knew from their presence I would be protected. Each angel was clothed in intricately woven tapestry robes. Ek Balam, or Jaguar-Star, the angel that appeared to be masculine, with sleek black hair, carried a large, elaborately carved silver shield and wore a sword in its tooled leather sheath. His flowing robe was woven from the rich colors of autumn. I could tell he was standing guard, protecting us in our time of Shifting.

Crystal spheres rotated around the second angel as if he were the center of their solar system and the source of their gravitational pull. Balameb, our teacher from the sky, wore a gown woven from yarn the colors of the sea. This angel possessed the powers to throw fire, shift wind, move mountains, and create the illusion of matter.

The third angel was dressed entirely in white. Sak-Be wore layer upon layer of lace that gracefully flowed down her body. She was stunning to look at; her beauty was unearthly. She was the largest of the three angels. Her wings spanned the entire cave ceiling as if cradling us all in her loving embrace. She had come to guide us down the 'white road' to our destiny. The angels' massive, all-encompassing presence filled the cave with protection and a sense of security.

As I sat next to Grandfather's motionless body, I felt light expand from the heavens both filling my chest and emanating from me. The light I had been looking for while trying to guide Grandfather in a healing direction now pervasively penetrated the cave. I looked toward the angels above me, and a sprinkle of glittering light showered down to me, opening my eyes to a higher level of awareness.

One by one the rest of the tribal members awoke and came to where I was now sitting, next to Grandfather's body. I had encircled his body with herbs and crystals. Again my face and hands rose to the heavens. For a moment Grandfather's spirit seemed to be present, but there was no longer a pathway for him to descend to his body. It was time for me to find my individual voice and my unique path to lead our people into an unfamiliar world.

As the sun rose high on the mountain behind the cave, we all erected a tall shrine and upon it we placed Grandfather's body. We prayed out loud for his safe journey to the afterlife, and we placed devil's tobacco around the shrine for his directed transition.

'The Shifting of the Wind'

TEARS OF GRIEF RAN FROM MY EYES. IN MY sorrow I vowed to do whatever it took to live the life of the awakened soul, to become the spiritual teacher Grandfather had groomed me to be. In the immediate hours after his death, I asked God for guidance.

By opening myself up to God, I realized Love was truly all there is. For the first time, I recognized myself as pure Love surrounded in Love with Love alone.

The following day, several more of our tribe's members chose to find their own path and departed the cave in search of a new direction. I was saddened saying goodbye to so many of my lifelong friends, but I knew the continuity of our community had been jeopardized, and I knew it would never be the same.

The next morning, Billy and Hope left the cave to walk to Antigua. They hoped to find Willy, who was to come from Indiana, and Logan, who Hope estimated should be getting close to Guatemala in *Ladyhawke*. I left the cave for my morning meditation walk. I could feel Grandfather's presence. He seemed to hover over my left shoulder just out of my peripheral view. I stopped walking and looked toward my left, but Grandfather moved back further behind me, once again, just out of sight. I looked straight ahead and asked, "What message have you brought me?"

Grandfather telepathically replied, "Nothing special, my precious one. I will be with you for the remainder of your life on earth. I have been sent to be by your side, to help guide the Corn People. I did not want to leave our tribe, but I was called to join our ancestors. The timing for me to shift from form to formless was not for me to decide."

I felt comfort in his presence as I continued to walk down the trail. I was enjoying the beauty and the warmth of the day, a day of new beginnings.

I stopped walking when I heard Grandfather say, "You must

help Hope. There is a reason she is with our people. Your newfound knowledge of the awakened heart needs to be brought to light for the pale ones. They are ready for your way of healing."

I knew he was right. I had already seen myself by Drew's bedside. It was obvious to me that I was also to teach Hope our ancient ways of healing.

Willy was waiting at the bed and breakfast when Billy and Hope arrived. He brought with him the information he had acquired from Lou Johnson, the Senator of Indiana. As a favor, the Senator contacted everyone he knew who might be able to help get the Copan Valley back for us. First the Senator contacted Internal Affairs, who contacted the U.S. Embassy in Honduras, who went directly to the President of Honduras for information. President Jose Azcona Hoyo had not heard of the sale of the Copan Valley, but he had heard rumors about the chief of a small tribe killing a military private there. The President promised to get his staff on it immediately and get to the bottom of the situation.

A note was found on Governor Lopez's desk stating he was not fit for his job and was resigning. In the top drawer of his desk, they found the contract selling the Copan Valley to Tony Cirrus. Internal Affairs pulled Tony Cirrus' FBI file and found he was wanted in Seattle for illegally transporting funds and machinery into Canada years ago. Internal Affairs contacted the Honduran President directly and told him Tony Cirrus, the new owner of the Copan Valley, was a wanted criminal in the U.S. That very same day, Tony Cirrus was detained in the San Pedro Correctional Center for questioning before he was shipped back to Seattle where he would stand trial. His illegal harvesting of trees was stopped.

President Hoyo reported to Senator Johnson that the Corn People did not actually own the Copan Valley; the Honduran government did. He was willing to let the Corn People continue being stewards of the Copan Valley for the remainder of his term as President, which was two years and nine months. At that point, he couldn't guarantee that the new President would make the same arrangements with the Corn People for the land. He suggested they try to buy the land so they wouldn't have to deal with the uncertainty in the future. He had been told the twenty three thousand acres in the Copan Valley was worth the modest price of the Honduran equivalent of twenty million dollars—a price the Corn People couldn't even imagine. They had lived off the land and bartered for outside goods for their entire existence. They had no concept of what it would take to raise twenty million dollars.

In Antigua, Hope received the email Logan had sent days earlier stating he was going to South Caicos to pick up the Shorts. She then read his next email that stated he was going to stay in the Turks and Caicos to search for the shipwrecks. She emailed him a message that she was in Antigua again but just for a couple of hours. While in Antigua, Hope also called her mother and was disappointed to hear the medical community still had not come up with a cure for Drew. Hope promised her mother she would bring me to Baltimore in just a couple of days.

Billy, Hope, and Willy arrived back at the cave before the last rays of daylight slipped behind the western mountains. Moon Jaguar finally let her guard down and she wept in Willy's embrace. It had been a trying month for her without her husband. Over the years, Willy's red hair had turned snow white, but his freckled, creamy complexion splotched with crimson had remained. His scrawny, boyish body was still thin, but his flesh had loosened and sagged with age.

Rolling Thunder, now the oldest member of the Corn People, had been busy organizing the elder men of the tribe to erect a temazcal, a type of ceremonial sweat lodge used to acknowledge my new leadership. He was the only surviving tribal member who had been alive when Roaring River had entered the temazcal acknowledging his guidance so many years ago. And only Rolling Thunder knew the ceremony was called 'the Shifting of the Wind.' Of course the rest of us had never heard the term before Grandfather started talking of it just a couple of weeks earlier; Rolling Thunder had kept this to himself, knowing that the ceremony had to be respected.

As the eldest tribal member, Rolling Thunder was to begin the ceremony and then turn it over to me. He was tentative because never before in the known history of the Corn People had there been a woman in the lodge during 'the Shifting of the Wind' ceremony, let alone a woman being the one honored to stand as the new guard for the tribe's protection. As the men constructed the temazcal to Rolling Thunder's guidelines, they also heated river rocks in a big, deep fire pit. It burned for hours, creating a large pile of glowing embers, heating the rocks to a red sheen.

Mid-morning I was taken to the river by the women in my immediate family. I was bathed for the ceremony. They softened my skin with pumice stones and adorned my hair with fragrant oils.

When the stones in the fire were sufficiently hot, I was dressed in a thin cotton robe and led to the temporary ceremonial grounds. All those who had not scattered in the confused winds gathered around as Rolling Thunder stood in the center of the cleared circle and faced me. He held each of my hands while saying, "We honor your wisdom and follow your guidance. We proclaim you chief and bearer of all truths. We look to you for healing and protection in our times of despair. Please allow us to be with you in your first residing temazcal." As he finished speaking, he released my hands and stepped back into the circle with the rest, leaving me alone in the center.

Ravens soared and called above us. I stopped to watch. Their presence was marked. They circled higher and higher in the thermal draft above the fire where the rocks were being heated.

"The ravens deliver magic," I announced before turning to the north and breathing in the ancient wisdom of those who had gone before us. Then, turning to the east I exhaled the breath of creation. Facing south, I closed my physical eyes and let the intensity of the sun sear an opening in my forehead for my true vision to enter. Turning to the west, I opened my eyes and looked to the future. Hope stood before me and I gazed into her soul. Rolling Thunder started shaking a seed rattle and chanting a joyful tune as he led the small procession of men who were to participate in the ceremony to the entrance of the temazcal.

Before following them, I reached for Hope's hand in a gesture that asked her to join us. She took my hand and we followed Rolling Thunder's lead. One by one, the men disrobed and entered the small dome. Hope and I were the last to duck in. I asked the young warriors outside who had been chosen as attendants to present me with one hot stone from the fire at a time until I felt we had sufficient heat for our journey. With long wood tongs wrapped in wet grass, I placed each stone in the shallow pit in the center of the lodge and then, before asking the attendants to close the door, I asked for the full bucket and the ladle I had brought to the ceremony.

With the entrance to the temazcal sealed from the outside, I immediately felt the heat from the stones penetrate my eye sockets. The air scorched the inside of my nostrils. It was pitch dark in the lodge except for the glowing hot rocks. The earth emitted a rich, wet, musky aroma. As my body relaxed into the heat, I began to recite the ritual story of passage from life into afterlife. I took a deep breath and these words rolled from my lips:

A long, long time ago there lived a young boy named Round Flower. He was the son of King Smoke Shell, who was the nephew of King Eighteen Rabbit, the last ruler of Copan Central. Round Flower lived by the Rio Amarillo in the lush Copan Valley along with his family, the Corn People. "King" was what they called the chief back then.

One day when Round Flower was an adolescent, he went to his father and asked him to explain what happens when one dies. King Smoke Shell didn't have an answer for him, so he sent him to the Medicine Man, Upturned Eyes. Back in those days, the one with the healing touch was not necessarily the one who led the tribe.

Upturned Eyes told Round Flower that no one had ever returned from the other side to report to the physical world what happened when they died. After a moment's thought, Upturned Eyes said to Round Flower, "I know of an herb you can boil to make a tea. Drinking it will take you to the other side. If you are strong enough, and it is not your time to pass on, you will return to us. Then you can tell the rest of us what is on the other side of life."

Round Flower thought Upturned Eyes' suggestion was a wonderful idea. He ran back to his father and expressed his interest in drinking the tea so he could return from death with the answer as to what is on the other side of life. King Smoke Shell couldn't believe what he was hearing. Round Flower was his only beloved son and the heir to his title.

*"But Father, I will return. I will return with knowledge of the af-
terlife,"* Round Flower *said excitedly.*

*Water Lily Jaguar, Round Flower's mother, heard what Round
Flower was planning to do, and tears of grief immediately began flowing from her eyes. She knew that no one had ever returned from the
afterlife. She was furious with Upturned Eyes for even suggesting such
a ridiculous thing. But Round Flower was determined to drink the tea,
with or without his parents' consent.*

*Behind the King's back, Round Flower returned to Upturned Eyes'
hut and made arrangements to drink the tea the following day. In
preparation Upturned Eyes took Round Flower down to the riverbank
and showed him which leaves to pick off the tall, mature hemlock plants
while asking the plant gods for protection and guidance to return to his
physical body after drinking the hemlock tea. Picking a sufficient amount
of hemlock, they returned to Upturned Eyes' hut and steeped the leaves
into a bitter-smelling tea. Upturned Eyes then sent Round Flower home
and told him to make peace with his family, in case he was not allowed
to return to the living after visiting the afterlife.*

*Thrilled, Round Flower ran home and told his mother and father of
his plans to drink the hemlock tea. His mother forbade him, but Round
Flower had already made up his mind. Upturned Eyes was also excited
for Round Flower to return from the afterlife so that everyone would
finally know what to expect upon death.*

*Water Lily Jaguar wailed in agony throughout the night. The entire
tribe was numbed to silence, already mourning the loss of their future
king. At dawn, Upturned Eyes led Round Flower to the top of the highest
hill behind their village. There he had erected a platform and padded it
with furs. As instructed, Round Flower sat in the center of the platform
while Upturned Eyes began to slowly shake the seeds in a dried gourd
and chant a prayer for Round Flower's visit to the afterlife and quick
return to this world.*

After I told this to the participants, I picked up a rattle and began
shaking it while chanting, "Protect our bodies as we travel to the
afterworld. And then safely return our souls to the forms we have
chosen. Return our souls. Return our souls." I repeated it over and
over, as Upturned Eyes had done.

Upturned Eyes handed Round Flower the cup of tea they had prepared the evening before and said, "Drink, my little warrior. Allow the poison to enter your tissues and quickly take you to the afterlife."

As I recited this, I ladled a large spoonful of liquid from the bucket in front of me and handed it to Rolling Thunder who sat to my right. I quietly said to him, "Drink," which he did. Barely able to see each person in the glow of the hot rocks, I continued around the circle, having each elder drink from my bucket. I could tell from the expression on their faces they weren't pleased with the bitter taste in their mouths. When I came to Hope, she looked trustingly into my eyes and she also drank the bitter tea. Returning to my place at the door of the temazcal, I took my turn and drank a ladle of tea.

"Lie down, my child," Upturned Eyes beckoned to Round Flower. "Leave your body for now. Travel to the afterlife. Do not forget to return to where you belong."
Everyone lay down, and I closed my eyes. Lying on my back, I felt sweat run from every pore of my skin. I took several deep breaths, allowing time for the tea to soak in. Then I continued:

Round Flower closed his eyes and for a moment he was afraid he had made a mistake. But it was too late. Round Flower quickly traveled to the afterlife, which excited him and enticed him with glee. He was joyfully greeted by his mother's mother and her sister and brother. Round Flower's father's great-uncle and his two small sons were also there. His father's grandmother and her mother's brother, relatives Round Flower didn't even know about, opened their arms in greeting.

One by one, each of the elders, along with Hope, drifted off into their own afterlife experience.

The sky above Round Flower was a more brilliant sky than he had ever seen on earth. The mountains were higher and more spectacular. The colors were fuller. There was music in the air—music more enchanting than anything he had ever imagined. Immersed in the beauty and joy of the afterlife, he never wanted to return to the Copan Valley. Round

Flower felt bad that he had promised his parents and Upturned Eyes he would return with the story of the afterlife.

And as soon as his heart slipped from the blissful joy that surrounded him, he fell into another world. It was dark and gloomy. Again there were many spirits around him, but this time they were hopelessly sobbing. Years of crying had etched deep crevices in their cheeks from the acid in their tears. In this world he wasn't warmly greeted by loving relatives, but was pawed at by desperate souls, trying to rob him of his life force, his glimmer of hope. He dodged their groping hands, and as his fear of them grew into anger, he found himself in yet another world raging with intense fear. There was fighting all around him. Clashing swords ripped oozing wounds into the others' flesh. Men and women were battling the manifestation of their fears.

Back in the Copan Valley, it had been three days. King Smoke Shell and Water Lily Jaguar mourned their son's death. They built a shrine for his lifeless body and placed him inside. In his anguish, King Smoke Shell banished Upturned Eyes from the village, blaming him for his son's death.

In the afterlife, Round Flower ducked from the slashing metal swords. He ran looking for a place to hide, but there was fighting everywhere. He could not escape the all-pervasive turmoil of war. He kept running and dodging to avoid injury. Heavily shielded men on horseback galloped toward him with outstretched swords and daggers. He threw himself out of their path at the last moment. Round Flower screamed with vigor and rage to build the power needed to fling himself from harm's way.

Again and again, he was approached by men who had flames of anger shooting from their eyes. He was exhausted and furious with himself for having drunk the hemlock tea. He didn't know how much longer he could run and dodge the threatening blows of the angry lost souls. Feeling done in, Round Flower looked up just in time to see the largest horse he had ever seen running in his direction. On the horse's back was a huge warrior dressed in metal armor. He raced toward Round Flower at an unbelievable speed. Round Flower was so tired he couldn't move. In the hot trenches of this dark world, Round Flower watched as the warrior got closer and closer. Feeling his end was imminent he closed his eyes, bowed his head, and asked for forgiveness for disobeying his parents. He felt deep love in his heart for his mother and father. As he felt that love, he heard Upturned Eyes say, "Return his soul. RETURN HIS SOUL."

At that exact moment, Round Flower opened his eyes. He was blinded by a bright reflection off the sheath of the sword that the massive warrior carried, and it briefly made contact with his flesh, cutting Round Flower's ribs above his heart. The intense sun blinded his vision for a moment, and he gasped for air. Then, there he was, sitting upon the marble slab he had been lain upon in his burial shrine.

Simultaneously, everyone gasped, releasing a huge sigh of relief as they all opened their eyes. I called to my assistant to open the temazcal door. The intense sunlight that shone directly into the lodge temporarily blinded all that were within.

"Please, would you bring us three more hot rocks? The biggest ones you have," I asked, wanting to intensify the heat in the lodge. After sealing us in the dark again, I continued.

Slowly Round Flower's eyes focused on his surroundings. He realized where he was. Above him was the small opening that had been left in the ceiling for his spirit to slip into heaven; but instead of his spirit slipping out, an intense ray of sun shone onto his face.

Round Flower rubbed his eyes and massaged his jaw. Slowly he rose to his feet and squeezed through the small opening in his burial shrine. As he walked off the mountain and into his village, everyone ran from him thinking they were seeing his spirit come back to haunt them. He entered his parents' hut. His mother, kneeling in prayer, looked up when he entered. She also thought she was seeing the ghost of her son. In fright she crawled along the floor to the far wall and said, "Please, Round Flower, I have only wanted the best for you. Why would you come back to haunt us?"

"But Mother, it is me, Round Flower, in the flesh. I have returned to my body from the afterlife. I have brought with me the story of what is to come after one dies. Please don't be afraid."

Water Lily Jaguar placed her face in her hands and cried, "Thank you." Bowing her head to the ground she repeated over and over again, "Thank you. Thank you. Thank you."

King Smoke Shell was in the men's hut when he heard the news that his son's ghost had returned. Fearing for Water Lily Jaguar's safety, he ran to their hut. When he flung back the skin that covered the entrance, he saw his wife and son in a tender embrace.

"Tell me it is not true that you have returned to do harm to your family, the family that so loved you." But even as he was saying it, he recognized his mistake and walked to his son with outstretched arms. "We must find Upturned Eyes." He wanted to exonerate him for his knowledge of herbs.

"We thought you were dead. It had been so long since you took your last breath," Smoke Shell cried.

"Father, the afterlife is an amazing place. What I felt was instantly manifest. Where my thoughts went, so did I. I have come back to learn the ways of the spiritual world from Upturned Eyes. It is so beautiful, Father. I must know what Upturned Eyes knows."

"My son, now you know more than Upturned Eyes knows. He has never gone to the afterlife and returned," Smoke Shell tenderly said to his son.

From that day forward, Round Flower sought a spiritual path for himself. After King Smoke Shell passed on to the afterlife, Round Flower led our tribe to a higher awareness of the spiritual world.

I ladled water from the bucket behind me, slowly pouring it onto the hot rocks. Steam rose, filling the lodge. Participants in the temazcal purged the toxic contamination accumulated in their bodies. We were all covered in a layer of sticky sweat that oozed from our pores.

Once again I asked the attendants to open the flap on the lodge. One by one each of us emerged, cleansed of our old beliefs and ways. We crawled from the dark womb as if we were being born anew. The women of our tribe surrounded us while playing slow welcoming tunes on their flutes and singing a song of love and adoration.

Hope looked around at each and everyone, seeing deep into their being. Her chin quivered as tears of pure joy rolled from her eyes. Every one of us brought back from the afterlife a message that would help us in this life.

That night I told Hope she was to learn to heal all hearts. I told her that in order to become a healer, she must learn to open her own heart first. It would be a lifetime of learning. It was what Grandfather had wanted.

"It is the practice he taught me, to listen to one's heart as it beats out the story that needs to be heard. It is the trick of healing the illusion of an illness. Very few can see the illusion; they can only see a cure or the absence when a person dies. An illusion of an illness allows humans to permit each other to shift from this world to the afterlife without a conscious decision to do so. It gives us an explanation for death, the way Grandfather was led to be struck by the truck, so we would have a story as to how and why he died; instead of seeing the truth—that it was the time and place for Grandfather to leave his body and continue down the flowing river, the journey for us all."

As I prepared to travel to the United States, most of the other tribal members prepared to walk back over the mountains to Honduras. It was a long way to travel on foot. The fear they had felt leaving Honduras and entering Guatemala was replaced with deep sorrow for the loss they felt, traveling without their beloved leader.

Stepping Further into the Unknown

SEVERAL OF US WALKED INTO ANTIGUA. WILLY was anxious to fly to Honduras and meet with President Hoyo. He wanted more answers about the Copan Valley. He wanted to fight for the land the Corn People had lived on for longer than there had been the modern government in Honduras. Willy couldn't believe the President of Honduras expected the simple primitive tribe who were descendents of the great Copan Central to come up with such a vast amount of money to buy the Copan Valley. He wanted to know why they were not already owners of the land.

Hope was relieved to see Logan waiting for us at the bed and breakfast when we arrived. He had left *Ladyhawke* at the marina in Provo before flying to Guatemala. I was struck by how handsome he was. I had a hard time not staring. His energy was infectious. His smile lit up his entire face. His large, hazel eyes sparkled with excitement. We quickly got acquainted on the way to the Guatemala City Airport. In the airport we went our separate ways, Moon Shadow went with Willy to San Pedro, as did Rocky, his wife, and baby daughter. I flew with Hope, Logan, and Billy to Baltimore.

I was nervous with anticipation. I had never been on an airplane before, or out of the tropical jungle of Central America. I trusted my cousin, Billy, and my newly appointed sister, Hope, and I knew they wouldn't lead me astray, but the newness of everything was still uncomfortable to me. Billy and Hope seemed completely at home in the large metal bird, so my fears subsided as I consciously tried to absorb their comfort.

When we landed at BWI, I was singled out and taken to the Customs Office. I could see the concerned faces of Billy, Logan, and Hope through the window that separated me from them. I silently asked Grandfather to be with me and guide me. The Customs Officers questioned me about the herbs in my medicine bag. I told them of my need to perform a healing on Hope's sick brother. They asked me if I was a doctor. I informed them I was the Leader and Medicine Woman for the Corn People. They had never heard of our tribe and my title meant nothing to them. I smiled and told them I had never heard of them either. My load was lightened; they took the medicine bag I had so carefully packed the day before with every herb I thought I might need.

The Customs Official informed me that all I had was noxious weeds, and they had to be destroyed. I left their office feeling stripped naked and confused by their lack of understanding of what the herbs could do for Drew. I thought everyone was aware of the healing powers of the earth and the fruits God pulled from it, but they seemed to think I was talking nonsense. Without my medicine bag I depended heavily on Grandfather's assurance he would be by my side to guide me through Drew's healing.

As I was allowed to leave the Customs Office, the puffy, pale man seated behind the desk said, "Be careful not to practice medicine without a license."

I wasn't sure what he meant by that statement and before I could question him, Hope grabbed my hand and led me into the crowd.

Concerned by our tardiness, Hope's mother was pacing at the luggage claim area. I knew who she was before she even spotted us. The energy was high in her body as if she didn't have a good foundation on the earth. When Ruth spotted Hope, she practically ran to her. A tear seeped from the corner of her left eye and she quickly brushed it away.

"We're here, Mom," Hope said, embracing her mother.

Turning toward me, Ruth enthusiastically hugged me. "Thank you for coming. I don't know how to thank you enough," she said with great sincerity.

"It is my pleasure. I hope I can help," I replied.

Then Ruth turned to Billy and said, "I have heard so much about you. Hope has the utmost respect for you and your family."

"As she does for you," he replied, lowering his head in a bow of admiration.

Logan wrapped his arm around Ruth and kissed her on the cheek before they began walking toward her car.

"I'm glad you could make it," she said, walking with her arm around Logan's waist.

"Well, of course I would make it," Logan replied.

When we left the airport, the earth was covered with snow and looked like a dead wasteland. I had never seen anything like it. The horizon was chopped up with the angular shapes of manmade forms. Without the dense canopy of trees I was accustomed to, I could see forever. Above me the sky was a massive, brilliant blue sphere. Even though the air was crisp and cool, the sun was warm and inviting and so bright that I had to squint continually until Hope gave me a pair of sunglasses to wear. For the first time I understood their necessity.

"Would you like to come to my house first to get settled and rest for a bit, or are you ready to go directly to the hospital?" Ruth questioned as she drove her car from the airport. We all agreed that we had come to see Drew, so Ruth anxiously drove to the hospital, maneuvering through the sloppy, half-melted snow. When the tires rolled over the frozen water, they made a funny, crunching noise. Along the roadway, the trees were all sleeping. Their leaves had left their branches.

As we walked in the door of the hospital building, an unfamiliar smell burned the inside of my nose. Ruth led us to an elevator and we went up to the third floor. I was in a mild daze, trying to absorb the unusual smells and sights around me. As we stood outside the door to Drew's room Ruth knocked, but then entered before it was answered. I was overwhelmed with the unhealthy environment in the building. It reeked of disease. I shook my head to try and clear the confusion of the oppressive atmosphere that was bombarding me. I went straight to the window on the far side of the bed and tried to open it, but it was sealed shut.

Hope went to Drew's bed. She gasped and raised her hand to her mouth when she saw his withered sleeping body. She was not prepared for how horrific he looked. The heart monitor next to his bed beeped out a mechanical rhythm. An IV dripped into the vein on the back of his hand to keep him hydrated. He lay motionless on his back, his mouth wide open. The distinct shape of every bone in his face was visible beneath his grayed, thin skin. His brow seemed over-extended, protruding above his sunken eyes in their sockets.

Drew stirred in his sleep, closing his mouth for a moment. With his tongue he tried to moisten his dried and cracked lips. Letting out an exhausted sigh, his unfocused eyes fluttered open. Hope quickly took the opportunity to see if he was now awake. She gently took his hand and gave it a light squeeze. Drew turned his head in her direction and when he saw her, he gave her a weak smile.

"Hey, Drew. How are you?" Hope asked.

He cleared his throat and licked his lips again before trying to speak.

"Okay," he squeaked as he raised his hand to point at a glass of water on his nightstand.

Picking up the glass Logan raised its straw to Drew's lips so he could take a sip.

"Hey man, you look awful," Logan said in a teasing voice, even though he really did look awful.

Bringing a fleeting smile to his lips, Drew weakly said, "Thanks, man."

Clearing his throat again, Drew looked from me to Billy and said, forcing out the words through a lot of phlegm, "Thank you for coming." And then sucking in a long deep breath, he continued, "Have you been here long?"

"Not long," Hope answered.

With weary sad eyes, he looked at his sister.

"I'm tired to the bone, Hopie," he said. "I don't know if I can fight anymore. I don't know if I want to."

"You must fight," Hope said. "You don't have a choice." Hope couldn't imagine losing him.

Drew had mixed emotions. On the surface he just wanted everyone to leave him alone so he could fade into unconsciousness and stop the pain and struggle. He had almost completely given up on his dreams for himself. Barely visible anymore were small sparks deep down inside his soul that still wanted to fulfill his vision of living in harmony with the earth and with a community of loving people.

His eyes had the look of defeat and despair.

"I don't know if I have the energy," he said as one small tear dripped from the corner of his eye.

Hope reached over and wiped the tear away as she fought to hold back her own.

Drew closed his eyes and his hand went limp in Hope's as he drifted away again. While he slept, Hope was unable to hold back her tears. They rolled down her cheeks. She buried her face in her hands as she sobbed. Ruth came to Hope's side and wrapped her arms around her shoulders.

Hope leaned down and kissed Drew on the cheek. She paused, resting her cheek on his; he felt warm in comparison.

Hope sat on the edge of Drew's hospital bed and held his limp hand. His hand had shrunk so much in the past two weeks that now they seemed as scrawny and brittle as willow twigs. The skin on Drew's once strong muscular form had thinned and turned gray; it had lost its elasticity and now hung loosely over his bones. Without a layer of fat beneath his skin, every bone and vein was visible. This once strong, supple man had quickly withered away.

Logan pulled up a chair and sat down next to Hope.

"What can I do?" he asked.

"I wish I knew," Hope replied.

The strident blare of an ambulance siren coming to the emergency entrance sent a shockwave of needles up my spine. The entire atmosphere of the hospital was so harmful that I had to concentrate and stay focused to not get wrapped up in the crippling energy.

After taking a long look out the window at the tops of the trees and the angular skyline in the background, I turned toward Drew. He was not the image I had seen in Hope's mind of the vibrant, strong man she held in her heart that day in the cave when I asked her to describe him. He was "The Bald Skeleton" Grandfather had talked of for so many years.

I walked to Drew's side, and I reached down, taking his other hand in mine. As I did so, he opened his eyes again, and we made eye contact for the first time.

"You will not get well here," I said. "This place will only make you sicker. Is there someplace else we can take him?" I glanced over at Hope.

Hope shrugged her shoulders as Ruth said. "Well, he is hooked up to a morphine drip. I would have to get special permission as a nurse to monitor that at home. The other fluids being admin-

istered are easy to monitor." She pointed to the plastic bag that
was connected to Drew's arm with a plastic tube.

"What is the morphine drip for?" I questioned.

"It is to control his pain," Ruth answered.

"Are you in a lot of pain?" I asked Drew, not sensing much
discomfort.

Drew was so weak he could barely speak.

He whispered, "Not really." And then after a long slow inhalation he said, "I'm more afraid of the pain than there actually being
any." Slowly he continued after another deep breath.

"They tell me I will probably starve to death before the bacteria kills me. I can now only swallow liquids. I have to drink very
slowly so the liquid can seep through the small space I have from
my esophagus into my stomach." His eyes were dark and very sad.
I could see the definition of his eyeballs sitting in their sockets. He
tried to smile at me, but it took more effort than he had.

I closed my eyes and began to rock back and forth, taking quick
bursts of inhalation. I could hear an unfamiliar voice speak to me
from the spirit world. It said, "My heart has become closed; I feel
the pressure building in my chest and rising up my throat. I no
longer have joy or desire. I'm angry with the people of this world
for not seeing the magnificent beauty all around us. I can't keep the
harmony of the earth by myself. I've been defeated. I give up. I no
longer want to try. I can think of a million reasons why I'm angry.
Yet I know I am just angry. I'm unwilling to drop the anger even
though I know it is killing me. I almost feel like it is my right to
be angry. I have lost all joy."

Opening my eyes, I looked back into Drew's. I knew the voice
was his spirit expressing itself to me.

I released his hand and walked back over to the sealed window.
I sat down on the floor and crossed my legs laying my hands, palms
up, on my knees. I felt guided to close my eyes and quietly chant.
The familiar guttural tones emanated from my mouth filling the
room with a rich intense vibration. I could feel an all-encompassing
light penetrate the room with an abounding Love, more powerful
than I had ever felt before. This Love was gushing through me and
around me with such intensity that I felt overwhelmed.

I opened a glass vial that hung around my neck. It was filled with an herbal tincture used to open the Eyes of God. Until this moment I had forgotten the vial hung from a leather cord around my neck beneath my blouse. It dawned on me that the Customs Officers probably would have taken it from me if they had known of its existence.

At Drew's side I dripped a couple of drops of liquid from the vial onto his forehead. He winced and opened his eyes into a wide stare. I knew he also was experiencing the Light of Love that pierced the lifeless hospital room.

"Everything is a give and take of energy," I vocalized, allowing Grandfather's voice to come through me. Drew found the strength to raise his hands with his palms facing toward me. I mirrored my hands to his, and we touched palm to palm.

Grandfather's words continued, "Back and forth and back and forth, energy moves through you. In its purity it is always moving, creating anew. When you resist the natural energy flow that is your true nature, you become stagnant and impure. Humans can be perfect vessels for energy to freely travel through in a vibrant, healthy state, or they can block energy and hold onto it, creating pain and disease. Very few of us are clear vessels, so where we congregate, the earth gets putrid and stale. To become an open vessel we must continuously let go—let go of beliefs, patterns, addictions, programs, fears, desires, anger, love, happiness, let go of everything... so that energy can freely flow through without an attachment.

"Drew, your ability to do this is needed on this earth. Do not let others discourage you to the point of resisting who you are. Go where your Love and openness flourishes. The earth needs your Light. You are here for a purpose."

I lost conscious awareness of what Grandfather was saying as the definition between my hands and Drew's left. The Love that abounded within me, through me and around me penetrated all of existence; I could no longer feel the separation of myself from the whole. Drew's dark sunken eyes became a fountain of Light. The room dissolved, as did everything else, into the magnificent glow.

"Just be," Grandfather continued. "Don't strive for what you don't yet have. Accept what is, and live in the present. By doing that, you ultimately will get the life you know is yours to have. When you strive for something, it is your small earthly self that is pushing you. Your small self stifles you, and what you are striving for will never be achieved. Just being is the fastest way to become. And from the place of truly being, you lose the desire to become. You just are.

"Open your heart, Drew. The stories that we put on an event limit the event and make it into something it isn't. Let go of the story of what is and allow the truth to appear."

Slowly Drew's hands relaxed, and tenderly he laid one on top of the other above his heart. Tranquility settled into him with a calmness that was felt in every cell of his being—a calmness without thoughts or words—and he slipped into a dreamless sleep. As he slept, tears of joy seeped from my eyes, for I had never experienced the merging, all-inclusive oneness so completely.

"The key to life is letting it go," the message from Grandfather continued to speak through me, and his words slipped into Drew's subconscious. "Let go of the past. Let go of your perception of how it should be. Let go of what you want it to be. Let go of all control over what is. Let go of your pain. It truly is that easy. Allow all preconceived perceptions to melt away from you. Be with what is. What is, is pure and simple.

"You can even be happy and content being in pain, but of course, only when you aren't holding onto your pain; it instantly dissipates. You can be happy and content in your sorrow and anger; but once again, it no longer resides within you when you are not attached to it. Life becomes a flow of peace and tranquility in awesome proportion. It becomes a wonderful marvel to observe."

As I listened to the words emanating from me, I knew what Hope's message from Running Filly had meant: "The spirits only go with you if you walk your path." In other words, if I walk the path I was born to follow, the path of a spiritual leader, the spirits would always be on the path with me. When I veer from my path, I also stray from spirit. It is when I deviate from my chosen path that I am alone.

As Drew slept, we left his hospital room.

"What just happened?" Logan whispered to Hope as we walked down the hallway toward the elevator.

"I think Drew was just healed," she said, leaning into him as he put his arm around her shoulder.

Billy and I exchanged smiles. He also knew there had been a healing. The following morning we said our good-byes and he flew home to Indiana.

Within two days, Drew was strong enough to leave the hospital without the morphine drip and return to Ruth's house.

Pausing for a moment on the covered entry of the white, two-story house where he and Hope had been raised, Drew could smell the familiar pine aroma mixed with the tinge of musty leaves that had fallen from the oak trees. Leaves blanketed the ground in front of the porch; and through the winter, they melded together into a thick carpet atop the rich, moist soil.

In the chilly spring air, Ruth wrapped Drew in several blankets and sat him in a recliner on the south deck so he could enjoy the fresh air. He held my hand as I sat next to him in silence.

Hundreds of cedar waxwings perched in the trees. The old, wood fence on the side perimeter of their property was lined with last year's thistles and long blue-stem grass that tried to brighten the overcast day by radiating a burnt-red glaze. With a gust of wind the birds twirled in erratic flight, filling the sky with waves of tan plumage pulsating through the air and settling again in the chokecherry grove by the water's edge.

In the days since my arrival in the United States, the snow had all melted. Small sprigs of tender green grass and blue crocuses had appeared.

When the sliding glass door to the house opened, Drew looked up.

"Hey Drew," Steve Jennings said, as he stepped out onto the deck. "How are you doing?"

"Oh, Steve, it is so good to see you," Drew responded, offering his hand to his friend. "I'm getting there. Grab a chair. Oh, I'd like you to meet Praying Dove."

"It's nice to meet you," Steve said, as he sat down on the other side of Drew and regarded me.

"Tell me what did you find in Tanzania?" Drew asked anxiously.

"It wasn't what I expected," Steve started.

Steve Jennings and his crew of journalists and cameramen arrived in the Chagga village three days after Drew had awoke him in the middle of the night. They started asking questions, but no one seemed to want to get involved. The medical tent had been removed, and no one would talk to Steve or his staff about the epidemic or rows of new graves on the hilltop.

"Could you please just tell me where Matthew lives?" Steve asked a young man on the soccer field.

The man shook his head, "No," and walked away. Steve didn't know if the head shaking was to indicate that no, he wouldn't show him where Matthew lived or no, he didn't understand what he was asking.

Steve sat beneath the acacia tree where there were several people lying on mats.

"Excuse me," Steve said asking a women sobbing in pain. "Do you speak English?" He sympathetically put his hand on her shoulder as she rocked herself back and forth.

His touch stimulated her to wail. He removed his hand, thinking just his light touch was inducing more pain. Cradling her face in her hands, it was obvious he wasn't going to get an answer from her either.

Frustrated, Steve was getting nowhere. He and his crew returned to their hotel in Arusha. He could tell there was a story that no one would talk about. Late that evening, Luke showed up at Steve's hotel room and asked to enter.

"I'm sorry no one will talk to you," Matthew's brother said while looking at the floor and avoiding Steve's eyes, "but we don't want any more trouble."

"Tell me what has been happening," Steve pleaded, promising anonymity.

"They beat my brother, Matthew.... to death," he said as he began to weep.

"What are you talking about?" Steve asked, shaking his head in disbelief.

"Matthew was the only one who questioned what the doctors were doing. He was the only one who stood up for us. And look where it got him. He's dead. Along with all the others." Luke spoke in a flat voice, but his face couldn't conceal his pain and anger.

"Tell me from the beginning. What happened?" Steve prompted. This was the point at which he would have typically turned on his tape recorder, but he knew if he had, Luke would have stopped talking, so he tried to take mental notes about what he was hearing.

"Five months ago, there was a group of men who were hanging around in the hills above our village. In that area, the underground spring that supplies our drinking water surfaces for a short distance before it goes back underground. It resurfaces again in our village. Then, at the rock ledge to the south of our village, the water disappears beneath the ground again. I don't know where it goes from that point." Steve tried to memorize the details.

"Within a few days after the group of men was seen in the hills, several people in our village began to get sick. Then it was only a couple of weeks before the tents arrived. So many people died," Luke said, shaking his head and putting his face in his hands. "It was happening so fast. We didn't know what to do."

Steve's heart sank hearing Luke's story.

"At first we assumed the doctors would cure us," Luke continued. "But only a few got better. Then Matthew met Drew, and the doctors got very anxious. After Drew left, Matthew began spending more and more time in the tents observing and asking questions. He told me Drew was right. Something was very suspicious. Then the switch happened very quickly.

"The doctors told Matthew they found a cure and wanted to give one last shot to the sick people in our tribe, as well as all the healthy ones in the village so we wouldn't get sick. Most people volunteered after seeing so many of their relatives die in such a short period of time. Those that were sick were getting better.

"Overnight, the doctors packed up the tents and left as fast as they appeared. Matthew wouldn't let it drop. He immediately went to the Arusha hospital to ask questions. He never returned, so I went into town asking for his whereabouts. No one had seen him."

Pausing for a moment, Luke wiped a tear from his cheek as he continued. "A group of teenage boys from our village found Matthew in the forest. He had been killed." Luke's voice cracked and it was difficult for him to get this last sentence out, "His head was bashed in."

Luke sat down and hung his head. Steve sat in the chair next to him. He didn't know what to say to console the distraught man. He knew Drew had stumbled onto something in which he shouldn't have gotten involved, but that is what journalists do.

Moments later Luke looked up. Through tears, he asked, "How's Drew doing?"

"He's not well," Steve answered shaking his head and wishing he had more details. "The doctors is trying everything they can think of, but still they don't have a cure. Drew can't remember what the doctors were administering that worked. I wonder if you could ask around and see if anyone here can remember what they were given."

"Dr. Hakem called it an antidote serum. That's all he said. I don't ever remember it being called by name," Luke offered.

When Steve was finished telling us about his trip to Tanzania, the three of us sat staring at the bushes along the water.

Tears dripped off Drew's chin. He had no words to say.

As the week progressed, Drew began to be able to swallow thicker fluids—smoothies and blended soups. His color and strength continued to improve. I could see a plumpness return to his tissues.

At a health food store I found, packaged in cellophane, most of the herbs the Customs Office had taken from me. However, these herbs lacked most of their vital energy needed for a complete healing. After boiling a cleansing tea, we all drank it with Drew. We achieved some benefits from the tea, but not as many as if I had been able to use the fresh herbs in my medicine bag. The one herb I couldn't find at the store was the one I knew he needed to purge the bacteria from his tissues, camu camu. I knew it was important for him to return to Honduras with me to receive juice from the camu camu fruit and drink tea from its leaves.

It was fascinating to watch how fast Drew was able to let go of his mind. By releasing his thoughts, he let go of his past and settled into a peaceful state that penetrated his being.

The following morning I awoke to the phone ringing in the other room. I could feel the budding of spring around me before I opened my eyes to the subtle emergence of daybreak. The chirping of house finches filled the immediate air. I saw the vague hues of color reappearing from the shadows of night, the birth of a new day. The birth of anything is always joyous. The new beginning filled with infinite possibilities, not burdened with the weight of what had been.

Ruth brought me a funny cordless phone and I could hear Willy saying his political contacts in the U.S. had helped him get a personal meeting with President Hoyo. The President signed a statement allowing the Corn People to be stewards of the twenty-three-thousand-acre river valley for the remainder of his presidential term, as he had promised. All charges against Roaring River had been dropped.

"Praying Dove, you are needed to sign the legal papers since you are now the official leader of the Corn People," Willy informed me.

"Yes, I guess that is true," I said, realizing it was time to return to the jungle.

Willy had already sent news to the rest of our tribe back in Guatemala, and at the border they were greeted kindly and allowed to cross into Honduras without questions.

Drew couldn't imagine my leaving so soon. After being very withdrawn and quiet most of the morning while I made preparations to fly to San Pedro, he asked if he could come with me. I could see his strength returning by the hour. I knew he was to come to the Copan Valley. Both Grandfather and I had seen the visions, so I eagerly invited him to come. I also knew he would benefit greatly from camu camu.

If Drew went to Honduras with me, Ruth wanted Hope to go and stay until Drew was stronger. So Drew, Hope, and I prepared for a flight to Honduras while Logan made arrangements to fly to Florida to retrieve *Maggie* and his submarine for his Turks and Caicos adventure.

Same Village/ Different World

I WAS BESIEGED BY THE POLLUTED THOUGHTS from the heavy congregation of people in the cities I had been visiting the past couple of weeks. Commotion from the barrage of densely packed human energy was overwhelming. I heard myself think and say things I had never thought of before. Realizing I was repeating the communal thoughts of those around me, not my own, I wondered how many thoughts were truly individual. How many were created without any input from the communal bank of knowing? People in the large cities of the United States were befuddled and very heated with anger about their situation. It took a lot of effort for me to stay in what I considered my own thoughts. I longed to be back in the Copan Valley with our simple lifestyle in tune with nature, where it was easy for me to be positive.

Drew held Hope's hand and slept on my shoulder most of the way to Miami where we had a layover, and then we flew straight to San Pedro, Honduras. Meanwhile, Max and Tina Short met Logan at the Miami airport.

I was concerned about the stress Drew was under. His body was sweating more than it should have been. In his sleep, he frequently sighed deeply from exhaustion. I trusted I would be able to pull the infection out of his tissues before they consumed his flesh. Still, I was concerned about his health declining from the strain of travel. When we arrived in San Pedro, Drew needed a wheelchair to get to the taxi by the curb. I had only been in the big city twice before, both times with Willy. Only because he talked about the city did I have an interest in visiting one. When I was a teenager, he took several of us from the tribe to visit San Pedro. Back then I was interested because it was not like anything I had ever seen before, and I was not so aware of the congestion and confusion.

From the pollution in the air, my eyes burned and the inside of my nose felt raw. The noise of the city roared in my ears. The pressure from the racket and heaviness of the air pressed on my soul and penetrated into my being. I was baffled by how poor the people in San Pedro seemed compared to the Corn People. They lacked the contentedness or inner peace that is the rich expression of wholeness. Here in San Pedro, like Baltimore, everything seemed to move too fast.

When we arrived in Honduras, Willy had rooms waiting for us in a small hotel on the outskirts of town. Drew immediately went to bed. Hope stayed with him while Willy took me downtown where we entered the law office of Jorge Agosta. He had prepared the papers as President Hoyo had instructed, and I was to sign as the Chief of the Corn People. I trusted Willy's judgment, not really understanding what I was signing. Mr. Agosta read them to me and tried to explain what they meant, but when it came down to it, he simply said I was agreeing as Chief of the Corn People to be the guardian of the Copan Valley. I was also agreeing that the Corn People had the option to purchase the land for twenty million dollars.

After signing the papers accepting stewardship, I walked with Willy a few blocks to a small restaurant where we bought packaged dinners. From there, we returned to the hotel where Drew and Hope were napping. I was deeply concerned for Drew's well-being. Traveling had taken such a toll on his body. I performed a small ritual to increase the healing energy around him. He had a hard time finding the strength to even drink the blended fruit beverage we had purchased for him.

After a fitful sleep for all of us, we took a taxi to Copan Ruinas where the car road stopped, and we had to walk the rest of the way to our village. Just getting into the green vegetation lightened the darkness that had entered my thoughts over the past few weeks. Hope was excited to finally be going to the Copan Valley. She told Drew the stories she had heard from Billy and Rocky that had enticed her to come and visit us even then. It was fascinating for me to hear her tell stories of my childhood that had been filtered through Billy's perception and then hers. I could pick out the events she spoke of, but it wasn't exactly the way I remembered.

Drew was very weak and leaned on Willy for support. Stopping several times, we slowly walked from Copan Ruinas toward our village. During one of our rests I spotted a camu camu tree, and with Willy's help, I gathered quite a few of its deep green leaves. The smell from the small, waxy, white flowers penetrated the air with an intoxicatingly sweet aroma. Beneath the tree we scavenged through the dry leaves for last season's dried, hard, leathery fruits.

With each step we took toward home, I could feel the accumulated tension drain from my form. The familiarity of my surroundings allowed my heart to relax and open. When we arrived in our village I quickly looked around as I walked directly to Grandfather's old hut, which would now be my home. The tribal members who spotted us ran to my side with greetings. It was obvious there had been a lot of looting and destruction of our village. I was not sure if Grandfather's hut had been spared from damage or if the tribal members who had returned home before me had already cleaned up his space. It was hard for me to immediately claim Grandfather's hut as my own, even though everyone else had accepted that transition. I didn't want to waste any time worrying about details because it was essential that Drew immediately start on the healing herbs.

Hope made a pallet of furs in the center of the hut for Drew to lie on. I began preparing a tea from the camu camu leaves for Drew to drink and a poultice from the small, dried, purplish-red fruits to administer to his abdomen. I stayed with Drew for the remainder of the day. Between preparation and administration of the teas and poultices, I chanted and prayed over his sleeping body. Hope was of great help running errands for me. She and Willy continued to gather more camu camu fruit and leaves from along the banks of the river.

One by one the tribal members visited me in my hut. They quietly greeted me with affection. They were respectful of Drew's need to rest so they didn't stay long.

I showed Hope how to pound the camu camu's flesh and its seed into a paste with a mortar and pestle, place it on Drew's abdomen and then cover it with a hot cloth that was soaked in tea. She caught on quickly and I was able to put her in charge of his daily regimen. The rituals of chanting and pulling in the light of healing from the universe were more difficult for her to grasp. I explained to her that it took a lifetime of learning to be able to perform healings like Grandfather had.

Over the following weeks, I rarely left Drew's side. He slowly regained strength. His presence was comforting to me after the physical loss of Grandfather. We shared tender moments as his deflated body flourished and became strong again. The camu camu fruit eradicated the infectious bacteria in his body, and the tumors in his digestive track began to shrink. He freely expressed his gratitude for my willingness to help him in his desperate state.

Drew observed the daily actions of the tribe and my leadership as I grew into the role. Within a month, I could no longer tell that Drew had been called upon by death. He began to help the boys in the fields, weeding and planting. He also started wandering further from the village with Willy to collect herbs and flowers for Willy's botanical studies and my remedies.

Before long it seemed like our daily lives in the Copan Valley had returned to normal and it was then that I missed Grandfather the most. The women in our family frequently talked about Grandfather late in the day when they prepared our evening meal. Moon Shadow and Moon Jaguar asked their mother Yellow Spotted Eagle to tell them stories about Grandfather and finally she revealed why he had been named Roaring River.

"I'm not sure why he didn't like to talk about himself," Yellow Spotted Eagle told her daughters. "As a child, I also questioned, like Praying Dove, why he was called Roaring River. One night I was sitting with him on the bench in front of his hut, where we frequently sat in the evenings. Horse Woman had also joined us and they were just idly chatting, so I thought it was a good time to bring up the meaning of his name. When I asked him, he looked to Horse Woman who just raised her eyebrows as if to say, 'Go ahead. Tell her.' Reluctantly he started, 'I was born Willow Leaf.'

"And then before he could continue, Horse Woman took over the story. 'One year the spring sky had unleashed a heavy rain on the Copan Valley,' she said. 'Water ran in small rivulets down the sides of the mountains and funneled into the great Amarillo River. As the river rose and filled its banks to overflowing, it disrupted even the mammoth Spanish cedar trees which began to be uprooted and tumble to their knees. Our village was flooded, and the Corn People had to move to higher grounds, out of the water's way until it subsided. In the chaos, Willow Leaf was separated from his mother, and before he knew it his young body of only three wet seasons was consumed by the river and swept away.

"'As night fell and Willow Leaf was nowhere to be found, his mother feared the worst and began begging to God for his safe return. Many days went by and still there was no sign of Willow Leaf. She began to lose hope and started mourning for his spirit. Two full moons had come and gone before a warrior of a neighboring tribe returned Willow Leaf to his mother.

"'The seasoned warrior had found the boy's lifeless body lying along the riverbank. He told Willow Leaf's mother he had slung the body over his shoulder presuming he was dead and proceeded to carry him back to his village for a proper shrine. But halfway there, he heard the most incredible roar of water like the river made when it was plowing its way down the mountain. This time the sound came from Willow Leaf as a stream of water shot from his mouth and he began to cough, arching up from the downward position in which he was hanging on the back of the powerful warrior.

"'Willow Leaf was returned to the Corn People when the waters had subsided enough for the warrior to travel to our village,' Horse Woman said very proudly. 'I remember this day like it was yesterday, for I am several seasons older than my younger husband. Before the great flood when he was simply called Willow Leaf, he was a docile young boy who rarely spoke. The story of Willow Leaf's return spread throughout our village and before the falling of the sun, Two Birds, our leader at the time, sent for Willow Leaf to be brought to his hut. Two Birds could see the change in Willow Leaf and declared he was not the same spirit and hence he was not Willow Leaf. He was now Roaring River. After the roar of the river flew from Willow Leaf's mouth he became loud and boisterous, expressing his beliefs and describing the visions of the spirit world he now frequently saw.

"'From that day forward Two Birds began grooming Roaring River to become our next leader.' When you were born," Yellow Spotted Eagle continued, nodding toward Moon Jaguar, "first child of Roaring River's only daughter, he had been leader of the Corn People for quite some time. Roaring River had calmed with age and stopped being as boisterous; he became like a Willow Leaf once again. But instead of reclaiming a used name, he became Grandfather to all, as you, his first grandchild, began to speak."

Retrieving the Treasure

I AWOKE TO THE BAAING OF GOATS JUST AS THE
first hues of dawn penetrated the darkness. Our pasture fence
had broken on the north side of the village and our livestock was
wandering among our huts. I could hear the hushed voices of the
shepherds trying not to awaken everyone in the village as they
herded the animals back to their corral. I could smell the familiar,
pungent aroma of camu camu fruit paste. Still asleep, Drew lay on
the other side of the room. With a contented sigh, sounding similar
to a large cat's purr, he took rhythmic deep breaths. I knew we had
won the battle for Drew and he would return to complete health.

When Hope awoke, she came to me and said it was time for her
to leave the Corn People. She also felt confident Drew was securely
on the road to recovery. Now it was time for her to help Logan with
the labor-intensive work of excavating *Josephine*. Hope was torn because she really wanted to stay and learn the ways of the awakened
soul, but she knew it was time for her to return to *Ladyhawke*. For
now she felt it was important to help Logan, knowing she would
one day return and work under my guidance.

It was a tearful good-bye for Hope as she left. Willy walked
with her to Copan Ruinas where she caught a taxi to the airport
in San Pedro.

After her flight, Hope walked down the secured hallway in the
Provo Airport; she could see Logan standing behind the security
guard. He was sporting the biggest smile she had seen on his face
in a long time. When she reached him, he was giddy.

"You won't believe what we have found," Logan blurted out, before he remembered to hush himself. He twirled Hope in his arms;
he was so happy to see her. As they hurried toward the baggage
claim, he quietly continued trying not to draw attention to what
he was saying, "I've got daggers and swords encrusted with gems.
A ruby the size of my thumb!"

He skipped and pranced next to Hope, not able to simply walk.

"Gold and silver coins from a multitude of countries. We found a silver chest full of jewelry. The more we pull up, the more there seems to be. I'm not sure how far it is scattered across the ocean floor or how deep we will eventually dig. So far the authorities have allowed me to claim a five-mile square, but I'm afraid the wreck spreads beyond our markers. And of course Goldie Locks is snooping around. He has found our site even with all of the evasive techniques we go through every time we leave Provo to come back to where *Josephine* lies. Goldie Locks and his cohort, you remember who I'm talking about." Hope nodded, remembering that Tina kept running into him everywhere. "They come out to the edge of our boundary and stop just a few feet on the other side. Sometimes they hang out all day. If we approach them in one of our boats, they high tail it out of there.

"Oh, babe, it is good to see you," Logan finished and planted a big, wet kiss on her lips.

Not missing a beat he continued, "Max and Tina have really gotten into this. You remember Larry? He's come out of retirement and is here helping me. He's teaching Max and Tina how to classify. They are so into it. Once the pieces are classified, we've been shipping them back to Miami where Dolf is sorting and storing the artifacts in a secured warehouse. Actually, I've got my entire crew back, everyone except Johnny. Everyone was excited when I told them what I had found. Dolf also has a team of historians preserving pieces for me in Miami. Most of the find is so unusual I think we need to display it somewhere. For three days we hauled gold bars up, one right after another. We just kept uncovering them."

Like always, Hope was immediately swept up in his enthusiasm and was eager to see what they had found. Logan was so focused on what he was doing that everyone working with him became focused on it as well, thinking it was their own interest, not just his.

"Every time I turn around, I run into either Goldie Locks or his friend. I'm surprised they didn't follow me here," Logan said turning in a circle scanning the crowd. "They seem to be everywhere I go. We never all leave the site at the same time. Everyone in town is talking about why we are here and what we are doing. I think Goldie Locks has been spreading rumors." Logan rambled on and on, unable to contain his excitement. Hope's luggage went around the carousel several times before they noticed hers was the only one still circling.

On the way to the car Logan temporarily switched gears. "Oh, I'm sorry, Hope. Tell me, how is Drew?"

"You wouldn't believe how fast he has recovered. He's put on about twenty pounds in the past three weeks. He has resumed health as fast as he got sick. I think Drew and Praying Dove are falling in love."

"Go Drew."

"When they sit together after dinner they hold hands and talk quietly to each other. He told me he still needed the healing that Praying Dove had to offer. I think he needs the love they share. I'm happy for him."

Logan drove Hope straight to the warehouse he had rented. Through the glass observing plate he showed her the figurehead they had successfully encapsulated on the bottom of the ocean in a pressurized case before hauling to the surface.

To Logan the most interesting aspect about the recovery was that the artifacts were not just from one time period or one part of the world. Since the women pirates had looted from a multitude of boats and coastal villages, *Josephine* held valuables from several cultures spanning a couple hundred years. There was a sword from the Far East that Logan found most curious. He wondered who had originally brought that sword to the Caribbean. There were gold and silver coins from England, Scotland, France and Spain. There were trading beads from Africa and a gold sphinx that appeared to be from Egypt. This certainly was the most widely diverse find Logan had ever come across. And if that wasn't curious enough, Logan also found stone arrowheads and other stone tools that appeared to be American Indian.

In the boat hull, they found several corroded metal chests with two and a half tons of gold bars. They were stamped with royal seals from England and Spain. The gold was estimated at being worth forty million dollars, not adding any value for being old or on the historic pirate ship *Josephine*. The weight of the loot Logan found on this small sailing vessel made him determine the pirates were on their way to unload their treasure, not out crossing an ocean. The weight would have been too heavy for the little boat to carry for long distances. Because of this, he was convinced the pirates had an onshore hiding place. Of course this sparked his interest, and he wondered if it had ever been found.

After touring the warehouse, Logan called Mickey, who was staying on *Maggie* anchored above *Josephine*, to let him know he and Hope were on their way out to the site. Logan wanted to know if Mickey needed anything from shore. While sitting at the navigation station talking to Logan, Mickey noticed the approach of a boat on the radar screen.

"Hey, I've gotta run. There's a boat out here," Mickey said.

"We'll be there soon."

Mickey went up on deck with binoculars to see if he could identify the boat. Through the night lenses he could barely make out the long sleek lines of a motorboat stopped a hundred feet on the opposite side of the barrier. The boat didn't have a single light on. Mickey watched as one of the crew went to the bow of the boat and dropped an anchor into the water. He continued to watch as three men put on diving equipment and slipped over the boat rail into the water. Through his binoculars he could easily follow the glow of underwater flashlights moving toward Logan's barricaded area. One man remained on the boat that appeared to be fishing.

Mickey went back to the navigation desk and contacted the Turks and Caicos Border Patrol, telling them about the suspicious looking boat. They said they were already in the area and would pass by to check it out.

It only took twenty minutes and the fast traveling Border Patrol boat pulled up alongside the anchored motorboat. From the deck of the Border Patrol boat, the skipper spoke loudly and with authority, "Permission to board?"

The man pretending to fish knew he had better give them permission or they would board the boat with force, so he replied, "Permission granted."

The Border Patrol Captain and one of his assistants boarded the small motorboat.

"We need to see your boat documentation papers, insurance

papers, and safety equipment," the patrolman said with authority.

The boat didn't belong to the fisherman and he had no idea who it did belong to or where its papers would be. He had seen a couple of life jackets down below so he ducked his head into the small cabin he couldn't quite stand up in and mumbled to himself, "What on earth? What am I supposed to do?" Lying on the settee were two lifejackets, so he handed them up the companionway. In his frustration he opened and slammed shut each and every cabinet. He was lucky to find a horn, but he never found flares, whistles, or a bell, let alone documentation or insurance papers.

"What are you doing here in the middle of the night?" the Border Patrol Captain questioned.

"Fishing, mon."

"For what? A sunken treasure?"

"How could I fish for treasures?" he answered, trying to act innocent.

"Do you want to come clean with me or do you want me to wait until your buddies surface when they run out of air?" the Captain asked, pointing in the dark to the obvious underwater flashlights glowing just inside the barricade that outlined Logan's claim.

"We're just curious. We mean no harm, mon."

"They're in a secured area. No one is allowed beyond the barricade. The man who has claimed this find could shoot you for trespassing and he would be in the right."

The Captain had his first mate take the patrol boat a few hundred yards away, so it would appear to the men in the water that they had left. It only took a couple of minutes for Goldie Locks to surface. As soon as he ripped the regulator from his mouth, he blurted out, "My metal detector is going wild down there." And then he noticed the two uniformed men, but not before he lifted the corroded shaft of a metal knife into the air.

Goldie Locks knew he was busted and reluctantly got on the boat. Slowly the other two men surfaced screaming with excitement before noticing the extra men on their boat. The loot Goldie Locks and his friends surfaced with was confiscated by the patrol. This time they were just given a warning to stay clear of the boundary lines with the threat of arrest if ever seen in the area again.

That night Hope was happy to return to *Ladyhawke* where she was anchored on a sand bar inside the boundary of Logan's find. Hope felt like she was home. The night sky was clear and dark. The half moon was not yet visible above the eastern horizon. Even the stars appeared as bright jewels against a dark velvet display card. Logan couldn't keep his mind off the excavation. He kept picturing what they had already excavated and what his overactive imagination told him was still to be brought up. While Logan and Hope sat in the cockpit of *Ladyhawke*, Logan continued in a manic sort of way to tell Hope about the past month he had spent away from her.

Goldie Locks couldn't stay away; he was drawn to the blocked off area like a hound dog is drawn to a fresh cowpie. Less than a week later during a drunken night at one of the local bars in Provo, Goldie Locks, the man with the tattoo on his head, and two new friends got into a cigar boat and raced to the coordinates of Logan's excavation, the coordinates Goldie Locks now had memorized. They anchored again just outside the boundary line. In their loud and drunken state, it took them quite a while to get ready to enter the water with dive gear. Before they did, they heard the approach of a motorboat. With the bright searchlights aimed directly at them, Goldie Locks instantly knew it was the Border Patrol again.

"Shit, mon. We can outrun 'em," Goldie Locks said. "Pull the anchor."

The man with the tattoos on his head ran to the bow of the boat and started ripping the chain-rode out of the water. As soon as the anchor was up, Goldie Locks grabbed the steering wheel and forced the throttle to its maximum position. The bow of the boat rose out of the water practically flipping the boat with the swift acceleration. The tattooed man flew from the boat, landing fifty feet away.

The Patrol Captain announced through a mega-phone who they were and demanded the cigar boat stop. As soon as Goldie Locks got the boat under control, it slammed into a submerged coral head, throwing the boat completely out of the water. Upon reentering, the boat hit another coral head and exploded into a ball of fire. As usual, Goldie Locks had been flying by the seat of his pants and not paying any attention to the charts of the area that would have warned him of the shallow coral heads. The Border Patrol stayed back while the boat exploded several more times before it completely submerged beneath the surface of the water, leaving only burning debris scattered on the face of the sea. The man who had been ejected from the boat was the only one rescued from the accident. Upon his arrest, it was learned that he was a wanted felon from the Bahamas.

The following morning Logan's dive crew found the other three bodies and immediately informed the Border Patrol of their location.

Logan speculated Goldie Locks hit the exact coral reef believed to be the one *Josephine* hit two hundred years earlier.

Creation

I KNEW IT WAS A SPECIAL EVENING THE NIGHT
Drew came to my hut. He had an extra glow about him from being
outside in the sun. He was relaxed and content entering my haven,
which had become his home. All afternoon I had been singing and
chanting a joyful meditative prayer. I could feel the harmony of our
village as music came from the men's hut and filled the air. There
was something very special about the music; it was as if every note
that emanated from their sacred abode mirrored my heart. It felt as
if the men were projecting my feelings outward for all to hear. Drew
seemed almost to be in a trance under the influence of the primor-
dial beat. They were expressing the pure universal sound of Love,
clearly speaking in the voice of our True Source's euphoric heart.

Drew looked into my eyes and smiled for several seconds. He
lifted his hands in front of himself with palms facing me like he
had on his hospital bed. Again I mirrored his hands by placing my
palms on his, but now the give and take of vibrational energy was
equal. This merging of energies had become a customary way we
greeted each other. Our hearts poured into each other through our
fingertips and music rang out louder, seeming to originate here
between us as the voice of Drew's heart met mine. Our souls were
exposed and their vibratory tone was audible. His hands felt warm
and his energy sensuously caressed and playfully stroked mine. There
was an intense creative force pulsing around us and stirring in my
core. We were the vibration of expansive Love.

I could feel Drew's throbbing creative flow. It appeared as waves
of light and sparks of energy vivaciously flowing through his body.
I gazed into his eyes and our music became softer and slower. The
warmth in the space between us was arousing, and for the first time
our physical bodies met. The expansive beating energy engulfed us,
undulating up and down the tonal scale with the rolling rhythmical
flute's voice and penetrating my core with the hard driving rhythmical drum. I could no longer hear which song was the sound of
my heart or Drew's. We filled my senses. It was impossible for me

to tell where each of our bodies stopped and the other began. It was unclear which was creating which; was the music creating a vibration field that we got swallowed into, or were we creating the beating resonance that pulled the instruments into tone?

From our lips, spontaneous singing began to harmonize with the wood flutes. The earth took a deep, intense inhalation as the music quickened and grew. It then expanded and intensified, building and growing until all was filled with an enormous tone. We filled the room and out into the cosmos. The stars and the solar winds blew through our hair resonating within us and around us.

As our expansion peaked, the singsong voice of the flute quickly quieted into a slow, penetrating sigh. "I love us," Drew whispered, as the last notes from the flute and the wind from his voice traveled out into space.

The warm night air blew across our intertwined limbs, exciting our skin into goose bumps. We spoke to each other with internal words that moved with the warm winds, from the place inside each of us that knows All-Knowing, and the place that commands all time. In each other's arms, we spoke from that place in silence.

Pure Love sparked into my womb and a soul incarnated with a calmness that was felt in every cell of my body.

My Beloved Sister

IT TOOK TWO YEARS AND SIX MONTHS BUT Logan was confident he had brought up everything that was left of *Josephine* and her treasure. After working ten- to sixteen-hour days, seven days a week, for such a long period of time, Logan agreed with Hope—it was time for a vacation. He wrapped up the job and shipped the rest of the excavated treasure to the warehouse in Miami. He had several of his employees take *Maggie* and his submarine back to Marathon before taking a well-deserved break from work themselves. Hope and Logan came to Honduras to visit Drew, his new family, and their wonderful friends, the Corn People. Many tribal members who had dispersed during the disruption two and a half years earlier had returned to live with the tribe once again and follow my lead.

Hearing of Hope's travels to Honduras, Ruth also took leave from her position in Panama and met her children in the Copan Valley. Drew was the proud father of his one-and-a-half-year-old daughter, Andrea Little Rabbit. She was a stunning baby; her thin hair was golden-brown and curled at the nape of her neck. Her arms and legs were thin and extremely long, as were her tiny fingers and toes. I had to take extra care with her sensitive, light skin. She broke out in rashes from the humid heat and was more sensitive to bug bites than most tribal children. Drew was once again strong and vibrant with health; he showed no signs of ever being infected in Africa. He had quickly taken on the burden of organizing the daily activities of our tribe and the preservation of the rainforest.

The remaining inhabitants of the Chagga tribe in Africa had regained good health. Steve Jennings and his crew of journalist never uncovered the source of the mysterious plague or the identity of the inexplicable pharmaceutical team.

Max and Tina Short moved onto their new Hinckley Southwester 43 sailing vessel in Bar Harbor, Maine. Sailing south, they were ready for another adventure.

The afternoon heat was subsiding when a mail carrier came to our village and presented me with a letter. I read it to myself before handing it to Drew.

"What does it say?" Mat Head wanted to know.

Drew began to read aloud, "The Copan Valley consisting of twenty three thousand one hundred ninety-two acres, has been purchased…" his voice trailed to a hush as Moon Jaguar sighed deeply. Mat Head stood with rage in his eyes.

"Why?" was all Yellow Spotted Eagle could muster.

"Let him continue," I said calmly.

"…purchased by an offshore trust. The Beneficiary of the trust is," Drew paused again not believing his eyes. He looked up at the small gathering he was reading to before continuing, "the Corn People tribe, descendants of the Xukpi people."

"What does that mean?" Yellow Spotted Eagle interrupted.

"Let him continue," I repeated.

"The acreage will be passed on from one generation to the next as long as the Corn People are an organized tribe and can prove to be of Xukpi lineage."

"Who paid for the land?" Mat Head wanted to know.

"It doesn't say," Drew answered turning the paper over in his hands looking at the blank backside.

We were in such shock that no one said a word for several minutes.

Hope snuck a quick glance and smile at Logan. He vaguely smiled in return before averting his eyes. I was the only one who caught their exchange. I knew in my heart where the money had come from to pay for our land. I also smiled, knowing they didn't want their secret to be told.

Acknowledgements

I would like to thank all of my friends and family who read my manuscript in varying stages of completion. Each was instrumental to bring this book to culmination.

I would like to thank my sister Marcia Losh for her gifted writing suggestions. She was there to offer support when I needed it the most. Her careful editing and re-editing made the story clean and honest.

I would like to thank my ever-talented sister Shelley Thornton for her insight into my thoughts, which allowed her to illustrate and lay out the cover of this book exactly like I had pictured, only better.

I would like to thank Jan King Garverick for her encouragement to continue the arduous task of finishing a novel.

I would like to thank Tori Miller for her editing expertise and insight. Her meticulous polishing pulled *Praying Dove* into the gem I had envisioned.

About the Author

After practicing the healing arts for twenty years and raising her son, Phyllis Jo Arnold retired to embark on an adventurous voyage with her husband. For ten years, they journeyed in their small sailboat from Maine to Venezuela, covering thousands of miles and encountering countless dangers. On their travels in Central America, Phyllis came to love the simple way the native people lived there. She has studied their spiritual and healing techniques extensively. When not on the water, Phyllis enjoys backpacking in the Rockies, the Alps, and Mt. Kilimanjaro. *Praying Dove* draws from her experiences and is her first novel.

Author Contact

www.PhyllisJoArnold.com
Phyllis@PhyllisJoArnold.com